SUNNYSIDE ROAD

SUNNYSIDE ROAD

Paradise Dissembling

K. B. PELLEGRINO

LifeRich PUBLISHING®

LifeRich Publishing is a registered trademark of The Reader's Digest Association, Inc.

LifeRich Publishing books may be ordered through booksellers or by contacting:

LifeRich Publishing
1663 Liberty Drive
Bloomington, IN 47403
www.liferichpublishing.com
1 (888) 238-8637

Because of the dynamic nature of the Internet, any web addresses or links contained in this book may have changed since publication and may no longer be valid. The views expressed in this work are solely those of the author and do not necessarily reflect the views of the publisher, and the publisher hereby disclaims any responsibility for them.

Any people depicted in stock imagery provided by Getty Images are models, and such images are being used for illustrative purposes only. Certain stock imagery © Getty Images.

Cover Design Inspiration by Holden Ackerly, NYC, and Atwater Studios Inc., Springfield, MA
Sunnyside Road Plot Design by AJP, Chicago, IL

This is a work of fiction. All of the characters, names, incidents, organizations, and dialogue in this novel are either the products of the author's imagination or are used fictitiously.

ISBN: 978-1-4897-1761-0 (sc)
ISBN: 978-1-4897-1760-3 (hc)
ISBN: 978-1-4897-1762-7 (e)

Library of Congress Control Number: 2018951116

Print information available on the last page.

LifeRich Publishing rev. date: 7/24/2018

Contents

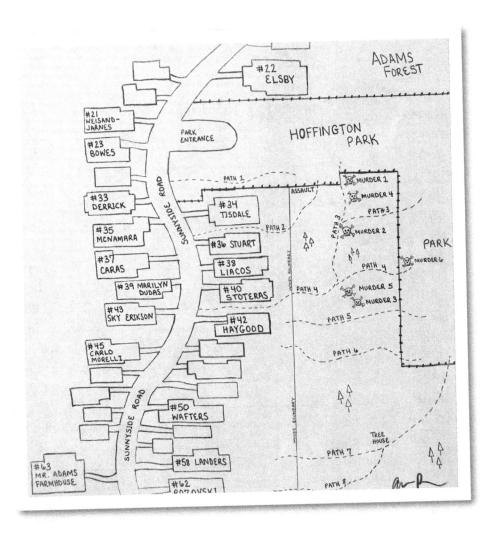

Characters

Sunnyside Road Residents

21 Sunnyside Road	Weisand-James Family
22 Sunnyside Road	Elsby Family
23 Sunnyside Road	Bowes Family
33 Sunnyside Road	Derrick Family
34 Sunnyside Road	Tisdale Family
35 Sunnyside Road	McNamara Family
36 Sunnyside Road	Stuart Family
37 Sunnyside Road	Caras Family
38 Sunnyside Road	Liacos Family
39 Sunnyside Road	Marilyn Dudas
40 Sunnyside Road	Stoteras Family
42 Sunnyside Road	Haygood Family
43 Sunnyside Road	Erikson Family
45 Sunnyside Road	Carlo Morelli
50 Sunnyside Road	Wafters Family
58 Sunnyside Road	Landers Family
62 Sunnyside Road	Rozovsky Family
63 Sunnyside Road	Mr. Adams

Nonresidents

Millie Banks, administrative assistant for MCU
Jim Locke, MCU detective
Petra Aylewood, MCU detective
Mason Smith, MCU detective
Captain Rudy Beauregard, MCU lead detective
Chief James Coyne, chief of West Side Police Department
Mayor Fitshler, mayor of West Side city
Mona Beauregard, Captain Beauregard's wife
Assistant District Attorney Marion Hetterman, assigned to case closing
Dr. Abbott, Hoffington Middle School counselor
Marnie Whiteacre, psychic from Agawam
Tom Blouin, instructor for federally subsidized survival camp program
   for kids

Prologue

Sergei scanned the landscape around his property located on Sunnyside Road, West Side, Massachusetts, and thought to himself, *This is not like Russia. No. This is not like in Russia!* He remembered when he and Mariska chose the large triple lot with the developer. It was the choicest lot on the shady street. Sunnyside Road struck him as a slice of paradise tucked into this mainly suburban city adjacent to the larger city of Springfield. He could have chosen a different site to build their home—perhaps in Northampton or Westfield or Holyoke or Chicopee. These were cities whose residential profiles were changed by the housing boom of the nineties.

He had viewed the transformation of centuries of traditionally worked farms in the area into a mismatch of architectural bastardization of residential developments. Granted, there were some pockets of new homes where the changes in development were positive, but that change was accomplished mostly in areas where there were owners with a surplus of money to invest and the city or town had strict zoning guidelines.

Sunnyside Road, in his view, was the most beautiful development in West Side. From all the choices available, Sergei had chosen West Side. He thought it was a thriving small city adjacent to the larger city of Springfield, whose population rivaled only the city of Worcester for lead cities after Boston. Sergei reviewed how long it had taken him to find this spot. It was a winding tree-lined street with birches, pines, spruces, fruit trees from the old preexisting farms, and many other trees, including, he thought, a few really old trees, maybe oak or elm. A wide wood backed up the homes on his side of the street, with narrower woods backing the homes on the opposite side of Sunnyside. All this ended in a park on his street side, followed by a forest.

There was diversity in home styles built, not like in Russia, with its concrete block buildings in the city and no real suburban areas he could afford in his home city of Buzuluk. No—not like in Russia!

He had built an important home here. He was respected here. It had not taken long. America opened her arms to him. And it was true; there was opportunity here. Not like in Russia! There, he was kept in his place.

He'd had some success there, had even earned a little respect there in Russia. But always the questions remained. Who would take it away from him? When would he be deprived of control over his life? Which potential government action could place him in peril? These had been the perpetual questions in the Russia he had left.

Yes, this was paradise. Maybe? Paradise or chaos! Maybe it was more like Russia than he thought. Murders abounded in this, his neighborhood. As he surveyed his domain and walked through what he considered his woods, he noticed the birds were flocking back. He thought that an early spring might be on the horizon. He needed some lightness in his life. He noticed new buds on some of the bushes, and for just a second, his heart was lightened as it occurred to him that new life was always possible.

But then the tension rose again in his heart. The winter had robbed him of his sense of safety. He could not allow that. But what could he do? No one had been able to do anything thus far. What do you do when a psychopath is working his evil? He was again fearful, as he had been in Russia.

1

Promised Land

CAPTAIN RUDY BEAUREGARD THOUGHT, as he drove down Sunnyside Road for the umpteenth time in fifteen months, that beauty often hides horror. He remembered the Broadway musical *The Phantom of the Opera*, whose hero was the reverse—horrible looks hiding goodness. At least that's what he remembered. He and or someone from his Major Crimes Unit team had interviewed most of the residents on the street multiple times. The interviews had followed about five murders, and now this new death possibly made six. All the events occurred within a period of about fifteen months. He recited from memory the visuals from the MCU's murder board:

M1	Tues, 12/8/2015, Jared Stuart, almost 12 years	Arrow through his ear
M2	Wed, 4/18/2016, Davie Caras, 12 years	Choked while held down
M3	Wed, 8/24/2016, Melvin Stoteras, 12 years	Strangled in the woods
M4	Sat, 11/19/2016, Merry Wafters, 12 years,	Drowned in three feet of water
M5	Tues, 1/24/2017, Jim Derrick, 12 years	Multiple hits with the back end of ax
Death	Tues, 2/28/2017, Jackson Elsby, 13 years	Fall from rock

As he passed number 62 Sunnyside, he thought of the Rozovsky family again. The family members and their interaction was a contrast to his family and his own personal history. He thought for a moment how fortunate they were to be an intact family, clearly working in concert for the good of the whole. Rudy remembered that Anya, Rozovsky's only child, was cherished by the whole Rozovsky family, especially by her babushka Albina. She seemed to be such a cheerful child and very beautiful with her short black hair and long, softly waving bangs hanging over her forehead. She also appeared well behaved, except when he relayed that to her family. Her babushka Albina, Mariska's mother, laughingly said, "Captain, she is good except when she's not good. Generally, Anya is an angel—a beautiful angel." Albina had told the captain that Mariska was forever by Anya's side, ever watchful.

Rudy did think that Mariska seemed to be a protective mother but not a helicopter parent. But what did he know about parenting? He thought, *I'm a parent, but Mona is the real force for parenting in our home. And for good reason. She doesn't have my baggage. Thank God for that!*

In interviews with the Rozovsky family, the MCU detectives learned that relatives would say, "Mariska, leave Anya's side. She is so well behaved. There is nothing to worry about." They reported that Mariska had what her psychiatrist and therapist, Dr. Ornstein, called "great anxiety" bordering on depression. She would not take the antianxiety pills prescribed. She told the detectives that she knew she should. She knew something was wrong. But the pills interfered with her ability to be a vigilant sentry for Anya. They learned that Dr. Ornstein continually asked Mariska leading questions about her childhood in Russia while trying to discover the source of her anxiety. He apparently explained to her that, often, issues arose in childhood that had ramifications for the follow-through in living life and had profound and sometimes negative effects on adult actions. It was only by examining those issues and their importance that a person was able to discover the source of the difficulties being experienced.

Rudy was told that Mariska carefully and adamantly stated that her parents were very good to her. Their notes quoted her as saying, "Yes, there were difficult economic times for our family, both in Russia and during the early years in the United States. But if Mother and Father couldn't take care of me, Babushka and Dedushka—my mother's parents—were always with us. Both were firm and kind and I dearly loved them. I remember always being happy and enjoying my family and friends."

Rudy, thinking about Mariska's reported story, was visited by thoughts about his own early life—the life before he'd met his parents, Lizette and Roland Beauregard. He shook his head to rid himself of that old fear. Now was not the time to remember; it was not the time to face, for the hundredth time, the moment of escape.

He had now reached the Elsby house. He was to interview the parents of Jackson Elsby for the second time since his body was found. He had further questions surrounding the circumstances of Jackson's death.

Sergei Rozovsky saw the unmarked car with Captain Beauregard driving and wondered what brought him to Sunnyside Road again. Why was he alone? Mostly the police came in twos, even when the police were detectives. *Well,* he thought, *ignore my racing heart—racing just because I see the detective riding on my street. My brain can't ignore it. How can I ignore what's happening around my home?*

Sergei regarded the joy he'd felt on the day when Mariska had agreed to marry him. He was pleased that he could give her a much-improved economic circumstance. He, like her, was Russian and, like her and her family, had immigrated to the United States with the help of the Lutheran Church, whose mission was to assist practicing Christians to continue their faith.

He was grateful for the assistance of agencies like the Lutheran Church and Jewish Family Services, which were the biggest support organizations in the area for immigrants from Asia, Africa, and Russia. He reflected that he and Mariska were loyal in their consistency to support their church, New Hope Russian Church, which was evangelical and the reason they were allowed into the United States.

He thought, *Our faith was suppressed in Russia. We've been true to that faith; we've attended services regularly and often much of the day on Sunday. We should because church is where I met Mariska. She liked my guitar playing and told me so.*

Later, afterward, Mariska had kissed him and said, "Sergei, you were ever so handsome and kind. How could I not love you?"

Sergei knew that he was successful. Didn't he own his own tile store in West Side? Didn't he employ five tile setters—three Russian and two American—along with many day laborers? He regarded himself as an important entrepreneur and a source of envy from his friends. He thought that this envy had been exacerbated when he'd married such a beautiful and fun-loving girl as Mariska.

Sergei was grateful that it had not taken long for Mariska to agree to marry him. He wondered how patient he would have been if she had not readily agreed to be his wife. After all, he knew that the community thought he was a good catch. He knew that Mariska respected his hard work—that a work ethic was important to her. He rethought how they had developed a life plan to follow after they were married, with help from Albina.

As was their custom, they wrote a personal contract with each other with assistance from their minister. The contract spelled out rules for mutual respect and financial planning. The contract said that they would both work for five years until they could afford their own home before they would have children. He welcomed having Mariska's mother, Albina, live with them. After all, family was the most important of all endeavors, the reason he worked so diligently to be successful. In Russia, family was often all the people had and all they could trust; family was why he pushed to succeed.

Sergei recalled that he and Mariska had agreed that maybe having two children (hopefully a girl and boy) at least four years apart, would be wonderful. The four-year difference would allow them to pay for college for each child and, thus, would not create a great financial burden. He remembered the Russian adage "Planning may bring something, but no planning will definitely bring nothing." Planning would help prevent unnecessary problems.

Sergei recalled the deep sense of pride the two of them had felt when they had become citizens of this new country. There were required classes that they attended for a year and all kinds of legislated paperwork. They had no problem with that; they were used to dealing with arduous government regulations and, therefore, tolerated with little complaint the new United States regulations.

For some reason, Mariska was allowed to be sworn in at the beautiful new United States Federal Building on State Street in Springfield, Massachusetts, while Sergei's application took longer. He was sworn in later in Worcester, Massachusetts. Despite their planning, his and Mariska's family experiences were internalized so that both he and she expected that life might be fraught with disappointments and worse. However, they believed that with thoughtfulness and careful living they could navigate life's difficulties. They were, after all, young and hopeful and willing to work.

As Sergei walked down the street a bit to see if the detective had parked his car, he could not put the reverie of his experience out of his mind. He must not let the vision of the police on his street negate his personal history. *Fear brings more fear, so stop it! Look at the positive*, he thought. In less than five years, he and Mariska were able to buy and furnish a home on this lovely street in suburban West Side, Massachusetts. He recalled the huge housewarming celebration, which some of his friends had called the "McMansion Special" party, and it was more than special. For it was on that day that Mariska had told him that she was pregnant.

His heart recalled that surge of happiness. *We were so lighthearted. We celebrated until two in the morning, which is not how we normally lived.* His memory brought tears to his eyes with the realization that the party was truly a major event in their lives.

After their little girl, Anya, was born twelve years ago, he had believed that there was every reason to celebrate. And they had with a large, Russian-style christening party, followed by first, second, third, and fourth birthday parties. He had wonderful neighbors who all loved Anya. He particularly liked the Landers family, who lived next door, as well as some other families who had girls around Anya's age. It had seemed that they were living the American dream—until now. Now he and Mariska and Albina had the old-country dark cloud overhanging everything they did; how could they protect their Anya?

And then the parties had stopped. Sergei remembered repeatedly asking Mariska, "Why no more birthday parties for Anya? If you do not want to work so hard, we could have American parties at Chuck E. Cheese's."

"No, Sergei, we've had enough of these extravaganzas," was her only answer.

He simply couldn't understand it. The parties were a bit over the top for children but certainly not extravagant, and they could afford to do it. His business had grown. He was considered an entrepreneur to watch, as noted in a cover story in a local business magazine. He thought, *I know something's wrong with Mariska. I begged Albina to talk to her daughter and convince her to relax and enjoy her life.*

Albina did try, but she told him, "Sometimes I think that America is overwhelming and too fast; there is too much going on to enjoy anything. And I don't love all these parties. Why invite all these children who aren't even relatives and all these strangers? They might take something. They are all too nosy. No, a small family party would be better. I know that you think I'm 'old world,' an 'old Russian lady.' But I've lived longer than you, and I am right."

He thought that Albina was no help at all with her foolish superstitions and distrust. And yet, with all this trouble, could she be right?

Sergei shook from a chill, although he did not believe it was from the weather. The late winter day felt like an early April day. He shook from shame as he recalled Anya's twelfth birthday party, which had not had a good finish. *No*, he thought, *my actions that day were based on concern for Anya. In fact, maybe concern was not a way to explain my reaction to Jackson Elsby's pushing Anya into the pool.* The party was held on a mild winter afternoon with the temperature at forty-nine degrees. It was warm enough to have the kids go outside by the pool but certainly not warm enough to swim. He, unfortunately, with the best of intentions, had had the pool people remove the cover for the party so it would look nice. *Foolish of me,* he thought. *My vanity at play!*

He remembered grabbing Jackson and threatening to drown him in that pool if he ever even thought of touching Anya again. He also remembered shouting and raving that whole evening, until Mariska screamed in rage at him. "Look at Anya," she said. "Look at what she did—shoving birthday cake in his face in front of all the guests." He cringed with self-reproach.

He didn't think that shoving some cake in that boy's face warranted Jackson throwing his little girl into the pool in her beautiful new dress on her birthday. He knew that Jackson was a bully, and bullying pretty little girls was dishonorable; but he had humiliated himself by treating a kid like that. He could not, at that time, control himself. That he knew. And that brought him such self-disgust.

He remembered Anya thanking him, happy that he had taken care of Jackson. Her words helped but did not relieve him of guilt when she said, "He had no right to do that, Papa. I was frightened." He thought, *She is such a sweet little girl. We are so lucky to have such a sweet little girl.*

It troubled him sometimes that Mariska seemed to be distant from Anya. He thought, *I can't understand it. Perhaps some of the chaos suffered by Mariska in her childhood won't allow her to stay close to the child.*

Sergei recalled that he'd had to insist on this party for Anya's twelfth birthday. Anya had been given permission to invite all her friends whose parties she had attended all year. He'd told Mariska that there was no reason for Anya not to have her own party. He'd thought, *It's been seven years. Surely a little girl can have a birthday party.* He remembered that Mariska was the most loving mother to

Anya, until Anya was about three or four years old. What happened to change her was something that he did not understand. That was not all that he didn't understand. Mariska did not embrace having another child. In fact, even bringing up the subject was contentious.

The problem, as he recalled from history, may lie in Mariska's early childhood. He reviewed what he had been told about Mariska's early life in Russia. Mariska had suffered as a child because her paternal grandmother was a former KGB agent and was considered by all members of the family to be a cold and evil bitch—always finding fault with her grandchild Mariska. Mariska's beauty, this grandma told her, would bring her sadness and agony someday. "Don't think a pretty face is an asset," said Grandma. "It hides the dark truth in many cases."

Mariska told him that she was certain that there was some truth in that grandma's statement. Her thoughts as she explained them were that "people expect great beauties to be perfect, which of course is not possible in this complicated life or even in a very simple life—if ever one of those simple lives even existed. Beauty is an accident in nature. I agree with my surly grandmother that beauty may hide a multitude of disagreeable traits."

Sergei was again morose, his mood ever darkening. He felt himself quite angry with his wife, something he never expected to feel. He thought that maybe he wasn't angry but that he felt powerless. He could not control Mariska and further did not understand her. Mariska often told him that she wondered why she herself was such an overprotective parent. Certainly she noted that her mother had hovered over her for safety and health reasons, especially when they lived in Russia, but not the way she did with Anya. She told him that she felt such great unease when thinking of Anya. When Anya had friends over or when they visited friends who had children, she found herself superwatchful. Children could be ever so mean and heartless.

She'd given into Sergei about the birthday party and had another birthday party for Anya, and look what had happened. Anya got thrown in the pool with her good dress on. She said that his anger was so threatening that she didn't recognize the man she'd married. He had always been calm and kind. The words he had spoken to that young boy—that was not her husband. Certainly that was not the Sergei she said she knew. He was being blamed, but what about Anya's behavior?

And then she told Sergei that maybe Anya brought on the skirmish. She said that it was clear that other children sometimes thought that Anya was mean and spoiled. But Sergei thought that even those children agreed that Anya didn't deserve to be thrown in the pool with her best dress on at her own birthday party. No, his anger and Mariska's problems were not helped by what fate had foisted upon them and their neighbors.

The last straw, he believed, had occurred two weeks after the birthday party, when Grandma Albina had brought in the newspaper, gesturing to a picture of a young boy, Jackson Elsby. Although Albina could not read much English, she knew the word "dead." Screaming in Russian, she had made Mariska read the article, saying, "We know this boy. What happened to him?"

Sergei remembered that they had all read the story, and a heavy blanket of fear had enveloped them all. The paper relayed that Jackson had been found dead the previous day at the bottom of a large rock in the Hoffington Park playing fields between Sunnyside and Old Towne Route roads. It was the sixth murder of children in about fifteen months at locations on or near Sunnyside Road. Mariska had been filled immediately with anxiety and started shaking, while Sergei had clenched his fists in anger and self-reproach.

On that same afternoon, Sergei recalled, Anya had returned from school with a paper flyer in her hand that listed the names of teachers and the school therapist, who had made themselves available to meet with the children from Anya's seventh grade class at Hoffington Middle School. The flyer was an invitation to parents to encourage their children to talk with an adult at the school, either one by one or in groups.

Anya told her parents that she and her friends were already

planning to visit with Dr. Abbott, the school therapist. Anya said the he was oh, sooo cute and was the only man in the school that the girls thought was worth talking with because, as she explained, "Dr. Abbott listens to us and doesn't ever criticize us."

He shivered as he recalled Mariska's immediate verbal reaction, "This is not the time to talk that way, Anya."

Anya's response was dramatic with an, "Oh not again. He is cute, Mama, and I'm not the one who is dead. I'm still alive."

He remembered later chastising Mariska, reminding her that Anya was only twelve years old, a time of preadolescence, which brings with it all kinds of silliness. He'd said that Anya was being silly, not necessarily deliberately being flip or insensitive.

Sergei told his family, "We should all go to the funeral. It's important to show our sympathy, especially because of my problem with the boy, which I deeply regret now. I apologize to you both, but we must deal with my error. Someone will tell the police about the birthday party confrontation. I am concerned for us all."

Sergei had driven the family, all four of them, to the funeral. The event had brought out the larger West Side community, as well as the Sunnyside Road residents and also, unfortunately, a mixed rabble of voyeurs. He had seen his little girl Anya cry and cry and cry, while Mariska, although tense, had stayed quiet and shown no visible emotion throughout the ceremony. He'd felt bothered by Mariska's lack of expression.

He'd thought, *Mariska is a woman filled with compassion. Doesn't she know that it's important to show compassion this day, even if she doesn't feel compassionate? It's important because I'm at risk; and if I'm at risk, then we all could be at risk. It is important for Anya. I remember how angry I was with this young boy, and rightfully so. Despite all the sympathy expressed by the funeral attendees, I believe that this dead boy would have been in serious trouble someday—very serious trouble, as he's been known to create rifts. Perhaps even the boys' parents secretly know this about his behavior. The funeral is a tearjerker. It doesn't matter how many times the area residents go through loss; the horror and drama of a new loss exacerbates any grief from previous losses. Who will be next is heavy on all our minds.*

Sergei had moved restlessly, not sitting quietly, but thinking of six young people, including Jackson, who had died—no Jackson, who had probably been murdered. The papers never said that they were all murdered, but everyone knew they were. He had thought, *They must think that we're all stupid claiming that one of the deaths was an accident and that there was no justification for the serial killer label. Ha, haven't the state police and the federal agents investigated? The victims are not just from Anya's class but also from the year ahead. This is not what I or my comrades from Russia thought could or would happen in America. America is supposed to be the safe haven, to which the world's refugees escaped.*

He remembered the first victim, Jared Stuart—how could children die that way?—so young. Police were everywhere in their town—nice police.

Sergei had seen the police in the back row, including the detectives and their captain. He remembered Captain Beauregard, who had interviewed them on several occasions. He also remembered two of the other detectives. Although he innately distrusted police authority, he generally thought that police in the United States were more reasonable than those at home, despite what some reports on the news stated. But today he was not reassured by police presence. Nothing so far had been resolved.

He envisioned his home on the street named Sunnyside Road— not as sunny as it had originally promised. No, now it foreboded what could happen next. It is not Sunnyside when a twelve-year-old is hit over the head with the back end of an ax. Jim Derrick's murderer had still not been found. He remembered repeatedly stating to neighbors that it was someone who was furious with Jim, who was known for stealing tools from garages and teasing animals and children. Jim had not been a nice young man, but he had certainly been too young to die. Karma for him, Sergei was certain.

Sergei knew from the news that the police had found the weapon.

It belonged to one of the neighbors whose whole family had been away in Florida for the winter when the killing occurred. It turned out that the neighbor was famous for never locking his shed. The gossip had it that someone had either caught Jim stealing from the garage and, enraged, killed Jim with his ill-gotten goods or, worse yet, had planned to kill him for thrills or some other reason. Jimmy was a strong boy and liked the girls. He had heard rumors that Jimmy must have known his killer and let him get close—close enough to kill him. He did not like the math; not just Jim and Jackson, but three other boys in or near the neighborhood and one little girl were dead. He reflected, *My Anya and Mariska had known them all.*

Sergei had sat next to Anya at the funeral and had wondered what she was thinking. He'd asked her in a whisper.

She replied, "Daddy, do you wonder if all the children here at the funeral are thinking about how bad Jackson and the other dead kids were? I think it looks like someone's actions were being directed to edit God's mistakes by getting rid of these kids. Maybe it's like Uncle Alex says. 'Taking them out.'"

He begged her to erase those thoughts, saying, "God would never plan killing children, Anya. Even if they were naughty now, they had plenty of time to change their ways."

Anya whispered to him, "Why were those kids so bad? Everyone was always talking about them and their awful meanness, at least five of the kids. Now everyone is crying. I don't understand."

Sergei had thought about the numerous police visits investigating all the events related to the dead children. He thought, *Anya's got something there. No one is saying anything negative; but that's the unstated rule at funerals, and Anya's just too young to understand.*

Anya had said under her breath but loud enough for Sergei to hear, "Once you die, they make you a saint."

Musing over events over the past year or so, Sergei remembered that Captain Beauregard had even questioned Anya, with her mother present as always. Anya had told her dad that she thought his questions were stupid but that she'd pretended to be helpful. She'd asked her dad, "Why didn't they ask what detectives on TV stories ask, 'probing questions'. It's been annoying to have police riding up and down Sunnyside every day, all day. They are always watching every house. Mom looked haggard when they came to the house, and she was in a shabby dress."

He recalled chastising her, saying, "Your mother never looks shabby. She is always beautiful."

Sergei discussed with Mariska just before the funeral the four boys and one girl who had died before Jackson Elsby. She had said to him, "Five children, in addition to Jackson. I'm not a statistician, Sergei, but these deaths certainly seemed like an extraordinary coincidence. All the other mothers are keeping an eye on their kids now. I remember when they used to laugh at me for staying so close to Anya. They assumed my closeness was a trait of all Russian mothers based on experiences in our home country."

Sergei explained to Mariska in depth that most of their neighbors had no knowledge of Russian culture and Russia. They thought her fears were a result of her upbringing in Russia. Americans thought all kinds of bad crimes occurred in Russia. Mariska had responded by saying, "They have it all wrong. If six children in Russia died in such unwitnessed ways, the people in Russia would be on the street crazed. Here the process seems slow and agonizing. Three of the six deaths are being very carefully investigated. Do the police think that, if they're annoying enough, someone will confess?"

An hour later as the family was leaving the graveside, Captain Rudy Beauregard, chief detective of West Side Major Crimes, had approached Sergei. He'd asked, "Mr. Rozovsky, I would like to interview you and your family about an incident you had with Jackson Elsby a couple of weeks ago. We have just learned about the event. I believe it was at your daughter's birthday party. We could do it at your home or at the station, whichever you prefer."

Sergei had stiffened but caught himself enough to say, "Please come to our home. We'll be available in an hour."

As the captain left, Sergei had thought, *And now they attack.*

I know police. How do I explain my actions at the birthday party? Exactly when did Jackson die? I seem to remember it was during the day. I'm always at work, so I have people to vouch for me. What the hell am I worrying about? I didn't hurt Jackson; I didn't kill Jackson.

He walked back to his family attempting to be calm enough to reassure them about the impending interview by the police.

2

The Cloud

DETECTIVE BEAUREGARD VISITED THE Rozovsky family at five in the evening accompanied by a woman detective, Petra Aylewood. Anya thought they took over the living room, making her dad look small despite his six-foot, three-inch height, which was silly because the detectives were shorter. Her mother and grandmother looked frightened. She was ashamed of the way they kept offering coffee and food and were repeatedly refused. It was not a visit. Why couldn't they see that the police were here on business? They were so old world. This was not Russia. Why couldn't they get it? Police needed proof here, and it looked like there was no proof for any of the murders.

Finally, Detective Beauregard resembled the detectives on TV. He now had a way of asking questions, Anya thought, that seemed unrelated but when put together formed a lasso around his potential prey, while the woman detective just stood and stared at the whole family. Her father attempted to be friendly to the detectives, but they were quick and abrupt, asking really peppering questions of her mother, father, herself, and even Grandmother, who did not speak English well at all. The family was questioned about each dead child. How well did you know him or her? Where were you around the time he or she died? What do you think happened? Did you have history with any of them? Many questions had already been asked in the past, but they went on and on and on. Anya thought they were trying to see if the family changed their answers.

Then the captain focused on Jackson Elsby and the birthday event. Anya told them, "Jackson has always been a bully. He teases girls all the time. He said that I wasn't nice to him. Well, it was my birthday party, and I told him that I was as nice as I could be to him. He was mad. Jackson ruined my new birthday dress; he pushed me in the pool in front of everyone. Even though they knew it was wrong, some of them laughed at first; then they felt sorry for me." Anya then started crying.

Sergei, who was already uncomfortable with the situation, jumped up, loudly protesting that he didn't want them to upset his little girl. Suddenly, Babushka Albina fell to the floor while clutching her chest. Mariska screamed and ran to her mother and hugged her.

Twenty minutes later the ambulance arrived and took Grandma and Mariska to the hospital, leaving the police and the remaining Rozovsky family thinking about the events of the day. Sergei was most disturbed that his daughter had had to participate in and witness these events.

⊰⊱

Detective Beauregard thought to himself that the Rozovsky family was a little off. He tried to understand their silent but deliberate distance from him, but he could not explain it to his satisfaction. He knew that his brain often attached potential motives; suspicion; and, yes, sometimes evil quickly, without evidence. Since he was more often right than wrong, he let his brain prevail. One minute, Mrs. Rozovsky is offering him coffee and dessert. In the next moment, she's answering questions in a most guarded manner. It wasn't that some of the other families he questioned weren't guarded. It was clear that some had dislike for at least three of the victims but, nevertheless, felt uncomfortable talking negatively about a murdered child. He thought that their dislike for some of the lost children colored their conversation, taking them from a typical family with an American guilty conscience to an "I hated the little brat, but I'm sorry he's dead" kind of thing.

But the Rozovsky family was truly a bit stranger. Not that he was unfamiliar with strange—especially when it came to family. No. Just thinking about where he himself came from brought chaos into his nice organized mind. However, he had survived; and with the help of Lizette and Roland, his adoptive parents, he'd developed insight that he was certain he would not have if there had been no bumps in his early years. Perhaps, genetically he was blessed with the half-full glass kind of outlook on life. No matter where it came from, he was certain that being an optimist was foil against the bugaboos of anxiety and depression.

Rudy thought about the Rozovsky's nice home, probably the showiest on the street. It had been built in two or three stages. The main part of the home was a large split-level that was better looking than most splits Rudy had seen. It was the gigantic front burnished oak door that led to a very large foyer that impressed him the most. There was what looked like a large addition built on the whole back of the house, leading through French doors to the fenced-in swimming pool; that then led to a beautiful, rather densely wooded area. He could see the Russian influence in the home, with the oversized crystal chandelier and matching sconces on the wall in the formal dining room and a lot of extra gilt on the furniture.

Rudy's wife, Mona, would not approve of such extravagant decor. She was a minimalist in house design. He thought himself lucky that that she hadn't thrown out his comfy oversized Barcalounger his kids had given him a few years ago for Christmas. At the Rozovsky house, all the chairs were oversized and comfortable.

No. His concern about these people started when he watched the women in the family. Sergei, the father, appeared to be a tough businessman with a soft spot for his family. But when the old lady fainted or had a stroke, whichever, it seemed just too convenient. The guys at the station would be thinking he was getting a bit aggressive in this case. He imagined them saying, "You'll be arresting a dog for serial murder next, Rudy." But there was too much going on. He thought, *That little girl, Anya, was too damn cute. But she was not easily approachable, not shy, but a little cold.* He concluded that she suffered from "only child syndrome."

As to her mother, Rudy had never seen a more repressed person in his life. For such a beautiful woman, and he thought that anyone would think her so, she appeared sad and insecure. He'd noticed her shaking just before the grandma fainted. Maybe that was the connection; Mariska was overly fearful about her whole family. Mariska appeared to him to be particularly attentive to detail whether it was in adjusting for pillows for where he and Detective Petra Aylewood sat or noticing and moving a gorgeous gypsy-style lamp on the table to a more perfect placement. Who knows what their history was in mother Russia? He'd heard stories about Russia and their KGB, which had another name now. He was certain that inflicting fear in its citizens was its goal. Perhaps it was just fear exhibited by these two women—although he believed that the father and little girl appeared to show no fear at all.

Well it was time to get to the bottom of this; that was for sure. The problem was no DNA evidence had been found so far. And witnesses had seen some of the victims at play and then just didn't see them anymore. In the case of the kid who fell off the fifteen-foot boulder and had all kinds of scrapes and damage on both sides of his head, well, the medical examiner believed that the massive damage could not be easily explained by falling from a rock. How that had happened he was uncertain, unless the boy had bounced three or four times against the rock on both sides in falling. Kids fall fifteen feet and survive. Even if the boy tripped and hit his head on the way down, why was there major damage on the back of his head as well as the front? No. The examiner said this smelled of intent to do harm.

So back to the station, he thought. *Let's looks at this family again.* The Rozovsky family knew every one of the dead children, and the cute little daughter had had some skirmishes with at least one of the victims. He didn't think that Sergei, the father, would take any monkey business related to his little girl. He was definitely a tough dude and very protective of his family. Still, he hadn't heard of Sergei having history with any of the other victims, and he certainly didn't look like a serial killer. None of them did.

The Rozovsky family received good news on the next day. The doctor said that Albina's condition was excellent; she had suffered a mild heart attack. However, he insisted that she clearly must have had symptoms previously that she had ignored. Sergei explained to the doctor that Albina never would go for a checkup, and she of course would never have reported to her family that she was unwell. Sergei was told that Albina had probably had high blood pressure and cholesterol for a long time before the attack; and if she didn't have such a strong constitution, the attack would have resulted in great damage to the heart muscle.

Albina would be given meds, a special diet to follow, and a menu of exercises to prevent another similar attack. Sergei groaned, as did Mariska and Anya, at the job ahead of them now. How to give Albina the help she needed given her old-world ways. She was suspicious about doctors and medicine and stubborn in her absolute conviction that she was the head of the family and would not take advice from those younger than her.

Albina said, "You have all become too American to suit me. You believe what outsiders say and what is said on the television."

Sergei was certain that Albina believed that the news on television was not reality but the government's twist to make people think a certain way. No. Sergei shook his head thinking about how to direct Babushka. But they were family, and if it was the right thing to do for Albina, they would do it.

Sergei remembered the story Mariska had told about how Albina had protected her from her father's parents, who were violent when threatened in any way. They thought that any changes in local rules made by the Russian CPSU or any lower-level government agency made the family's life impossible. Her father's mother would raise a tirade, blaming all the younger people in the world and constantly screaming, "The old ways are the only ways to be trusted." Mariska's father, Albina's husband, who had died years ago, constantly had to explain that the changes required by the state in farming really had brought some resources to the family.

The story as reported said that Mariska would scuttle and hide behind the only wardrobe the family had in the house and stay there for hours. Mariska sometimes said, "This childhood experience is the reason I'm always so nice to everyone, always avoiding conflict. Perhaps it is why I'm so attracted to you, Sergei. You have no problems with conflict."

He remembered replying to her, "Mariska, you see potential problems everywhere before they even present as a problem. You spend all your days moving out of the way. Sometime you must face the problem aggressively and immediately without thinking too much."

She had retorted, "No, Sergei. You do not know. I only see problems that exist, often when you're not even aware that there is a threat. Perhaps, I've inherited the great Russian triad of sicknesses—suspicion, guardedness, and fear of joy. Maybe this is the source of all my fears around Anya. You, Sergei, Anya, and sometimes even Babushka are optimists, thinking that all will be well. If only I could believe as you do, but I can't."

⸻◆⸻

They were leaving the hospital. Mariska was trying to make Babushka comfortable, but thinking all the time, *It is our job to run around, to take good care of Babushka, as she has always taken good care of us. I'm very good at taking care of things, as good as Grandma. I can instill order in any situation.*

Mariska thought about when she had first come to the United

States and found work with a Russian-owned cleaning service. The service had residential contracts and more lucrative contracts for commercial buildings. It didn't take long for her supervisor to put her in charge of two to three other cleaners in a commercial building. The owner-manager told her, "Mariska, you have a license and own your own car. I need that, but even more than that, I need you to pick up some of the good new immigrant workers who have no transportation. Your English is very good, and that is a plus. You will be a site supervisor."

But Mariska also knew enough to work along with the workers, dividing the work fairly. She knew that if she also worked with the others they could not complain about her, and she didn't mind the work. It was mindless at times, but it gave her brain the space to dream. She dreamed of her own home someday. She dreamed of a husband and children. That dream was worth all her hard work. Yes, Mariska had prayed. And, yes, her prayers had been answered.

3

Pain

AMY LANDERS, THE ROZOVSKY'S next-door neighbor, watched through the lace-curtained windows as the detectives left the Rozovsky home. Seeing them on her street distressed her. They reminded her of the dead children. How many were there—five or six? She had known them all, for her son, Henry, would have been just a year or two older. It was true that she didn't know all of them well, but she could feel their parents' loss; oh how deeply she could feel their loss. Her Henry had died over two years ago of a severe case of juvenile Crohn's disease. His intestines were so damaged with infection that had gone systemic that he just did not make it through surgery. The pain of watching his suffering over the years previous to his death and dealing with his sweet, compliant nature continued to encourage the deep anger she suppressed in her heart. Why hadn't Henry yelled at her or ranted about the pain or cursed God? Instead, he would tell her husband, Jeffrey, and her that it would be all right and that he was not afraid to die. Who was the child here, certainly not Henry?

Deep in the recesses of her brain, she wondered, if he were angrier, could he have put up a better fight? Did she and Jeffrey wait too long in making the surgical decision? Should they have gone to Boston for the surgery? Her daughter, Suzanna, told her, over and over that Henry was an "old soul" and lived between two states of being, the before and the now. She personally thought that Suzie was reading too many of those "over the other side" kind of books. However, now that she had also lost her husband, Jeffrey, her sorrow was sometimes overwhelming. She was so alone. Suzie was now not just her only child but the only other soul living in the home. She would listen carefully to everything Suzie would say; Suzie was all she had left of what had been a perfect life.

Amy also knew that all she had left of Henry were their conversations and his powerful words and her holding him when he was in pain. Jeffrey had died differently, of a massive coronary; he was dead before the ambulance came. She had not had a chance to hold Jeffrey in her arms. She'd never thought he was at risk. Memory was all that she had left. She also knew that she would never not listen to Suzanna—that conversations were all that were left to the survivor after death. She often tried to remember words spoken by Henry and Jeffrey; and when she couldn't, she would explode in despair, crying.

Amy wondered as the police drove away what her neighbors had to say to the police. Mariska had told her that Anya knew all the children. *How dreadful*, she thought, *to know so much about loss at such a young age.* But she thought that that little girl, Anya, although pretty, was one strong little girl. As Amy's mother would say in denouncing some of Amy's friends, "That girl knows too much too early." Amy didn't know how Anya could be "too knowing," as her mother, Mariska, rarely let her out of her sight. She always thought the Rozovskys were a good family whose members all showed great respect for their neighbors. And they had all been so very kind when she and Jeffrey had lost Henry and later when her wonderful Jeffrey's death had added to her pain. They'd sent home-cooked food over daily for weeks. She'd tried to tell them to stop, but Mariska had explained that that was what they would do in Russia; that was all they could do.

The Rozovskys were well off, always adding something new to their home. They had an in-ground swimming pool and had certainly improved the front of their house so it was now what she would call "grand." Amy thought, *How happy we all used to be—my neighbors and my family.* Her loss seemed to her to have cast a spell over the whole area, for the deaths/murders—she didn't really know which or what—of so many children had started happening shortly after Henry's death. She looked toward the woods in the back of her home and was slightly startled at her thoughts. The connection of her beloved Henry and Jeffrey's deaths with the deaths of six children; well they could not be related.

Amy thought that the woods in the back of the houses on her side of the street were seductive to all the kids who lived on Sunnyside Road. Their houses backed into over a quarter mile of woods that then led to the park. Her children had loved playing in the woods with the other kids on the street, and they had built an enormous tree house that her husband had had to reinforce for safety sake. It was not the prettiest tree house she had ever seen, but it was certainly the biggest. The children had also camouflaged the tree house so it would be difficult to see if someone was just trudging along in the woods. The woods were dense, and it was necessary to follow little trails to get through, but there were many little trails, each named after one of the families for the child who'd either made the trail or found an old trail. The trails were not labeled, and she suspected that each kid named a trail and another kid had a different name for the same trail. She thought that inflation of ego started early in life.

The woods had always seemed like the perfect space for children to play, so close and safe. She laughed inside at herself, thinking of all the worry she had had over safety concerns when the family illness, which some in her family had lived with all their lives, had killed her gentle son. It had never occurred to her to worry about that earlier. No. She'd worried about locking doors, setting the alarm, getting her kids' rides for all their events, and pulling them in from play before dark. Now she thought, *I see that perhaps the woods were not so safe. Didn't one of the boys die on this side of the woods opposite the Liacos yard? Another boy was found way down near the woods.*

Amy shook as she realized that no one was ever safe, and she started crying as she thought about those other parents facing the overwhelming loss of their children. Now they would suffer.

It just wasn't healthy for her Suzanna, who was now so cynical, to have to bear witness to so many children's deaths. These murders ripped open the wound left from Henry's death for both of them; for Suzanna, maybe this was more than she could bear. Underneath her daughter's pleasant exterior was a girl who was seriously burdened with grief; and to be honest, she was her father's daughter. Jeffrey and Suzanna were twins in spirit, and now one twin was gone.

Suzanna had gotten mixed up with a group of kids after Jeffrey's death—a group that really did not have Amy's approval. At the time, Amy had known that Suzanna may act out from anger and grief, but she was surprised at her choice of marginal friends and her dabbling in pot and whatever else. She had tried to get Suzanna to therapy. Instead Suzie was drawn to readings about the afterlife and the souls floating around in the universe.

She'd once queried, "Mom, maybe when I have children, Henry will be one of them or maybe even Dad, although that would be really weird."

Amy did not find this consoling at all.

———◆◆◆———

Detective Petra Aylewood liked to think that she had a little different perspective on crime than Rudy, her boss. Her nickname given by the department was "Bolt" because she moved so quickly. Everybody in the department had a police-given nickname. Hers was appropriate, as all the nicknames addressed something about the habits or traits of the cop named. She was, to the observer, the faster-moving decisive member of the two detectives when they were working a case together. Although Rudy was Petra's boss, it often seemed to observers that he was the slower of the two. Early in their partnership, she assumed that the fifteen-year age difference was the reason. Later on, when she spoke to some of his previous case partners, they laughed at her. Rudy, they said, was a foxy turtle. Just when you think he's going nowhere in solving a crime, he puts his finger on the perp. And, *boom*, he's got the collar.

The force called him the "Auditor." He chased every bit of evidence, building a file of details that was really helpful when a case went to trial. And like any auditor, he only needed a few samples from which he would extrapolate volumes of thoughts directing him to a perp or two or three.

Petra realized that her first five years in this police relationship was spent getting educated. Rudy was her teacher, and he demanded a dogged searching for details. He would log these details into a computer spreadsheet whose matrix left the rest of the detectives, other than their IT detective, Mason Smith, and their staff secretary, shaking their heads. It made sense to Rudy. Every detail from his notebook found a place on his spreadsheet. It didn't matter what other computer programs the department used; Rudy still compiled details in his own way. He said that it wasn't duplicate work that he liked; he didn't like doing the same thing twice. Instead the spreadsheet was another view offering a lens that was different from his notebook and the murder boards.

Petra often commented on Rudy's old-fashioned ways and how they were odd and unexpected for such a young man. He was almost or barely fifty years old.

Their city was small, and the murder rate was not high. But every murder brought political pressure on their heads. The thing is that the homicidal—at times—actions of a nineteen-year-old druggie—say, killing someone while robbing a convenience store—were crimes cops were familiar with. This type of crime they had at least seen before. There was a whole list of investigative points that they would follow, which would normally lead to an arrest. But killing kids, well, that projected in her mind the face of evil.

What kind of monster were they looking for? She looked for the hundredth time at the murder boards. She'd never seen so many boards, for it now appeared to be really six murders in one murder investigation. She thought of Rudy and his insistence that these were serial murders. She thought, *The FBI agent suggests we not label them as such because of the potential of pandemonium in the community. That's a joke! There are five, maybe six, murders of twelve-year-old children around Sunnyside Road in fifteen months. The state police and the task force have ruled out just about everyone who services the area or who has ever been known to hang around. We have a serial murderer. We just don't know the motive yet.*

Rudy had told her many times to review and review and then review the work over and over and over and then sleep on it and review again. He had some kind of respect for the sleeping process. In sleep, while the body was at rest, he believed that the mind could relax and play. He called it "mental creative inspiration or MCI." Petra thought she had seen it work for him. She hadn't had much success herself.

So for the sixteenth time she grabbed a stale coffee and settled in for another review of the facts and assumptions. It was at least more interesting than filling out processing reports for comparison with time sheets before Millie found something off. Millie was the staff admin or secretary and receptionist for the Major Crimes Unit (MCU), and she was a nitpicker for discrepancies in reports.

The city was too small to have a separate homicide unit. In fact the MCU was made up of two units merged into one—Armed Robbery and Burglary and Homicide. The work of the merged MCU was now in need of two more officers. West Side had about 125 to 135 officers and about 15 detectives assigned to various units, one of which was a drug unit that also interfaced with the DARE program. It was a fact of life in 2017 that drugs were in the schools.

Petra felt she was one fortunate cop to be in Major Crimes, particularly as she was a woman. Major Crimes Unit was the gold standard, the rainbow, the plum; and her appointment to it had caused an eruption of some grumbling in the squad. She knew that her ability to work with Rudy was one reason she had been chosen, and many had been surprised when the chief had okayed Rudy's choice.

She was Rudy's choice, which certainly surprised her. She didn't know him, and although she'd applied for the position, she had thought at the time, *I've a snowball's chance in hell of getting it.* She had never asked him why she had been given the position. It wasn't to add diversity to the unit. The captain didn't care a hoot about diversity. He only cared about performance and trust issues. And he certainly wasn't trying to make a move on her; he just wasn't that kind of cop.

The other two detective members of the unit were okay, but she thought that they took little responsibility for moving cases forward. She did have to admit, though, that Mason Smith was a guru with the computer. He was called "Byte" by everyone and to his face. Jim Locke, the fourth detective, knew more about what was going on in the whole surrounding district, not just the city, than even the street beat cops. He was a kind of touchy-feely guy, always concerned with what people thought and why they did what they did; kind of moved too slowly for her.

It seemed to her odd to call West Side a city. It was officially organized as a town. It was now the size of a small city but was still legally a town. Her colleagues, Jim and Mason, were really skilled at foreseeing potential problems in the town. They could just review local trends and area macros and know where the city's resources should be directed, including police and fire resources. The mayor and police chief would often ask them what they thought as they were putting their budgets together.

But make a decision or form a conclusion that would be helpful to solve something? No. They were useless. They had skills, but her skills were a little more traditional cop skills. Rudy, in fact, once said, "Petra, you have a big future as a cop; your short time with the Boston Police Force has given you creds that other cops can't argue with. With enough time on the job, you will go far—much farther than I will or that I would even wish to go." She wondered, *What exactly is he saying or really meaning?*

Petra knew that she was smart and a street cop in many ways, but she still couldn't figure out why Rudy had taken her on the unit. She often thought that her nice middle-class background was not overly helpful in prepping her for police work but that maybe all the pain surrounding her failed marriage with its disappointments and unmet expectations was truly instructive. Well, as she had learned before, she would do the hard work diligently and endure. So she went back to the murder board. One section of a board listed a summary of the murders.

Five certain murders and one question mark—all were children around twelve years old, five boys and one girl. The murders had happened more or less a few months apart, except for the last one. The initial murder had occurred on December 2015, while the latest murder had happened now in February 2017—all occurring in a span of fifteen months.

She thought, *The problem is that all the murders were in or next to Hoffington Park.* After all the investigations following the previous murders, there just wasn't a lot of riffraff left hanging around that area. Granted, the park could bring in the perverts, but the department would know anyone with a history. Those soccer moms who frequented the park called the police on anyone who even looked suspicious. There had certainly been much more activity in the area at the time of the first and second murders than there was now!

It is a bit odd that three of the boys murdered were not well liked, while the other three kids were accepted pretty well by most everybody, she mused. The boys who had been disliked had apparently created a lot of disharmony in the classrooms, at sports, and at parties. Maybe, some officers had thought, it was someone cleaning up the neighborhood before these kids grew up and created havoc. They had even looked at the neighborhood residents for Goody-Two-Shoes types with missionary zeal. No, none of that. The only rabid interest shown by these neighbors was for soccer, football, and dancing. So middle class, so surprising, as she'd never thought that serial murdering was a suburban hobby. *Rudy is right. I don't care what the Feds say; there is a serial murderer lurking in the area.*

Petra worked the murder board again, thinking, *Jackson Elsby's death, which we know was a murder, is the last in the series. While we wait for the ME's final report, looking at all the other murders is important. There is a connection; why can't I see it?*

She looked at the pictures of Jared Stuart, the first victim, and thought that he would have been a great-looking man someday if he had lived. Already five feet five inches tall at the age of almost twelve years, he was certainly tall for a boy of his age. She thought that he probably looked older too. She knew, and that knowledge was reinforced by the FBI profiler's report, that a series of murders almost demanded a strong connection in the profiles of the victims to be considered serial murders.

She remembered the first statement made by the FBI profiler who had been called in after the third murder. He'd said, "Sometimes it's the similarity of the victims by age or physical appearance or sex or disability or anything that will help you with a motive. Sometimes it's what was done to the body before, during, and after death that will help you with a motive. Sometimes the perpetrator just loves to kill for any reason, and in that case, the only connection to the victim is proximity and the murderer's knowledge of the victim."

She thought, *Could anyone just like to murder children?* She sighed as she thought of the stress put on the department by these murders over the past fifteen months. By murder number three, the Hampden County district attorney and the state police were organized into a task force. By law in Massachusetts, the district attorney and the state police technically have supervisory oversight of all murders taking place in most of the state's cities and towns outside of Boston, Springfield, and a couple of other cities. The theory was that those cities had the resources and force size that gave them more capability to conduct professional murder investigations.

She laughed and thought, *We can all thank Whitey Bulger, the Irish mobster from Boston, and his deranged agreement with FBI agent John Connelly for this law. Nobody on the local level trusted the FBI after that horror show.* The investigative task force included the district attorney's office, with their assigned state police detectives; other state police; and in this case, the West Side police. And when there were serial murders involved, the Feds were also included.

Petra believed that the result was problematic for the West Side Police Department. First, the state police were in charge along with the DA. All overtime was given to them and not to the department's personnel. And there certainly was overtime. What killed her was that the overtime was often given for travel for "staties" who drove in from Boston every day. Four hours of driving to and from, all paid for under the task force budget, allowing minimal overtime for West Side's police. And they all hated the attitude from the state cops and the Feds. She did think that if it weren't for the political skill of their chief and mayor there would have been a major eruption in the department.

She remembered when she was bitchin' about the unfairness of it all that Captain Beauregard had given her a primer on when and where to express emotion on the job. He'd said, "Detective, you understand issues you are able to control and those you are not able to control. You don't like this; neither do I. Build bridges for yourself with the chief and the mayor and the district attorney. Build bridges with all in authority, just as you do with the community. You will be in a better position then, when you rise to the top. And you will get there." She wasn't sure if the captain was blowing smoke her way, but the captain was not known for blowing smoke.

One of the big problems, she thought, in this kind of a situation is that neither the troopers nor the FBI know the area locals, and they often stomp all over everyone, creating a public relations nightmare for the local cops. Witnesses talking with the staties were less likely to open up or, in some cases, more likely to change their story, whereas local police knew when they were talking bullshit. It was the local police who know what was going on in a town, not the staties or the Feds. They knew the people and the environment. Their instincts were often ignored because as they were told, "Instincts are not scientific."

Petra read a note attached to the board that said, "There isn't a vendor in town who services the Sunnyside Road area, which is one of the main street accesses to Hoffington Park, that hasn't been investigated." She thought, *The Task Force is, even if it sounds contradictory, too all over the cases; and the murders haven't stopped.*

Although there is one strength in bringing in the state police, she conceded. *And that is the district attorney's ability to pressure for results for DNA or trace evidence testing.*

Petra knew that the department itself had a couple of guys who understood what was important—for instance, what may be able to be tested to potentially get a result that was useful. However, neither the West Side Police Department nor most police departments in cities and towns in Massachusetts had forensics laboratories. Boston and Springfield had laboratories. But the DNA went to the state lab in Maynard. Trace evidence currently went to the state lab in Sudbury. But the FBI had access to everything. In fact, they were opening, in the Chelsea FBI facility in April, a new regional computer forensics lab for fighting cybercrime.

Petra supposed that the previous investigative activity was mainly helpful, as the troopers and the feds were able to rule out as suspects just about every outsider who ever visited the park or Sunnyside Road for any reason; and they now know all the legitimate reasons for folks to be in the area. Who were left as potential suspects? She shivered thinking about the remaining possibilities—maybe a brilliant psychopath living there or related to someone living there or who'd formerly lived there or who legitimately worked there and flew under the investigative radar.

Petra went back to the list on the murder boards and read about Jared Stuart, a practical joker who always tried pulling stunts on the girls in his class or wherever. Jared was said to be very bright and had been moved forward in his class. Some of his jokes weren't funny, but he was pretty good at getting out of any blame. Hoffington School administrators could still not prove that Jared had ruined the back of Evelyn Liacos' dress. Apparently someone had coated her assigned seat at assembly with gluey and ink-laden tissue paper. The paper had stuck to her dress and left a mess that she did not notice until she got up from assembly. And then she was mortified when she realized that everyone was pointing at her and laughing. And her new dress was in ruins.

There was a problem in proving who did it for the principal. Nobody had seen who put the tissue on the chair. There was a movie played at the assembly, so it was assumed that some kid who sat in the row behind Evelyn was the culprit and had done the dirty deed while the lights were out. All the kids and teachers knew it was Jared, and Jared was assigned a seat in the row behind Evelyn; but there were eleven other kids in that row as well.

The poor girl, Evelyn Liacos, was so embarrassed that she didn't return to school for a week following her screaming obscenities and running after Jared right after the incident.

Of interest to Petra was the fact that both Evelyn and Jared lived on Sunnyside Road, and Jared's body was found in the dingle behind Sunnyside on the park side. Jared was always at the park. He would cut through the path right by his garage, which angled to the park.

Was Jared's death an accident? Everyone at the station thought no. He was killed with an arrow driven through his ear. The only archery going on at the park was an adult club that met during March and April each year. No one was doing archery in December. Furthermore, the arrow tip was of metal, commonly supplied by places like Wal-Mart, and used in target shooting and field shooting.

The only kid who was interested in archery in the neighborhood was the Landers boy, who had died before any of the killings occurred. Using a metal arrow tip gave more accuracy to the shooter. But the police could not imagine a kid as a serial killer, although the FBI profiler did not rule the possibility out; he just thought it unlikely because of the lack of trace evidence at each scene. Besides their only archery guy was dead.

There had been a search conducted on all the garages that backed up to the first half of the woods on the park side on Sunnyside Road, hoping to find arrows or tools to make arrows but without success.

The police spoke with Jeffrey Landers, whose house was much farther up on Sunnyside; they'd searched his home, with permission, in an attempt to locate a wrist sling that Henry had been seen using before he died.

The officers did not find anything that was helpful. In fact, all the normal archery gear was still hung on the wall in a place with a sign written above stating each item's use. Jeffrey Landers, Henry's father, had explained to the detectives, when interviewed, that he had purchased all of Henry's archery equipment, and it all was still neatly stored in the garage with a marked place for each item.

Forensics found no fingerprints on the arrow, which made the possibility that the death was accidental less unlikely. Even if the perp wore archery gloves, it would be normal to notch the arrows before shooting. Also, there was no guarantee that the person who owned the arrow was the person who killed with it; but knowledge of one could lead to the other. And besides, not only were there no fingerprints at the first crime scene, there were no fingerprints at any of the crime scenes. No footprints—there were no footprints at any of the sites except for the place where Merry Wafters had been found. There were tons of kids' footprints around the water that was the site of murder number four, if, in fact, it was murder.

Detective Aylewood, trying her hardest to stay on point, scanned the board for the murder number two victim—a twelve-year-old boy who looked like he was in second grade. He was known to be a little hanger-on, one who would do anything to be accepted by the other kids. His name was Davie, though his baptismal name was David. Even his parents, sister, and brother called him Davie. He apparently was a happy kid, who generally didn't cause trouble unless he was put up to something by the bigger kids' group at school. She knew from his file that he was much loved but perhaps had not found a perfect place for himself within his peer group yet.

Detective Beauregard had asked Detective Jim Locke to research Davie, and of course he had. Jim knew everyone, from coaches and teachers to court personnel to soccer moms and wealthy professionals.

If you joined him in questioning a witness, you learned the meaning of simple but probing questions. He would come away from an interview with a history of a couple's marital disputes over the past twenty years. He was patient and empathetic, but his questioning took time. Jim, called the "Shrink" by the department, was a soft-spoken man who really liked his job. Getting to know what made a person tick was always his goal.

Jim had previously asked Petra out for a drink one time. She was immediately concerned that, with his skills, he would learn too much about her; she still wasn't ready to let someone too near. So instead she had given him a weak excuse that she was babysitting her nieces. She kind of regretted it in thinking about it later that evening. She'd spent her night alone when she could have been enjoying an evening with a really nice and pretty good-looking guy. She knew how damaging her seven-month marriage to her high school boyfriend had been, and it was still affecting her. She was too gun-shy to go on a date with a decent guy.

To be truthful, she thought, *I don't want to get involved with a colleague on the force. No. I've seen too many of those relationships. There were too many problems with police having police-to-police love affairs, and she was a girl who didn't want problems.*

Petra remembered that Jim had said getting to know what makes a person tick was always his goal. She didn't want him to know what made her tick. No, she didn't want anyone to know that. She would then be vulnerable. Jim rarely swaggered like most cops, except when he'd recite his personal detective mantra, "The why, the why behind the action is the motive, and once you have that, the rest is dogged police work."

Detective Mason Smith or "Byte," the force's IT guru, would then follow right after with his own mantra, "My computer has saved thousands of pairs of officers' shoes."

Petra thought that in her experience it was unusual to work with three colleagues who were just downright nice and were workers. When they got info to help in a "perp quest," they were just pleased with themselves. This lack of ego was unique on the force. She hoped that Chief Coyne would be able to see that they were committed workers who were not glory hounds and would probably never embarrass him or the department. Besides, everyone knew that Chief Coye was a pretty fair boss most of the time and gave great advice. He was called the "Consigliere" or "Sig" for short by all the cops. He took care of the legal issues for the department but was also a most astute political animal.

She commended him for that and thought, *I need to develop some of his subtleties—be slower in my judgments and kinder in my words.* The chief could be rough if a cop didn't stay on the straight and narrow, and it was known that he strongly felt that problems should be solved within the department. Petra agreed with him on that score. Most of the cops knew that it was better to fall on your sword with him than to attempt to bullshit him with some nonculpability story. Right now, the Sig was beleaguered, and his only direction to anyone was to just get the friggin' perp. So why? Petra asked herself. What is the why behind killing a harmless little kid like Davie Caras?

Rudy had joined her, bringing fresh coffee for them both, his a decaf. They were discussing some aspects of Jackson's death when the captain asked her where she was at in reviewing the murder board. She said that she was only on murder number two, Davie Caras.

The captain said, "Have you noticed, Petra, that the ME suggested that perhaps we're dealing with a left-handed perp. His report shows extra damage on the left side of the larynx on the choking of Davie Caras and what he believes are angled blows from an ax showing a force from a left-hander perp in the death of Jim Derrick. He also thinks left-handedness may be consistent with the more severe damage again on the left side done in strangling Melvin Stoteras, the third murder victim.

"I had uniforms review the records and make some calls to residents to ask who was left-handed in the families living on Sunnyside Road. Mason is including results in our murder matrices. I was surprised to find that there were twenty more girls in the area than boys in that age group and a greater than average amount of left-handedness in the population. Some statistics on left-handedness show an average of 10 percent in a population. Sunnyside's residents have closer to 28 percent of those asked. It is something to think about as we go forward, although maybe not important at all in the end, but another detail."

The captain told Petra that, despite the previous investigative work done by the FBI, he had asked Detective Jim Locke to pursue garnering new information on Davie Caras and also asked Detective Mason Smith to research archery. Could a kid under thirteen years old shoot an arrow with such accuracy as in the murder of Jared Stuart, the first victim? How strong would the kid have to be? Could a girl be the perp? What level of archery skills would he or she have to have?

Looking at Davie, the second victim, they both thought that anyone could have choked him. Davie was so small and frail. He had been choked with a piece of wood pushed into the trachea area. The kid was mostly under water when he was found in the small stream. That piece of wood was never found. Perhaps the killer took it with him or her. Again there was no evidence. Why would anyone do that to such a small kid? It would take a bit of time pressing on the piece of wood before Davie died. Why was someone so angry or vindictive or what? Why? Could a kid be the perp and choke Davie? Was it just a case of availability of weapon? If a kid was the perp, was the kid willing to murder anyone and happily press the wood into Davie's neck while watching him struggle? Her gut told her, no.

Davie was always there looking for attention from anybody, everybody. Did this attention seeking bother the perp? Perhaps he or she wanted all the attention. Perhaps Davie took some of the light away. Petra hated using the Feds' word, "unsub," short for unidentified suspect. She thought it took away all humanity from the victim, as if the victim wasn't important enough for a perp to have had a motive for murdering him or her—that he was just a murdered victim by an unsub.

At that moment, Jim walked into the murder board area of the private conference room and said, "Hey exotic Petra, let's talk about Melvin Stoteras, the third victim. I just spoke with a few older folks, all in their seventies and eighties. I think it would be worthwhile if we made another field trip to Sunnyside."

Petra groaned and reminded him that the Jackson Elsby murder was now on the agenda and said, "Jim, how many hours will this take? It's three o'clock."

Jim said, "It'll take what it will take. I don't mind your company."

On the road, she asked whether he had gained more info on Davie. His answer was that his source interview was a bust.

4

Insight Perhaps

JENNY LOOKED OUT AT the garden beds that she had been working on for the past week. There had been a spell of warm weather allowing her to turn soil and hope for continued warmth. She felt the pain in her shoulders resulting from her two hours of work transferring some of the old soil from the raised beds to the low ground at the edge of the woods. That process was easier than the next one, which required adding some new garden soil and humus to the beds and then turning all the soil over in the beds. Having raised beds seemed useful in preventing weeds and animal damage to the crops, but there was still work. She'd paid over $300 for each of her five beds.

She planned to finish with the soil in the next two days; so, if there was more snow, it would be of no consequence. She could plant early lettuce in April, and by June, the lettuce would be ready to harvest and new plants, maybe pepper, would take their place. Her arms ached from her gardening efforts, but it was a good ache. It made her feel alive at age seventy-nine years.

Albert, her husband, had no interest in plants—just in people, dogs, football, and philosophy. They had no children; neither wanted them. Neither had a childhood where children were valued. Perhaps that skewed their view of any personal assessment of children's necessity in their lives.

Jenny wondered today if Albert may have had a change of mind. If he had married his high school sweetheart, Rosie, would he have had children? Rosie now had an enormous family with five great-grandchildren. She wouldn't mind great-grandchildren, you know, just skip the first two generations in between; and childcare would not be a requirement of the elderly. Everyone knew the elderly couldn't be trusted with babies. Just watch TV and see the elderly falling over or needing an attached alarm or the grandma holding a baby with a wolf's head signaling the passing on of whooping cough. Pity the poor wolves now being blamed for passing on whooping cough.

Albert certainly was interested in all the children on the street. He knew all their names, ages, interests, and problems. Some kids actually sought him out to discuss "teen issues." She had no time for that kind of nonsense, and if she were honest, she'd admit that his interest in all those kids disturbed her; she felt no such interest. She dearly loved her sister's kids once they were adults, but who wanted to deal with pregnancy, babies up at night, children sick with vomit and diarrhea—all with the expectation that the parents would be able to cope? She secretly thought that most parents hated their children at least half the time. And as far as the discipline required, especially with teens, she knew that it was daunting.

Jenny had done a stint as a high school teacher when she was in her thirties during her career discovery period after her ten years in retail. Both fields were not for her. The one year of contract teaching at the Noble Academy two towns away was enough to assure her that young people and Jenny were incompatible.

Albert thought that her real issue was her need for personal structure—that she was excessively compulsive. He probably got that idea from those Facebook quizzes he was always taking. He said that she always required order and liked neatness. She could not argue with him on that issue, but how OCD could she be when she could easily sink her hands in the soil in the garden without hesitation? In fact, she felt an earthly connection that she did not feel with most people.

She hated her land disturbed, even to the point of always finding fault with Ross Landscaping Service who mowed her lawn. Jenny was not as strong as she was before, and so she needed help—not a lot of help. She knew Ross Landscaping Service was as good as she could get, but did anyone monitor their employees anymore? Other than wearing a Ross Landscaping LLC T-shirt, the men had their drawers down by their thighs and looked hoody and sloppy. They were probably just out of the county jail from their appearance.

She remembered when the police had searched her section of the woods. The woods were not really hers. If they were, she would have fenced the woods to prevent all the bratty children from running around and playing God knows what in there. The woods were in a land trust set up by the development builder. They were not buildable because the area included wetlands and required some distance from the homes on that side of Sunnyside Road. Her woods were pristine.

Jenny had cleared half of the section of the woods backing up her home of brambles, choking undergrowth, and tree limbs. She'd moved or thinned the woods' beds of pine needles to make pathways throughout the area. The woods were deep and thick, and although they were not technically *her* woods, she groomed the area as if she were the owner. She never asked permission to clear the area, and no one bothered her. She was proud that she had created a wonder to walk through. *And*, she thought, *they really are my woods; I take care of them.* Walking through these woods reminded her of why she could only live in New England. She had been quite upset when some group from UMASS environmental graduate class had brought her pamphlets on maintaining the environment for insects and bees. Basically they were nosy and questioned her about who had cleared some of her woods. They instructed her on the need to keep the undergrowth there, as it served a purpose for insects. Well, Jenny knew when to play dumb, and they went away.

Jenny remembered the many times the police had scoured the woods after the death of each of those children. She'd tried to assure them each time that she would know if anyone was in her woods. They had not even tried to listen to her.

She'd told Albert and her neighbors that the police made a mess, breaking good boughs off trees and moving pine needles with their big boots. Albert was not sympathetic. He'd said, "Jenny, five children are gone, and we have just learned that another child is dead; that may make six murders. They can search anywhere, inside or outside our home, without a search warrant."

Furious, she'd told Albert, "It's my house, too."

Jenny thought that Albert was bonkers over some of those kids. He'd cried when the boy Henry Landers had died. Albert said that Henry had the heart of a saint and a lion at the same time—true and brave. Well, she wouldn't know. She had never even talked to him. How could she know? But she thought she knew a lot about his sister Suzanna. Oh, she surely did, just by watching her saunter down the street.

When Jenny had taught at the academy, she had observed the young women there. She thought that they were just a bit full of themselves, always sauntering as if they were on a catwalk. That is, the girlie girls always sauntered, and Suzanna was a girlie girl in her looks and walk. But she was always clearly pretty strong in her opinions. Albert said that she was a cut above the rest—one who knew her own mind. She would always stop and talk to him. Everyone did. After all, he was always by the driveway in the front of the house. She herself was always working in the back big yard and woods, not shooting the breeze with neighbors and their children.

Life is unfair, she thought. Jenny had majored in English. And when she'd taught at the academy, she had not been able to compete with the coach, who taught civics or psychology, using film as a crutch. No. She'd had to prepare lessons and read all the materials and books required, not watch a movie. And when she'd finally found her way to her career in journalism, she'd had to work really hard before her peers appreciated her in-depth knowledge of plants and gardens.

Her husband, however, had been a professor of philosophy in the state university in the next town. His full-time schedule was twenty hours a week, and the rest of his time was given to interpreting the world for whoever wished to listen. He had summers off. He used them to get free travel with the students to whatever country held the international philosophy convention for the year. She had to admit that she had gone on many of those trips, and it was clear that the students thought of her husband as a special mentor and even a guru. She used to feel that way about him, but she really hated his spending all his time with other people when he could help her in the gardens. Oops, the master calls.

"Jenny, Detectives Locke and Aylewood are here; they would like to talk to us both."

She shrunk at the thought that he could remember their names, and he couldn't remember the names of her roses. *So goes marriage,* she thought. "Coming, Albert," she said as she took off her flower-printed garden gloves and matching hat to walk into her living room.

Albert and the detectives were talking quietly when Jenny entered the room. Fortunately, she thought, everything was in order. Albert hadn't tossed the pillows off the couch to lie down and read. Heavens above, maybe he had and had repaired his mess before the doorbell rang. That would be a new wrinkle; that would be a first for Albert.

They all greeted her, and Detective Locke began, "We're here about the latest incident that I know you have heard about from the police, your neighbors, or the news. Our concern is about Jackson Elsby, the twelve-year-old boy who was found dead by the big rock in the park. The cause of death has not been determined as of now. So we are just interested in more general questions. If you would be patient while we review information with you, I'd be grateful. I'd like to start with a review of the death of Melvin Stoteras, the boy who was strangled in the wood behind your house about eight months ago."

Jenny spoke up. "Detective, I've never understood how that could have happened, as I am able to see almost every move in the cleared path in my section of the woods. I didn't know Melvin, but maybe

Albert does. I read that Melvin wasn't strangled near the rock, so why are you questioning that old case when you have a new possible victim?" She thought, *Let them explain things to us. Maybe there's a connection. They aren't the only ones who are able to apply logic.*

Detective Aylewood responded with, "Mrs. Haygood, we are here about all the deaths. And, yes, we are most interested in knowing about Jackson's death and want to know what you know about him. But we need to hear if you and your husband see any connection, not discussed previously, among the children."

Her Albert quickly explained that Jackson Elsby lived way down at number twenty-two, and he was unsure that he could even identify him if he saw him. He had much to say to the detectives about Melvin, and without a pause, he continued to do so.

"Melvin was a haunted little boy, growing up in a dysfunctional or at least difficult family. His father is an orthopedic surgeon, a member of that fancy country club that's adjacent to the neighborhood, and is known as a ladies man. His mother, Vivian, is a part-time singer and voice instructor and quite something to look at. Sounds good, but not so good! I like Vivian much more than Chris. Chris is making a play for the young widow, Marilyn Dudas, who lives directly across the street from him. But I think that Marilyn is a pretty straight arrow, and so Chris hasn't been successful. Detectives, Chris is the kind of guy who never appreciates what he has and is always looking for more. If I were Viv, I'd get out of that marriage."

Albert relayed the history of the family, including that the Mr. and Mrs. Stoteras had three children, with Melvin as the youngest and only boy. There were definitely problems in the home. Melvin was troubled by his relationship with his dad, who always presented himself as a perfect head of the household role model, always in charge. It didn't help that Melvin was an only son who did not physically resemble his father at all. Melvin was a slim, nonathletic boy who was an average student. He did seem to want attention from the girls but didn't appear overly successful. Albert thought that Melvin, at twelve, was just interested in girls because they were a safer bet as friends.

Unfortunately, his method of talking with them was by teasing and annoying them, looking for someone to bother with him.

Albert often talked with the boy when he saw him on the driveway between the houses. Melvin would cut through a path from the fields through the woods to his house, which was between the Stoteras and Haygood houses but was not technically inside Jenny's section of woods. He seemed to enjoy Albert asking about whether his homework was finished and, one day, showed him a test in social studies that Melvin had done well in.

Albert continued the story, saying that Melvin didn't like math and science. He said his father was never interested in a grade that was not in math or science. Dr. Stoteras regaled his son with stories of how much effort it had taken him to become a doctor. He took every opportunity to share with anyone who would listen how he'd met a wealthy Jewish doctor who regularly came into the restaurant where Chris worked for dinner. The elderly man had sought Chris out when he'd learned that Chris was in a local college taking a premed program. The doctor followed his progress for a couple of years, making a few suggestions here and there. And when Chris was in his final semester and taking medical school entrance testing, he called the doctor for advice. The doctor was thrilled to help in his efforts and used his influence in support of his application to the Tufts Medical School Admissions Department. Chris was successful.

That success had triggered Chris's obnoxious habit of pushing to get anything he wanted. Chris never stood in a queue for anything. Standing in line was for those mopes who had no energy. Melvin was, in Dr. Stoteras's estimation, bordering on that kind of lethargy— letting the world go by him and never running to catch the train to the future. He often told his son Melvin just that.

As he spoke, Albert shook his head. "What a loss. Melvin was such a kind boy and a dreamer, whose only savior was his mom. He might have survived his childhood if some evil and disturbed person hadn't killed him. Why him of all people?

Detective Locke asked Albert if he had thought more about any of the other murders, as clearly Albert had a feeling for and a sense of the neighborhood kids. Albert reminded him that the police had been to him several times to question him, because he talked to most of the kids on the street. He didn't think he knew anything more.

Albert couldn't stop himself from asking Detective Aylewood, "Have you police vetted all the vendors on the street? And do you have more profiling info on the killer? I'm just so darn frustrated and horrified that children are continually being murdered on my street, where my home is, where I live. I find myself reading all kinds of studies on profiling. And as a researcher, I have not been able to find any quantitative data to prove that profiling before a suspect is arrested actually matches the caught perpetrator in a serial murder."

Detective Aylewood immediately responded, "I think that profiling may point you in the right direction, Mr. Haygood, but it is a broad direction and mostly based on reasonable assumptions. First, profiling is used if there is some certainty that there is a serial murderer at large. We don't know that yet."

Albert and Jenny both looked annoyed. Albert loudly stated, "Of course there is a serial murderer afoot. You think there are six different reasons for six different children living on the same street to die in a little over a year of nonillness? Hell, what would be the statistics for that to be coincidence? Please don't treat us as stupid."

Detective Aylewood continued, "For instance, if there are five sexual murders of women all the same age, then perhaps you could assume that they are connected. The perp or perps would have at least one man involved with a negative history with women. Matching commonalities of victims or essences of the particular kind of crime has always been a police procedure. Profiling has success because some very smart people put together more statistics and more interpretations based on history. But history only gets you so far."

Detective Jim, as Albert would normally address him, looked at her with a really big smile and said, "Petra, you're right on the money. Professor and Mrs. Haygood, you must understand that other than the children's ages and the location of their homes and place of death, there is no definitive evidence to suggest motive outside of hatred of twelve-year-olds."

He then told Albert and Jenny that they might return after they'd picked up reports on any of the victims that showed discrepancies in the public's views of the children. Perhaps Albert could do an analysis for them, as he had known most of the children. "After all, we're interested in all aspects of the children's lives; there must be something there that will assist us."

⇒◆⇐

Outside the Haygood home, Jim told Petra how really insightful he thought she was. Her response was a turn of her head to him with a look that asked, *What are you talking about?*

He was undaunted by the look and said, "You know not everyone can see the limitations of the song the FBI always sings about the profiling concept. You really understand that it is all in details matched with logic. You get it, Petra; not every cop does. It's understanding what you see under the microscope, not what you want to see. That's always been the limitation on investigations. We all see the same evidence. Some immediately attach motive to a particular person because, historically for example, the spouse is the first person of interest or profiling suggests a particular person.

Rudy, for instance, is a collector and rearranger of evidence. He does it over and over. It's annoying to the rest of us who like a quick solution. The chief likes quick solutions, but Rudy can never be pushed into one. Why is he so successful in closing cases? I think it's because he never gets trapped into a decision, relying on a view from an early biased lens. Rudy wants to see it all. And you, Petra, you work faster than Rudy, and you're often there. But I notice that you hold back sometimes on closing. You want to be sure that you're right, and that's good most of the time. I think you have good gut reactions to evidence but don't trust your instincts."

She turned as they walked to their sedan, and she wasn't smiling.

"Who the hell are you to tell me that I don't trust my instincts? Hold it. Stop walking. I've years as a cop in Boston before coming here. I'm a street cop with developed instincts. I don't have to think about every decision ten times before making one. Where do you get off saying that to me?"

With a smile, Jim said as he entered the car, "Well, Petra, I profusely apologize for misspeaking. But if you did really trust your instincts, you'd have a drink with me. Your instincts tell you I'm trustworthy and nice, but you hold back; instead you will probably tell me that tonight's the night you wash your hair or your niece needs you to attend some game. And I know you have nothing planned tonight. So what about it? Let's have a drink at Moriarty's and talk about the case, or at least let me buy you a drink in contrition for my sin."

Petra shook her head and, with a giggle, replied, "You guys always seemed to think that putting us down is a demonstration of your masculine protection. You underestimate us, and I don't like it when you do that to me, Jim. Not one bit."

But as she glanced over at Jim she did feel a pang of loneliness, an itch, and a pinch of nagging desire that she usually tried to ignore. "You know, Jim, you're sometimes quite the asshole." She smiled.

He looked surprised.

She said, "Don't look at me. Keep your eyes on the road. So, you want me to have a drink with you? Well, okay. But be careful what you wish for. And by the way, I thought you were all talk. On to Moriarty's!"

Jim silently answered to himself, *On to no holding back!*

As he continued driving, he thought, *Well, now I have the opening. I'd better not blow it. She's a bit sensitive and has a history. She doesn't trust easily. No problem. She'll see that I can be trusted.*

As they entered Moriarty's, a cop's bar, Petra was overwhelmed, as always, by the noise. In fact, it was louder and noisier than usual. She noticed the low-level decorations of team photos for all the kids' sports the bar supported, and with shamrocks no less. The bar was busy. They joined a group of cops celebrating after a raid with a loud drinking party and laughing at how they'd scammed a group of druggies operating out of a second-floor flat in the Russian section of town. The Russian group of drug dealers was thought of as being pretty intelligent but arrogant. They closed ranks with each other even when they didn't like one another, which made the cops think they were smarter than average drug dealers. Jim thought the real story was that it was in their history to mistrust any government and work in concert to confuse any authority. He espoused that theory to Petra and she agreed, thinking, *Well, that's the first agreement between us today.*

The Russian dealers certainly didn't trust the West Side cops. When the dealers were caught, the cops thought it was vindication that they were smarter than the Russians. Both Jim and Petra laughed at their colleagues' cockiness. Petra thought, *A cocky cop is almost a dead cop.*

They both believed that these Russians had been caught because their clients were teenagers who could not shut up. Petra laughed at them and said, "Most teenagers today need an audience to live out their lives. A girl's dress isn't pretty unless her girlfriends say it is pretty. They need a posted selfie to guarantee that they lived the moment. I never want to return to those years of insecurity and confusion."

Jim couldn't agree more. They both believed that teen years were about walking through a minefield loaded with hormonal blasts, insecurity, and confusion surrounded by psychological bullies. Therefore, it probably was the teen drug users who gave the dealers' names to the cops, not the cops' natural brilliance.

Looking around the bar, Petra thought that West Side was a nice place, even this bar. Despite being a cop's bar, it had representative patrons from business, ladies clubs, and college kids. And it was a cop's bar. Moriarty, himself now retired, was the third generation of a family to own the bar; all the others were also cops.

While on her second boilermaker and his second beer and out of starvation, they both ordered the same food, the special of the day, pastrami and Swiss cheese on dark rye with mustard and a large dill pickle. Petra said, "In this suburban city, I find another cop who loves pastrami. Unbelievable, who could have predicted?"

She ate her sandwich quickly, hoping to dull the fuzz affecting her brain from her drinks, while Jim thought, *God, she's all rosy and soft away from the station.*

Jim chided her, referencing the salt intake in pastrami and the calories.

Surprisingly to her, Petra flirted with, "Why, do you think I'm too fat?"

His answer was too quick but said with great sincerity, "I think that you're fine, quite fine, Petra." Although he really meant it, he immediately regretted saying it. He thought, *Too fast, you stupid fool—just too fast.* But maybe he was wrong; maybe it was okay, because she didn't answer and she didn't run out of the bar.

After a long pause, they discussed the cases.

Petra said, "Let's make a list of the categories that we use to solve crimes. Let's think of it as a regular case without all the connected horror. You know we make errors in judgment when we're emotional."

Jim answered, again too quickly for his own satisfaction, "Sometimes, maybe not in this case, emotion is important; it is at least a catalyst both in doing crimes and in solving crimes. So maybe we should think of the emotions of various kinds of perps to figure out whether any of those emotions would make sense as a motive or an accelerant for action. We'll do that after we have all data confirmed."

"Like in the novels on the seven deadly sins," she retorted.

So they categorized and reviewed what they remembered on type of victim, perspectives on the victims, age of victims, normal enemies of the type of victim, sex of victims, families of victims, adults who regularly interacted with each victim (schoolteachers and so on), and school chums of each victim. They examined any even imagined evidence in each murder site or lack of evidence, the season of the murder, the weather on the day of the murder, the time between each murder, the month of murder, the time of the day, the personality of the victim, irregularities around the murder scene or time, and on and on. When they were finished, they had twenty categories. Some overlapped but not in all cases, so they set any overlapping data into a separate category.

Petra started laughing and pointed out that Rudy must be brought into this. "You know, Rudy probably has already thought a lot about this detail, but he's going to love our categories for his damn matrix. Let's give the list to him tomorrow. It's Friday, and we can let Mona have a rest for the weekend as he sits by his computer inputting and studying data and not going over budget figures with her."

Jim loved the gist of it, especially thinking about Mona and Rudy, whom he believed had a perfect marriage with complete respect for each other, although they were truly an example of the tortoise and the hare.

Jim suddenly jumped up, stating, "Time to move to another location, Petra."

With a bit of disgust in her voice, Petra said, "Look, Jim, I'm not barhopping tonight; I'm not going to any choir practice tonight." Choir practice was a long-standing police tradition, as first cited by the author Joseph Wambaugh, that supposedly offered comfort and an opportunity for cops to decompress after a shift. Choir practice practiced meant any group of cops drinking together whether the drinking took place after a shift or not. Petra secretly was distressed, thinking that this nice evening would turn into too much booze and too much information. Although she often attended choir practice, and it was a favorite cop activity, it was not her favorite. *With too many drinks*, she thought, *cops ramble about themselves and tell anyone who'll listen all their problems.* And she did not want to know Jim's problems—yet.

"Petra, Nah, not booze. I want dessert. I have a gift card from my mother for Cold Stone's ice cream parlor in Springfield, you know at the Basketball Hall of Fame."

"What are you, Jim, a mama's boy? You mean your mama's paying for me to eat ice cream. Are you two jointly tied at the hip? How the hell old are you? I don't even know her. I don't know, Jim. You must agree it's a bit bizarre."

And then she saw the slice of pain float through his eyes, momentarily addressed, but certainly there and thought, *I guess it also means he doesn't lie. No normal American red-blooded cop would admit to his mother's support of his ice cream habit.*

Jim pretended not to take offense and nodded in agreement. "Ice cream is my major bad food habit. I think I'm addicted. Every time I'm sad or stumped over a problem or happy, I want ice cream. I don't smoke and don't drink much. But I've gone to every joint that sells ice cream in this state and Connecticut and, well, anywhere I've ever visited."

Petra was a bit nonplussed but also quite happy, thinking that if he wasn't a skirt chaser or gambler or prescription drug addict, then she might look seriously at this guy who only had an ice cream problem.

Jim then said, "Don't worry about my mama, Petra. I'm blessed with a good mama who knows when to butt out."

Petra reddened but said, "Let's hit the high-calorie psychotherapy. But I'm telling you now, if you're one of those multicolored sprinkles guys, I might throw up."

Jim, chided with, "I'm sick of all you women with your chocolate fetish—brownie Sundays, chocolate sprinkles, hot fudge, and on and on. And then you probably require coffee ice cream or Friendly's Swiss Almond Chip. You love to add a bit more caffeine into your pleasure. Let's go now before we argue about the kind of nuts to choose. I'll bring you home after our lustful ice cream eating."

She thought about the two of them in the car on what felt like date night. It wasn't for work, and she could no longer pretend that she wasn't interested in him. "Oh, what the heck, vanilla ice cream boy, let's go."

5

The Brood

THE MCNAMARAS LIVED AT 35 Sunnyside Road on the opposite side of the street from the woods next to Hoffington Field. Freida McNamara knew that the family culture she insisted on, as well as the size of her family, was a little unusual for the folks living on Sunnyside Road. What was rare for the neighborhood is that they had eight children, and the children were specifically organized in a fashion unheard of in this upper-income neighborhood. Every member of the McNamara family had a supportive role in both household duties and, particularly, in duties to each other. Some older kids were assigned a younger child to assist with homework. All the children were encouraged to do a kind deed daily for someone else, both within the family and outside the family.

She and Frank truly believed that kindness started in childhood and that their role as parents was to instill kindness in the children. It was easier with some of her kids' personalities than with others, but she thought it was taking. Freida believed that raising children in 2017 was particularly difficult, with distractions such as Facebook, Instagram, and Twitter competing for her kids' attention.

Freida believed that the environment for having children in this millennium encouraged some trends; many tended to think that it was special to have one child and exciting to have a second or even a third and perhaps even a fourth child. After that, most parents simply said enough was enough. For the McNamaras, they always had room for one more—until there were eight. Often there were laundry baskets by the dining room table, while the daily assorted laundry lay on the dining table.

On this day, Freida was sorting socks by size in shades of gray, navy, brown, and black for the six boys in the family and brighter colors for the only two girls, her twins. There were only three sizes assorted on the table, one size for the little ones, one for the medium-sized boys, and finally large for the big boys. The assortment for the girls tended to be in shades of pink. Freida felt that, in having only two girls, she had a responsibility to cater to their gender.

The two girls, Carol and Claire, were eleven-year-old twins, and they were next to last in birth order. She mused how the kids were still comfortable with her clothing choices. In fact, all the kids seemed to go along with every aspect of their family-defined rules, even accepting most discipline with equanimity. *Surprising*, she reflected, *because I was a royal pain in the ass as a young girl; lucky I don't have me for a daughter.*

Freida tried, within their circumstances, to allow her children some freedom, but even that goal had been squelched by the horrors of the child killings in their area. Frank, her husband, was adamant that the children go places with at least two kids together. So far, each killing had been of a solitary child.

Freida and Frank had grown up in a tough area of Dorchester and were acutely aware of the dangers of young gangs and bullies. That was the reason why they had purchased a home here in West Side in an affluent area. It had not been easy. They had lived here for twelve years. Frank was a licensed construction supervisor who did extra outside work as a carpenter for the first five years in order to afford the lovely large home. If they could have sold the home now, they would have. She remembered conversations among several neighbors bemoaning that they couldn't get out of their houses. Who would buy in their neighborhood now?

She thought, *Frank and I would do anything to protect our children or anyone's children. But we simply wouldn't have the resources to move if we took a hit, which we would if we sold this home now with the deflated housing prices.*

Freida couldn't understand why someone in the neighborhood had not emerged with some evidence related to the child murders. And now there was most probably a new murder. She was thirty-five years old and very proactive. She had even entered the woods the other day through the lot next to the Landers home. There was a path, actually many paths, through the woods that most kids and adults used to get to the playing fields. She often thought, in the past before the killings, how lucky the residents across the street were to have homes backed up to the woods. Imagine just being able to let your kids explore the woods; instead, she had to worry about her children crossing the street. Their yard was one of the narrowest on the street, and its size probably contributed to the bargain purchase price they had paid for their home.

Also, the house had been previously occupied by two elderly women who were hoarders—not like on television but a mess nonetheless. Again, as she often thought, her neighbors across the street could just send the kids out to play in the backyard bordering the woods, while her children, when they were very young, could not do the same. They had to play in their small backyard. And when they were old enough to let cross the street to play in the woods by themselves, she still worried, as she could not see them.

Despite all her past worrying, she simply couldn't imagine the concept of children being murdered in her neighborhood. She never dreamed that the murder of children could be a possibility, except for the few cases she heard about on television. She had heard about missing children like those pictured on milk cartons, but they mostly were never found. How could this have happened? Who could be that evil? How were these particular children chosen to be murdered?

Her older boys constantly barraged their parents at the dinner table with psychological theories they had read about serial killers. Frank would try to change the conversation to protect the younger ones. He didn't want them to be frightened, but they were all frightened. Everyone in the neighborhood was frightened. What had happened to those children could have happened to her children.

She thought about how much of her waking time was spent planning where her children were every minute. Having eight children was a lot of work but nothing next to cataloging their whereabouts. No child on the street was able to visit three doors down without a parent connecting to the other parent, both at the start and end of the visit. What signals were they giving to the children? How do we teach independence now so children feel they can try things without overworrying?

She could hear in the background a television reporter interviewing police about the investigation into Jackson Elsby's death. Clearly there was no new or helpful information. She shut off the sound. She couldn't take any more. Would she melt down? She thought, *A mother with eight kids can't afford to show stress. The kids have enough to deal with seeing death among their friends. Kids shouldn't die at age twelve and certainly shouldn't die violently.* No, she believed that they would all pay a big price some day from living under this constant stress, especially the kids.

She asked herself, how were others coping? Many with children were economically able to afford drivers or nannies. But some families required two parents working, so the time period in the afternoon after school and before parents returned from work was a time when children might be alone. And Freida knew that children alone, even the best of them, could talk themselves into just about anything for an adventure.

She again looked at the woods. She now viewed them as a conspicuous danger; but to the kids, they were just their play area. It didn't matter what parents said; the kids still all crossed the woods to the playing fields in groups to meet other kids. Her boys for sure would think nothing about crossing those woods and fields alone, no matter what she told them. One thing was certain—after the first two murders, kids outside the neighborhood no longer roamed the street. There were no burglaries or thefts in the neighborhood, and the number of family get-together barbeques had diminished noticeably.

Freida was always checking her front window, viewing the houses and woods across the way for foot traffic. She made sure she connected all her neighbors' faces with names, which had become relatively easy now after so many neighborhood crime watch meetings, funerals, and meetings held by the police.

She looked out again and saw a man in a cap and heavy work jacket running between the two houses across the street. She didn't know him. He did not look familiar. In fear, she called her neighbor directly across from her, who did not answer. She called 911; God, it took almost three minutes through several connections to get to the West Side police. The answerer took a description and said a cruiser was in the area and would be there shortly. She knew that she would have to be available for an officer to speak with her, maybe within the hour. It was probably a waste of time, but what else was there to do? She felt her heart beating triply fast.

Two years ago, she didn't allow Colin and Mark cell phones because they were not yet in high school. Now all the children had cell phones, even baby Mike who was only eight. She remembered the Russian lady up the street, Mariska, and how she used to secretly laugh at her watchfulness of her only child, Anya. Well now she understood. Mariska probably had experiences in Russia with this kind of horror. She would never criticize parents, ever again, for their attentive care of their children. She now had her kids texting (a concept that, three years ago, she would have laughed at). They all had telephones with limited access and would text her husband or her updates on their location or would text the other children.

She really worried only about the boys for a while. But then when that little girl Merry was killed on November 19, 2016, well, it just extended her fears. Freida checked her desk for the folder with info on all the killings. She hid it from the kids but to no use. Some of them had their own scrapbooks of the killings. None of her kids were safe. Freida put her head in her hands and sobbed.

Freida often thought that raising children was an art form, and all the pediatric science listed in all the books on children could never help parents understand their role, which required giving heart, soul, and understanding for the benefit of their children. It was quite easy to feed children cereal, half a banana, and a glass of milk every morning; throw in some toast. It was very easy to dress them, even in high style, each day and for special occasions. Easy—that was the easy and fun part.

Wiping their nose when they were sick may be a little bit more difficult. Certainly when several of her children were vomiting simultaneously and having diarrhea daily, it was stressful, but it was a stress that was understandable. And when one of her children broke an ankle and one had to navigate through the medical system at the major hospital in the next city, one felt tried and sometimes was brought to tears. But what was really difficult, what must always have been difficult for parents through the ages, is to understand how a particular child could be chosen for death. Traditionally, one wailed at God, saying, "Why did my kid die when others lived? Why is my child a victim of this disease?" But to be chosen as a murder victim, well, that concept was incomprehensible to her. Was a child chosen or was it random? No, she thought, random wouldn't hit six children on one street.

Her twins, identical twins, who probably had DNA more closely identical to each other than any of the other children, were not at all alike. Carol could cry at the drop of a hat if you touched her. Her sensitivity to physical pain was notable. "The Princess and the Pea" must have been her story. Her twin, Claire, would never cry no matter how she was physically assaulted. Despite that difference, Carol, the physical wuss, felt no psychic pain at all. You could scream at her; you could say horrible things that were not true about her; other little kids could put her down. And that girl just didn't get bothered at all. Her sister was quite another situation. She would cry if you looked at her the wrong way. "Nobody likes me" was a daily complaint.

She worried constantly but thought that the only eleven-year-old killed was the first murder victim, and he was almost twelve years old. All the other victims were twelve or almost thirteen years old. She knew that she couldn't count on that. Besides she knew that the twins were close enough in age to the victims—close enough to scare her beyond sensibility.

Freida then thought about how she used to believe that the murderer only chose boys, and then a girl was murdered. No. She thought this whole thing was based on pure evil. She didn't care what her son Nick said about some of the boys; no one murders little children unless they are evil. She could not see a motive. How many kids could you be enraged by enough to murder? If you hated kids enough to murder them, why wouldn't you realize that you would eventually be caught? Upset as she was with this investigation, she knew that the murderer would be caught eventually. No one was that smart.

And Freida didn't believe that there was no evidence. Nor did her boys. Nick constantly was listing potential motives. Of all her children, Nick would never give up, whether he was building something or writing or debating with anyone, including her and Frank. He had lots of ideas. Among them, he said you couldn't look at each individual murder. The police should be looking at it "globally." What was to be gained in murdering six children? Nothing. Therefore, they must all have pissed off the murderer. What kind of murderer would be so easily pissed off? The murderer must be pretty smart because the whole town knew there was very little evidence. So he concluded vehemently that the murderer was a smart, easily pissed off nutcase.

Freida gave him hell for using that language.

Nick said, "Mom, kids are being murdered; language is not very important now."

Freida thought, *What does the absence of evidence tell you? It must say something to the detectives. She thought that Detective Beauregard was smart. He gave nothing away but noticed everything. Absence of evidence, for example, in raising her kids was an important clue to catch their little mischievousness.*

A few years ago, before the murders, she recalled when the older boys were disappearing every afternoon and not returning home until supper. Absence of the boys was a clue that they were up to something. And then she was downstairs doing the laundry and noticed that her husband's workshop looked awfully clean. The absence of mess enticed her to investigate. To her surprise, some wood and tools were missing.

Strange! she had thought at the time. Freida told Frank about her suspicions, and he agreed that the kids were up to something.

They decided not to grill them. Why give the boys any information when it would only encourage them to circle the wagons against their parents? Frank, instead, one afternoon, followed the boys on foot about a mile and a half down Sunnyside to where the woods narrow on the other side of the street, finally ending in about five acres of forest. The boys had built a tree hut high over a four hundred-foot dingle. It was angled over the dingle and was certainly not safely built with enough weight at the bottom. At the bottom of the hut were his missing tools.

Well, the boys saw a side of their dad that they normally never saw. They should have known, because the safety of his kids was always a primary concern for Frank.

Down came the tree hut midst the tears of his sons and several other boys. Frank had found it harder than he'd thought it would be to tear the hut down. They had actually dug three-foot holes in the ground for the stilts to support the hut. Their choice of stilts, however, would not be able to continue to do the job. He was just in time.

One of the boys, Jim Derrick, was really upset about Frank's discovery of the fort. Derrick resisted helping the boys, who Frank had insisted help him carry all the wood and tools back home. Frank and Freida were vigilant thereafter.

So what was missing from the crime scenes? Freida thought that if she saw Detective Beauregard she would ask him that—about what may be missing. He was nice, and she didn't think he would mind.

⟹•◇•⟸

Mona Beauregard was having a bit of difficulty putting up with Rudy this weekend. He had come home with two briefcases filled with records, and she unfortunately knew what he planned to do for the weekend; and it was not helping her wash windows, turn the soil in her gardens, or wax furniture. Mona really didn't always like Rudy doing his work on the weekend when she thought that he should do it during work hours. She knew, however, that what made him great as a detective was that he was a focused professional detective.

On the other hand, it appeared to be her role in this marriage to be the great balancer. It also appeared to be her role in this marriage to be the travel planner, the decorator, the strategist for answers to the children's questions, and the determiner of the future. Was her marriage worth the effort and did it balance out? Was it worthwhile or not?

She remembered something she had read. "Make a list," said Ann Landers, the advice columnist. The list was to have two sides—one side listing all of the spouse's good traits and the other side listing all of the spouse's bad traits. Mona knew she could really, really bomb out the one list with negatives. She could list all the times he wasn't home sitting next to her in the evening, all the teachers' reviews of the children's work he missed, and all the overseeing of work in the house and around the house he didn't do. To boot, she could add that he wasn't even aware of the processes required. The list could go on. It did get tiring.

Mona again thought about what Ann Landers would say. Look at both sides of the list, and Mona did. The trouble was that Mona cared about four things in a husband, and Rudy supplied those four things. He was trustworthy. He was kind. He was patient. He was generous, both within their means and spiritually. She knew in her heart that he was never avoiding responsibility or work; but still she was often left doing the work for the house and the children and assuming responsibility. When he was focused on a case, she could get him to agree on any issue. She also knew that Rudy's life was a mission—a mission to make society better.

She thought, *These kid murders, they're not healthy for my Rudy to be involved in.* He was protective of children, and she understood why. His need was fired by his history. He both denied his history but then couldn't forget about it. She remembered Lizette sharing information about Rudy, about what had happened before Lizette and Roland had adopted him. She explained a little about his struggle when he had first come to live with his adoptive parents. Lizette and Roland had decided to send him to a therapist, but he hadn't spoken until the fourth session. The therapist let him play with a family doll set for the first three sessions until he was ready to communicate. He kept tying the two boy dolls to chairs. The bigger boy's hands were tied, as well as his feet. The little boy doll's feet were tied but not his hands. When Rudy finally talked, he said, "The lady yells at the big boy. Sometimes she lets him go to school. When he gets home, they talk loud and she ties him again. The little boy is sticky, always sticky."

Lizette had teared up as she'd told the tale of how the boys had been found. The police were responding to calls from the neighbors in the apartment building; they had not seen the mother and sons for two days. When they were let in by the building super, both boys were practically starving and needed water. They were tied to their chairs. She and Roland had tried to adopt before, but at that time, they were considered too old to qualify for a baby.

She never found out what happened to Rudy's brother; she assumed it was his brother. She would have taken him too, but she was told that the boy had problems and there was a special placement for him. The mother, as far as she knew, was never found, and information on her was scarce. All Lizette knew was that the mother was new to the city of Holyoke where the children were discovered.

Her Rudy had a past that he was not ready to explore, and Mona was certain that he would eventually be ready; what that would mean for them all was unknown and not something that was constructive for her to dwell on. She smiled, thinking, *I'm nothing but constructive, but that is how I cope day by day.*

So Rudy avoided another weekend of home maintenance, and using a little guilt, Mona got Rudy to agree to go to Maine for a three-day trip with the Police and Fire League. It was reasonably priced, and he did agree. But to be honest, she told him about the trip when he had his head in some old evidence, and she didn't tell him that they were going with the league. It perhaps wasn't quite fair, but she enjoyed the company of many of the women in the league, and the trip was, after all, not pricey; it included good restaurants and shopping.

The unsaid result was that she would not complain about this weekend because, on Tuesday, they would be traveling. A wife had to choose her battles. Besides, one never really could win an argument with Rudy. He was adept at bringing in evidence and counterpunching your perfect case. She often felt sorry for the hoods and criminals in town.

⟫◆⟪

Mona and Rudy arrived early for the bus on Tuesday. No problem for Rudy, who had brought part of the Elsby case file and was diligently working on it while they waited for the bus to fill. It bothered Mona that he was doing work on what should be an interactive vacation with her. She tried not to thing negatively, but her brain was abuzz thinking, *I've left my older sister Imelda in charge of the boys; I again have to plan everything. And here is Rudy, content sitting inside by the window on the left side or west side as they were going north.* No sun was in his eyes, and he was also able to avoid all the small talk among the mostly cops wives or girlfriends. Just a few male cops, maybe ten in total, had deigned to travel. *He'll be sleeping next, just like the other men. Not surprising they sleep while we women discuss the agenda for the next two days.*

———◆———

Rudy, meanwhile, was actually reviewing what Mona had told him about the trip. He knew that they were staying at the Cliff House in Ogunquit for a night and then at the Casco Bay Inn for the rest of the trip, as it was cheaper, although not quite Maine iconic. He knew, without being told, that they would visit Stonewall Kitchen, and that was all right with him. His favorite fig jam and cranberry chutney would be coming home with them. They would also spend some time in Portland.

He smiled, thinking, *I love the waterside, but I'm sure that Mona will insist on dragging me to all those pretty little galleries— her words not mine. Mona will see new designs and paintings, and something new then will develop in my house—maybe not in a week, but within a month.* She called her little trips, "Inspiration." He called them "money suckers." *But,* he realized, *I personally love this part of Maine, and I love lobster, which I am certain we will have for at least one dinner. No, Mona has it right again. I'm happy I'm here.*

One item on the agenda was half a day twenty minutes away in Freeport, where he would stock up at L.L.Bean. He was planning. *I'll order boots in double D width there, and they'll send them home if they're not in stock. If anything goes wrong with them, well, I'll just mail them back. I really love their men's outerwear. Most everything is sensible; wears well. This is my store. I won't complain about shopping there. Yup. I can get through this trip.*

He just hoped that Mona would find a lunch place (two days for lunch were not included in the trip cost) where he could get a hamburger. She tended to go to these earthy crunchy places with "great soups and salads." *I've never once been satisfied with soup and salad,* he thought. He looked over at Mona and saw that she was happily gabbing with a friend. He was happy; he was always happy when Mona was happy.

Rudy scanned the group on the bus and realized that he was one of a few who were having difficulty settling down to touring. A few guys had a bit of trouble with alcohol, so they were waiting for a stop for a quick one. Maybe a few of the women were thinking the same thing. *Well*, he thought, *not my problem. I worry only about children being murdered. I know I have and will probably always continue to have difficulty letting go of work, but maybe that's not necessarily a bad trait for a detective.*

The rhythm of the bus was calming to him, and it was also helpful. Despite his slow gait, Rudy knew that his apparent slowness was a learned response, counteracting his facile mind, which if he did not control it, could lead him to jump to conclusions too early. No, he thought, he was a hare on tranquilizers imitating the turtle.

The bus stopped suddenly, and his mind turned to murder. Murder was the great stop to life. Who wanted to murder six children? And we are looking at six murdered children. The ME had assured him that the injuries on the last death could not have resulted from the fall alone. The kids weren't even teenagers! He personally thought kids today were kids until they were twenty-eight years old—always wanting with no thought to cost or appropriateness. *Could there be a teen or a twentysomething who just wanted to kill with no thought to cost or morality and, therefore, no guilt?*

If the perp felt no guilt and the perp had been interviewed by one of the detectives, he was sure that the lack of guilt was the only way the perp had been able to fool his detectives or himself. He perused the idea. *Maybe the perp doesn't feel guilty because no sex was involved. This society is obsessed with sex.* Most young people thought it was all okay, except that it wasn't okay to two-time someone. Maybe the perp was disappointed in his love life. But that would mean that the perp was a woman or a gay man. *Would fit*, he thought, *except for the little girl's death.* And how angry could an average young person stay? The child murders took place over fifteen months.

In the afternoon, after they had settled in at the Cliff House and enjoyed a ladies lunch, they took off for L.L.Bean. Rudy's ability to shop had time limits. He addressed his boot and shoe situation, told Mona for approval, and three pairs were ordered. He felt wasteful when he thought of his mother cleaning houses to buy him one pair of Keds and one pair of dress shoes each year. He now had eleven pairs of shoes and boots. He looked at jackets, but his outerwear at home never wore out, and after his rich shoe purchase, no, he couldn't abide more purchasing. Enough *was* enough.

Sitting down on a nice bark chair that rocked, Rudy decided to do what he loved best—what his main hobby actually was. He chose a perfect spot that he soon realized allowed him to see three directions of walkways of customers. It was such great sport. Families were standing around deciding how much to spend on each person with always one person wanting more than their share. It was that way in the universe. One family really impressed him, except for the second youngest kid. He was a really cute blond, tousled-hair boy, who at first sight appeared to be perfect—until Rudy saw something disturbing.

The boy's sister and brother were getting more expensive jackets than the one to be bought for him. His father explained that the jackets the siblings were getting were not stocked in his size. They walked over to the cashier to cash out, and while his sister and brother each held their jackets, the kid sneakily took a magic marker from the counter and damaged both jackets. Rudy waited for the kids or the parents to see the damaged jackets, but they did not. Further, the clerk didn't notice it. That was bad enough, but the kid, whose name was Brian, said to his dad, "You know I really like my jacket now." The father beamed but the mother looked around carefully. Rudy thought, *She looks suspicious. She knows something's up.*

Rudy didn't know what to do. Mona would kill him if he got involved during vacation. He walked over to the clerk who was bagging and said to the parents, "I thought I saw a flaw in one of those jackets." Everyone examined the jackets and found the damage. Dad told the two kids to see if they could find other jackets in their size.

This slowed up the counter traffic. Brian had stopped smiling by now, and Rudy noticed that his mother was carefully watching him. Rudy now saw that she knew what she had on her hands.

Brian was about ten or eleven years old. The kids returned with their new jackets, and the family cashed out, but not before the mother came over to thank him and said, "Do you know how that happened, because I'm pretty good at inspecting merchandise before I buy?"

Rudy said, "Probably it'd be good to get Brian to a shrink before it goes too far."

She looked him squarely in the eyes and said thank you to him and walked away. He was impressed with her ability to see a truth she did not want to see. *I don't do half as well as that mother. I don't really want to go back and examine that woman who left us and that other boy tied to the chair. This woman is a hero, and she is just as frightened by the truth as I am.*

But for now he had something else to handle. He thought about L.L.Bean's merchandise loss and felt some guilt but not a lot. He hoped he wasn't becoming one of those liberals who believed it was okay to take from big corporations. No, but he did believe in decision making based on the particular situational ethic involved. Rudy didn't know if his take was the best, but he knew that the mother was aware of her son's problems, and she would try to get help. How she would do it without her husband's knowledge, he didn't know. He did know that the husband did not want to see this problem.

In his house, he intuited, *Mona would not let me get away with not sharing the horrors of childcare. No, she was clear that I'm to do my part. I agree. L.L.Bean will have to take this hit because I'm not going to report the problem. This is just another example of my playing God, not cop. Do I want to be God? No. Yet I don't trust God. Hell of a way to live.*

That evening, while Rudy was waiting for Mona to dress for dinner, his mind replayed Brian's calculating and jealous ploy. Brian had done the damage instantly, using tools around him. He hadn't planned it. He'd reacted out of jealousy and maybe sibling competitiveness. Regardless of the motive, his actions were nasty, criminal, and intimated of some kind of at least moral instability. He surely had done some nasty things before. His mother's reaction reeked of knowledge that Brian was a problem. Did his mother or his father play a role in past denial facilitating this little boy's actions? Brian had reached a point where destroying others' property seemed not even worthy of considerable thought. Would the mother or father continue to cover up his misdemeanors until Brian someday became a juvenile or adult in the criminal justice system? Could he ever become a murderer? Would his jealousy or greed ever reach the point that he could murder? Could it even be in the realm of possibility that this mother or father would ever murder to cover Brian's actions?

Brian's behavior bothered Rudy. He was afraid for this family. *Hell, why can't I push the potential awful scenarios from my brain?*

Fortunately, Mona was finally ready for dinner.

6

One View

A GORGEOUS DAY AT the beginning of March with the temperature rising to sixty-five degrees found Carlo Moretti lying sunning himself on the chaise lounge on his rather grand veranda facing Sunnyside Road. His house stood out on the street, given its Italian country design. He reveled in his Italian background and history and surrounded himself with Italian decor. His wife, Marion, although of Irish and Polish descent, went along with his ideas. He thought that Marion liked everyday life and had no need of a little adrenalin rush. He needed that rush. He thought maybe that was because practicing law required it, and his body needed the drug daily.

Purchasing furniture was problematic, Marion had once explained to him. "Carlo, I have a house to clean, my kids to keep in touch with, lunches with my friends, and involvement with the museum in Springfield. I just cannot make those kinds of decisions. In fact, decision making is not for me. Darling, that's why I married a lawyer. You can make those decisions for me." And she would give Carlo that beautiful smile till he melted.

He'd then tried to bring her into the process by bringing color charts or settee and chair shapes home to attempt to force her into the process. Occasionally, she pointed out something she hated, but that was the limit to her participation in decor or landscaping. She did point out that, for a man who was infatuated with Italian design, he seemed to want every New England evergreen on his grounds. He understood her reasoning. When they had traveled to Italy, Spain, and Portugal, there were few trees still existing after centuries of woods stripping for fuel and construction. He wondered sometimes if he might be part Russian. He truly loved woods and evergreens, and when they visited Russia, he was entranced with the country's forests.

Carlo thought that if he were honest he'd admit he liked this part of their marriage. He liked decorating and gardening, but not flowers like the older lady Jenny Haygood was always fussing with. He liked grand designs and gardens that just needed trimming once a year and weeding. He admitted to himself that he limited the weeding by bedding the gardens with nice earthy black soil mulch. Not that he himself would ever weed. He had Russ Garden Service weed and trim when needed. Funny thing about Marion, she used to love to weed and trim; she said it was therapeutic. Oh how he missed her.

It's been over a year since she died, he thought, *and the pain still hits me right by my heart when some ordinary thing brings her back to this world. Never, never, never could I ever have believed that she would die first! She was eight years younger and always looked so young. It's fucking unfair.*

He considered his life. Their kids both lived in Tennessee now. Ian lived in Nashville and was a surgical oncologist at Vanderbilt Medical Center. Alison worked as a CFO for AT&T Mobility in Johnson City. Both had spouses at one time and two children each. He secretly thought all four grandchildren were brilliant and beautiful. One girl named Jane looked just like Marion. He sometimes caught his breath when he looked at her. Jane was nine years old and so sensible. She was the peacemaker of all the grandchildren, the sharer of toys, the school mistress, and the hugger. She was Marion. Thank God that Marion got to see all the babies before she died.

Carlo couldn't understand why his daughter was still living in Tennessee. She could work for AT&T Mobility or some related company in Connecticut, Massachusetts, or Rhode Island. He knew she'd moved with her husband Paul because of his position as an assistant dean at Eastern Tennessee State University. But they were divorced now; there was no reason to stay. No, Alison felt that the children needed their father, and living nearby facilitated that. If the kids were so important to him, Carlo thought, Paul wouldn't have cheated on Alison with one of his graduate students. "The hell with him," he told her. "Move home." Carlo could help her out. He could certainly find her a better husband—one who wasn't a skinny milksop with doggy brown eyes that all the young girls fell for. He had told Marion that Alison shouldn't marry Paul, but Marion wanted Alison happy. Marion pointed out that Alison was a typical geek and shy around the opposite sex, and if Paul made her laugh, he couldn't be all bad.

What a joke, Carlo reminded himself. Alison made over $250,000 a year with additional perks, and that's why Paul liked her. In fact, he paid no child support, and she gave him alimony. He'd laced into her, "Why with a lawyer for a father, how could you go along with this horrible divorce settlement." Her answer had actually made him feel a bit better. "Dad, I now know that Paul is interested in money and control and, I suppose, young women. You know he could be mean. I have made it very clear that, if I find he's said one little negative thing about me or my family to the children or interfered with my direction for the children, then I will paper him to death in court, and he will lose his alimony and maybe visitation rights. I know things about him, and I have kept records—and he knows I know—that would allow the court to look at our situation differently. He will behave, and I feel better knowing I have some method of preventing him from interacting negatively with the children. On his own, he only sees the kids one weekend a month instead of four. He won't be a problem, and the alimony is a small price to pay for my peace of mind."

Carlo took off his $350 athletic shoes and socks and sunk his feet in the cool grass. He would have loved a swim, but it was still too early to open the pool. Feeling the earthiness under him quieted his nerves as he remembered how he'd never understood why Alison didn't realize how good-looking she was. Neither did she seem to know how funny and how very smart she was, as was clear to everyone around her.

Carlo thought about his own career; he was one of two senior partners in a general service law firm of seven lawyers, with a total of twelve paralegals and staff. Over the years, he had enjoyed a plethora of large criminal cases, but he really loved business practice cases. He had also handled divorce and real estate, both of which he was happy not to be doing anymore. The problem with real estate, unless it was an interesting big commercial case, was that it was repetitious, monotonous, and required a detailed mind constantly in focus. Divorce work required him to be either a daddy to his client or a dictator, depending on the client. He didn't mind counseling a client, but some of them were so emotional, they couldn't see what was right in front of them. "She really wants to get back together; it's her mother creating havoc again." Or, "She loves our sex life; it's not about my money. I just haven't been paying enough attention to her." One stupid story after another had been recited to him in his office. If only you could leave emotion out of a divorce, the results would be better for both parties.

The worst cases were when a spouse had a social worker mentality, often found with teachers, nurses, and counselors who thought that they couldn't leave the other spouse homeless or destitute, which was almost never the case. Those cases fired him up because his clients were hurting themselves. So he and his partner agreed that he wouldn't do divorce work anymore. He mused, *Alison is typical of some of my clients—treating Paul like a child who needed her help regardless of his behavior. That divorce broke Marion's heart.*

His son, Ian, was not the soft touch that his daughter, Alison, was. In fact, Ian was all logic. He was kind, but he had the lawyer's gift, despite being a doctor, of assessing a situation quickly and immediately acting to address what was needed to be addressed. Ian's two boys were cool; one was athletic and the other a musical nerd. He was lucky with the children and grandchildren and daughter-in-law Sandy; he liked them all.

He looked across the street at the park behind the houses and thought about this great criminal justice horror story his neighbors and he were experiencing. He'd known most of the kids killed, either through their parents or by just talking to them when they walked by. Teen boys were always asking him about drug laws, and he would smoothly give them information while inserting penalties and the current policing to catch kids, telling them that kids in the suburbs were not good at drugging and getting away with it. It was perhaps a bit of a lie because he believed that the ability to get away with anything was really related to in-your-face gall, intelligence, and a lack of guilt.

The kids who were killed were just twelve years old. He had only just seen the little girl as she walked by, but she just looked awfully cute and didn't look like an instigator. Some of the boys were brats, with maybe two of them with a delinquent future. *God, there are a million future delinquents out there, but they don't get killed at twelve years of age.*

He'd never heard that any of them were drugging. *I guess you never know,* he thought, *but there has been so much talk after almost two years of investigation that something would have emerged if they were on real drugs. None of them had had a surgery with a recovery long enough to get addicted. Nope.*

Although Carlo had often had a go at the police, he respected West Side's Major Crimes Unit. They were police with a solid reputation as tough but fair; and they generally were not underestimated by serious local criminals up to no good. As a unit, the MCU detectives had a reputation of being straight up for police. No. Carlo's experience with criminals and the special branch of criminals called murderers was that there was always a motive. Even with the crazies, if you got inside their heads there was a motive. Even if the motive was to just see someone suffer, it was a motive. *And when you throw the little girl in the mix, motives for these serial killings get complicated,* he mused.

His experience with crime and motive told him to examine a list of possible motives. They could be greed, jealousy, power, control, sex, envy, anger, rage, hatred, defense, fear, disgust, contempt, and so on. Some of them could be included in another one. But he wanted to think about them as connected to twelve-year-old children.

Let's start with greed. What did six twelve-year-old kids have that a perp would want? Nope, not a good potential motive in this situation! Most of the kids could get anything that another kid had. What about power and the next one control, both intertwined, could these be motives? Possibly, but they didn't all fraternize on a regular basis with each other. *I'll hold that possibility aside,* he decided. *What about sex? No.* He ruled that out. His police buddies had said that no sex was involved with the bodies, whether before or after death.

The next two were always possible in any death. Anger and, perhaps, rage could be involved. But rage required an emotional relationship with either the victim or a situation, which would normally result in some evidence at the scene. Carlos decided to allow that all the children had been murdered. Although the news had not confirmed this last kid as murdered, he'd heard that the kid had been. And it made sense. Six kids on the same street in such a short period of time; probably the sixth death was not an accident. Falling from the rock could be an accident, but there were supposedly multiple hits on the boy's head, not easily explained by a fall. Perhaps he fell and the hits were administered to ensure death. So this killing might have involved extended intent—maybe a second smashing attempt after the push. *But anger could be a motive if the perp was predisposed to easily anger by small actions,* he mused. *Twelve-year-old kids say and do stupid things because they're not completely socialized into the world. Yeah, anger could be a motive.*

How many twelve-year-olds could anyone hate unless there was a mental case in the area? Maybe someone who had a traumatic experience at twelve years old or was hurt by a twelve-year-old sibling when he or she was young? That was assuming the perp is an adult or teenager.

Self-defense didn't work because Carlo couldn't imagine some person being attacked by six different twelve-year-olds, including a sweet girl; and again, there was no evidence. The same was true of fear. Could any one person be in fear of six children? *Suppose the perp was a kid.* Wouldn't matter. These kids were not a gang. Disgust and contempt are perhaps possible motives. Who could be disgusted by or feel contempt for six different kids? It would have to be a troubled person. And again why these kids? On the whole, they looked like pretty good kids. Who had such a history with all of them to be disgusted? Maybe there was an event witnessed by the perp that triggered something in his or her mind.

Carlo looked at a couple of his trees and then again viewed the trees on the other side of the street. At different times of the day, their shadows shaded different parts of the yards. He loved trees. He thought, *Maybe I'll walk the street at different times of the day to see the entrances to the woods and park and figure out how any perp could have access without being seen. I'd have to account for different seasons, but evergreens are always there even in the winter.*

Marion would want him to use his mind to assist in finding this person. She had known about the first murder, and she'd cried for the boy's parents, as she had cried for Henry Landers when he died. *Maybe I'll talk to that Detective Locke. He's a thoughtful guy. I can't talk to Rudy.* Carlo had a current criminal case where Rudy would be a witness in the trial against his client. His role was to make Rudy look foolish or at least careless, and that was always a difficult job when Rudy was a witness. He couldn't compromise his client by furthering a relationship with the detective who'd closed the case for the cops. No, that only happened on TV. *I'll move forward on talking to Locke. Jackson Elsby's death, death number six, is just too much. In my heart, I fear that it's someone in the neighborhood. In my fucking neighborhood! I'll have no peace until the monster is found.*

God damn it, he found himself thinking about property values on the street. They'd all plummeted. He couldn't sell his house if he wanted to. Then again, he would never sell. *This was Marion's home. I'm here for the duration. I'll make it my business to talk to Jim Locke.*

⋙◆⋘

Jim Locke called Petra on the radio and said he would pick her up for an interview scheduled with Dr. Abbott the Counselor at Hoffington Middle School. He would explain later. He didn't ask if it was okay. She noticed that she didn't say it wasn't.

Petra said as she jumped in the vehicle, "I hope this isn't your idea of a date. You can't have an interview at a school and have it pass as a date, you know."

Jim was thrilled at this banter. *Does it mean that she wants a date? Was the other night out a date?* They had alluded to it at the ice cream parlor, but he'd thought that he would have to work much harder to entice her to go out on a real date. Well, a gift was a gift, and it wasn't even Christmas.

Petra asked him why they were meeting with Dr. Abbott again, for probably the fourth time. Jim replied, "Not just John Abbott but also with Evelyn Liacos."

"Well what about the new death, Jackson Elsby? Will we be talking about him too?"

Jim explained that the captain wanted him to clear up some details on Evelyn. They were to conference on the direction of the Elsby case later. They then discussed their history with both John and Evelyn. Jim explained that there had never been an interview with Evelyn beyond a review of her history with victim number one, Jared Stuart. He thought that interviewing Evelyn with Dr. Abbott in the room would reap several benefits: First, Evelyn would be more comfortable with Mr. Abbot there, as all the girls were giddy over Mr. Abbot, who was, by any standard, quite good-looking. Second, Mr. Abbot had a PhD in psychology. And third, Mr. Abbott knew all the other victims, many of the parents, and in fact most of the children who lived on Sunnyside Road, including Jackson. They both were thinking that perhaps they'd get a glimmer into more of the goings-on at Hoffington that could influence their view on the murders.

John welcomed them and they said hello to Evelyn, clearly a nice looking and acting twelve-year-old, who explained very quickly that she was almost thirteen; in fact, she would be thirteen in May. This she said as she looked adoringly at Dr. Abbott. Jim had asked John earlier if he would let Evelyn's parents know that they would be asking questions about Jared's spiteful joke on Evelyn during the school assembly. The parents had told John that the interview between the police and Evelyn was fine with them.

Petra initiated the questioning by asking Evelyn if the kids had stopped talking about the dress damage event. Evelyn laughed and said, "Detective, it's not important anymore now that all my friends have been killed. In fact my mom says that, after what has happened to all the kids who died, lots of things we thought were important just aren't even on our radar anymore."

Petra quietly said, "Evelyn, were all these victims your friends?"

"Well, they were all in my class one year or another. I was on the Community Service Committee with four of them."

Petra continued, "What was each like in doing events? Tell me how they worked with you and the others and whether they were helpful."

Evelyn relayed how, at the Community Service Committee car wash on Route 20, Davie Caras and Merry Wafters were real workers. Davie and Merry would stand in the road with signs waving in drivers. They were the ones who had smart phones and had put the car wash on Facebook and Instagram. They would talk like salesmen and got many more cars waved in than when any of the other kids tried. So they were left there all morning that day, and their excitement never changed. Jackson Elsby and Melvin Stoteras were car washers, and they did a good job.

Evelyn said, "Davie was just a good kid; he was a great kidder, but all the kids knew that he didn't mean anything. At least I thought all the kids knew. Although I have to admit that often he was really annoying. Sometimes he'd get in trouble with the teachers, but they knew he just wanted to be noticed. Maybe he got noticed by the murderer.

"Melvin was kind of an information geek. He knew everything about history and society. He used to talk with Dr. Albert, who lives on Sunnyside, about philosophy. Dr. Albert was really nicer to Melvin than to any of us. Sometimes I would be with Melvin, and I'd listen to Melvin and the doctor. I learned a lot and I'll never hear talks like that again. My mother says that it's an opportunity that was a once in a lifetime for me."

Dr. Abbott then asked about the other two boys, and Evelyn was quick to say that Jared Stuart was just awful to be around. He was always putting someone down with his not so funny jokes, but even her mother said that he wasn't bad enough to murder. Some folks on the street, though, thought he was a thief and nothing but a troublemaker. Jared's family was never home and maybe that was why he was always in trouble.

Jared was worse than Jackson Elsby. Mr. Rozovsky really got mad at Jackson on Anya's birthday party after Jackson pushed Anya in the pool when she was all dressed up and looked beautiful. "We were all shocked and afraid of what her father would do to him. Even Jackson was nervous; Mr. Rozovsky shook him and screamed at him. Jackson was really sensitive about any criticism. If he thought you were ignoring him, then he would get even in mean ways. That's why he threw Anya in the pool. Anya had not bothered with him during the party; in fact, he was the last person to get a piece of birthday cake, and when he complained, Anya shoved it in his face. But I don't think even Mr. Rozovsky or Anya would want him dead, do you? I can't even imagine killing someone over that. That's only in novels, right, Mr. Abbott?"

"Anya could let you know when she was mad at you. It's easy to resent Anya because she has everything and knows it. One time, I wore the same shirt as Anya at the West Side Christmas Party for Middle School kids, and Anya didn't speak to me all night. I didn't even know she had that shirt. Her clothes are always more expensive than mine. I wondered if maybe she was mad that my mother had bought me something as nice as hers. Sometimes I think that Anya doesn't understand that she makes me angry. I don't like being put down. No, I don't like to be treated badly."

Dr. Abbott then asked Evelyn if she could think of something that all the children who had died had in common with each other. This question confused Evelyn, and she responded with, "Do you mean, besides age, going to Hoffington School, and all living on Sunnyside Road?"

Dr. Abbott said, "Well, did all those kids annoy one person or were there altercations with the kids who died and maybe another person, such as a neighbor, teacher, student, parent, or older kid? There have been some sightings of a man entering the park through houses on Sunnyside; have you seen anyone talking to a stranger?"

"Well," she said, "first of all, Dr. Abbott, you of all people, know that all us kids have been told not to talk to any stranger, not to ever go near the park alone, and to run home in groups if we saw someone suspicious. But I do know that Claire McNamara, one of the twins, who is younger than us, was always being bothered by Jared and being teased by Davie because they both knew it bothered her; they could be really annoying if they knew you got upset, and Claire is sensitive. They only bothered Claire when she wasn't with her twin. Nick McNamara, Claire's older brother, had a talk with them both, and Claire was left alone after that. Nick is really nice and friendly with everybody."

Petra then asked Evelyn, "What do you know about Jim Derrick?" She was thinking, *Jim is the only one of the six murdered children who Evelyn hasn't mentioned.*

Evelyn wrinkled her nose, looked down at the floor, and groaned. "Dr. Abbott will tell you about him. He stole anything he could get away with, and he was never caught. I think that he stole things he knew you wanted. He and Jared were bad, but when I talked with my parents about it, we kinda agreed that it was to get attention."

Evelyn then told a tale about Jim Derrick being a pervert. He was seen by Dr. Stoteras peeking in Mrs. Dudas's windows at night. She said, "You know, Mrs. Dudas is really pretty." No one knew how he was found out because Jim Derrick told the boys that he was looking in her bedroom window, which is in the back of the house, and Dr. Stoteras lived across the street. The kids said that Mrs. Dudas, who they all liked, probably called Dr. Stoteras when she heard something outside. They said that any lady living alone would do that, but Jim Derrick said that Mrs. Dudas was in her bedroom the whole time, and he didn't see her cell phone in the bedroom. Anyway, he was a lot more careful and stayed away from her house after that—except, strangely enough, Mr. Stoteras's garage door was broken a week later. Jim said that he thought Dr. Stoteras was weird and a stalker."

Petra asked Evelyn, "Have you heard other things about Jim Derrick with girls or ladies?"

Evelyn thought about it and shook her head. Evelyn then asked Dr. Abbott if she could leave, as she had an exam next period, and her mother would kill her if she missed it.

The detectives and Dr. Abbott discussed Evelyn's interview. John said that he knew Jim Derrick was a bit of a klepto. And Evelyn was right; he was never caught with the goods. He was surprised that he had never heard the story about Mrs. Dudas and Dr. Stoteras and wondered if that could explain the rumors about them. He personally thought that Mrs. Dudas would have nothing to do with the likes of Dr. Stoteras. He also shared that she had expressed to some friends of his that Dr. Stoteras was an obnoxious braggart.

Petra asked John to think about a common motive or motives that he could list, in light of these particular six children being murdered. What could possibly be in common was the question.

John said, "The police have asked that same question before and you just asked it of Evelyn. I mean, not besides someone who just hates twelve-years-old, like a middle school teacher or a neurotic parent who can't stand the competition. Is that what you want to hear?"

Jim Locke said, "Yeah, like that. You're a counselor. You're sitting on professional knowledge about these kids. Have they all been in your office for something? If so, was the something relevant? Have you watched them interacting in unusual ways? Anything? And, John, like you, we ask questions, often the same questions, over and over. Maybe we'll get a different answer, implying maybe a lie; or maybe a new thought will be brought forward. Just like in your field. Be patient with us."

John thought for a moment and said, "Do you really think a kid could do this or a parent or a teacher? I was only kidding with my remark. Well, to answer your questions in order, all of them have been in my office for infractions, except for Merry, who came in for counseling. She came in for counseling with three other girls, but they spent the whole time giggling and talking. It's part of my job—letting them know I will listen to even some of their silliness.

"But I'm really wondering about the issue with Claire McNamara. She is overly sensitive but willing to fistfight anyone. I rarely see her without her twin, and I never heard about Davie causing anyone that much trouble. Jared was a pain in the ass with the girls, but bad enough that Nick McNamara would intervene? Nick is a stand-up guy and not one to be overly worried. However, the twin girls in that family are well taken care of by the brothers. Probably it's nothing."

Petra mused that maybe Nick McNamara would know more about the boys. John said, "Don't talk to him unless you've checked with the parents. They are very protective parents, second only to Mrs. Rozovsky."

"Well," Jim asked, "what about Mrs. Rozovsky and Anya?"

John said that no school personnel or students had ever had any trouble with the family. He thought that the mother was overprotective, always there waiting for Anya after school or events. One time Mrs. Rozovsky was ill, and she called the school to request that a teacher bring Anya to the curb outside and meet the Uber driver. "Christ, Anya could have walked home with the other kids, but Anya was always to be with someone."

Petra asked, "Do you think Anya is a good kid? Do you have any worries about her and her family?"

Dr. Abbott said that he had absolutely no negative information on the family. "In fact, the father is very generous and supports the school's athletic events, paying for travel and helping some of the underprivileged kids with uniforms. The mother, Mariska, would cook for anyone suffering from any malady, and she's just a pretty and very nice lady. She's neurotic about Anya's safety; anyone can see that. Anya herself just seems to be about herself. She's one of the silly girls in her class. No," he said. "I have nothing to say about them except I am always tense when Anya and her mother are around. Mariska is so watchful, so alert, that I look around for trouble."

Jim then explored Nick again, with questions about whether or not Nick had a temper. But John stopped him in his tracks with, "Nick McNamara is a young man with enormous common sense. Could he get angry? Have I ever seen him angry? Yeah, there was the time when a player for another school deliberately tripped Nick in a basketball game, seriously knocking him against the bleaches. He pulled some muscles and was in pain for a couple of weeks. Despite the pain, Nick came out fighting, but I would have too. The other kid was out of line."

Petra said, "Well, What about Merry? Can you stretch your memory and come up with any problems she might have had with other students or teachers or parents of other children?"

Dr. Abbott said, "Wrong idea, Petra. This kid was a wonder and it breaks my heart thinking of her dying. I can tell you this: She was one of the most liked students in the school—liked by both girls and boys. Her parents were just as well thought of. I can't think of any reason anyone would murder Merry. Maybe the perp did it by mistake, or he or she just enjoys murdering. I cried when I heard she had died."

Detective Locke then threw out the concept that perhaps Merry saw something or heard something that put her in danger. "Who were her friends?" he asked.

John Abbott said, "Just about everyone, but she hung around

with Evelyn, Anya, Judy Tisdale, and some of the younger girls, like the McNamara twins, who live on Sunnyside Road. I remember that, before the murders, they, with the exception of Anya, would all walk to school together. Now mostly everyone is driven to school."

Jim asked, "What about Judy Tisdale. She's the selectman's daughter. I remember talking to her with her family after Merry's murder, and all she did was cry. Is that normal for her?"

"Yeah," John answered. "She's a timid little soul—all A's and really nice. I can't see her ever being aggressive and certainly she couldn't hurt an ant, but she's smart enough to hear and see what's going on around her. I never talked to her about the murders. She didn't come in for counseling with the other girls, but I get reports on all kids who are out of school for longer than two days without a doctor's note. It's my job to call the parents. Judy was out a week after each death. I called each time and was told by her parents that she was overwhelmed by loss. I offered counseling, but my offer was refused. However, I wouldn't take that as a bit of evidence. Judy Tisdale is a rare and sensitive soul, incapable of hurting anyone."

Jim and Petra left Hoffington School and returned to their Crown Vic, debating whether there was anything relevant in the new information they'd heard. As Jim drove, Petra again checked her notes against his memory. At exactly the same moment, both stated that maybe they should interview Judy Tisdale.

Petra said, "She's the only one not to be interviewed by us. She was never available; only her father spoke with the police. In fact, her name never surfaced before, and she was not at any of the memorial events. That in itself is unusual. We need to see for ourselves."

"Great," Jim replied. "Her father will never let us do this easily. Just a request to talk to her by herself would be like lighting a fire. Maybe we could say that we're hopeful that she could shed some light on Merry's thinking before the murder—that we know so little about her. Let me make contact. I see him at the gym. I'll approach him and ask his help. I'll tell him that you'll talk to her so she won't get nervous. Let's see where this goes. It's late, partner. What about I bring you back to the station and then meet you at the Fort in Springfield for a drink and some apps?"

Petra laughed and said, "And you mean ice cream afterward, I suppose?"

7

Talk!

WHEN CARLO CALLED DETECTIVE Locke and suggested they meet because he had some thoughts about the murders, Jim asked him why he wasn't calling Rudy. Carlo pointed out that, although he and Rudy were old acquaintances, they were in the midst of a tough criminal case; perhaps it wouldn't be wise for them to see too much of each other.

"It's a small city, West Side, with ignorant tongues wagging and creating trouble. No. I just have just some thoughts about the serial murders, and if I don't share them with you guys, my wife Marion will return from the dead and keep me awake until I do."

Jim responded with, "I knew Marion, and you were a lucky man to have her for so long."

"Not long enough," was the sad answer from Carlo.

"I'll be right over if that's okay," was Jim's response.

But it was not okay. "Meet me at my office; I don't need any questions asked about why the police are at my home. I have no hard evidence, but my gut's telling me to talk to someone."

Jim agreed, thinking that a gut response was one of his best friends. Instinct overcame culture and encouraged the flow of information. They agreed upon Saturday morning at nine o'clock.

On Saturday, after pouring the perfunctory coffee with a shot of amaretto, no tea in this office, the two settled down to a discussion. Jim knew that any conversation on any matter with a lawyer, especially an Italian lawyer, would be a circuitous trip down memory lane of criminal history in the area. Jim looked forward to it. He knew that Carlo sat on a world of criminal sociology, and his conclusions would be important if he knew anything about these murders.

Jim really didn't think that he knew anything, because there wasn't much to know that wasn't already in the papers. However, he could not blow off Carlo's past legal ability to counter the government successfully in court, even on occasion, countering Rudy's overly logical brain.

Carlo was worth an investment of time. In fact, he knew that conversations with the best, like Carlo, were always helpful in some way. Or as Rudy would say, "Fresh eyes are always needed. It's like a jolt of lightning that forces your brain to reassess what you thought you knew. One of the biggest problems we have as police is we can be too focused, too myopic. Always let new info in."

So he had his excuse if anyone ever asked him if he had met with Carlo. He would also tell Carlo that he should not represent the murderer if he were ever caught. He didn't think Carlo would represent this murderer even if he were asked—too close to home and not a perp Carlo would understand.

Carlo started with his history with perps. He also discussed the environment for the murders. "My street, Jim, it's my street; and its surrounds me—where six kids are found murdered." He told Jim that he had walked the street at various times of the day to view shading of the trees that could hide entrances to the woods. The trees that allowed someone to hide would have to be evergreens, since two murders occurred in the dead of winter. Also, he asked, "Have you detectives looked at the light at various times of day to see who could have traveled the street and not be noticed?" Carlo then discussed in detail his history with crime motives and their application to child murders.

Carlo had only represented child murderers in domestic situations.

Therefore, he didn't believe that his history there was relevant, except that, in every case he handled, the murderer was enraged. Also in each of those cases, the enraged murderer had left evidence behind. Carlo asked, "Not so in this case from what I've read. Is that correct, Jim?"

Jim let Carlo know that he was right.

Carlo then said, "You know it takes a great deal of dislike or hatred for an adult to murder a child, and in this case, children, in cold blood. So I think that the person would have to be psychologically impaired but also quite intelligent. Leaving no evidence speaks of planning, and planning requires intelligence—unless in this organized chaos we call our world, the perp accidently left no evidence. I mean there could be situations where there was no planning, an immediate reaction to a situation, and then the murder, after which the murderer just walked away and was not noticed. Are you following me, Jim?"

Jim nodded, demonstrating that he was certainly interested.

Carlo then said, "In that scenario, the murderer felt no guilt, and the murderer was not noticed? Who could feel no guilt in murdering children? And what murderer could not be noticed six times. Do you see where I'm going?"

Jim replied, "I see the validity of your logic, but I think you're ahead of me. Are you saying that, because we've not found any child hating nuts who are great planners, the other direction to look is accidental situational killings that are, therefore, not planned but still result in no evidence?"

Carlo nodded in agreement and said, "Jim, at what stage in life do we learn to feel guilty? Some of us don't ever feel guilty about anything. There are men out there who cheat on their wives and then bring the wife home a birthday cake without a moment of hesitation. Some of my clients think nothing of swindling the little guy. Some police think that it's okay to beat up on a perp when no one's looking. I have one wealthy woman client who steals regularly. For her, it's a game.

"I think the world believes that only sociopaths could do these things, but it's my experience that some people feel very little guilt and must look to the culture outside to even begin to understand the extent of horror resulting from their wrongdoing. So what group of people can we say may, as a whole, have a lower guilt response than society as a whole? Think about it. Young people are more concerned with immediate rewards. Young people do not always appreciate what cultural expectations exist out there. I believe that we are not as good as our parents and grandparents about teaching kids right from wrong. Television and video games and our materialistic culture may infuse in young people the idea that all you have to do is take what you want, whatever that may mean."

Jim shook his head and said, "Carlo, you are jaded, but don't think that we haven't passed that idea around in our discussions. I do believe that we haven't pursued it, mainly because of the lack of evidence at each scene. We didn't think a young person could be that careful. And by the way, how young is the young you're talking about?"

Carlo thought for a bit and said, "Old enough to wield an ax, take advantage of a situation, and act with little emotion; knowledgeable with archery; and able to choke someone while holding him down. So I think it would have to be a kid at least the age of the victims or a parent or guardian of a kid around that age or a sibling of a kid around that age. I have such problems with the ability to kill kids. All my perps would stop at hurting a kid; if one did, it was a drive-by shooting. I have had parents kill kids while enraged, in severe depression, or heavily on drugs or alcohol; but the kids were not really the main target. Sometimes the killing was just a way to get back at the other parent or the in-laws or their own parents. How much strength, Jim, would it take to choke the Caras kid or to hit Jim Derrick with the back end of an ax?"

Jim really didn't want to answer. He thought, *There is just so much exploring I can do without something getting back to someone in the station.* Carlo could be pretty closemouthed generally, but he clearly was mentally involved in pursuing this case. Jim didn't think Carlo would stop discussing this case with others. He knew that Carlo wouldn't knowingly compromise him or his position, but his thoughts about the cases not only informed Jim of a new view on things but also that Carlo was slightly obsessed with the cases. And he knew that any new view discussed could hit the papers as progress that really hadn't been made yet.

To end the interview, Jim said, "Carlo, I'm going to write this up as an interview with you, not as an attorney but as a Sunnyside neighbor. Normally, we have two detectives interviewing, but I'll just say that we were chitchatting, and you started discussing your concerns. That way, I can use all the information you've given me and follow through on your ideas."

Carlo responded with, "I forgot about process for a minute and probably didn't give my meanderings any probative value. I just know that Marion would want me to share my thoughts on this, to take every opportunity to help in this matter if possible. Go ahead your way. And thanks, Jim. I didn't want to put you in an untenable situation. Rudy would kill me."

Jim replied with, "Not to worry," and left.

As Carlo walked Jim out of his office, he asked whether Jim had ever married.

When the response was in the negative, Carlo said, "If it feels right, if she just feels right to you, just do it; marry her. I did, and I never regretted it, even now when I'm so lost without her. You're a good-looking guy, Jim. Don't shy away from marriage."

Jim nodded in the affirmative and thought that Carlo always had perfect timing.

⫘⬦⫘

Rudy pulled in all the department detectives for a review of evidence, in light of the John Abbott, Evelyn Liacos, and Carlo Moretti interviews. He had spent an hour questioning Jim on his interview, alone, with the lawyer Carlo Moretti. He did not like it, not one bit, and Jim's answers did not quite satisfy him. He thought, *Anyone but Carlo Moretti. Carlo is sly, goddamn smart, but sly; he's a man who knows how to work just about anyone. But what could be Carlo's interest if he isn't representing a client? And I don't for a minute believe that Carlo would rep this serial murderer killing on the street he lives on.*

Nope, Rudy decided. Carlo wouldn't hit that close to home unless he suspected someone or knew the murderer or the murderer's family. He respected Carlo enough, however, to be interested in his take on a young person killing the kids. *We've thought about it,* he reminded himself. *It makes sense especially if it's a serial killer. A kid could be a connection or a kid's parent or sibling.*

He didn't want to think that. *We have to come up with something.* The mayor was wondering whether they had the stuff in Major Crimes to do the job. Rudy's headache from yesterday was back. Mona would call it a stress headache. *I love this job; but there are a few out there after it. I love my family and my life. I need control of it all. I can't go back to not knowing things and feeling dirty. I can't go back there, to that apartment.* He sometimes still felt tied to a chair, especially when he couldn't control a case.

This morning's meeting would be a review of the spreadsheet that was developing, which included possible motives and connections on each crime. The software system the department used was only helpful if you asked a direct question to search for multiple characteristics to match to one, two, or three other pieces of data. The department now had pin boards, string theory boards, and Excel-backed programmed electronic murder boards. But programming them for all the data on these murders, although an improvement over the plain murder boards, still did not allow a connection of all the dots for the massive amount of data. At least they couldn't do it—probably needed more tech classes.

Rudy had personally developed an Excel sheet in the past for the murder board with all his ideas used as variables; but he had a problem. He didn't know how to link all the multiple murders with one perp. He struggled with the morass of details. He was normally so good at details, but there were so many linked murders in this case; he just couldn't see the end game.

Jim, Petra, and Mason were busy debating each new idea. Rudy thought, *One thing about Mason that I particularly like is the noncritical, nonemotional, but tactful manner with which he keeps everyone on tract. Perhaps it's his computer techie training, but he's like a collie dog with sheep bringing everyone into the pasture.*

Today, Mason was a happy man. He told them all that he thought he could develop a program that would help—and he had the time right now to do it, which was unusual.

Rudy, after looking at the lists before him, his own spreadsheet, and the murder board asked, "Mason, how the hell can you help us? We don't have a suspect; we have a street of suspects and maybe a school of suspects."

Mason explained, in depth, that all he needed were twenty possible suspects, which, in this case, could mean maybe twenty families that could include someone who could murder. He pointed out that if they could just hone it down to twenty and give him everything they had on each family set, he would find the best data to analyze. If they could agree on the data, he would run a statistical variability study that would perhaps allow the detectives to narrow their search of families or students, and then he could get serious. Even if this wasn't perfect, he assured them that their information would be more succinct and more telling. "Stats are everything, guys," he said.

Jim got really excited because he knew Mason was tooling economic analysis onto soft subjects, such as anger, character, and so forth, which was what he as a psychologist had studied and understood. He firmly believed that these murders would be solved by knowing more about people and understanding connections.

Petra was skeptical, not because she thought that Mason couldn't perform math and computer miracles, but because she liked direct evidence, such as footprints, alibis that weren't right, and lying and stammering witnesses who could point you in the right direction.

In the end, the detectives knew that Rudy would go with Mason's idea. And so he did.

Rudy set them all to work deciding what was important. Jim

pointed out that, with all their data, they only really had good information for far fewer than twenty families. He also pointed out that they should reinterview all the families they would put on the list and all the victims' families. He also wanted Dr. Abbott to be reinterviewed and hoped that some of the multiple family members could be interviewed at the station. Perhaps they could separate some of the members and ask each exactly the same questions based on Mason's focused information—see if there were any deviations in each person's answers.

Rudy then set about discussing the detectives' new prospective interviews. He tasked Petra and Jim to walk the street on a weekday and weekend three times a day. Since the deciduous trees were blooming now, it would be more difficult to imagine the treed winter landscapes. He pointed out that only one murder had happened on a weekend, and they should review their data for the Merry Wafters case to see what had been happening in the neighborhood on a Saturday that no one saw anything.

"Check the time of day. Analyze any info we have on any families included in the list on that day. Everything about the Merry Wafters case is odd. In any interview questions, make sure that Mason has included an assessment of guilt question. Come up with a list of questions to ask in the interviews that covers all of Carlo Moretti's points. Work with Mason on this. And, Petra, I want you to look more carefully at Jackson Elsby's case. We've all walked the scene. I'm ticked it took the ME so long to determine his death as not accidental. We've done most of the on scene work; but you're a good cop. Think about where to go next and connect with me."

Rudy also suggested ferreting out, in Mason's new matrix, what families or kids or whoever needed immediate rewards and seemed to lack any guilt. He also insisted that they assess the culture of the families and who had enough physical strength to wield an ax.

Finally, he stated, "And whatever you do, interview Judy Tisdale before we start interviewing anyone else. Since this is her first interview, and Petra will be the sole interviewer, Jim, you also go and keep Mr. Tisdale busy with questions on politics. First sit by and watch the interview, explaining to Tisdale that a detective rarely goes on a solo interview. Then when it gets boring, you suggest that you're thirsty and get Tisdale to move to the kitchen for coffee. Petra, really throw softball questions in the beginning! You know how. Your job is to get a feel for the kid and her knowledge of her friends and the victims. Judy has been absent after each killing, so assess if she ever feels guilty about anything, Jim. Also you can try to get Tisdale to gossip about other parents and neighbors. He's good at that."

Rudy was on a roll and continued, "One thing strikes me. We have to go back and look at the time of each murder. We've talked about it before when we were assessing the truth behind each alibi for every resident on Sunnyside for each murder. As I recall, the five murders that took place on a weekday happened in the later part of the afternoon from about three thirty to five, while the Saturday murder happened at ten thirty in the morning. Check what happens with school, sports, and in the neighborhood in late afternoon. Seems there's a pattern there, except for maybe the Saturday morning murder of Merry Wafters—another anomaly we face in her murder."

There was renewed excitement in the murder room. The detectives worked together for several hours developing questions and planning the timing of each interview. Petra started making calls scheduling some of the interviews. Then she and Jim took to walking down Sunnyside for the first midday walk.

8

Politics?

DETECTIVES LOCKE AND AYLEWOOD were able to schedule an appointment with the Tisdales on Good Friday, as all the kids had the Friday off before Easter. At the Tisdale address, the two detectives surveyed the classic colonial-style home, sided in gray shakes; they liked the large and inviting entrance, with large black shutters full-sized to match the door they bordered. Jim thought, *Good maintenance here.*

They discussed what kind of approach Petra should use, and Petra was adamant that girl talk, rather than direct questioning, would be best with a twelve-year-old, almost teen girl.

Jim laughed, saying, "Bolt goes girlie girl now."

Petra kicked him in the shins, fortunately before Mrs. Tisdale opened the door.

Mrs. Tisdale greeted them, conducting herself as the perfect hostess. She immediately offered them a variety of refreshments. Jim, keeping with their plan, quickly refused with the old "We've just had coffee."

Jim suggested that they get right to work so as not to cause too much intrusion into the family's long weekend. After some discussion, it was decided that Mr. and Mrs. Tisdale and Jim should sit in the dining room, where they would have a view of the interview and could hear the questions posed to Judy.

Jim pointed out that it would be less stressful for Judy to work one on one with Detective Aylewood, citing that Judy seemed like a sensitive child. He further stated that a little distance from Judy and Petra was warranted. It would be prudent because the adults would not be hovering over Judy while she tried to respond. Jim shared with the parents his background in psychology and his past successes in dealing with children. He pointed out that it was important that adults, especially parents, be careful not to bring out any issue that seemed to upset a child. He said that he realized that Judy was very bothered about the violence and especially upset over the death of Merry Wafters, her friend. He went on to explain that giving Judy the opportunity to share her knowledge of all the victims and her friends and exploring their pain may be therapeutic.

The Tisdales actually agreed; they said that she has been less willing to participate in school activities since Merry's death. Mrs. Tisdale said, "I was so comfortable with Judy having such nice friends like Merry, Anya, Evelyn, Claire, and Carol. I always felt that they were all safe in the company of each other. I was as devastated as Judy was when Merry was killed. Judy is our only child. Gerald and I have tried to bring her a joyous childhood. She is shy but a happy girl. God knows how all this has affected her. I was actually pleased when you called to talk with her. In fact, Gerald, didn't I tell you that we needed someone with more distance to talk with her?"

Mr. Tisdale nodded his head but protested that maybe a shrink would be more appropriate. Mrs. Tisdale responded very quickly, "Gerald, there is more therapy with Judy speaking with the police; Judy won't think that she's being treated differently from the other kids. The police interviewed all the other kids, but you wouldn't let them near Judy. You kept her home forever, and I believe it made her more fearful. She will think that she's being helpful in talking to the police—that maybe she can contribute to solving Merry's and Davie's and the other murders. That, I think, will do a lot for her. At the same time, she is getting all her thoughts out of her mind. Right now, she's been going over and over them; you know, Gerald, that is redundant behavior and not good. You know she's a bit OCD. In fact, I think that she'll be more helpful to Detective Aylewood if we all go in the kitchen and have some coffee. And don't talk to me about legal protection, Gerald. Nobody could implicate Judy in any violence and you know it. So let's let her experience life for once."

Jim couldn't believe how quickly Mrs. Tisdale, or Betty, as she requested they call her, arranged the scenario to his specs. Life happened without his expert management, and he already knew more about the Tisdales in five minutes than he'd ever expected to discover.

In the kitchen, which was tastefully decorated in a traditional way, certainly warm and inviting, you could see Betty's, not Gerald's, influence. Gerald now took charge with questions on the progress of solving these "despicable travesties."

Jim turned the questions into questions to Gerald. "You know everything about this area and its people. What can you tell me? What's unusual about this area and/or its residents?"

Gerald then discoursed on the requests by neighbors to have the city fence in the playing fields next to the woods. He had asked the police to attend a neighborhood meeting to discuss the efficacy of fencing in Hoffington Fields. Despite their fears, and perhaps because the police pointed out that only two of the murders had taken place in the fields right near the woods, the neighbors did not go ahead with their request. As a selectman, Gerald explained, his job's major focus was forwarding information between parties, and he suggested that he always worked in partnership with the police, as he had this time. The neighborhood did not forward the request to the city.

Gerald said that, in the period of the first three murders and before, there were lots of complaints in the area about a group of weird people who were supposedly practicing witchcraft. But it had turned out to be costumed pot parties. It was something new some of the college kids in town were into. "All weird activity is gone now. With all the patrols, troubles moved to the other parks in town."

Jim was impressed that Gerald had given credit to the police. These were different times. Jim was certain that, despite Gerald's service to his community, which included many issues related to crime, he had never been in the midst of serial murders in his own neighborhood—all new territory to experience.

Gerald then said that, when he looked under his microscope, he realized that every family on the street was not normal. To his credit, he then wondered if there was any definition of normal. His family was living the American dream he said. "But look at my Judy, who is painfully shy; look at what she has to live with now. With six murders in my neighborhood, nobody will ever buy a house on this street. For a long street, no houses have turned over in over a year. I double-checked every neighbor. How could any of us be normal after this? I don't drive quickly down Sunnyside Road anymore; instead, I look to both sides of the street to see if anything is going on. In fact, our town is on all the national television shows; one news outlet called West Side a child murder capital blight. It casts a bad light on this town."

Jim tried to bring Gerald back to specifics, asking what he knew about anyone on the street or the victims. Gerald basically reiterated info that the police had already received.

Jim questioned him about Jim Derrick and the widow Mrs. Dudas. Gerald was in the know. He said that Jim Derrick was a thief and that Mrs. Dudas was a lovely woman. He also said, "Dr. Stoteras is a flaming asshole who has a wife who is almost as honest and straightforward as my Betty. I don't honestly think that Dr. Stoteras ever valued his son, Melvin; his loss was about something he owned that was taken away from him. His wife Vivian, however, is really suffering."

Gerald felt that Vivian Stoteras was as sensitive as his Judy. He also believed that there were changes in that marriage after Melvin's death. He heard that she wasn't taking a lot of bull from the doctor anymore. The Stoteras daughters were friendly and outgoing girls and they were seen out with Vivian at many events; the women in the family were often seen together now, but not with Dr. Stoteras. "This is certainly a new and welcomed development. Everyone loves Vivian but suffers Dr. Stoteras. Maybe Betty can cast some light on that family, as she knows the girls. The girls are a little older and very mature and especially friendly to anyone who liked Melvin."

Betty said that Melvin had been taken good care of by his sisters and that Judy had really liked Melvin.

Jim asked, "Who didn't like Melvin, Betty?"

Betty immediately said that Melvin sought attention with the girls, not with the boys, though boys of his age actually liked him. He was funny like a comedian and was very fast moving. He was small. "But you should see him run," she said. Judy thought that he could probably outrun any of the other boys. Betty believed that if Melvin thought he was in trouble he would have made a fast escape and said, "Truly, Melvin must have trusted his killer."

His sisters, called Penny and Cali for short, were tall girls and as trusting as Melvin. Betty didn't mind at all seeing Judy with them. She said, "I actually believe she is emotionally more their age, although not nearly as knowledgeable about the world."

Jim was surprised to see Gerald quietly observing the conversation. He had a new view on this marriage and now believed it was a marriage of equals, a conclusion he would not have made earlier today. He then asked, "Who were Melvin's best guy friends?"

Betty quickly named the Weisand-James boy, Jonah, and the Bowes boys, Riccardo and Maynard, whom she thought were really sensitive young men and sensitive for a reason.

Betty firmly stated, "This is just my opinion, but Jonah has two fathers who carefully have educated him to never laugh at anyone who is different. The same could be said of the Bowes family, with Riccardo and Maynard Bowes, who are sons of the only interracial marriage on this street. Their mother is Puerto Rican and their father is African American. I asked the boys one day how they got such different names from each other. They relayed a cute story of balance in their home. Mom did all the work in having the babies, so dad said that she could name the first baby. She chose Riccardo as a beautiful Latin name. When the second son was born, Dad chose Maynard for the first African American mayor of Atlanta, as Mr. Bowes was originally from Georgia. He wanted the boys to know that hard work bore good fruit." Betty added that Mr. Bowes had often said that hard work had enabled the family to buy into this lovely neighborhood; that was said before the murders.

"All of these boys are wonderful," Betty added, noting how Jonah's two fathers were always covering for neighbors who were late picking their children up from the playing fields. If some neighbor's kid was instructed not to leave the park until the parent got there, then Jonah and one of his dads would wait until the parent showed up. Contrary to all the political rhetoric Betty heard on television and the Internet, she believed that her neighbors, all of her neighbors, were good people. "This murderer is a sociopath; no question about that!"

Betty further pointed out that she'd read reports that listed statistical evidence that 1 to 3 percent of the population in the United States was a sociopath. "There are all kinds of disagreements about what creates a sociopath," she explained. "But it's believed that if there is a biological tendency to not feel guilt and not get upset when hurting people, then that tendency could be further developed if the child experienced a traumatic childhood or lacked love during early development."

Surprised at this direction in the conversation, Jim asked Betty what her field of study was. With an embarrassed look, Betty said that she was an economist, who before marriage had worked for the federal government in economic research. "I've always been a research junkie. Before Gerald and I met, I made my living doing what I loved to do. I think I impressed Gerald with all the info I would quote; he, if you haven't noticed, is an info junkie."

<hr />

In the other room, Petra and Judy were discussing the latest fads. Judy was showing Petra her favorite fashion magazines, *Teen Vogue* and *Seventeen* and was pleased that Petra knew of them and had even read them. Judy seemed to bloom when she discussed fashion. Petra was surprised at Judy's insight into what worked best on which figures and which colors were most flattering on different models. She asked Judy where her interest came from and was a bit surprised to discover that it came from Anya.

Judy said that Anya knew everything, not only about fashion but also about any subject. Anya was a walking Google. Petra explored Judy's relationship with Anya and Judy insightfully said, "I'm shy; Anya is not. Even if I know the answer in class, I don't volunteer. Anya doesn't volunteer either, because the teacher won't call on her because she always knows the answer. Anya says it doesn't matter that we aren't called on because everyone knows that we know the answers. I told her that I don't always know the answers, and she laughed and said, 'Neither do I, but no one knows that.'"

Petra then asked Judy if the boys who were killed may have been bullied or bothered by someone at school.

Judy said that she'd heard a television reporter the previous evening say, "Everyone knows that you can't say or do anything today without someone who doesn't agree with you wanting to hurt you." She said, "I see my dad being very careful in his dealings with the public. He says that if he isn't careful with what he says people may react against our family. So, Detective, I'm very careful with what I say, and I get angry that I have to be so careful. Don't tell my mother. When I told her a little bit about what I thought, she yelled at my dad. He was just trying to protect us. But to answer your questions, I know of no one bullying the kids who died."

"Judy, do you spend a lot of time with Anya?"

Flipping the pages in her magazine, Judy answered, "Yes, but there is, or was, a whole group of us girls who all live on Sunnyside and go to Hoffington Middle School and hang out together. It used to be such fun before. Anya, Merry, Penny, Cali, Evelyn, Claire, Carol, and me had each other; at least one of us was always available. We had each other."

Judy continued, "I'm a little bit shy in meeting people, but I have a smart phone, and I keep up with all the kids who have them. I think that's why Claire, Carol, and Anya like to hang out with me because I update them on all kinds of stuff that the other kids with smart phones wouldn't bother to explain. Mrs. McNamara and Mrs. Rozovsky will only allow their girls to have flip phones. I know that Mrs. McNamara has eight kids and maybe can't afford smart phones, but the Rozovskys have everything. Mrs. Rozovsky will not allow Anya to have a smart phone until she is sixteen years old. It's kind of unreasonable if you ask me. Anya is very well behaved."

Judy said that the girls saw a lot of Melvin and Davie. "Melvin was even a better information guru than Anya and me. He knew everything, and he was so funny catching us when we tried to pretend we knew something when we didn't. He was never mean. We liked Davie most of the time, except when he got too clingy. The twins were turned off on Davie. They said that he could be a stalker someday."

Petra concluded her interview with, "Judy, was there ever a time when you didn't feel quite right with any of your friends?"

Judy answered with a story about Penny and Cali and a senior in high school, Suzanna, who all came by together one day and told all of them, after Melvin had been murdered, to stay away from all the boys. She admitted that she listened to them and always stayed away.

She then said, "Merry told us that what Suzanna said was nonsense; the murderer, in killing Melvin and Davie, was letting us know that he would kill anyone. She said that she suspected the murderer could be someone we saw every day. She would not say any more. We were frightened because Merry never said anything that wasn't true."

The detectives wound up their interviews, and after some hugs from Betty, they returned to the station.

⟫⟩◆⟨⟪

Millie, MCU admin assistant, called Vivian Stoteras to arrange a meeting with the detectives and Vivian and her daughters. Millie did not ask if Dr. Stoteras was available and set the time for right after school. The detectives were hopeful that maybe the doctor would not be there. Petra said to Millie, accompanied by smirks from the rest of her colleagues, "Maybe God will answer our prayers."

Detectives Aylewood and Locke arrived just as the kids were returning from school. Penny and Cali were pleased to have avoided Science Club, which their father made them attend and which they simultaneously said was, "Oh so boring."

Jim began the conversation with the girls by asking them how they were holding up after Melvin's death. They shrugged their shoulders. To change the subject, he requested that they review for him what they knew about the other victims.

Cali, the older girl, quickly responded with, "You mean murders, don't you, Detective? They weren't just plain victims; they were murder victims. There could never be a reason to murder Melvin; maybe my father could if Melvin flunked a science test."

Vivian immediately rebuked her daughter with words to the effect that their father was devastated and probably would never recover from Melvin's loss.

Penny, who appeared the quieter of the two girls erased that thought with, "Cali, Mom, you both need to get out of our family situation. We need to help with any stuff we may know but don't know we know. Detectives, just ask the questions. We'll talk about Melvin in the end. You understand that Melvin was the glue holding this family together, and the murderer just couldn't have hated Melvin. Nobody hated Melvin."

So Petra, pausing for a moment, asked a series of questions about the relationships the kids had with all their peers who lived on Sunnyside and who were within five years of their age.

Cali without a moment's thought questioned, "Why these kids? Why aren't you looking at the kids on the street that are in college or the ones working? Are you saying someone our age could do this?"

Jim moved in immediately to explain that it was important that the police completely understand all aspects of the victims' lives, about what was important to them, who caused problems for them, and what routines were normal for them. He softened the tone, he hoped, saying, "Police work involves review of information already garnered. We look for changes in what has been told to us or additional new information; then we go over it all again to make connections. That's what we do. We are always looking at details—details that eventually direct us."

He questioned the sisters about having joined Suzanna in telling Judy, Merry, and their group of friends to stay away from all the boys after their brother died. The girls quickly acknowledged their actions but explained that, after the deaths of Davie and Melvin, they thought the murderer must be a boy who was bigger and respected by all the other guys. Therefore, it seemed logical not to go anywhere with any of the guys, unless you were with a group of girls, which was exactly what their parents had also told them. "Then when Merry died, the one day she was alone, well, we all thought she should have listened to Suzanna and us. Merry was just the nicest girl from the nicest family," said Cali.

Petra then asked, "Who do you think Merry was thinking about when she kind of refused to accept your advice? Did she seem different than before? Were there any boys who appeared to raise her suspicions? What happened the day Merry died? Where were all the girls? A lot of questions I know, but would you think about them all for a minute and then answer them as well as you are able?"

Cali and Penny were quick to respond, saying that Merry had acted very differently after the deaths of Davie and Melvin. She'd told them that the murderer had to be someone from the street who knew all about them. She'd said that the most important pieces of evidence were the archery method of death, killing Davie and Melvin when there was no reason to ever kill those two boys, and the killing with the back end of an ax. Penny said that Merry was an amateur detective, "like the sleuth Nancy Drew." Merry was given her mother's Nancy Drew series of detective novels when she was eight, and since Merry was an avid reader, she had finished them all in two months. She was always very logical in her thinking. Cali said, "I asked Merry, shortly before she died, if she suspected someone in particular, and she didn't answer, which was not at all like Merry." The girls both said that Merry could keep a secret; she had to because of her home life.

Jim said, "What was going on at home, girls? Merry has an older brother in college, and the parents seem very nice and certainly are hurting from their loss."

Penny responded with, "Merry is from her mother's second marriage, and her mother's first husband, Louis, drives the family crazy. He shows up sometimes if he finds out that Merry's father is traveling, which he does all the time. Merry and her mother wouldn't tell her father if Louis was seen in the neighborhood, because Merry's dad would get some kind of 209 paper against him, and Mrs. Wafters said she couldn't live with the embarrassment. Merry and her mother would never say if Mr. Wafters was traveling. They didn't want Louis to find out if they were alone in the house, and Louis lives in town."

Petra then tried to discover whether the girls knew Louis's last name, but they didn't. Merry had said that he was a rich contractor and drove a big truck and that he had never married again. She said that she heard her parents arguing about the fact that he was no good, and he used to hit her mother when they were married.

Jim asked the girls if they had ever done archery, even though, in the early preliminary investigation after Jared Stuart's death, there was no evidence of any kid but Henry Landers being interested in archery. None of the kids on the street, according to their parents, had taken lessons in archery. He and Petra were surprised by the girls' answer. The girls said at the same time, "We took archery lessons from Henry. Well, we didn't pay him, but he taught us how to shoot at targets. All us girls did, even the boys, Melvin and Davie. It was really hard work. Merry, Anya, Claire, and the two of us were the only ones strong enough, besides the boys, to do at all well. It was fun at first but got a little boring."

Petra asked, "Did you ever try out the wrist sling?"

Cali said, "No, Henry said it was his cousin Pete's wrist sling, and he'd promised to not let anyone besides himself use it. He said it was dangerous because, when he used the sling to get accuracy, he used a special more dangerous type of metal arrowheads. Pete was older and kind of strict acting so we didn't touch it. He had also brought some bows and arrows to use while he was visiting. Pete was from someplace in Pennsylvania and was only here for two weeks."

Jim then asked where Henry stored the wrist sling and was told by Penny that it was put on the shelf on the left side just inside the garage door. Both Jim and Petra had been with the uniforms when the Landers garage was searched, and they had seen no wrist sling. They would search again and have a conversation with Mrs. Landers about archery classes.

Vivian Stoteras said to the girls, "You never told me you were playing with bows and arrows. I had no idea. This may be important information, and you didn't share it. You must tell adults what you're doing, girls. I will never stop you from experiencing life, but you must have known that Jared Stuart was killed with an arrow. You should have known how important it was to tell the police everything you know."

Cali laughed. "Mom, this is the only time the police talked to us alone, and we would never talk in front of Dad; you know what a jerk he can be. He'd control everything. 'Girls, you know you never did archery,' when we did. He'd deny it and tell us to shut up. You, Mom, of all people, how can you tell us that we could ever win an argument with him?"

Jim and Petra tried mitigating the family discussion by saying that the girls were helpful and that if they thought of anything additional to please use the phone numbers on their cards to contact them directly.

Vivian was ashen as the two detectives thanked her for having her daughters meet with them. Her expression told them that she deeply regretted her decision.

Petra shook her hand and said, "Your daughters were very helpful and we thank you again. I do believe that they spoke truthfully and fearlessly. You should be proud of them."

In the car, Petra said, "She is afraid of what her husband will say. What kind of married life is that?"

Jim replied, "Not to worry. Vivian and those girls will not breathe a word of our interview. They're used to keeping secrets from Dr. Stoteras. And as to the parents married life, well it takes two to tango. She's probably in the process of making changes. Melvin's death has shaken the balance of power there, I think."

The two reviewed their interviews and agreed that it was time to go back and visit all the kids again, specifically in reference to the Merry Wafters and Henry Landers families.

9

Fitting In

WHEN PETRA AND JIM informed the captain about the new information garnered from their interviews with the Tisdale and Stoteras kids, he decided that there should be reinterviews with Mrs. Landers and with Mrs. Wafters and her husband. "Jim, you and I will conduct those interviews today."

Petra was ticked off thinking, *Why am I being excluded?* She tried to interject about how she had pulled out a lot of the new information from the children. But the captain was adamant and reminded her for the tenth time that there is no "I" in team. She really hated his using all those old-time junk phrases. She thought, *Just tell me the truth, Captain. You think I move too fast.* But she did not tell him her thoughts, although she was pretty sure he knew what she was thinking. In fact, when Jim said that there was no reason all three of them couldn't go, she was embarrassed. She knew that the department would generally not waste more than two detectives on one interview. Further, she was afraid that Rudy would discover that she and Jim were dating. At least she thought they were dating. In fact she thought that this was more than dating. She thought that she was falling for Mr. Nice Guy. Could he really be what he appeared to be?

Petra reminded herself, *That's the problem with being a police officer; you tend to have trust issues with all your relationships. When my sister-in-law tells me I look nice, do I believe her? No, I find the nearest mirror to see if something is wrong with my outfit. And now I question the captain when I know there is no fairer guy. I've no trust.*

After the guys left to see Mrs. Wafters, Petra left the station; she didn't go too far, just for a little walk. She remembered what her therapist had told her years before, "Always break the angry cycle, Petra. Move, walk, go to the store, do tai chi. It doesn't matter what you do. Just break the cycle. The brain needs a short rest, like rebooting a computer."

Petra, still smarting, realized that she always had trust issues. Where did that come from? She came from a nice home and was loved, but she was always insecure. And then when her marriage to her high school boyfriend fell apart, she blamed herself. But she didn't cheat on him; he cheated on her. He cheated with her best friend! Who was to blame? Not her, but she had blamed herself anyway—until one day, for no particular reason she could think of, she woke up, got some counseling, and believed that she may finally be on the right road. It had been many years since that day, and yet today that old insecurity had come back.

She calmly reviewed her thinking. *Maybe Rudy taking Jim over me was simply an example of the old boys' club. Or, if I am more realistic, it was the fact that Jim and Rudy together will surely be able to pull out more information than ten detectives. Time to grow up, Petra! Time to grow up!* She wondered whether the captain and Jim ever had thoughts like this. *Nah, Jim is a rock of psychological balance. And the captain, well, other than his habit of washing his hands frequently, he's grounded. Christ, he moves so deliberately; maybe that's how he addresses handling issues. Not like me. They don't call me Bolt for nothing. I react too quickly practically all the time.*

⋙◆⋘

The two detectives were greeted at the Wafters home by Mrs. Wafters, who knew them both and had coffee service waiting for them in the family room, a large room connected to the kitchen. Introducing herself as Lorraine, she served them pastry with their coffee. Both could see that this polite service was a ritual that made her comfortable with them.

After telling her that they were here as part of the process of reinterviewing all the victims' families, the captain asked if she could please talk about her daughter, Merry, and her friends. Lorraine thought she would do better if they asked specific questions, saying, "If I talk about Merry at any length, I dissolve into tears; that won't help you, Captain."

Jim took the lead as preplanned and said, "Everyone in the neighborhood seems to agree that Merry was not only the most likable young girl but also very intelligent and aware of what was going on around her. We've been told that she really liked Davie Caras and Melvin Stoteras and was seriously moved by their deaths. We also have been informed that she was an amateur sleuth. And her friends said that she seemed troubled just before her death. Did you notice any change in her before her death?"

Lorraine just sat and cried and apologized for crying and then cried some more. After a few minutes, a composed Lorraine in a slow and definite voice spoke about her daughter. She said that Merry was a gift to her and her husband. She was the best baby, a wonderful child, the most thoughtful child, and wise beyond her years.

However, Merry kept her own counsel, and she was afraid that she had trained her that way. "You know, Detectives, my husband and I both had previous marriages. Cliff's wife had died, and he had a wonderful little boy Zachary, who was six years old when we married. We love each other, and our lives are wonderful together with one little exception. My ex-husband, Louis Campola, is a controlling and abusive man. I barely escaped that marriage intact. Cliff's gentleness and kindness really were the sources of my recovery—that and Zachary. When Merry was born, I felt redeemed, but apparently redemption is not forever. We are a severely wounded family. Zach wanted to quit college to stay with me. He says he doesn't want me to die like his first mother. Cliff is carrying on, calling me twice a day to see how I'm doing, not playing golf to be with me, and bringing me home little presents. We have not recovered, but not for a minute will I deny that Merry could have known something and not have told us.

"We are a bit secretive about our lives because Louis, my ex, shows up on Sunnyside whenever he hears that Cliff is traveling. He won't come near Cliff because he knows that Cliff's work as a national political consultant may give him big-time connections, and Cliff would get him audited or interfere with his construction contracts with the state. Cliff wouldn't, but he lets Louis think that he would. But you can't stop Louis from driving around here when he knows Cliff is not around and when he's been drinking. So the children and Cliff and I have always been quite circumspect with that information.

"I truly, just recently thought about my role in training Merry. I never wanted to bring charges against Louis, because I didn't want to ruin his business, and I didn't want the shame of my neighbors knowing that I used to be an abused woman. You know, Louis just can't stand that I left him. And now my daughter's dead. And maybe if I were more open, maybe I could have prevented her death."

Lorraine started crying again when the captain gave her a tissue from the box next to her and, in a soft voice, said, "No, Lorraine, no one could have prevented this. Merry's death is probably not related to your personal circumstances, because her death is one out of six murders. There is a relationship between the murders, which is really difficult to understand. But it is about a very seriously twisted person who feels nothing and knowingly murders children for some reason personal to him or her. As far as Louis is concerned, I am perfectly willing to have a conversation with him about his presence at any time on Sunnyside Road. I don't think that he will bother you again."

The captain remembered, *I know this punk Louis Campola from high school, and he is a bully, was always a bully. Time to renew our acquaintance!*

"Lorraine, love your family and remember what a wonderful child you and your husband raised. We will be leaving now. Oh, one last bit, of all Merry's friends, was there any one who made you nervous?"

Lorraine looked at him and said, "It couldn't be one of the children. They are all perfectly nice and well behaved. Yes one or another may be shy or a talker or boyish or a bit too ladylike, but those are traits, Captain, not flaws. No. The children are all lovely children. Merry liked them all, and they liked Merry. Detective Beauregard, I can't go there."

Lorraine thanked the detectives and insisted they take two of her pastries with them for later. Normally they would have refused, but Jim responded quickly, "You're special, Lorraine, thinking about us. We will work to find out who could have killed your wonderful Merry."

As they walked to their dark blue police-issue, nondescript sedan, Jim asked Rudy why he hadn't explored the son Zachary's life and Cliff's life for more info. In return, Rudy reminded Jim that the various police forces, including the state police and the West Side Police had taken statements from all the neighbors after the second dead child was found. They all had what looked like solid alibis for most of the murders. It was not likely that anyone of them could have killed only one or two children while someone else killed the rest of the kids. He concluded that you have to "know when to hold them; know when to fold them." Jim groaned at Rudy's use of old-time jargon, but there was no correcting Rudy.

Jim thought about asking whether maybe Louis Campola hated children and maybe that was motive enough. Then he realized that he would have stopped murdering children after Merry's murder unless he'd learned to like to murder. Jim decided that he would at least check to see if Campola had ever been seen in the neighborhood around the time of the murders.

Rudy mused out loud, "What is it about nice young women and the poor choices they sometimes make in husbands? Those loudmouth bastards always fool them."

Jim nodded in agreement, thinking about Petra.

Their conversations led to a discussion about where to direct their interviews next. Rudy immediately said, "Mrs. Landers is next. Let's find out about archery lessons. Maybe she can check with the cousin to see if he took the wrist sling home. I really am frustrated with our efforts, especially since we didn't find out about this earlier. Another thread hanging that we should have chased better. Where the hell is the great success of the FBI's data crime collection? They didn't find about it either."

In fact, he thought, *the state police with their guidance did many of the initial interviews with the neighbors after the third murder.* The bureau had come in early on the case because West Side's mayor was very close with the head of the FBI for western Massachusetts. At first, it was just an ad hoc meeting to give advice, but after the third murder, the agency assigned staff. Every stiff in town was questioned. Every neighbor and visitor to Sunnyside was questioned. *Christ, we've been given advice at every turn. We've followed it all but had no results. Why have there been no results?*

⟫◆⟪

Suzanna was just arriving at her home as the unmarked sedan drove up. She waited for them. The captain appraised the appearance of the young lady, noticing that her ripped jeans fit well with her tight, short winter jacket. She wore stylish boots; at least he thought they were stylish. *What the heck do I know about style? My oldest son says I just know "looks good versus looks awful," but I think he underestimates me. This girl would look cool to him as well as to me.*

On entering the house, the detectives were led to the exquisite kitchen that had hosted previous interviews. Jim thought, upon seeing Amy Landers again, *What a handsome woman she is.* True to his last experience in this home, Amy was ready for them with requests for coffee, tea, cake, and fruit.

Suzanna remarked that she wished her mother was ready with such goodies every day when she returned home. The detectives could see sorrow shoot across her mother's face, as if she believed she wasn't a good enough mother. Suzanna, noticing the pain her remarks had caused, went and hugged Amy, saying, "That's because she's busy making gourmet meals for us, and I'm stuck with sampling as she cooks. Detectives, it is a really terrible job to have an enormous appetite and then to be ordered to be a food sampler. It does horrible things to my waistline."

They laughed, and the tone in the kitchen was relaxed. As Amy ground coffee for a really "fresh" cup of coffee, she then also asked if they wanted tea. She showed them a Teavanna glass teapot and coaxed them with the option of a really "nice" spiced chai loose tea ready for the hot water. The detectives knew it was from Teavanna because Millie in the office had one and would sell the detectives its benefits on an everyday basis.

When all was done, two grateful detectives tucked into some homemade apple-orange coffee cake; as they were downing their delectable goodies, Suzanna said, "How can we help you, Detectives? We want to help."

The captain suggested that Detective Locke tell them about some information they had gathered that was the source for this visit. Jim began with a reminder that Mr. Landers had said before he died that he had never bought an archery wrist sling for Henry and that they, in their search of the garage, had never found one.

Suzanna interrupted with, "I was not here for the search, and I didn't know that you were looking for a wrist sling. I can say that Dad never bought one, but my cousin Pete brought one with him along with other archery equipment when he came to visit, and he let Henry use it. But I'm sure he took it home with him. He's OCD bordering on neurotic about his things."

The detectives saw a shocked look on Amy's face, who, in a shaken voice, said, "Wait here, Detectives, while I call Pete and his parents. There is a problem here. The family called after the visit looking for some of Pete's equipment, including some special wrist sling that was missing. I'll make the call, and you can talk to them. Okay!"

Amy immediately connected with her sister-in-law and turned the phone over to Captain Beauregard, who asked if any member of the family had ever found the equipment they were looking for after their last visit east. They answered that they had not. The captain informed Amy, and her face confirmed her early fears as she digested the news that Pete didn't have the wrist sling and was missing a bow and arrow as well.

Pete's family told the captain, "We didn't haunt Henry about it because Henry took really sick right after our visit, and we all thought that the family had enough to worry about." Amy said a last goodbye and thank you and finished her call.

Suzanna said the obvious, "Detectives, if they don't have it, it should be here. Henry's carefulness with all his equipment is legend. And he would have been even more careful with any equipment of Peter's. Pete is difficult, and I can't even imagine what a problem there would have been for his parents in normal circumstances, when he discovered his equipment missing. God, I can't believe that, even hearing that Henry was sick, he would back off harassing until he got his 'stuff' back. Maybe he has some redeeming qualities after all."

Mrs. Landers then remembered. "Oh my God, when we last talked to the police, they went over our habits in locking the garage, and I'm the one who leaves it open sometimes during the day. If someone took it from here, why didn't that person take all the archery equipment? Some of that equipment is very pricey. My husband never understood any carelessness in security. It's just as well he's not here now, I guess. He always shut the garage door. If that wrist sling was used in the murder of Jared Stuart, how can I ever live with myself? I never thought that a wrist sling was unusual equipment. In fact, if I hadn't gotten a call about Pete's archery equipment, I never would have even processed it as something I knew about. This was long before the first murder. We were under such stress with Henry so sick and then dying. I sometimes think Henry's death was an omen for trouble approaching us all. My husband was the next to die, and then all those murdered children. What do they call it—the black cloud overhead?"

114

Amy started crying, and the detectives watched as Suzanna, in a very adult manner, said, "What would Henry say, Mom? You know what Henry would say to you. He would talk about Karma. I have thought about these murders, and I say what was said by the author of *The Adventures of Sherlock Homes*: 'Violence does, in truth, recoil on the violent and the schemer falls into the pit which he digs for another.' Mom, you are not the perpetrator. Detectives, I don't normally remember quotes, but I just did a paper on Sir Arthur Conan Doyle, and with these murders, his quote seemed to satisfy something in me. I need to believe that this murderer is digging his own grave. He chose the weapon, not you, Mom. Henry would be upset with you. Now stop this nonsense. Let's remember that the wrist sling is used by some archers to improve their aim, but most don't use it."

Suzanna also thought that Henry and Pete were impressed with the looks of the sling, which was decorated with braid, as it made for a current archer fashion statement. At least that was her view on it. It was the holder of the bow with the arrow who had done the dirty deed. "Mom, Let's stop this nonsense and answer any remaining questions the detectives have for us."

Amy tried to smile as she said, "Well, Suzanna, this killer has dug a lot of pits and has not fallen into one for himself. I, God forgive me, want him buried soon."

The detectives took this opportunity to explore again just who could easily walk into their garage without notice. Suzanna said it could be anyone. She also pointed out that the Russ Landscaping Service guy often left his truck in front of their house whenever he was working this end of Sunnyside. It could be a barrier to anyone driving by, as it was a pretty good shield to her garage entrance. But that was only during the day. Sometimes the truck belonging to the Rozovsky's pool service guy was there at the same time, and that gave double coverage. At night lots of visitors parked anywhere on the street. She did say that her father had always locked the garage at night before he went to bed. In fact, he was a bit of a stickler about locking up at all times. "He's no longer here, and we are not that careful," she added. She thought the best opportunity would be in the afternoon, from two to four thirty. It was a given that her mother would be gone then, mostly shopping or banking. She then would come home and shut the garage door for the benefit of my dad and her old habit and start cooking for dinner at six thirty. "Mom's totally predictable."

Rudy returned to questions about Henry's archery lessons that he had given to the kids on the street. Amy and Suzanna said that Henry would teach anyone about anything he knew. He was also a Spanish scholar and who knew where that had come from because nobody else in the family spoke Spanish. He used to play CDs in Spanish and make the kids repeat everything, whether it was spoken or music with lyrics to sing. He taught a whole bunch of kids about archery, but many of them didn't come back because Henry said they thought it was boring. The detectives pursued the subject and asked which kids did well at archery and came back over and over.

Amy was quick to say, "I often brought lemonade out to them, so I know the regulars. Anya from next door; the twins; that shy girl; Merry, the girl who was killed (she and Henry were truly simpatico in spirit); Penny and Cali; Davie; Melvin; and a few others. They were very nice, but none of them lasted long. It's a lot of work, and Henry said that, like any game, you had to like it and then practice to be good."

"Who do you remember was really good or came around regularly to practice?" was Jim's next question.

The answer included one of the twins, Claire; Penny; the boys; Anya; the shy girl, who was Evelyn; and a few others as well. Included too was Suzanna, who Henry had said could be good if she wasn't so spacy; to this, Suzanna nodded in agreement.

Rudy noted silently, *May as well check whether any of these kids were left-handed*, but then asked, just in case anyone knew. Suzanna said that her father and her brother as well as she were left-handed. She added that one of the twins was too, but she couldn't remember which one, although she thought it was Claire. Merry, Anya, Evelyn,

Melvin, Penny, and Nick McNamara were also left-handed. "I know this because some of them tried the wrist sling, which I think was set up for use by Henry and Pete. Henry was left-handed. Pete's parents are not left-handed. Henry gave us some kind of an eye test to see if our dominant hand matched our dominant eye. Mine did not. Henry said it was important in choosing bows and in understanding how to improve accuracy. I just wasn't that interested in pursuing my skills and really only got some rudimentary training."

Suzanna then embarked on a conversation with the detectives that basically questioned whether they were seriously looking at the kids and inferred that if they were then it was scary. She and Penny had told the girls and Merry to travel in groups before Merry was murdered, but Merry wouldn't listen. "I was surprised at that because Merry was really smart and very interested in all the facts related to the murders. She would tell us all the details from TV and Facebook, and believe it or not, she even read the newspapers for info."

Rudy questioned Suzanna about whether Merry shared any specific ideas about the killers or had any clues.

Suzanna said, "Merry said that whoever killed all these kids had a motive that was 'very personal' to the killer. She thought that maybe the kids could have threatened the killer's self-esteem or denied the killer's desires in some way." She said that Merry was quite definite about that and had said that the police needed to look into relationships. "I think that there is just too much talk about self-esteem these days," she added. "Everyone in our neighborhood has an adequate background."

Her mother stopped her there with, "Suzanna, you of all people know that we never know how much suffering our neighbors face or how much each of us suffers in our own soul. Look at us! We used to have everything. And what do we have now? Two big chunks missing in our lives. Now, material things mean almost nothing to us."

Rudy and Jim left shortly thereafter, and Jim questioned their info on the wrist sling and metal arrows. He said, "We may be off the mark about that. Let's go back to the experts again and see why they think a wrist sling was used, who normally uses one, and whether metal arrows are normally used with a wrist sling—whether one was just used in this case or whether they're used all the time for target shooting. And if it's definite and not overly common in use, then we have to find the wrist sling used. It must be somewhere. Also, there are just too many left-handed kids and adults on this street. How many of them are left-eye dominant and is that important? Are we going to give eye tests, even supposing forensics is able to tell us the perp is left-eye dominant? Let me give the forensics lab a call and see if they're certain that a wrist sling was used. There is certainty that, in at least two of the murders, evidence says the perp was left-handed. I have a headache."

Rudy looked at Jim and said, "Jim, you talk too much and worry too much ahead of time. You need to step back a bit from this interview. One murder involved archery, only one. Sounds like the weapon was a choice based maybe on the perp's plan, but certainly on the immediate need—the need to kill. So Henry's classroom may play a role in this; maybe someone was taught to be good enough to use the weapon effectively. That someone may have been a fair shot and had some skill. That's all we can possibly infer now. Let's have Byte do some searching and analysis regarding all this stuff."

10

Some Bloom

AT THE STATION THE next morning, Jim regaled Petra with details on Rudy and his interviews and quickly captured her interest in the archery details. She immediately googled eye dominance and found a test for it. It involved moving one's hands and focusing on something and then alternating closing each eye.

"Aha, I'm right-handed and right-eye dominant. And you, Jim, must be confused all the time; you're right-handed and left-eye dominant."

Just what this information meant about the killer was still not understood by either of them. Maybe the whole theory was nonsense.

They headed for a late Saturday morning meal at the Tea Room in town that specialized in Russian crepes. The large windows on the left side had roll-up wood blinds. Bolt quickly rolled one down, leaning over a heavyset matron who thanked her, saying, "I didn't know we could lower them."

Petra thought, *I guess I can't put up with things as well as this lady does*, and replied, "Can't see with the sun glaring over at us. Thanks for letting me do this."

The waitress, Peggy, who knew all the cops from the station, laughed and, in a loud voice, said, "Ya coulda asked me. Ya know it's my job to give good service. Ya want to get me fired?" She laughed again. Peggy would never get fired from this job. She never got an order wrong, and she was always happy.

Petra ordered potato and farm cheese pancakes, eggs, and bacon, while the weird one ordered crepes filled with ricotta cheese with fruit all over and sour cream on the side. "This dairy thing must mean you're Scandinavian or something," Petra said after the waitress took the order. "And you're having chai tea, not coffee like any normal cop. You are weird. Or have I already said that?"

He smiled, all the while thinking, *She hasn't walked out yet. And this is another date, even if it's not evening. Maybe I can stretch it to a hike at the reservoir and an early dinner and who knows what else? A show, some kind of show! I'd best move slowly.*

While they downed their food with gusto, the two detectives discussed what foods they would try the next time they deigned to visit the Tea Room.

Petra started on the kid versus adult for a perp conversation. She did not want it to be a kid, especially not a kid from this neighborhood. "After all," she said, "if a kid from this neighborhood could be a serial killer, what hope is there for kids whose childhoods reek of abuse or for kids coming from war-torn areas in the Middle East? I mean, I'm going to be a whole lot more cynical if the killer is from Sunnyside. I know that, whoever the perp is, he or she is not easily identified. Could it be one of the parents? I'd rather that. Maybe one of them is a sociopath who has fooled everyone for years."

Petra continued, "We've gotten alibis for most of the neighbors but have never really followed up to completely check the alibis or conducted work interviews on the parents of all the children—I mean discovering what their work history is or what their fellow employees think of them. Maybe we should do work investigations on all the working parents. After all, people from work often are quite able and may be willing to tell us about strange behavior, especially if a person has worked at one place for a long time. And if a person has a spotty work career, that alone may tell us about family stress levels. Perhaps we could talk to retailers about the nonworking parents. Store clerks are often great students of human nature. Maybe some of these people have seen some strange behaviors that are not in our original six area interviews."

Jim told Petra that Rudy had stopped him in his tracks and told him to slow down and step back and look at the big picture. Jim concluded with, "Maybe this is the time to look at Rudy's and Byte's charts for nexus. Let's think about this over the weekend. This is the first weekend, other than the usual Saturday morning, that we haven't worked in a long time. Spend the day with me, Petra. Maybe a hike and a good early dinner will help us develop distance from this mess. I'm willing to go in for a couple of hours Sunday in the afternoon to develop strategies for the week. I'll bet we'll find the Auditor and Byte in there as well. What do you say?"

Petra thought it was a good idea. After a short discussion, they agreed to take a walk in Szot Park in Chicopee, where there was not enough acreage to call the walk a hike.

Three hours later, after many stops—including a shopping trip to CVS that took Petra a half hour and a hike in the park, where they spent most of their time watching people and their dogs and determining which dogs were well trained and which dogs they liked—their stomachs took over. They headed over to Springfield for some good Indian food at a storefront restaurant on Main Street. By that time, Petra and Jim were both busy talking about dogs again and their love of ethnic food.

Petra turned to him later as they were leaving the restaurant and said, "I think I like weird."

Jim responded, probably not in the subtlest of ways, "I surely like fast like a Bolt. Oops! I didn't mean anything by that. I just meant your nickname."

She smiled. She didn't take offense, which really surprised them both.

It was now past six o'clock, and Jim said, "Want some ice cream, Bolt? Help feed my addiction?"

Her answer stopped him in his tracks, and he thought he was

at the movies when she said very, very coyly and totally unlike her, "That's not the dessert I'm interested in, Jim."

He questioned hopefully very, very quickly, "I cleaned my place last night. Would that be okay?"

"Yup. That would be fine," was his best recollection of her answer, and they were off to the races.

Petra thought, *It's not a bit awkward.*

He opened the door, threw his jacket and her handbag on the ground, and kissed her, slowly pushing her against the tall bookcase near the door, and there was excitement as they tore their clothes off.

"Slow down, Bolt, we don't want a race. I love this part—touching you everywhere."

Jim's hands are kneading my breasts, pulling the nipples until they stand up to face the cool air before he crushes my body against his. And then he repeats the series, interrupted only by his hands alternating between my belly and ass. He seems to be everywhere, with his lips on my neck and then on my breasts and finally at home plate. I want him now, she thought, *but I don't want him to stop this. Why doesn't he have ten hands?*

Petra begged Jim to enter her, saying that his mouth was not enough.

"Not just yet, baby, not just yet."

Jim's in control. I've let him take control. Oh, Jim, please know that I'm ready. Please!

Jim somehow knew and said, "Petra, hold on, Bolt," and he entered her slowly, carefully. And he, with measured lifts, pushed in and out until he groaned from her nails scraping his back and she screamed, "Oh my god, Jim."

Petra stayed the night, and it was quite a night. She later thought, *Sex is best when you're in the know—not a kid anymore!*

Jim thought, *She has a mighty fine ass. She has beautiful breasts. She is in wonderful shape and so soft.*

In the morning light, while she was sleeping, he watched and saw no cynicism in her face. In fact, she was almost innocent looking.

Innocent looking she may be, but she was mighty creative in making love. She was what his father would call "a keeper," and he intended to keep her. He had known before; she was it. He didn't think he needed to know more.

Jim was quite aware that Petra could be difficult, certainly stubborn and quite sensitive; but she was what she appeared to be. He knew that. Best of all, she was a kind person. He guessed that her allure and her beauty were both inside and out. He went to the kitchenette and made coffee, eggs, bacon, and toast. Grabbing a tray his sister had given him to add some decoration to his stark condo, he placed napkins, his best dishes (he laughed, as they were his only dishes bought at Home Goods by his mother), and utensils on the tray, organized in what he envisioned as artful. Into his bedroom, he brought the tray, hoping that his girl would feel that he was treating her like a princess, which was how he thought she ought to be treated. He hoped he'd have many more opportunities to bring her breakfast in bed.

He opened the blinds to a sunny morning—a good omen, maybe. He thought the heavens were shining on them. She woke, a bit confused at first, and then gave him the most wonderful smile. "Breakfast in bed! I hope that's not all I get this morning."

Jim set the tray down and said, "Breakfast first, Bolt, and then we'll see what you're up to."

Five hours later, after breakfast and lovemaking in the shower, Jim and Petra were dressed and ready to face the world. It was two o'clock when they stopped at the grinder shop on Route 20 and picked up to-go cold cut grinders for sustenance, which Jim would take to the station after he drove her home to get her car.

At the station, they found, not surprisingly, the other detectives studying data. Jim told Rudy and Byte about eye dominance, and they all did eye testing on themselves but soon put the foolishness aside when they realized that eye testing of the perp was not going to happen. The detail the department now had on the kids and their parents was voluminous and not all clearly connected in an understandable fashion. But Byte promised that, by Monday, he would have something for them. The captain pointed out that the latest murder needed addressing. The chief was making calls.

Rudy then said that it was also time to talk to the other murder victims' families. "Our focus now is on any interaction among these kids and parents that is new information. If we have a connection to a few of the cases, we may see something that casts a light on Elsby's case. We also have not recently talked with the Rozovsky family, and we should; after all, Mr. Rozovsky did have a major incident with Jackson Elsby."

The captain believed that they would never be able to isolate Anya from her mother or her father or her grandmother, and for sure, he didn't want to witness another heart attack. He concluded that probably Petra should go alone. Rudy said, "It should be a conversation about Henry and archery and the other kids. They live next door to the Landers house. Anya and her mother probably know more than they think. Also, see if Anya's mother is always with her now. And let's hope that Mr. Rozovsky is too busy with work to stay home for the interview. He is severely overprotective of his wife and daughter. Plan it for Tuesday afternoon. Chief Coyne demands all of us to be here tomorrow for a meeting."

⸺◆⸺

On Monday later in the afternoon after the meeting with the chief, Petra was on her way to get some rich pastries for the MCU. Her task of fetching wasn't sexist. The detectives and Millie each took turns, except for Rudy, who didn't eat pastry and would have made all the wrong choices anyway. Rudy could not be trusted with this serious errand. Further, they were afraid that if Mona discovered that they let Rudy into a pastry den of temptation they would have to answer to her. Everyone would work to prevent Mona from ever learning that Rudy was deviating from his diabetes diet, eating pastry. It was understood by them all that Rudy lived only in fear of Mona, as they all did. Petra thought, *I shouldn't encourage Rudy's sugar habit. He's the best supervisor I've ever had, and he chose me; I want him to not have health problems. The captain's the best!*

Petra was halfway to Dunkin Donuts when she heard the alert tone with a signal 7 for a call to all officers in radio contact. The dispatcher knew enough to also call Major Crimes, as well as to send available Alpha Sector cars over to the Sunnyside entrance to Hoffington Park for an assault in progress. An ambulance would meet them there.

Petra caught her breath. She contacted Millie at MCU and was told the captain and the others were on their way. While talking, she grabbed the flashers for the roof, turned on the siren, and sped the two miles to the park in record time. Her brain and her emotions focused on only one thing as she thought, *Hoffington Park again! Assault! Not another murder, not another one; please God, don't give us another one. I know all those kids now. Please God, not another one.*

The park was a mad scramble of police cars. Rudy took control, along with the uniform captain who had arrived first. Petra wondered if dispatch didn't give the uniforms a heads-up by a second, for they often were the first on the scene. She knew this was crazy because dispatch was always in real time, at least in her department. Uniforms, with Rudy and the captain's assistance, were already moving everyone back from the area in which a young girl, Carol or Claire McNamara, lay.

Petra loudly announced that she was certain it was Carol not Claire. She distinctly remembered figuring out the difference between the two when she'd interviewed them. Carol was dressed in a skirt, and Petra had never seen Claire in a skirt; also this girl had a birthmark on her right hand. "It's Carol McNamara."

Jim caught up to her and assured her that the twin (he wasn't sure which one) was still breathing but had a nasty gash on the left rear section of her head and was unconscious. Some guy had been walking to the playing fields on the edge of the woods, when he'd looked into the woods, and seen her. Lucky it was. He was a coach, and he'd given CPR and called 9-1-1.

Petra whispered to Jim, "Question the 'good actor,' Jim, and see if his story has holes."

The ambulance siren announced its arrival, and Petra thought as she watched them just how fast and efficient the EMTs were. She knew they were all thinking the same thing. We don't want another kid murdered, not now in West Side. Why oh why have we not been able to catch this sucker?

Rudy walked the area where the girl had been found. He started scanning and inspecting. There were only a few necessary people now in the area. The uniforms were doing a good job at keeping the public at bay and, thank God, keeping the press on the perimeter. It was a difficult ground to inspect, located as it was just inside the woods. He guessed that the girl had been hit with a large rock or a rounded or maybe pointed end of some type of weapon. Maybe they were twice lucky this time. The girl might live, and there was a weapon used—only the third weapon, if you didn't count the piece of bramble used for choking in one of the murders. He thought, *A weapon found is an opportunity for additional evidence; maybe there'll be DNA or fabric or anything to help direct us toward the perp. It's imperative that we find this weapon, unless the killer has taken it from the scene.*

The scene was not easy. There were pine needles and broken branches from the winter all around. It was still a partial winter landscape. Although it was almost technically spring, spring was jumping only sporadically at them this year. However, the area was softened somewhat by low greens sprouting.

This section of the park, so near the Sunnyside Road drive-in entrance, was not used nearly as much as the entrance to the park located on Amosville Road. This entrance was mostly used by kids and families from the middle school who were familiar with the entrance. The kids had been at the park since a ten after three. He knew from their previous investigations that, whatever sport was being played, the middle school let the teams out of school a bit early to get to the park—early enough to get them home before any shadow of darkness. Hoffington Park was used by the younger kids in the day and by adults at night and on the weekends. It was now 4:10 p.m. There must have been many people milling around during the assault.

Rudy saw nothing suspicious in the area where the body had lain. He called Petra and Jim to bring their eyes to the scene. Petra told him that the assault victim was Carol McNamara. He asked the two detectives not to kick up anything, to just do a visual inspection. He'd then bring in "Weasel," the uniform, after they were through. If something existed, Weasel could find it.

"Did you see the injury, Jim?" Rudy asked.

Jim said, "I saw Carol as the EMTs brought her to the ambulance. She clearly had a fracture and depression in her skull, but I don't think just a rock could do it. It took some dynamic force to crack the skull that way. It looks to me as if a tomahawk or maybe a pointed, narrow rock might be the weapon. I didn't see any debris other than pine needles on her besides blood around the injury, but I saw no blood splatter. Even on the ground when they moved her, I only saw a little blood on messed-up pine needles. Forensics has just arrived."

The three detectives agreed that there was more to this crime scene than met the eye.

Captain Beauregard requested that Petra have four uniforms in a concert of parallel lines go through the woods looking for a weapon. He chose the woods first because the uniforms had informed them that witnesses in the parking entrance had not seen anyone pass after two girls came by around 3:25 p.m. Uniforms had already started checking and had done a visual check on the trash barrels but had seen nothing pertaining to the assault. Petra had also bolted over there to take a quick look and had also seen nothing. Their guess was that the perp had gone through the woods. They all knew that the good afternoon light wouldn't last. Rudy really pushed them to look for the weapon or a rock with blood on it.

About fifty feet into the woods going toward Sunnyside north, there was a small brook. Next to the brook Petra saw a rock with a pointed shape on top of the leaves, not under them. She called Jim over, and they stooped down to look at the rock. Petra put on white department-issued surgical gloves. She picked up the rock. The blood had a reddish hue to it; it hadn't yet dried. She gingerly felt one of the splotches with her gloved fingertip. She could see that the liquid, which she assumed was blood, was still moist. "Voilà! I think I've got something!"

She took a clear evidence bag from her jacket pocket and bagged and tagged the rock. Petra viewed the scene and was haunted as she envisioned the pictures from the nightmares she'd been having. *How many children do I have to see mauled in my dreams? I've seen junkies dead in alleys in Boston and accident victims dead by the road. And yet I can't erase the pictures of these children. This has to stop.*

Jim came up behind her and lightly touched her back, saying, "We'll get him, Petra."

She looked around, assuring herself that they were alone, although she could hear her colleagues tramping around in the woods nearby, and told Jim about her repeated nightmares.

Jim turned her body with his hands, forcing her to face him, and quietly said, "Nightmares indicate how deeply affected we are by our life's circumstances. You'd have to be a hardened criminal to ignore the devastation of children being murdered. Please always let me help you; I want to help you and be here for you. Together we will do better. Petra, we will get this guy."

They sent the evidence bag for analysis, knowing, as Jim said, "I doubt that we'll find fingerprints." He then stated, "Look at the shape of that rock. It looks to me like river stone. It's the type that we were taught in scouting to find in order to make a tomahawk. I wonder if kids still do that today."

Petra lit up. "I'd never have thought about a tomahawk. You're not all ice cream, are you?"

As she said it, Petra realized that she was flirting, and she wasn't the only one who noticed. Rudy's famous right eyebrow did the uplift, and maybe there was a smirk on his face. Petra thought, *I had better cool this nonpolice banter.*

Back at the station, Rudy directed them and four uniforms who came into second shift to leave immediately to interview all the kids and families other than the McNamara family. He wanted to know everyone's whereabouts from three in the afternoon on. The information for alibis was to be followed from three o'clock on, in five-minute segments. He had instructed the uniformed captain to have uniforms take written statements from anyone walking in or near the woods and fields during that period. He himself would follow the McNamara family. He wanted a uniform at the hospital 24-7 who would watch every visitor. And he would have Chief Coyne connect with the chief in Springfield to ask if someone could cover for restroom opportunities for his guys.

Rudy knew that the Springfield chief and Chief Coyne often sat together at the Massachusetts Police Chiefs' dinners and got along pretty well. Chief Coyne had already come down from his office to Major Crimes to let Rudy know that anything they needed—overtime, computers, or anything at all—would be authorized. Rudy was comfortable knowing that the chief trusted his fiscal and operational judgment. He also believed that he needed all the help he could get and would have to answer to the Task Force and the Feds on any sloppy early investigation. He was sick of their implied superiority, even during their display of their best public relations behavior.

While Rudy was driving to Springfield to the hospital, he got a call that the stone that had been picked up had blood on it and forensics would call him immediately if they got a match to the victim. Rudy was not surprised to receive this information but found it useful for when he met the McNamara family, the whole family, at the hospital's intensive care waiting room.

As Rudy was approaching the unit, he was pulled aside by one of the nurses into a small side room. Carol's doctor had been informed that he was in the building and was there waiting to tell him of Carol's condition—which, although better than originally thought, would not allow for questioning now. She was still out.

Mrs. McNamara was a mess. Freida was shaking. The other twin, Claire, was crying. But it was Frank McNamara, the dad, who looked haunted, as if he were cornered. Nick, one of the sons, had the same look as his father.

Rudy expressed his concern for Carol, but with apologies, also told them he needed their assistance. He pointed out that time was of the essence—that he needed their help while the day's events were fresh in their minds.

Claire, still crying, said, "I'll never forget this day, and I'll never forgive myself. I should have waited with her. She always waits with me. I'm the fighter. No one would touch her if I was around. I told her I was sick of waiting around so she could make google eyes over some of the older boys playing in the field. We're in seventh grade and had been let out early today; instead of going home, we stopped by the fields. It was Carol's idea."

Claire went on to say that she herself had wanted to go home and change and join practice with a group of kids playing softball on one of the empty fields. Carol did not like sports and was happy just watching the older boys—really just watching her brother Nick's friend Mark. It was silly because Mark would never look at her. Claire said, "I told Carol that Mark is four years older. But she said, 'That's okay. I like to look at him; he's so cute.' Lots of girls in our class do that. Anya likes our brother Nick, who is three years older than her, and Carol thinks that's stupid because it's our brother. Anyway, Anya, Judy, and Evelyn had joined us by then. We waited about five minutes, and then I said I wanted to go home. Anya said her mother would be out of her mind on the street looking for her. She said that her only hope was that her mother would fall asleep sometimes in the afternoon and would forget to walk to meet her."

Rudy interrupted her about the time, and she said that they'd left the park at about three thirty. Anya was rushing. Claire said, "Anya's mother is always looking for her, and I guess it gets pretty embarrassing for her. Anya is pretty speedy and left the park through the woods by the pathway to the Haygood's house to Sunnyside, while Evelyn, Judy, and I walked out to Sunnyside through the drive entrance and then split to go home. I changed, got a snack, and was just leaving to return to the park when I heard the sirens and then Mom screaming from a call she got from the police. It was after four o'clock. He must have tried to kill Carol right after I left."

Rudy stopped Claire and said, "Claire, what makes you think it's a man who attacked Carol?"

Claire swallowed hard. "I ... I ... well, I just assumed."

The captain frowned. "We assume too much sometimes. We want to see what we think we should see when the opposite could be true."

"How do you mean?" Claire asked.

The captain said, "We need to have evidence—that someone saw a man or heard a man's voice or perhaps heard heavy footsteps in the woods nearby, something that would indicate a man, Claire. We, right now, just don't know who attacked Carol. But please continue with your story."

Claire said, "If I know Carol, she regretted not leaving with me right away. Besides, she'd be afraid Mom would kill her. Mom has told us not to leave each other alone, and mostly we don't. But today I did. I'm so sorry, Mom."

As Claire dissolved further into tears, Frank McNamara moved away from his family. The action signaled that he wanted to talk privately to the detective. Rudy moved from the group.

When alone, separated from the others, Frank let Rudy know just what he thought about the police force's inability to stop this fiasco. "I'm from one of the worst sections of Boston, from a seedy section of Dorchester, and let me tell you there's no way this could happen seven times to kids in a single neighborhood without a full-scale riot. Both of my daughters have been traumatized, and my sons feel helpless; shit, I feel helpless. And Freida is reconstructing all our past choices that brought us here. Get this guy, or so help me, God, I'll organize a neighborhood vigilante committee. No more sitting back waiting for the police, the politicians, or the Feds to step up. Get it done!"

Rudy, with the most control he had ever been able to muster in a confrontation, said, "Do you think you're alone in your feelings of helplessness? I've talked with all the victims' families and all the professionals working on these cases and all the neighbors and other citizens, and we also are sick with the lack of progress. We are moving toward some conclusions. Perhaps inching along would be a better description. But Carol is alive and maybe will remember a conversation she had with someone. Maybe she felt someone familiar coming toward her from behind, even though the area is wooded. Maybe Carol knew and trusted her attacker, which was why she didn't run away. Maybe the attacker was interrupted by someone else in the woods."

And, Rudy thought, *finding out just who or what that was is most important. In any case, I must talk with Carol the minute that she's able to communicate. And if there is a blood match between Carol and the blood on the rock, I want to know whether there is also trace DNA on the rock that could have come from the assailant. If the lab finds DNA that doesn't belong to Carol, they could try to get a hit through CODIS.*

The captain continued his conversation with Frank. "This case is different from the others. This is the first time that we have been on the scene immediately and have over twenty witnesses at or around the scene. I ask you to please take care of your daughter and not escalate community feelings. In fact, we will be much more successful if you tell your neighbors to share with the police any visual information on Claire and Carol from 3:25 to 4:30 p.m. and about any children and adults in the area and their movements. Your assistance is important. We need your help to stop this carnage of innocent children."

Frank said, "I know that the doctor called you and that you know that Carol is alive but hasn't woken up yet. Did he tell you that she is moving her legs, one side normally, and they told us that's a good sign? The doctors have warned us, however, that her memory may be impaired. They said that even if there is no brain damage the blow by itself could cause memory loss around the time of the blow and maybe for a short time period before and after. As to brain damage, she also has some spinal fluid leaking, which they said is a worry for potential infection. One doctor—I don't even know if she was trying to be kind to us—said something about spinal fluid leaks may be countering the enlargement of the brain from the hit, possibly mitigating damage. She does have a fractured skull. She was hit hard. I'll do what you want, Detective Beauregard, but I give you a week. If you don't make any progress, then I'll haunt you and the whole damn neighborhood." He turned and went back to his family.

Rudy walked down to the uniform watching the action in the ICU and was accosted by Nick McNamara. He realized as the boy addressed him that Nick probably was the really cool guy the kids had talked about but that he was also a formidable presence for someone so young, maybe fifteen years old or more. Nick calmly started a discussion about his sisters and why anyone would want to hurt them. He reiterated that Carol was mentally tough and sarcastic—someone who, as his grandmother would often say, "doesn't suffer fools lightly." She was mentally tough but physically afraid of her own shadow.

He said, "Claire is different. She's aggressive physically and great at sports, but she'd cry if she thought she hurt your feelings. This killer got both of them by physically assaulting Carol and overwhelming Claire with guilt."

Captain Beauregard queried, "Nick, do you think that Carol was the intended victim? Maybe Claire, aggressive as you describe her, has enemies—someone who wants to get even for some past altercation. Do you think that's possible?"

Nick reacted, "Yup, Captain, I suppose that's possible—unlikely, but possible—because lots of adults can't tell them apart, while most of the kids can. Also, Claire can fight and then not hold a grudge. She's not a girlie girl, you know; so I guess I'm not answering your question 'cause I don't know. But I'll tell you this: I think this perp knows us. He really knows us. It's someone we know. He—if it is a he—knew enough to get Carol when she was alone, and he was smart enough to choose Carol over Claire. You have to know them both pretty damn well to know the difference. So if it's a mistake, then the guy is a stranger. My sisters dress differently, although I suppose some kids who go to school with them still get confused. It's a kid or adult in the neighborhood, and I'm afraid of my suspicions. I mean, I'm not certain who it could be. But if I become certain, I'm afraid of what I might do. I really love my sister, and I really liked Merry. Davie and Melvin were really good kids. I want to kill the bastard, and I wouldn't feel guilty doing it."

Rudy could see Nick suffering from a vision of himself acting in a way that, for his whole life, he had been socialized against. He thought, *It's agonizing to think about how all these kids are marked for life. I suppose they all will develop some coping skills, but those same skills may interfere with future choices, limiting youthful daring. They now know real fear. That kind of fear normally develops over a lifetime if at all—not by twelve or even fifteen or sixteen years old.*

Rudy put his hand on Nick's shoulder and said, "If you weren't upset by this, Nick, you wouldn't be a red-blooded male. It is normal to want revenge, but you're smart enough to know that revenge has never gotten anyone any satisfaction. Forget about revenge. We'll take care of this; it's our job, not your job. Okay?"

Rudy all the while was thinking, *In this case, you would make your family suffer even more. He's a good kid, part of a good family. God damn blessed until today. Why do all these kids have to suffer? They'll pay a price. Haven't I paid a price for being tied to a fucking chair for who knows how long—as much of that time as I can remember? I still have to think before I rise from my chair whether I should move. Is that normal? Maybe that's why I'm so slow moving. Hell, forget about it.*

The captain tried to keep the dialogue open with Nick and said, "You have a perspective on these kids and their parents, and we might be missing something. So here's my card. Call me if you think of something else."

Nick smiled. "You mean a connection—you're missing a

connection. You know I have some learning problems? They say I'm really smart but have mild dyslexia and left and right mixed dominance, and I notice that I understand really hard stuff but don't connect between ideas and words easily. Word problems in math are the hardest for me, and yet I can do calculus. Sometimes, it's just a connection in the material that I need. I understand about needing connections, Detective Beauregard, and I'll give this some thought. I'd better get back to my mom and dad now. They'll be looking for me. Please don't tell them what I said."

Rudy watched the boy walk away. Here was a kid with real empathy. Here was a kid he'd want for his own. He wondered how well his own kids would do under the circumstances. He'd probably discuss Nick's conversation with Mona tonight if he ever got home tonight. Mona would love this kid too. She had insight, and she had a background in special education. She had worked until the children had arrived, and she planned to go back when Roland started college in the fall. *Mona's the best on finances,* he reflected. *She thinks we'll need more money next year. Smart lady. Has kept her teaching and special education certificates in place.* He realized he'd never heard her complain about work when she was working and figured she'd just seamlessly go back to work as she'd planned. *I'm a damn lucky man,* he realized, *lucky to have talked Mona into choosing me for a husband. I always knew she was for me. It was touch-and-go at first, our getting together. But, slow though I may be, determined I also am.*

After checking with the stationed uniform, Rudy spoke with the charge nurse and requested that at the first sign that Carol was conscious they were to call him. He gave his card with his cell phone number handwritten on it, something he normally didn't do.

The nurse then said, "Detective, will this ever stop? I don't live in West Side, but my sister does. She used to always tell me that West Side was a sleepy city and that I'd be safer there than here in Springfield. She worries about me because I now live alone. My husband passed two years ago, and my children both work in Boston. I have wonderful neighbors. Now I feel sorry for her. She lives in that lovely neighborhood about a quarter mile over from Sunnyside. You know, Detective, hospital employees always have sick jokes about everything. It's how we cope with some of the stuff we see. So now the new joke is 'Nothing's sunny on Sunnyside, not even on sunny days.' Silly, isn't it, to make fun when these awful things are happening?"

Rudy smiled and said, "Humor has always been one way to live with horror. I think that it's probably normal."

On leaving the hospital, Rudy got a call from Chief Coyne. He had scheduled another meeting for Rudy and the other detectives to attend on Friday morning. Joining them would be selectmen and the mayor.

Chief Coyne was unnerved as he inferred that his and Rudy's jobs were on the line. The chief said, "Rudy, he's talking to the FBI again. They've helped us in eliminating a lot of possible avenues, but they haven't solved any of the murders. I told that to the mayor and he said, 'Neither have you and Rudy.' The shit's hit the fan. We may be able to hold them off for a few days because I explained that I understood that you'd made some progress. I told them nothing, inferred progress, but you had better have some good stuff on Friday. I'm cancelling a scheduled police conference in Philly because I'll get killed by the press if I go. By the way, you didn't answer your cell, so I went ahead and cordoned off Sunnyside from anyone but the residents, including the press. Unusual for you not to answer your phone, isn't it, Rudy?"

Rudy explained that he was with the victim's parents and the sound tone was off. He said that it was a difficult meeting and required concentration. Chief Coyne clicked off without a goodbye, which was not normal for him and not a good thing. Feeling the stress, Rudy then remembered his wife's blistering scolding about doing the little things to take care of himself for his family's sake. He stopped at the hospital cafeteria for a cup of chili with cheese and some Syrian bread. *Never overeat when stressed, but always have something in your gut,* was Mona's advice.

He headed back to the station. Something was nagging him, and it was geography. Time to look at the map again on these crimes, time to measure linear footage, time to attach time to footage; it was time. The FBI had been asked after the second murder to get involved, but other than some conversations on the phone, the agency hadn't done so until the third murder. The case had gone up the chain to the National Center for the Analysis of Violent Crime, or NCAVC. He remembered that this division of the FBI had three departments. The BAU, or the Behavioral Analysis Unit, had sent an agent. Jim Locke had spent the most time with him as the special agent, trained in psychology, developed some profiling on the potential perp—or the unsub as the agent called him. The profiler assigned helped interview individuals associated with the murders, including some of the kids. The profiler gave some guidance on who might be the most viable suspects but determined it would most likely be one or more young adults familiar with the area. The special agent had not been willing to label the killings serial murders because he said there was no strong evidence that a serial killer was even involved.

Rudy laughed. *I know damn well it is one murderer or maybe a pair. I can't prove it yet. The news knows it's a serial murderer. The public knows it's a serial murderer. Maybe a child psychologist could be helpful—maybe give us some info on the type of kids in this neighborhood and what would motivate their parents. I know, just know, it's someone in the neighborhood, if my gut is doing its job.*

11

Door to Door

DETECTIVES AYLEWOOD AND LOCKE had brought Byte out of his hidey-hole to assist the shift captain in organizing some uniforms that were to take statements from Sunnyside residents, visitors, and players at the park. All license plates of cars present at the park had been previously taken by uniforms upon arriving at the scene. There was no lollygagging around here. Every cop wanted this perp.

Byte was a genius at organizing data and crowds, although he hated interviewing. He said his mom, grandmas, great aunts, aunties, sisters, sisters-in-law, wife, and daughters interviewed him so much during his life that he knew he was not a master of their skills. Instead, he was a master at being interviewed. He had taken his laptop with him, and he checked data for really good alibis for each home for at least three murders. Good alibis, to him, required someone outside the family circle to support a story. Byte said that he knew no one in his family would ever give each other up for a cop or anyone; therefore, he reasoned, probably most folks felt that way.

There were a few homes in the whole area whose owners (and the homes on this street were all owner occupied) had never been interviewed. Some hadn't been included because they were out of town during all the murders or were sick in the hospital; others' capacities were limited due to age-related illness, blindness, and the like. Mason sent uniforms to all those homes, directing them to get information about today and the goings-on in the neighborhood.

As a child, Mason had been caught doing what he was not supposed to be doing by a half-blind, half-crippled old lady who had taken her broom to him and chased him all the way home, resulting in his getting severely punished by his mom. No one in the family had ever forgotten his escapade with the old lady, and it was repeated at every holiday gathering. Someone would start the memory, laugh, and say, "Hey there, Mason, any old ladies chasing your squad car lately?" Laughter would last for ten minutes. No. No one had greater respect than Mason for those folks who are not rushing to work or school but who sit around watching what was going round. And he told that to the uniforms. He said, "You guys are going to hear something we don't hear or know. It's a sure thing. Now get going." He was keeping tabs on their progress, answering questions, and shepherding the blues down the street.

Meanwhile, Detectives Aylewood and Locke were interviewing all families on the street that had children, leaving any victims' families until last. Petra was working the odd side of the street and Jim the even side. If there seemed an obvious discrepancy in information, then the other detective would go back and do a reinterview. By design, the detective doing the interview would inform the family that his or her partner would be along shortly. This was said to prevent the family from getting nervous about maybe having two interviews in one night.

As Petra approached the walkway of number 21, the Weisand-James two fathers were standing outside with Jonah, apparently waiting for her. They quickly acknowledged that they knew who she was before she showed her shield and introduced themselves as Neil Weisand and Barnett James and Jonah Weisand-James.

Undeniably upset at the assault on Carol, Barnett explained that they all loved the McNamara family. "The McNamaras have their shit together. They know what's important in life. I was on duty today for Jonah, and I'm ashamed that I didn't follow Carol when she left the park. I'm normally diligent about watching over the kids when their parents aren't there. I always wait by the Sunnyside entrance to the park, which is, as you know, at the end of the residential portion on the even street number side of Sunnyside. Normally, I walk over. If I or Neil (if he were on duty) needed the car, we would walk across the street for it."

Petra asked Barnett and Jonah, who were both at the park that afternoon, who else they had seen. The list was no different from what she had already seen. She then asked about the period during the time when the other twin, Claire, had left with her friends and the discovery of the assault, whether Barnett had noticed anything unusual, maybe odd activity. Where was he standing? Did he hear any noises related to the assault or afterward? Did he watch the girls leave and could he describe how he had seen them leave?

Barnett was thoughtful before he answered and questioned, "Why? Do you think that these girls were involved, because I find that difficult to believe?" His answers regarding the girls leaving and the directions they split up corroborated her previous information.

Barnett appeared disturbed and said, "I want to deny this because I didn't do anything about it, and I'm ashamed. I heard, right after the girls had left the park, noises in the woods, like running toward the entrance. And then I heard someone running the other way. This was after Anya had cut over to the woods to the other walk path to Sunnyside. I can't spell out the time exactly—just what I said. I'm going to beat myself up over this. Neil and I have always tried to be vigilant in watching over all the kids in the neighborhood. Maybe someone else heard something. Try talking to Vivian Stoteras. She was near me at the time."

Petra questioned, "You said you heard running toward the entrance and someone running away. Was more than one person running toward the entrance and only one running away? Or did I hear you incorrectly?"

Barnett said, "There definitely was more noise coming toward the entrance and maybe ... a time lapse, like coming toward and then coming toward again and then running the other way. Oh my god. Maybe I heard the assault. Please talk with Viv; she may have heard something too."

Petra left the Weisand-James family consoling each other. She told them to please keep this information to themselves, as it was important that independent support for corroboration be found. She asked them not to contact Vivian Stoteras or anyone else. They said they wouldn't, and she believed them. Fortunately, Jonah had gone in the house when Barnett was interviewed. She may trust Barnett and Neil. But kids? No they could not, at that age, generally, shut their mouths.

Petra had begun her walk on Sunnyside, starting at the low numbers and working forward, while Jim started at the high numbers working backward so that it wouldn't be obvious there were two detectives working the street. They then would visit the victims' homes together. Petra visited several homes without success. They knew from previous inquiries that the neighbors expected them and that some would not answer the door or would have nothing to add.

Petra was still alone on her end of the street when she made her next stop, two houses away at number 23, the Bowes family home. She had skipped a house whose owners didn't return from Florida until May 15 every year. Mr. and Mrs. Bowes lived with their boys, Riccardo and Maynard. Petra interrupted a family homework session in process at the dining room table. Each family member had work in front of him or her, and the smell of some Latin cooking was in the air. Petra loved Spanish food and felt the first spasms of hunger she'd had that day. It was now seven in the evening.

The first thing the two boys asked Petra was whether Carol was going to be all right. Their parents shushed them and offered to help if Petra could explain what she needed.

They reported that Mrs. Bowes and the boys were at the park at the time of the assault. They didn't see the four girls leave the park, but they did see Carol leave the park. Mrs. Bowes knew it was Carol because she was wearing a skirt, and Claire, the other twin, never wore a skirt. She was surprised to see Carol walk out of the park alone and more surprised that Barnett didn't stop her from leaving with his usual, "I'll walk with you."

Petra asked if Mrs. Bowes had heard any rustling in the woods behind the houses on Sunnyside and was told that she was watching the boys on the field, and maybe she heard something, but she couldn't be certain.

Maynard then said, "Why would anyone want to hurt Carol? She could be sarcastic, but Claire was the only one who would fight. Carol would run away from any fight." His parents tried to shush him, but he was persistent and repeatedly said that no one disliked Carol.

As she walked up the Sunnyside Road, Petra thought, *Jim must be in one of the homes.* However, she never caught sight of him. Her final interview was with Mr. Adams, whose house at number 63 was a two-hundred-year-old farmhouse, the only house that predated the modern housing developments, other than a small 1930s cottage on the other end of the street. It was his land that had been used for the development. He'd sold the land in several large parcels on Sunnyside to several different developers, while staying put in his old colonial home. His home was dated from 1850, according to the plaque on the front porch, and it was in perfect shape. Mr. Adams was quite definite that he wanted little to do with his neighbors and explained, at least twice, to Petra that developing the land was best done while he was living. If he waited, his heirs would bulldoze his house as well and would sell to the highest bidder.

Mr. Adams chose three different developers in five-year time frames, in the hopes that the area would have some architectural diversity. His sales contracts required that developers save existing trees and not impair the building site, and he paid attention that they kept their word. He then persuaded the city to take the woods into a perpetual trust as a protected wetland area with the help of the Massachusetts environmental people. He didn't think that his neighbors understood the protections he'd built into the developed area for their benefit and for future residents. "I've planned for a beautiful neighborhood, and my plan worked; now no one wants to live here because of the murders. You can't plan for everything, can you?"

Petra immediately slanted the conversation, in the hopes of developing a relationship with Mr. Adams, by reinforcing the wisdom of his work and on the beauty of his home and the neighborhood. She then expressed that her concern was for the living, the neighborhood, and the ending of the killing of children. She invited him to share with her his thoughts and insights into the children, their parents, and any unusual occurrences he had ever witnessed in the neighborhood.

Mr. Adams relayed a verbal dissertation on his history with trusting government agents, even the police.

Patiently, and smiling understandingly at his remarks, she said, "Mr. Adams, you save trees and the woods for the future. I want to save kids for the future. Worthwhile work, don't you think?"

With a slight tear in one eye, Mr. Adams responded, "I lost a daughter twenty-five years ago. I wouldn't wish that on anyone, but I don't know if I know anything. I am observant. But why don't you just ask me specific questions? I am far better at answering questions than guessing at what's important to you."

Petra started with the time frame around the assault. Mr. Adams lived diagonally across the street from the Rozovskys and liked the family, despite the overdone Russian house, which he called "the Rozovsky's Dacha." He said that the grandmother was a good gardener and kept a manure pile behind the trees and that the little girl was a cute and smart kid who could take care of herself, which made him wonder why Mariska was so watchful. He really liked Mariska, whom he called by her first name. He said she was just as nice as any neighbor could be and was always cooking something for him.

He said, "I'm careful around Sergei. I think he could be a tough bugga, but he takes care of his own, and everyone who uses his tile company says he's a good businessman to work with. The Landers family, next door to Sergei's, are wonderful people. Mrs. Landers and

Suzanna have suffered great losses. Their Henry was one in a million; so is Suzanna."

Petra questioned him about Henry's archery classes and was surprised when Mr. Adams said that he took classes from Henry. He said that Henry was as good at teaching as he was at anything he put his mind to. Petra questioned whether he was right-handed or left-handed and whether he had ever used Henry's wrist sling. He responded that he was right-handed and he had never seen a wrist sling over there. He said that he had seen many kids over there taking lessons but only a few lasted, like everything else these days; if it's not immediately rewarding then kids go to something else.

Mr. Adams did say that the girls and boys he saw there regularly were all neighbors and seemed like good kids. "That Merry Wafters is such a loss. And a couple of those boys—well, I suffer thinking about their parents' loss. I even feel sorry for that jackass Dr. Stoteras who lost a boy. I thought about who could do this. Don't think that I'm so involved with myself that I don't think about these killings. I look at everyone now who lives on Sunnyside and wonder, *Could this one be the sociopath?* Not healthy for me to think this way at my age, but I do. You see, I believe it is someone in the neighborhood—someone who knows the park and the woods. It's just a matter of time."

Petra jumped in with, "What do you mean, 'It's just a matter of time'?"

Mr. Adams quietly said, "Look, the police have ruled outsiders out. I know that from my friends in high places."

"Mr. Adams, I don't know who told you that, but at this point, we haven't ruled anyone out—outsiders or people in the area."

"Well, Detective, I've ruled out outsiders. So I think someone who is really evil and/or certifiably crazy, with no previous known criminal history is the murderer. It's probably someone young because someone older would have shown their 'spots' by now. As to someone younger as the murderer, I believe that's likely except for a couple of issues. For someone young, no matter how bright or cunning, to be able to successfully cover their tracks six and now seven times would be a stretch. Besides, I don't think young people are able to plan long term. Young people, despite the planning taught them in their video games, only plan for not getting caught. Put the spotlight on one, and he will squirm. I've been around a long time, and I think you're getting there. I am here to help you, but I don't know anything more I could tell you. I'm uncertain but think we will know shortly who this evil murderer is! I hope that little girl, the twin Carol, is going to be okay. The ladies at my church called me and said they're praying for us and Carol."

Petra doubled back down Sunnyside to see Marilyn Dudas, who had just driven by but had not been home earlier. Bolt really booked to catch her in her driveway. The interview was not particularly fruitful. Marilyn was at work during this day and felt she could not add anything to her previous statements. She was quite upset over Carol's assault. She said that the McNamara twins were really good girls and never fresh or impolite. Petra could not fault Marilyn's stressed attitude, and she also understood why Dr. Stoteras would want a go at her. *She is remarkably good looking*, she thought. Then again, Vivian, Stoteras' wife, was also a looker. *Men! They're never happy.*

⬖◆⬗

Jim trudged up the front walk of the Rozovksy's garish home. Smiling slightly, he shook his head, thinking that some people with money just couldn't help showing it off. He stepped up to the grand oak door and pressed the doorbell button. Mariska opened the door a crack and peered out.

After Jim showed his identification, he was welcomed by Mariska, with Anya and Grandma behind her. Sergei was not yet home from work but had called several times according to Grandma, who in broken English said that they should not talk to the police until Sergei was there.

Grandma said, "You a nice policeman, but Sergei should be here when you talk to us."

Anya laughingly said, "In Russia, the man is in charge of the house and what anyone would say. Isn't that right, Mama?"

Mariska frowned at both Anya and Albina and invited Jim to sit down.

Mariska's face was scrunched up from crying, and she was clearly very upset over the assault of Carol. She reiterated what everyone else had said about Carol. Jim asked them all their whereabouts from three o'clock on. Mariska said that they were all together after Anya came home from school. She said that she had fallen asleep and then went to look for Anya. And when she didn't find her, she returned home. Jim asked Anya if she had come straight home, and she said she had. In fact, she was home before her mother returned.

Albina started talking to Anya in Russian, but the child firmly restated that she was home before her mother got home. Jim asked Albina if Anya was there before Mariska returned and she said, "I don't know—in the bedroom."

Mariska explained that she must have missed Anya when she was walking. Jim questioned how that could be true, when Anya said, "I walk a good part of the way in the woods and the rest of the way on the street. Mama must have been on the street at that section where I was still in the woods, and that's why she took longer to come back."

Jim then asked for a timeline for each of them in their walks to and from the park. His questions centered on what Anya had done after she, Judy, Evelyn, and Claire had left Carol at the field. What were Albina and Mariska doing during that period? Anya said that she had cut over to the next path through the woods out to Sunnyside while the other girls had left through the driveway to Sunnyside. She explained that this way was shorter because it was a diagonal and exited just before the Haygood house.

Jim questioned Mariska, "I was told that you always met Anya after school and walked her home."

Mariska sighed, "Detective Locke, I have always met her after school, but sometimes and lately more often, I have been falling asleep; and I don't know why. I drink a cup of coffee to keep me awake, but it's not working. That's why I was late today in meeting Anya. I woke and saw the time. It was 3:29 p.m., and I ran to meet her. I missed her, and then when I saw all the police cars, I ran home to see that Anya was safe. I didn't go into the fields. I was afraid of what had happened. Thank God, she was home when I got home. Thank God she was safe."

Jim again asked them all how Mariska could have missed Anya. Anya explained again, "Mama maybe was walking on the street when I was taking the path by the Haygood house. I didn't look back, so I couldn't have seen her. I wanted to get home before she came and got me, but she had already left. And Babushka was mad at me for not waiting for Mama."

Albina, speaking in an emotional manner in Russian to Anya, was stopped by Mariska. Jim thought that there was a lot here that he didn't understand.

Jim then questioned Anya on her relationship with Carol. Anya said that the twins were a little younger than she was, but they all hung out together and got along fine. She thought that Claire would be the one someone would hurt because she was a "brute" physically, although nice enough.

Jim wondered aloud whether Carol had any problems with anyone in school or in the neighborhood.

Anya's answer was, "People had problems with Claire, not Carol. Claire is thin-skinned, and it's kind of silly, but she can't take any kidding at all. Carol says cutting things. Claire never says mean things, but will hit anyone—anyone she thinks is giving her a hard time or to protect Carol. You can be a wise guy with Carol but not with Claire. Carol is actually a sissy, you know, afraid of everything. It's weird how the twin thing is. I'd hate to be a twin. The only good thing is they always cover for each other. Maybe someone was getting even with Claire by hurting Carol. Or maybe Carol was a wise guy to the wrong person. Carol was even sarcastic with our teachers."

Jim asked, "Anya, can you remember anyone or any incident that Claire had with another person who may have wanted to get even, who seemed to be very angry? Maybe Claire had enemies and the attacker thought Claire was Carol."

Anya said that there were lots of kids afraid to fight Claire and mostly don't because Claire is pretty likable.

Jim's next visit, to the Landers family, wasn't fruitful. Amy was not at home at the time of the assault, and Suzanna said that she was at a school drama club meeting. He then visited several homes on his side of the street and made a list of passers-by during the three o'clock to later time frame. Several had seen Anya walk by around three thirty, although none were absolutely sure. They had also seen Mariska on the street coming back from the park without Anya. Most had gone to the park when they'd heard the police and ambulance sirens and then listed for Jim all the neighbors they had seen during the specified time period that they recognized.

His interview with the Haygoods was interesting. Jenny was her usual self, distancing herself from all activities in the neighborhood. She did say that, after her three o'clock cup of tea, she had gone back to the edge of her woods to cut brush and had heard someone in the woods farther back. Whoever it was, she said, was not on a path but had cut through some brush. She could not see the figure because there were so many evergreens with full bottoms in the way, but she was quite certain someone was passing. She said she'd walked the woods and found broken branches and moved pine needles that were not there the day before. She could not say how long she was in the house having tea. "But normally I take anywhere from fifteen to thirty-five minutes—no longer."

Albert had been driving home from a meeting at the university when he had seen the activity at the park. He'd stopped and had been very upset to see Carol being moved into the ambulance. He had known it was Carol because he said she had a different look than Claire. He could always tell them apart. He said, "Carol has a sharp, logical mind. She is a fearful young girl, particularly of physical confrontation. I don't know how she let anyone she didn't know get close to her. She'd normally run at the first sign of problems. Detective

Locke, she must have known and trusted this person enough to get caught from behind. They said that she was hit on the back side of the head. That's true, isn't it?"

Jim did not answer but responded with, "Dr. Haygood, who didn't like Carol? Who had daily friction in dealing with her? Do the twins get along with each other? What about her relationships with Anya Rozovsky, Judy Tisdale, and Evelyn Liacos? Do any of the boys in the neighborhood have a problem with Carol?"

Albert could not answer all the questions in depth but did say that the twins really did get along well. Carol was talking boy talk lately, and Claire did not. But he didn't think it was a big deal between them. As to the other girls, he never saw anything. He really only knew Carol, who'd joined her brother Nick and his friends a couple of years ago when he'd met them over at Henry's house.

Jim's last interview was at the Tisdale's home, and he found Gerald being consoled by his wife and daughter. Apparently he was at the Park when they found Carol, and he had watched the ambulance take her. He said to Jim, "I've never seen a little girl, so small, a little girl I knew, a good little girl, a victim of violence. How do I explain to my constituents how we can live with this? It was bad enough with Merry and Melvin and Davie. But I didn't see them!"

Jim thought that Gerald was like many good people he knew. They had to be a personal witness before they could really feel the horror of violence. Gerald did not see anything related to the assault but gave a list of everybody he did see at the park.

Judy and her mother had no information. Judy had come home from school when she'd left the park. Her mother had run an errand and could not tell exactly when Judy arrived home. Judy said that it was only a couple of minutes after she and her friends had exited the park because her house was right there at the exit.

Mrs. Tisdale said, "She is safe again, but what about the next time, Detective Locke"?

Jim left to grab some grub for Petra and himself, called her, and met her at the park to conference before deciding whether to visit the previous victims' families tonight or the next day. It was now eight o'clock at night, and they decided that it would be better to wait. Furthermore, they would consolidate the info they had gotten before they went forward.

Jim and Petra's phones rang almost simultaneously. The call confirmed that the blood on the rock was Carol's blood and that Carol had regained consciousness. The sandwiches were put aside as they raced to Springfield to the hospital.

12

Hospital

THERE WERE SEVERAL SPRINGFIELD Police uniforms at the entrance to the hospital working to restrain reporters and a couple more at the desk at Bay State Medical Center. Around and in the ICU waiting room when Petra and Jim arrived, there were West Side Police uniforms, Chief Coyne, the mayor, Rudy, and Mason. A uniform was also stationed at the corridor, preventing people from entering the waiting room. This room had been cordoned off by hospital personnel, and a nearby room was used for patients of other families. The doctors and the family had said that only one person could attempt to talk to Carol, who was awake, and that she was doing well, although she was confused. The family thought that Petra, as a woman, would be less intimidating and wanted her to interview Carol. Rudy agreed, and the others acquiesced.

Petra was relieved to see Carol doing well, better than she had thought, although the girl said she was a bit numb on her right side. Petra pulled up a chair next to Carol's bed. She saw a big bandage sticking out on the left rear of Carol's head behind the ear and a lump outside her left eye. Bruising had started and swelling as well.

Petra initiated the conversation with, "Looks like you've been in Iraq on the front lines." She touched her hand softly saying, "Bet you feel like crap."

Carol, however, said, "Going to be nice to those returning soldiers. They feel a lot worse than me, but I do feel like crap."

Petra tried to reassure Carol that the doctors said that, in time, she would be fine.

But her answer negated the effort. "I don't feel okay at all. I really hurt and have all kinds of problems. I can't remember. I have a wicked bad headache, and one side doesn't work right. Who would do this to me, Detective?"

Petra did her best to be sympathetic but was chomping at the bit for an interview. She said, "If you don't feel like an interview now, I don't want to tire you out. I'll wait. But, Carol, you are our only witness."

"Just get on with it, Detective. Tell me what you know, and I will try to figure out what happened. Don't worry about putting words in my mouth, but I need you to tell me exactly where I was found."

Petra paused for a long moment, unsure as to whether Carol was ready for even the most basic questions but certain that she did not want to lead her. Still, she was the first really excellent potential lead. "Did you see who did this to you?"

Carol shook her head ever so slightly and let out another soft groan.

"Easy," Petra said.

"Didn't see anything. Heard some footsteps behind me, and then ..."

"Then you got hit?"

"Yeah."

"And that's all you remember?"

"Yeah. Pretty stupid, right? Some guy hits me wicked good, an' I don't even see him."

"How do you know it was a guy, Carol?"

"Well who else would do this to me?" Carol's voice trailed off.

Petra wanted to get the story from Carol's memory first and knew the tape was turned on. However, she also realized that Carol needed some support. "You were found just inside the edge of the woods at the entrance to the park heading facedown, with your head lying on its right side and the gash showing on the left side. You were diagonally positioned as if you were heading up the street but you were in the woods. In trying to remember, maybe you can tell me why you weren't going down the entrance road to Sunnyside to your house?"

Carol tried to smile, but it was a bit twisted, and that attempt to smile informed Petra that her facial muscles weren't quite working right. Carol responded with some difficulty, "I always cut through that slanted path that comes through the Stuart driveway, and then I cross the street to my house. It's shorter than coming out the park entrance driveway to Sunnyside. Everybody walks that way if they're going up Sunnyside. Some kids go up by the stream for the path that comes out before Haygood's driveway if they live farther up the street. I'm not sure what I remember, but I know that's what I would always do. I do remember rushing; you know, my mom gets angry when I don't stay with Claire. I should never have stayed behind."

Carol tried to move herself up in the bed but was having trouble with her right arm and leg. Petra questioned whether she had any feelings on that side, and Carol said, "Yeah, a little, but it's not right. It doesn't work right. I can't move right." She also told Petra that the nurse told her not to move too much—that it was too soon and that she had suffered a concussion. Petra then asked if she could prop pillows behind her to spare her having to move, and Carol gratefully told her to go ahead.

Carol's next memories seemed to center on her hearing something behind her. She heard a crackling in the woods but did not turn around. She said, "There were so many kids in the fields with coaches and parents that I just thought that someone else was over by my left behind me. "It's funny," she said. "Don't you think? If someone was over to my left—he must have been on the left because all the pain is in the left side of my head—well, the only path the man could have come down would be from the Haygoods' driveway and from the stream. Who would be coming down that way?"

Petra questioned whether Carol had heard the blow coming or if she'd heard any voices, and she said a definite no.

Petra tried to jump-start Carol's memory about her activities that afternoon. Carol was sensitive about having been at the park longer than Claire to watch the older boys. She said that she just liked one of the boys, and her sister said that she was stupid if she thought a boy that age would be interested in a twelve-year-old girl. Carol thought it was okay to "look" and had asked her dad. He had said, "You're too young right now to go out with boys, but it won't hurt to watch how boys behave because their behavior is often very different from girls' behavior. Honey, right now boys your age are more interested in cars than in girls. Wait a bit, and then you won't have to worry if someone is interested in you. You'll know."

Carol said that Anya would have still been there, but she was afraid that her mother would be angry. Anya was mad at Claire because Claire had said that her brother Nick would never look at a little girl. Anya had a crush on her brother Nick. Carol said, "You know, Detective, Anya is really gorgeous and the most mature, you know, of us all. I think that Claire is wrong and someday Nick will be stunned by Anya. He says he doesn't like her now and that she's a self-absorbed princess, but I think that will change. Anya was really angry with me for saying that Nick would never be interested in her because Nick likes blondes. I just said that to bust her. Who doesn't like blondes? Then Claire said the same thing to Anya, but Anya probably wouldn't say anything to her because Claire is intimidating."

Petra questioned Carol. "What do you mean intimidating?"

"Well, Claire's a jock. And Anya is, like Nick says, 'a princess.'"

Petra's next questions related to whether Carol had any enemies at all. Carol said, "I never fight with anyone. I suppose that I'm sarcastic at times. Maybe I use my mouth instead of my fists; it seems just as good at keeping any bullies in line. I don't know why anyone would do this to me. Doesn't the guy know that if my brothers find out who did this he'll be dead?"

Petra, realizing that Carol could no longer concentrate and was very tired, left her cell number and told Carol to call her if she thought of anything that would help. Petra tried to reassure her that she was safe by explaining that an officer would be there around the clock. "Carol, your work is to relax and get well, not to worry."

Before she left, she asked Carol to have her mother do an inventory of her belongings and, based on Carol's memory, check to see if anything was missing.

When Petra joined her colleagues in the waiting room, she was accosted by the family. Claire asked if Petra had learned anything new. Instead of answering the question, Petra asked Claire some further questions about the afternoon timeline. Claire reiterated that she, Judy, and Evelyn walked down the driveway to go home. At the driveway's end, she'd crossed Sunnyside, while Evelyn and Judy had gone up to their homes a few doors up on the same side of the street.

Petra sought an explanation as to why they hadn't taken the diagonal short pine needle path to Sunnyside. Claire said she would have, but Evelyn's mother didn't want her in the woods, and Judy thought it best to go with Evelyn and her. Evelyn, Judy, and she used to take the path all the time. But since Merry's death, Evelyn had been forbidden to take any path through the woods. Claire said, "She wasn't scared of the woods; she was just scared of her parents."

Petra, on the off chance that Jim's theory was right, asked her if she or her friends had tomahawks.

Claire's answer startled them all. She said, "Yeah, last summer the city held a survival camp at Hoffington Park in the early mornings from eight to eleven. We all went. It was awesome. We learned to make weapons from materials commonly found in the woods. We all made tomahawks so we could cut things—you know, like for a tool. We were learning about the American Native Indian tribes. They used tomahawks as tools and weapons. Our instructor in the survival course wanted us to know that most things around us can be used to help us to survive, if necessary. He said, 'Remember, iPhones don't always cut it in the woods—cell tower interference!' He was really cool. Why are you asking me, Detective? I thought it was just a rock thrown at Carol."

Petra did not answer Claire's question. Instead, she asked if Claire still had her and Carol's tomahawks. She was told that their dad had confiscated the weapons. He'd told them that they were not in the woods and didn't need weapons for normal living.

Petra asked who else had attended the camp, and the list included most of the kids who were in seventh grade at Hoffington, along with her, her twin, and Penny and Cali.

Frank then said that he wanted to talk to the police alone. They went into the hallway and listened while Frank drilled them with question after question on the weapon used in the assault. "You told us it was a rock. Was it a tomahawk?"

The captain assured him that it was just one of the many possibilities, but police work required them to explore every possibility. He then asked Frank, "Do you still have your daughters' tomahawks. If so, we'd like to have them. And if any of your other kids attended the class, could we see theirs as well?"

Frank said that he had both tomahawks locked up. "I told the twins that I would return them on their wedding day to help keep their husbands in line." He groaned at his memory of the joke. He would bring the weapons to the station on Tuesday. None of his other kids had attended the camp. It was the only time the camp had been held, at least as far as he knew. He thought it was some federal funds used for introducing kids to the wonders of the woods. Frank with a most dejected look said, "Fucking federal programs. Who would believe it as a possibility? It looks to me that if a tomahawk was used then the killer is a kid or a parent."

Rudy told Frank, "Don't be too quick to form a conclusion from one little question when we don't know what weapon was used." He then gave Frank his best wishes for Carol's recovery.

The detectives quickly left the hospital to return to the station and synthesize information from the interviews taken that day.

At the station, the very tired detectives split the sandwiches Jim had purchased for Petra and himself. Fortunately, Jim had ordered chips and sides. The food fed their growing energy, and they dug into the data retrieved. Mason had left the hospital earlier and had included all timeline info gained from the uniforms' interviews into his various spreadsheets. He'd also developed the map that Rudy and the detectives had requested of the Sunnyside houses, listed residents, murder sites, geographical interests, park, and woods. Mason, in showing them the color-coded map, said, "I don't know, but it seems to me a lot of stuff is going on in one section. We already knew that, but it's clear that someone knew these woods. That someone was local, could pass and not be noticed, and probably lives on Sunnyside."

The other detectives nodded but shrunk a little bit inside.

Jim Locke responded first with, "We didn't want to see it. We've interviewed the perp or unsub as the Feds say; we've interviewed a sociopath. It's almost impossible to recognize a sociopath in the short term. It's now been a long term. We should be able to make some educated guesses and do some squeezing. What do you think, Rudy?"

Rudy's answer was not a surprise. He reminded them that the whole city was traumatized, and Sunnyside residents were on the border of acting irrationally. "We have to have a bit more evidence. Petra, you did good work using Jim's suggestion that a tomahawk may have been the weapon. I want calls made to every kid's family who attended that park camp and have every tomahawk picked up. I want that done tomorrow early in the a.m. before they're all at work and school. We have working numbers. I want all the tomahawks tested for fingerprints or fibers and, if there is a reason, for DNA. Jim, I want you to get hold of the camp counselor who taught the tomahawk class. Hopefully, he will be able to tell you what kid may have been particularly interested in the tomahawk as a weapon and who made a really good one. Also, call forensics and have them test that rock as a fit in a tomahawk to be used successfully as a weapon. Don't answer questions, Jim. Ask them!"

To Petra, he said, "You work with Mason with your interview notes and Jim's interview notes. Later, when Jim gets back, he can go over his interviews with you both and give some of his more subtle interpretations. He'll see some things; you'll see some things. Together, hopefully, we'll have a move in one or two directions. I'm not comfortable squeezing this population until I know more about any weapon used in the assault. Meanwhile, I'll inform the chief, and together we'll hold the political Huns back—for a short while at least."

Rudy then sat down with Mason and requested that they google tomahawks. He inquired loudly, "Let's see how easy it is to learn about making a tomahawk. I know that Jim says he made one when he was young, but I never did. My mother never let me near anything that looked like a weapon. It's time for us laymen to figure out whether this theory holds water. How much strength would it take to make a gouge like that in Carol's skull? Call the ME and see what he thinks? It's going to be a long night."

⟫◆⟪

At ten o'clock on Tuesday morning, a slightly refreshed detective crew met in the conference room. Millie was busy handling all the phone calls, taking messages, and answering as best she could all other matters for the next few hours. She was directed to say that the detectives would return calls within twenty-four hours and within two hours for serious matters—unless, of course, there was an *emergency-emergency* matter.

Rudy used the agenda, not normal for his style, and held them to it. "This is no longer the time for free flow thinking," he said in a raised voice, again not usual for him. "Understand me. We only have a few more days before the mayor, the chief, the Feds, and the community will have our heads, and I don't know where that will lead. So work with me."

His agenda listed the following: tomahawks and their efficacy as a potential weapon in this case; geography of the area around Sunnyside and timing for walking the area; location of murders and assault; analysis of walkers around the area based on witness statements from three o'clock to a quarter to five the previous day; analysis of the previous day's interviewees' attitudes; and new directions to take.

Jim had recovered fifteen tomahawks so far, including weapons from all the kids who had attended the camp who lived on Sunnyside. Forensics had checked the weapons for blood and had found none. These weapons were made with found stones, and they were river stones. The shafts were pieces of thick branches. Some he knew to be from rhododendron bushes. He knew this from years of cutting his parents' and grandparents' rhododendron bushes. Most had a curve to them. He could just imagine the instructor taking the kids on a field trip through the woods. The only thing was he didn't think it was through the woods behind the homes; there weren't enough rhododendron bushes there.

Jim wondered if the class had journeyed down the woods at the end of the street, where the woods blossomed into almost a forest on the even side of Sunnyside Road. Jim said that none of the stones showed evidence of grinding. The handles were rough cut, thick branches with bark scraped off at the bottom for use as the handle. The handles all showed sanding; some were smoother than others. The shafts were all about sixteen to seventeen inches long and wide enough so the notch could be made in the top to fit the river stones. The notch cut was anywhere from two and a half to three inches deep and just wide enough for the stones. The stones were set in the notch and reinforced, some with twine, some with natural vines, and some with rawhide.

Jim said that they looked exactly like the ones he had made as a kid but inserted, almost as an aside, "Once you've made one of these, it would be easy to duplicate many more. In fact, the stone we found in the stream with Carol's blood on it is remarkably similar to these stones. I'm waiting for the instructor to call me back. I think it would be difficult to find all of these stones so similar in shape in one area, unless there is a section of riverbed in the forest I mentioned. We should check that area. Perhaps the instructor went hunting for them and saved them for his camps; it's more likely, though, that he made the kids do the work."

Jim stated that he was disappointed that all the weapons were found with stones intact. "Some weapons have narrower heads on them, and some have fatter heads. I don't know, again about the supply source. Perhaps there were several stones available. Maybe the instructor gave two stones to some people. As to whether someone could use one of these weapons and make such an impact on Carol's skull, it's possible. I made one that's pretty similar to these tomahawks and had Petra try throwing it. We used a tree stump behind the station for a target. The arc created when she threw the tomahawk would not allow her to hit her target. If someone were really good at throwing it, maybe it would be possible. But I think that the weapon wasn't thrown." Jim remembered helping Petra throw the tomahawk, thinking, *Doesn't matter if she's a tough street cop; she throws like a girl. Sure gave me a great opportunity to teach her how to throw it. Hope nobody was watching us.*

Jim reported that he'd talked with a guy from forensics who knew a lot about homemade weapons. He said that these types of tomahawks were not really made for throwing. They were made for chopping; they were meant to be a tool. "When Petra went closer to her target and chopped," he added, "well she very easily did some damage to the partially rotted tree but still intact stump in back."

At this time, Millie buzzed Jim, referencing a call from a Tom Blouin, the survival camp instructor.

The group spent the time, while Jim took his call, discussing tomahawks. Mason said that, when he was a little kid, they'd use stones for stripping bark from trees. And of course, with the right stones, they did lots of damage with their homemade slingshots. He remarked, "Parents don't understand that kids have a lot of time on their hands, and they don't know what their own kids are up to. If I had learned in some camp how to make one tomahawk, you can bet I'd have made more."

Rudy asked Petra how close she was to the tall tree trunk when she'd hit it with force.

She said she was less than three feet away, adding, "And I know what you're getting at, Captain. How could I be so close and not have Carol notice me? I thought about that. Remember, she was hit on the back side of the head on the left side. Now follow me for a minute and visualize. It couldn't have happened if I were in front of Carol, for she would have seen me. I don't think it could have happened if I were right-handed. I tried, and I think to get the full force of the blow, she would certainly have seen part of the perp's clothing and would have remembered it. If I sliced with the tomahawk to the left rear of her head with my left hand, I could stay behind her and get a good blow in. She would not have been able to see the blow coming."

Petra then pushed Mason and put him in Carol's place and showed what a right-handed person's blow to the body would require. It wouldn't work without Carol seeing some movement or an arm or clothing that would have given her a chance to run away. Also, forensics seemed to think a left-handed person had given the blow. "When I tried doing it left-handed, I could strike the blow with full force and still be behind Carol. The other aspect of this is that the rock in my tomahawk came out after each blow and had to be reattached, which goes along with a rock with her blood on it being found next to the stream. If the unsub threw away the rock, maybe we can find the tomahawk shaft out there along the woods. I think it's worth getting Weasel in again. Show him what these tomahawk shafts look like. Maybe dogs can find the shaft; there may be blood on it. We can give the dogs a sniff of Carol's blood."

The Captain directed Mason to call Weasel.

Jim returned to the conference room, and by the look on his face, the other detectives knew he had some news; they weren't certain what kind of news he had. He began with an analysis of the instructor, Tom Blouin, an absolutely dedicated environmentalist who spent his life developing programs to sensitize children, teens, and adults to the importance of protecting and understanding the trees and forests around them. He tried to include some Native American history in the classes. Tool making was used to add fun for the kids and to keep them involved.

The program Blouin conducted at Hoffington Park was developed to keep alive the history of survival tactics used in northern woods and forests. The kids get totally immersed in how to build shelters, find food, fish, discover healing herbs, make tools to survive, use a compass and their GPS on their cell phones, and do anything related to improving their knowledge of the wooded environment. In his camps, kids were never bored and didn't want to leave to go home for lunch. This was true for the kids in the Hoffington Park camp.

Blouin did conduct a class in which he taught tool making. Other than some twine and rawhide, all the materials were found locally. He detailed that they did a search on the larger woods or what the kids called the forest at the end of Sunnyside Road after the park on the even-numbered side of the street. There was a wide stream down there called Adams Stream after the original owners of the woods and all of the area. The stream was a treasure of river rocks, and the kids all picked up stones and put them in their backpacks. He said that they all tried to find vines for tying. They got some, but they were told they would have to figure a way to cut them or pull them out of the ground. Some of the kids were pretty creative.

Blouin recalled that there was a group of girls who would not give up. And of course, some of the boys thought they were wilderness nuts like on television, and they certainly never gave up.

He had told Jim, "I have a tomahawk made with shale rock, which was sharp, and I let them use it to cut bark off the handle and to cut branches for the handle. These were made to show the kids how easy it is to make a tool that would work for survival. The girls loved my shale tomahawk because it was easier for use in sharpening stones, but I explained that it was not a tool they could make. It was much too sharp for kids that age to use without supervision. The girls were the ones who got the best river stones to use. I mean they found longer and more pointed river stones for their tomahawks."

Jim had asked if any of the kids stood out in his mind, and Blouin was quick to answer, listing one of the twins, a black-haired pretty girl, a girl named Merry (he remembered because he loved that name, and it matched her personality), a quiet but smart girl, and a funny little boy who wanted a lot of attention. He would look for his notes and see if anyone else stood out. He said that those kids were really good at making their tomahawks and also good at using them for making lean-tos and cutting brush back and chopping heads off fish when they caught them and had to clean them.

Tom had said that if a tomahawk was used in an assault and it was similar to what he had taught the kids to make, he would be in trouble with the US Forestry Department that sponsored his program. It could move to eliminate the program. He'd said, "And maybe they should. I mean I never thought these tools would be used to hurt anyone but a dead fish. Maybe someone found one and used the tool—maybe a Dutch uncle or some weirdo. These kids who attended the program were really good kids. I do all kinds of programs for suburban, rural, and inner-city kids. These are good kids."

Jim had asked how long it took to make one of his tomahawks and asked him to go through the process for him.

Tom had described it. "We spent a lot of time finding the right kinds of thick bush branches that they would be able to cut with my tomahawk or break off. It would have to be around two inches in diameter because, when you take off the bark for the handle, it comes down to about a quarter inch or more reduction in diameter. It has to be strong enough and yet allow the kids to hold the handle. I like a bend to it. We don't do throwing tomahawks. Even I would never let the kids make those. The Native Americans made two types of tomahawks. Actually, the Native women often used the chopping tomahawks for domestic work. The men used them also but used the tomahawk designed for throwing for hunting. Talk about a near occasion of sin. These are work tomahawks that the kids made. After we choose the stem and cut to length, then we strip the bark off the hand grip end and the ax head end. That's why I like rhododendron bushes. There's a whole mess of them in that forest, and you don't destroy the bush by cutting some branches. They are also overgrown, so they have nice thick branches. I've used birch sometimes, but they require more work to prepare.

"Next I teach them to measure their stone against their branch and make sure they can cut a notch that will not destroy the end of the branch but will still fit the stone. They have to do this without measuring tools. They try to cheat a little. One had a Home Goods measuring tape that her mother told her she should not be caught without. I nixed using that. I told her this was the wilderness, not a shopping trip. The kids caught on fast that the rock had to be set down far enough to prevent the river stone from slipping out. Then the job is to tie the stone firmly in place in the branch stalk crevice with vines. In this case, we couldn't get enough vines, so I let them use some rawhide I had. When I ran out of that, we used twine. Twine will let go on impact, even if you tie it tightly. It doesn't hold like vines and rawhide. When we use rawhide, it has been shrunk first so it doesn't stretch."

Jim had concluded with questions about any aberrations in any of the kids' behaviors that Tom might have seen. He really couldn't remember too much. There had been lots of kidding about the twins always helping each other first and how it wasn't fair that they helped each other first and on and on, till he stopped that nonsense. Tom had added, "It's common that kids that age find the world not fair all the time!"

Rudy asked Jim what could be concluded from this interview, given that part of the weapon had been found; that it was probable that it was connected to this tool making; and that it was possible, even plausible, that someone left-handed could have inflicted the injury on Carol without too much difficulty. He directed, "Who had access to the weapon and could have so quickly been there to assault the girl? Was it just an opportunity to kill that the perp took? Was the perp in the woods prepared to attack any kid who came that way? Anya came that way shortly before Carol. So why wasn't Anya attacked? Jim, did you learn anything in the interviews that would help clarify anything?"

Jim's response was that they needed to look at all the timelines for the day, including any interviews that suggested knowledge of noise in the woods.

Petra and Jim's notes gave the detectives some interest in pursuing timelines again. Mason was now in the game, with a sheet showing possible times for the six murders and a pretty definite time for the assault. If the detectives took Claire, Anya, and Evelyn at their word, along with those who saw them leave the park and two of them entering Sunnyside Road, the assault couldn't have happened before three thirty. "We know that the call to 911 was made at 3:55 p.m. If Carol left the park, like she said, no more than five minutes after her friends, then we have a window of 3:35 to 3:55 p.m. for the assault. I think the coach found the girl probably a few minutes before the call, so more than likely the end time was about 3:52 p.m. That's the time period for the assault."

The captain directed that they look carefully at conflicts in time based on neighbors' reports. "We have a really decent analysis of when the assault occurred. We think we have good records on who was near the area. We'll never get a better opportunity to pin this down. Get going."

Millie broke in as the captain was speaking with a call from Weasel.

Rudy took the call on speaker. Weasel had Willi, the police dog, and several uniforms ready to search the park. In response, the captain directed Petra to get over there and control the search. "I don't want any screwing around there if evidence is found. You're fast, Petra; make sure you keep up with them. Get some of Carol's bloody clothes from evidence for the dogs."

Petra let Weasel know that she would be there in five and told him to wait, as she would have the evidence bag for the scent. She enjoyed the twenty or more minutes running crazy after the dog. Weasel really had to be strong to control Willi after he let the dog smell a piece of Carol's bloody clothing.

And the dog found a stick, resembling the handles on the tomahawks, stuck in the ground near the Stuart's yard in their rhododendron bushes. No question, it never would have been found but for Willi. Forensics now had the handle. Their work could confirm quickly the success of the search. But Weasel was certain that the dog would not have found it if there wasn't something about the scent that got him going. Weasel rewarded Willi and both cops were satisfied.

Petra knew that if this was the assault weapon, then someone had been behind the Stuart house shortly after the assault or had gone back later, which would have been awful chancy.

⊰◈⊱

At the station, Millie again called Rudy. This time it was to take a call from Chief Coyne, who was counting the minutes since his last update. They agreed to meet later that day.

Later, Petra called in her report on the piece of wood. Rudy told her that, after she dropped off the evidence to the lab, she was to return to Sunnyside and hike all the distances currently being looked at on Sunnyside and on each path in the woods. "Your goal is to time both slow and fast walks on the street and to discover any difficulties in walking or running the pathways in the woods."

Meanwhile, the other detectives had been pursuing other remaining interviews and working on building all the evidential questions from all the previous crimes to fit into this new focus.

Mason reminded the crew what had not yet been stated. He said, "What is the motive? It looks now like one of these kids did it or one of these parents. But you have to ask why. I'll build a circumstantial profile of possibilities. But circumstantial may not cut it if it turns out a kid did it. So please isolate a perp with some kind of motive."

They all groaned thinking that Mason's role in life was to find the shortest and easiest path to solving crimes without any understanding of their work. Mason, on the other hand, was certain that he was the underappreciated member of the bureau.

Jim remembered and said, "Motive! Remember that real-life movie about the cheerleader's mother who was jealous of her daughter's competitor in cheerleading."

Debate ensued on how relevant that movie could be to these cases. Just how jealous could any parent be over twelve-year-olds' activities? This was Jim's strength. He could discuss all day psychological rationales that individuals build in their brains that would motivate them to do stupid things and say stupid things. But murder?

Although Rudy's agenda had not been completed, the captain called a meeting for eight o'clock the next morning. Rudy, at the time, reminded them that overtime was being covered. "If you have an idea, follow it. See you in the a.m. And remember—we're on a roll here. But remember too that cases are solved by paying attention to every detail."

13

Suffering Families

THE FAMILY HOME OF the first victim, Jared Stuart, was situated between the Liacos and Tisdale homes. As Jim rang the bell, he noticed that there was a walked-on pine needle path to the left of the garage and wondered if that was the path used by some of the kids and by Anya the day before. The house was set back from the street, and one black shutter hung at an angle. Adding to the specter of disrepair were banged-up garage doors and a damaged front door around the lock. He had never noticed this damage from the street view before. His first thought was, *Maybe one and perhaps more members of this family are drinkers; seen this kind of nice home not kept well before in such situations.*

It was always a puzzle to Jim how some alcoholic families kept the outside of their home perfectly so nobody would suspect the emotional chaos inside, while others didn't really care what anybody thought. You would think that if someone could afford to live in this neighborhood, there would be some sensitivity to what the neighbors thought. He also had heard rumors about Jared's parents. He really only knew a couple of specifics about Jared. Jared had three older sisters who were all out of high school. Jared was known as a thief by just about everybody. So he was probably a spoiled baby of the family. *It can happen, maybe could have happened with me,* he thought.

Mrs. Stuart answered the ring. She did not appear to welcome him at first but then smiled; introduced herself as Camille; and invited him into her living room, which was rich in oriental rugs, jardinières, beautiful drapes, and a profound sense of order belying the home's external condition. She asked Jim to call her Camille and expressed her sense of horror at another assault. She could not give him any information about the previous day because she had been attending her grievance support group offered at a church in Chicopee. She chose that group to attend because, "I simply can't face my neighbors and friends. They all knew Jared, and they are judgmental about him. I guess that's normal, but it's not helpful now—not for me now."

Jim, with sensitivity, questioned Camille about Jared and his friends. Sighing with tears in her eyes, she said that he was not an easy child. She often wondered if, perhaps, she had more understanding of girls or if Jared's coming later in life had affected her parenting style. "You see," she said, "Jeb and I waited for a boy. We stopped trying, and then out of the blue, I was pregnant. Such joy at first! He proved to be a difficult boy. He sucked my energy. He needed constant attention, and if it wasn't given to him, he created trouble. He did it in school also, but later his personality seemed to be smoothing out— shortly before his death. My husband, Jeb, was impatient with him sometimes. He expected Jared to like what he liked, but Jared didn't like anything we liked. He was always interpreting the world from a different framework than ours.

"Frankly, I thought if we could get him out of college that he would make a great negotiator; he was fearless and walked where angels wouldn't walk. But! But! Jared was taken from us, and Jeb and I will probably never be the same. Jeb went on intermittent benders after Jared's death, while I cleaned and cleaned and painted and wrote and did anything to keep my emotions in control. He was such a handsome boy." And she cried.

Jim asked her about Jared's constant joking and did she think that someone hated him for that? She smiled and said, "You must be talking about the Evelyn Liacos incident. The problem with parenting

Jared was that he was a wise guy but in a funny way, but way too smart. I always had difficulty catching him. I often knew he was guilty. Try, however, catching him. Jeb would convict him without evidence. We sent him to a shrink after that event and after someone accused him of stealing. I don't believe he had a theft problem, but the shrink did think that he needed a lot of attention and close supervision. Jared was so difficult to live with that both Jeb and I left him alone much too much; I now see that.

"The therapist suggested that we find something that interested him, and we did. We enrolled him in the drama workshop in the Forest Park area of Springfield, and he loved acting, scene setting, and all that. It was a bit of a ride, but he loved it; at least that's what he said. I think the whole experience elated us all. We enrolled him only six months before he was murdered. I just don't get it; why anyone would murder our Jared?"

Jim said, "Let's talk about that, Camille. I know that these questions have been asked before, but be patient; you may think of something. Think about jealousy, competitiveness, victims of his joking, or some other issue. Does anything come to mind with his friends or with neighbors on the street?"

Camille said, "Jared did have words with Nick McNamara about teasing his sister Claire, but Jared promised Nick he wouldn't even talk to Claire. Besides, Nick is really mature, and I don't think he hates any kid. Jared liked the girls but was too young to like them in the boyfriend kind of way. We noticed that, when he went to drama classes, he had a lot of friends who were girls, and they were jokesters just like Jared. I think that the girls in his class at Hoffington School were not into that kind of creativity, except maybe Merry, who saw and understood a lot for a little girl. Outside of the Liacos affair, I can't think of any kids he had problems with. Jared didn't like Carol and Anya. He said they were stuck-up. He thought Evelyn was a sissy and would sing a ditty to her that I know annoyed her because I saw her face one day when he was singsonging it. I spoke to him about it later, and he just said he was having a little fun, but she did not like it at all.

He liked Davie but didn't like Jackson or Melvin or Jim Derrick but never said why. Probably he was just a little jealous. They took some of the attention away from him."

Jim wanted to hear the words in the Evelyn song. She shared it to the best of her memory but could only remember a few lines. "Evelyn is a real big sissy, always acting oh so prissy, treating boys like bugs 'neath her feet, but gushing over the old man, teach."

Camille laughed at the memory and shared, "Apparently Evelyn liked the school counselor at school, and all the girls did from what I've heard."

Jim then questioned her about Melvin, as he was a pretty harmless kid; she said that Jared had problems with Melvin, who was always psychologically examining Jared's relationship with Jeb. Melvin would say that it was similar to his own relationship with his dad, Dr. Stoteras. She explained, "Jared was having none of that. His view of Jeb, his father, was that they were just different from each other, but his dad loved him, and he knew that. Jared really disliked Dr. Stoteras and hated the suggestion that Jeb was anything like Dr. Stoteras.

"You know, Detective, Jared was very loving to us. He needed so much hugging; he is so missed by us. I think my husband is doing better. He actually joined a Big Brother program with the Division of Youth Services. I think that's what it's called. He says maybe he can help another boy like Jared who needs attention. He says it's better than dreaming about how he can kill Jared's murderer. I think we're doing better.

"The girls, fortunately, are in college and separated by the everyday of it, but they also have their scars. Mostly those scars consist of regretting telling us when Jared was alive that he was the spoiled baby. Oh it's always the words we regret, Detective." And she cried and cried!

Jim held her as she cried. *Not in my job description*, he thought. But sometimes it was a necessary field requirement to comfort those in distress.

The Caras family, next on his list, was standing at the front door when he arrived. Jim felt no need to introduce himself. The parents expected him or some detective. They asked how Carol and the McNamara family were doing and said how lucky they were to have Carol recovering so well. Mr. and Mrs. Caras did not feel that they could contribute any more than they had previously. Jim questioned them about all the girls and whether Davie particularly had problems with any of them. Mrs. Caras quietly answered, "Davie followed all the girls, particularly Evelyn, Judy, and Anya." Davie was, she said, small for his age and was like everybody's annoying but awfully smart little brother. "If that gets you killed," she added, "then why are there so many annoying kids left alive? He was a good boy. He actually was competitive in school; but he was so loving, just so loving!"

Next in line was the Stoteras family. Guardedly, Jim pushed ahead and found them all at home. They had been discussing the assault, and the girls had a specific idea for a motive on the killings.

Cali started with, "Detective Locke, just think about some of the murders. Penny and I think that Melvin, Davie, Jackson, and maybe even Jared all just wanted attention from anyone who would give them attention. They were stupid and wiseassed. They liked stupid funny stuff—you know like the movie *Super Bad*, jerky stuff. And they annoyed everyone, repeating scenes from movies, jumping out to scare you—just dumb! That really was the only common thing we see.

"We think that Merry had an idea of who the murderer might be. I can tell you that if she did, she would have tried to have a confrontation. She was brave.

"As to Jim Derrick and Jackson Elsby, well they were just delinquents, and maybe they went over the line with someone. We think the murderer is overly sensitive and had his feelings hurt or is a parent that didn't like his kid being kidded. But that doesn't explain why he would kill Merry, unless he knew that she might know who he is, does it?"

Jim thanked them for thinking seriously while Vivian scowled at her daughters and said, "No one kills because of hurt feelings, girls."

Dr. Stoteras disagreed. Surprisingly, he said, "People are much more sensitive than we think they are. Some of my patients get sick because they seek approval from their families and only get it when they're ill. No, the girls may be on to something."

When Jim left the Stoteras family, he was tired. But he continued, moving on to the Wafters family; the Derrick family; and finally the Elsby family, where he found Mr. Elsby drinking and, well, "three sheets to the wind," as Jim's father would say. Mr. Elsby said that Jackson was a good boy, perhaps a bit sensitive, but a good boy. He had heard the story about the altercation with Anya and her father's reaction and said, "Sergei Rozovsky is lucky I didn't kill him. Imagine doing that to my kid. I should have beaten him before this happened."

Jim looked at Mr. Elsby, who at five and a half feet tall would be chicken feed to Sergei's over six feet in height. He wondered what Mr. Elsby was like sober. Elsby said that all these kids who were killed, with the exception of Jim Derrick and Jared Stuart, were harmless little bastards.

Mrs. Elsby entered the room, apologized for her husband, and led him off to his bedroom. When she returned, she said that she had nothing to add. She finished talking to him with a goodbye and, "I don't care anymore who did it. It won't help us. And frankly, I don't think you'll find this murderer unless you accidently catch him in the act. I can't see, as they say on television, a motive. And without motive, well, what do you have? Nothing! Good night, Detective."

Finishing his interviews, Jim reviewed his notes, disappointed in their content. Perhaps he understood the kids a little better or maybe not. He called Petra, who was finishing logging all her walking of trails. They agreed to meet at Springfield's Fort or Student Prince German Restaurant, an old-time bar and restaurant, where they could talk if they could get a booth in the bar. Those booths, he thought, afforded a lot of privacy for talking. He agreed to pick her up at her house to allow her to change from her athletic shoes. After all, Petra shared, "This is a date."

⋙⬗⋘

Vodka martinis were sitting in front of them with fried Camembert cheese and potato pancakes with sour cream and applesauce. As they caught their breaths and took in the other's face, each then grinned stupidly. Petra thought that she was in love, and maybe love made you stupid. She certainly had been stupid when she'd married her husband for love. In that case, she just hadn't seen what the whole world saw. Her husband was considered a jerk by about everyone who knew him, even her family. But this was different. Jim was well liked. Jim was certainly not a jerk by anyone's standards.

The only question Petra had was why he had never married. So she bit the bullet and asked.

He smiled with that slow smile. He did not rush his answer. Finally, he responded, "You never wanted to know much about me before, Petra. Does this mean you're interested in me for the future—a long-term future? I sincerely hope that, because I see a future for us. I'm a slow starter, Petra. I was a C student for twelve school years—never an A and never a B but, then again, never a D. I went to Holyoke Community College and majored in criminal justice because my school adviser said it wasn't too difficult, and my school record supported his advice. I ended up taking psychology and criminal justice. I liked both.

"After that, I joined the army and spent three years as an MP. I think I needed the discipline the army gave me, because my parents thought that anything I did was okay. They were wrong; they should have had more controls on me. I believe that kids need more direction and more push, especially if they are like me. I had very little motivation. My father was a CFO, and my mother was in retail. They're both retired now. My siblings are all very ambitious, working for the good life. I was at the tail end of my family—the baby who everyone assumed could rear himself. Maybe my parents were tired, or maybe the others' success took all the pressure off me. I think I grew up finally when I was in the army. When I left the service, I got work as a salesman for a paper company and did really well."

Petra interrupted his reverie with, "I can believe that. You've sold me. Why didn't you stay there and make lots of money?

"I mightn't have met you, Petra, if I'd stayed there. Do you want to know more?"

She nodded. His summary of his life continued with his saving quite a bit of money he earned in sales and then continuing his education at Westfield State College, now University, again in criminal justice and psychology and then picking up a master's in psychology.

"Along the way, I had some girlfriends, but no one kept me interested for long. I wasn't ready. Petra, I'm a slow starter, but I always finish what I start."

Jim explained that he had taken the police exam and had done very well, actually finishing at the top. He also did well on the civil service exam too. He applied for the first job in criminal justice that was hiring, and it was in West Side. He got an offer, and he took it. "If I hadn't, I'd probably have gone into counseling for some nonprofit do-gooder organization. You know, Petra, I wasn't ready for you before, but I'm ready for you now."

All the while, Petra was thinking, *Slow in making moves—yes, you are, Jim. All this time at West Side Police Department, don't you want to move forward? You haven't taken the lieutenant's exam. Is sergeant enough for you? It's not enough for me. Fuck, loving another cop sucks.*

Despite her thought or maybe to fight her thoughts, Petra reached over, took his hand, and said, "I'm ready too, Jim. I didn't plan this, but then again I'm not that good at planning. I normally am all action and reaction. My journey has always been unplanned. But someone must be looking out for me because, here you are!" *And*, she thought, *I really mean it.*

Instead of dinner, they ordered desserts after their appetizers. His was a typical male choice of apple strudel and, of course, vanilla ice cream, while she chose Bailey's in her coffee.

Enjoying their time together, they saw several Springfield detectives walk into the bar for a weekly meeting they had with one of the member's brother-in-law who was a prosecutor. They stood over Petra and Jim's table, peppering them with questions about the assault. One of the detectives, Mark Spaulder, was particularly interested. He said, "Just wait a bit while we get settled over there. I have some questions about your case; everyone has questions about it. I won't keep you, but you have the case of a lifetime. You have a book, if you can ever solve it. Maybe I can give you some suggestions. Please stay a little longer. Wait while I get settled with these guys and place my order?"

They agreed. They were in no hurry.

Spaulder rejoined them and talked a bit about having been Jim's buddy in the service. Petra thought that she'd never met two more unlikely buddies. Mark then asked pointed questions that let them know he had really been following the case closely. Not everything he said was in the papers or on the news.

Petra in a firm voice asked how he knew so much. His smile ticked her off, and his answer more so. "No secrets in this business, Petra."

Someone inside was talking, and it wasn't the four detectives on the case. Jim was certain that the FBI was talking to someone at the Springfield force. Mark asked if they had whittled things down to maybe one or two directions. When neither of them jumped to the bait, he said, "Have you called in a psychic yet?"

Their startled look was his answer.

"I see no is your answer. Look, Jim, you know I'm not a nut and probably don't believe in psychics; at least I don't think I believe in them. However, we used one when we had that serial killer who was murdering all those young women in our city."

Jim asked, "And ... well, did the psychic lead you in the right direction?"

Mark wiggled a bit and answered with, "Not exactly. It doesn't work that way, you know. After we caught him, we realized that the psychic was right on several points, but it didn't help us solve the case. That was done by old-fashioned police diligence, like always. The thing is that we really didn't take the psychic seriously enough.

If we had, we could have saved us a couple of months of shoe leather. We still would have needed good police work to find the perp. That's not why I suggested that you bring in the psychic. You guys are taking a lot of heat over there, and I know what I know. And the word is that the Feds are coming soon, and you guys will be chump change then as investigators. The one thing the psychic will do is show that your group will do anything to solve these murders. Right now, you have a public relations disaster. This will slow it down while you do your work. And maybe, just maybe, a psychic will come up with something."

Petra said, "Yeah. And bringing a psychic in could backfire. The news would love that. I can hear it now, 'West Side police stumped in six murdered kids case. They bring in a psychic.' It sure wouldn't make the public believe in us. I can tell you that!" She was thinking, *Normally psychics are brought in by families when a vic's body hasn't been found and the police feel obliged to go along with the family's wishes. Doing what Mark was suggesting would preempt that. Maybe, on the other hand, if things don't go well, then hell, let the Feds deal with the psychic.*

Jim asked Mark for the name of the psychic used by Springfield police. He was told not to worry. They would have her call and offer her services, if she had not already called them. He also said that if she called them, it would save them from looking like they had nothing. It could be inferred later that the detectives would not overlook any help offered.

Petra laughed a little too quickly, quipping with, "The Captain's going to love this."

Spaulder tried to go a bit further fishing for info on the case. When that proved unsuccessful, he said goodbye. They thanked him for his help. As he was leaving he said, "Put me in your book, okay?"

Petra and Jim started discussing the "book." They both were thinking variations on the same thought: *How could we write a book? How could we let the world know how we and everyone stumbled along in the dark with so little direction?* Petra said, "If there's a book in this,

I know I would need a whole lot of distance before I would have any objectivity. I've never written a book before. Have you?" she asked.

Jim smiled at her and thought, *There Bolt goes again, booking ahead too soon.* "Not to worry, Bolt. There's time for everything. There's even time for us. This is our time. We'll be killing ourselves for the rest of the week until Monday, so let's go to my apartment for the night. And by the way, did I tell you that I love you? If not, I do. I want to rush this relationship along. Remember, Petra, I don't normally rush into things, but now, I know what I want. Okay?"

Her nod was a yes, but she said nothing. Jim noticed maybe a glint of tears in her eyes.

14

Dogged

THE PLACE WAS ABUZZ. Millie had laid out all their calls by issue, in order of priority. Petra stifled a yawn as she entered the bullpen, taking a long swig of black coffee as she moved. There was a buzzing about with no queen bee to serve on this early Monday morning. "Hey, Bolt," Jim Locke said, pointing the business end of a Bic at her, "you late for a reason?" He raised his left eyebrow and shot her a mischievous grin.

Her fresh answer would help keep the guys guessing about Jim and her, "For me to know; for you not to find out." She went to her desk, set the cup of coffee down, and plunked into her seat.

Every one of the detectives, with the exception of Mason, had a pile. Mason had been in the office the previous afternoon working on compiling details—maps, times, distances, and the detectives' notes—and calling attention to "needs to check." NTC was a category that all the West Side detectives used at the end of any interview, reminding them that their gut was telling them there was something of interest that needed corroborating or felt funny or something of that nature. Petra and Jim both had notes from the chief, the mayor, three selectmen, and at least five other citizens about the case.

Rudy had arrived a half hour earlier and using his cell phone was in deep conversation with Chief Coyne. Rudy had that slow and determined voice, portraying his knowledge and skill; they hoped it was enough to keep the chief satisfied for a while. If not, then the chief would bring in interference in the form of using the Feds or the state police to muddy the waters. Rudy thought, *Once they come into this investigation, they'll arrest quickly if there is even a possibility of a connection and no alibi, or they will again drag the murder investigations into areas that we've eliminated—ad nauseam.*

Finally, Rudy clicked off the phone and motioned them, including Millie and Mason, to the conference room. Petra and Jim raised their messages to him saying, "Mayor, chief, selectmen." But before they could utter another word, he motioned them to move, yelling, "And don't worry. I've covered all your asses with the pols."

Once in the conference room, he informed them that this was the time to buckle down and make some procedural decisions. Rudy wanted them, in a few sentences, to each tell him, their concept of the next, most important step. Silence reigned.

Finally, Millie spoke first. "Ya'll have to realize that I'm stuck with communications. I'm not complaining, but folks are getting pretty hot under the collar when they call and I don't have any really good answers. Now, ya'll know I'm good at my job. I can put people in their place or schmooze them with the best; but it's getting out of control. Now, I've had to handle calls from a psychic named Marnie Whiteacre who claims that she helped the Springfield Police Department with a couple of cases and has worked with police in Boston and Fall River as well. She lives in Agawam, and, well, she sounds kinda normal if ya'll ask me. I need to call her back."

At that point, Jim said, "Millie, you must be upset. Youuuur Alabama ya'allin is getting to me. Calm down. Put her off for an hour. We have to discuss it."

Rudy then told Millie that all the other calls would be returned ("don't say by whom") after four o'clock that afternoon.

Rudy, looking way too perturbed for him, questioned his team about this psychic bullshit. Before he could sound any more on the subject, Jim and Petra shared Mark Spaulder's conversation. Each gave a perspective, but both appeared to think it might not hurt to talk to the psychic. Rudy, to his credit and their surprise, immediately saw the public relations aspect of allowing Marnie Whiteacre to visit. But he had a condition. "Let's allow our chief and mayor to make the final decision. Do we know anything about her? Is that her married name? It sounds either English or American Indian. Mason, do a check on her. You know, does she pay her bills? Her property taxes? Have kids? A record? I have to know something before I bring her to the big guys. This isn't Springfield. I'm grateful she lives in Agawam. If she lived in town, we'd never know what she heard from our own guys. You might also want to make a few calls, Mason, to see if she's a cop junkie. Do that, and we will all meet in an hour! I have something that's bothering me, and I know it's about the case. Let me think on it a bit. See you all in an hour and be prepared with some answers."

⟫◆⟪

Rudy took this time to do some thinking. *There is personal stuff all over these crimes. I don't get it, but it's there. I have another goddamn headache; always get them when I can't move forward. Funny, I think I know why I'm physically so slow. Tied to a chair all day as a little kid probably trained me not to move; but my mind did what my body couldn't. My mind was always working even then. Makes sense! But when my brain is stalled then fear sets in; that's when I get these headaches. Well, I'm not going to a shrink. Had enough of that as a kid! Time to visit Mom. Yup, Lizette is finally going to get her way.*

Rudy's mom wanted him to look to his past and examine issues. "Rudy, we love you. You love us," she would say. "But repressing fear will make you sick. Your kids need you. Mona needs you. Your dad and I are in our eighties. We'll be dead soon. Please let's explore your history together, so you can live without these ghosts of what you think may have been or would have been. Maybe you will like your brother or half-brother or stepbrother. You need to know more and stop running away."

<hr />

When the detectives regrouped, there was food—great food for cop foodies. Millie had been authorized to bring in sandwiches and salads from Panera's. Rudy was kidded about this budget-breaking feast, and they all dove in, stuffing their faces, with only Mason eating a Thai garden salad, about which he took a ribbing. The others recalled that old stupid remark that stated, "Real men really do eat quiche," and sang it in unison.

Mason made some remark about working with people who didn't play with a full deck. He then relayed, "Whiteacre is clean—no record, no cop junkie, pays her bills and taxes, has no kids, is a nurse infamous for knowing things, and is very well-regarded, if a little spacey."

Rudy said that, after the meeting, he would raise the subject with the mayor and the chief and let Millie know when and if she was able to schedule a call. He hoped to get Whiteacre in today, because he was willing to listen to anyone with any new perspective that seemed to be reasonable. "We're solving these murders this week," he said.

He then told them that he'd figured out what was bothering him. He said that, shortly after his trip to Maine with Mona, he'd had a rather disjointed conversation with Freida McNamara. Freida had said she'd done a mental review of the crimes and that her own experiences had taught her that the solution lay not in what they found or were looking for but in what was missing from the crimes besides the obvious fingerprints, footprints, and the like—what should be known and wasn't known. Was there silence when there should have been noise? Was there no activity when there should have been activity? What normal action had not occurred?

The Captain then jumped to Jim's interview with Carlo Morelli. "We need to review his concepts on motives. Something's there we're not seeing. Or more likely, something's there we should see. Now that you've all eaten, go to a separate corner of the room with Mason's spreadsheets and a copy of recent interviews. Try to mentally create what should be at the last three murders and the assault that isn't or what is that shouldn't be. What is different from normal goings-on? I give us an hour. By that time, we'll have an answer on the psychic, and we'll have something else. I just know it."

The detectives didn't argue because this was Rudy somehow putting the puzzle pieces together, and not one cop here or on the force would ever interfere with that process. In fact, it gave them all hope. It meant that they were on the way. They were about to solve these cases.

An hour later, Rudy entered the conference room with the mayor, Chief Coyne, and a very pretty older woman dressed as if she had just walked out of Northampton, which was most notable as a funky college city. Marnie Whiteacre was introduced to them, and the mayor quickly gave her a prepared sheet about the privacy requirement of everything they shared with her. The sheet included statements about the almost total limitations required in dealing with the press and when it came to writing anything associated with the case until the case was solved and the perpetrator tried and convicted and expectations for her own professional behavior.

Marnie asked if she was to sign it now and was told yes. After she scanned the document, she said, "This is the same document I signed for the Springfield and Boston police. I'm pleased that you communicate with the others, because you will know what I can and what I can't do."

After Marnie signed the document, the mayor asked how she would like to proceed and was cut off by Chief Coyne.

The chief suggested that Marnie and the detectives be left to reach an understanding on investigation information and to conclude how much help, if any, Marnie could give after the informative session. He was quite specific in saying that notes were to be taken and his office was to receive them by close of day. He would then share anything of interest with the mayor, not his office, but with him personally. The detectives saw that the chief was letting them control what came out of the session and were pleased. The detectives were then left to do their work without the mayor or the chief.

Rudy gave Marnie a quick summary on the six murders and the assault, using a computer program the department used for public information. Marnie stopped him. She explained that she had already read everything printed in the papers, listened to and watched all radio and television reports on the cases, and had been following them since the beginning with the first murder.

Rudy then gave her the direction they were going in and asked if she was willing to listen in, without speaking, to their session planned for the afternoon going after specific points of inquiry.

Marnie was more than agreeable and opened her laptop to take notes.

Rudy, with no hesitation, stopped her there with, "Pencil and paper only. And I take it back when you leave. Okay!"

She smiled and agreed.

The three detectives had agreed on the following list of questions:

1. Tom Blouin has said that some of the kids in the camp made two and sometimes three tomahawks. Would it be worth additional questioning on which kids did that and then searching for the stones inserted in the tomahawks? If some of them showed recent use or sharpening, then it may be helpful. To Rudy's point, maybe some were missing that should be there or vice versa.

2. For all the alibis for the families, how many only had family members corroborating their presence or absence? Mason was pleased with this one because, as he often stated, "Family protects family, even when they might be guilty."

3. What did the detectives think about the noises in the woods around the time of the assault on Carol?

4. What is important in a psychological profile on a preteen sociopath or psychopath? See what the differences are

between teen and preteen sociopaths' profiles and the difference in parents' profiles of each group. Find out what typically makes a child of that age or the parent angry enough to become a serial murderer. Rudy could not help but remark that he didn't think there was a real answer to this question.

5. What will show up in a psych profile on anger issues between twins?

6. What was the workplace view on all parents of the preteens in the group currently being investigated?

7. What is relevant in terms of the location of the victims or access to the wooded paths or times for traveling each path?

8. What is the possibility that someone was directing anger at Claire by assaulting Carol, since it was well know that Claire was overly protective of Carol and would be extremely hurt by the assault?

9. Were Jenny Haygood's alibis solid? What could be found in her background? Her house has easy access to that section of the woods, and she has a history of resentment of young women and perhaps all kids. Check her work background.

10. Had there been a match of the arrow from the first murder with Henry Landers' cousin Peter's equipment?

For every area of questioning suggested above, the detectives supported the foundation for their questioning. The ten items presented took about ninety minutes and left them drained at the thought of how much more work they had to do.

Rudy turned to Marnie and asked if she had any thoughts.

Marnie directed her gaze at them all slowly, turning from one to the other, and said, "I am impressed with your collegiality with each other and wondered if the length of these investigations brought your team together in such a positive fashion."

She then went on to say that her knowledge on psychopathy versus sociopathy was limited to a rough understanding that psychopaths appeared to have more planning involved, while sociopaths worked more on impulse. How that would affect children versus adults was not well understood. She had read some works by well-known psychologists who suggest evidence shows that, in children where self-control may not be well-developed at even eleven, twelve, or thirteen years of age and where there was a biological predisposition to sociopathy or psychopathy, there could be dramatic acting out for even slight disappointments or to get what seemed important to the child.

In an adult, she felt that these crimes evidenced psychotic behavior, and there should be some signals in their personal lives. Since this was such a small population that they were currently working with, the adults would be the easier ones to investigate, and it looked to her that there were really just a few of them to scope more closely. However, if it was a child who was able to commit these six murders and one assault without leaving any evidence, then the waters between psychopathy and sociopathy, as currently understood, were really muddied. "But I don't think finding a term for these actions is the important thing," she added. "I have a PhD in Psychology, am a licensed clinical psychologist and social worker, and I can tell you that actions by perpetrators, ordinarily, do not fit nicely into a listed psychological checklist.

"You already know the tendencies of psychopaths. They prey on others. They are often charming and good-looking, and they fool most people immediately and for a while. It is only over time, through the evidence or the victims they leave behind, that their true self is revealed. You guys see more of them than the average person, and it is your gut that often picks them out, maybe on the fifth interview. They want what they want.

"In a child, those wants may be very small—something you can't even imagine could be a motive. They will do most anything to get what they want. If we're dealing with a child here, we're dealing with someone who has already mastered manipulation of family members, teachers, coaches, and others. If it is a child and he or she has not been caught after six murders and one assault, then my assumption is that he or she is quite intelligent, manipulative, a planner, and shrewd. This person has no sense of guilt. This person lacks empathy. This person is narcissistic.

"However, you've probably already been told all this by the FBI," she noted, adding she knew a former colleague of hers, who was with the FBI BAU (Behavioral Analysis Unit), had been in town several times over the last year. "So I guess nothing I've said is news, is it? It is, however, worth thinking about at this time—now that you have your sights on a small group of potential suspects.

"My role is as a psychic, and you probably don't know how I work. I won't bore you with my history. And time is important, so I'll give you a short statement of how psychics work and how I may—and I say *may*—help you."

Marnie had been a psychic as early as she could remember. "My grandmother was a psychic. The family valued what she called her gift and let me hang out with Grandma a lot." She explained that each psychic's gift seemed to be in specific areas, not that there couldn't be multiple areas. She personally believed that many people were potentially psychic. She thought those folks who appeared to be intuitive, if exposed to creative freethinking as children, could perhaps have developed into psychics. Marnie told some stories of little children seeing and hearing things when they were sick or playacting and thought of herself as an adult trained in childhood social connectivity.

Her particular gift was in clairsentience, which was the ability to pick up energies and emotions from people or places or things. Mostly, they occurred in her mind. She sometimes saw visions, was highly intuitive, and believed she was also what's called, "psychometric," which meant she had the ability to receive information from the energy of objects, photographs, or places. This went along with her clairsentience. She had ESP or extrasensory perception and used all her senses in a heightened way. She said this allowed her to create a synergy in results that was not easily explained. She best explained her abilities by saying, "I have a profound awareness of my surroundings, kind of like Sherlock."

She assured the detectives that none of these gifts were extraordinary. "Now how can I use these gifts to help your cases? I have been aware of something related to these crimes from the first death. On that day, which I remember quite vividly, I was seeing a patient when I started drawing an arrow. I always doodle, but to my recollection, I have never drawn arrows. When I read the first report on the killing of that young boy with an arrow, I knew I had a connection. But it's important to know that I needed more evidence to convince myself that there was a connection, so I held back. In each of your cases, except for the fall from the boulder, I doodled something related before the reports in the news mentioned the object of my doodling. In the fall from the boulder, I felt trauma as if I were repeatedly hit. I felt serious anger behind the hits. I normally feel no physical pain, just psychic pain or emotional pain. In that particular case, I ended up with a severe headache. When the assault on the latest victim happened, I actually felt pain in the left rear side of the head. I have brought with me my daily journal, which I always keep, explaining anything unusual that happens to me. I write about it soon after events happen. I even wrote about doodling an arrow. You may think it's silly, but I have to document my experiences to even convince myself that I'm prescient. I have had recurring dreams before each death; but I didn't understand that they were related until the fifth death. The dreams seemed innocuous enough. I was in a wood with pathways and a stream, and I kept jumping from one to the other. In each jump there was a young person telling me to come over, and when I did, a new youngster called to me; it didn't raise my awareness that I was needed until the fifth death."

Marnie then suggested that, to best assist the detectives, she would like to visit the murder scenes with someone who knew what happened. She would then describe what she saw when she was there. For instance, she may see something when she touched a rock. She wished to touch the three weapons if possible. She inquired whether there were some particular potential suspects, saying that she may be of help if she was allowed to meet them or at least get within five feet of them. She thought that she might have feelings about them. She offered her assistance at any time. "The results of my offers may not give you evidence, but I can guarantee you that I can feel things that you can't feel, and those feelings may direct you. Look in my journal. I have a note in there after the fourth murder saying that it was someone on the street. After the fifth murder, I wrote it was a child or a woman. If you check your calls, you will find that I called your phone line and left my number telling you that. But the return call was just a thank you and rather brusque at that. I don't want to waste your time or resources, so if you can't have someone accompany me to visit the murder sites, then I will go alone. But I do think I may be of help to you."

They all looked to Rudy. They didn't roll their eyes. They weren't acting antsy. Rudy just knew that they had taken her seriously—as seriously as any cop could take touchy-feely stuff. Rudy said that they only had two more days. He would personally give her an hour and a half and then bring her back to the station to inspect the murder weapons. She could then write her report. If, by tomorrow, the detectives had any more questions with which she could offer assistance, they would call her early and make arrangements to meet her at the station. "That is it; that's all I'm able to do," he told Ms. Whiteacre.

He secretly thought, *It's a waste of my time.* But it was ninety minutes; he had wasted that amount of time many times.

Rudy directed his detectives to start investigating per the list they had discussed. He wanted them to contact the psychiatrist that the department used to look at the psychology of twins and preteens. He thought that Jim would be most comfortable doing that.

Mason was to check the data on alibis and try to find holes in family alibis.

Petra was given the duty of investigating Jenny Haygood's

background and also writing up which routes were most likely to have been taken by the killer on each killing, particularly the Saturday killing. Also, he asked her to review the sixth killing of Elsby and made the observation that the victim lived on the other side of the Hoffington Park entrance, which was farther down Sunnyside Road. He wanted her to review who had seen him that day and at what times. The detectives then broke to follow their missions as instructed by Rudy.

15

Found!

RUDY ACCOMPANIED MARNIE TO the murder sites. He parked the cruiser and walked to the first site, which was just inside the park near the woods. He'd participated with the FBI in many information sittings with some strange specialists, but this was a first. Mona would want to know all about this.

Marnie walked around the site several times without talking. She stooped and touched several stones in different areas and held her head. She then walked over to a space under a tree and picked up a stick, which she then dropped as if it were a hot potato. The stick was more like a piece of wood from a building. It was about eight inches long and three inches wide. "Captain Beauregard, please check this wood. I feel it. The murder was a long time ago, but I feel something."

Rudy didn't laugh but took the wood and put it in an evidence bag for later. He told her that it couldn't be the murder weapon because wood was used for murder number two, and this was the site for murder number one.

Marnie retorted, "It doesn't matter. This wood piece speaks to me. Maybe the murderer moved it over to site one because he or she knew it wouldn't be searched."

Rudy wondered, just what was going on at the park today. *Was anyone watching them, like the press?*

They then went through to the other sites. He gave her space. She exhibited strange mannerisms, at each site holding her head. But at the last site for the sixth murder, Marnie cried out, "Oh God he suffered. He was hit more than once. The killer was very angry, and I feel that the anger is unreasonable—that the killer is too sensitive and not emotionally mature." She looked at him again and said, "This killer is very angry."

Marnie then wanted to see where the assault took place and when she saw the nearness of the site to site number one, she said, "This is near the killer's stalking area, where the killer is most comfortable. I think the killing of the little girl Merry was an accident, well not quite an accident—maybe a push and then more. I felt no anger there at that site. It was a mistake but had to be finished. I don't really know why I think that. I feel extra heaviness at this site, at the assault site."

On the way back to the station, Marnie Whiteacre said, "Captain, I think you should search for your brother. Finding him is important for you."

His response was almost seething with sudden anger. "I think you should stay on the case, Ms. Whiteacre."

Rudy brought the psychic back to the station and left her with Millie and the weapons, all the while thinking, *Fucking waste of time. But how did she know?* He would follow through, and he would think on it.

At the station, Petra wrote and sent a report to the other detectives informing that she had gone to see Jenny Haygood under the guise of her hearing noise in the woods behind her home on the day of Carol's assault. Jenny walked Petra down a double elbow path in the woods that she had made. It went circuitously from her yard to the park. The path was narrow. And Petra, despite what Jenny had said, could not be certain that any person could see someone more than ten feet away. It was now over a week and a half after Easter and some deciduous trees were early greening, and there was already full undergrowth. It was also late in the day. The assault was around this time on Monday, this week on the twenty-fourth of April. It was now Wednesday, the twenty-sixth.

Petra questioned Jenny, and Jenny said, "I know these woods. There are diagonal paths from the Rozovsky and Landers homes to the park, leaving no reason for anyone to go through my woods at all. My path goes from my house to the park. There are two straight paths from my upper next neighbors before the Landers home, but those people are never home during the week. One couple is only here from Easter to Thanksgiving, and this year they spent Easter with their son in Colorado. I know because Albert fed their cat. They have service taking care of their home. The neighbors lower down use the path by this side of the Stoteras house and the one on the other side of the Stuart house. That's why I know I heard noises because there is never anyone near my yard or wood."

And she was absolutely convinced that she'd heard people in the woods. Petra asked her if what she heard could have been an animal, and she was immediately faced with that "schoolmarm" look and, "Detective, animals are much quieter than people. It was the sound of breaking brush by vertical people that I heard, and I am most certain of that."

After some follow-up questions, Petra learned that Jenny thought the footsteps of the person she heard was someone who knew the woods. The only people, besides those big-footed police, who ever came near her woods were kids from the street building forts and lean-tos. She had more than once torn down some stupid brush they had lined up. The kids knew enough not to build in her woods. She said, "Maybe if the police looked carefully, they would find some 'edifice' built nearer to the park or up by the Landers house. Mrs. Landers would let the kids do anything." She said that the one she had taken down was well camouflaged and required careful looking to spot it.

Petra then asked Jenny if she remembered a lot of foot traffic in the woods behind her house on the days of some of the murders. Jenny said that if she had, she would have reported it—that she couldn't remember now. She said that she wasn't questioned regularly until the third murder. So if she'd heard anything, the police would have her answers in their interview notes.

After that, Petra left Sunnyside and made some calls to Jenny's former employers, who glowingly referenced her work product. When she got down to asking about personal interaction, she was told that Jenny was a loner who never, unless it was part of her duties, participated in any social events or activities connected to work. It was one reason she had left the private girls school, which required faculty presence at most events. The school also said that Jenny wasn't sympathetic to the younger women's needs.

Petra found no evidence of any incident between Jenny and the girls and no events related to Jenny.

Only one person remembered Jenny's service in retail and she said that Jenny was ever so organized and a worker. She was impatient with difficult customers, but she always did her job.

Petra, after writing her report, immediately investigated the police notes for the last four murders. One of the officers who had surveyed the street she knew well and felt confident that he would have asked all the right questions. She accessed his report and found the two interviews with Jenny. In both, Jenny had reported someone was in her woods. She then found the officer's notes for Jenny's previous interview from an earlier murder and found that she was at the doctor's on that afternoon.

Then to complete her assignments, Petra reviewed the murder board for the sixth murder of Jackson Elsby. It turned out that Jackson was always at the park when he was not at school. There were several sightings of the boy by neighbors on Sunnyside that day, sightings late in the day after school. He apparently went home and immediately returned to the park. He was at the park by 3:40 p.m. and then was found at the bottom of the rock, which was just inside the park near the wood. That day was rainy and chilly, and there were few people in the park. The rock's location was further up behind the Liacos and Stoteras homes near the path from the driveway of the Haygood home, which the cops had labeled path number four. She wondered why he was so far up in the field when there were so few people out that day. The police reports did not address this issue. The officer reporting on scene had found a brand-new volleyball, but Jackson was not seen with a volleyball, and no one owned up to missing one. She finished her written report just as everyone returned from the field.

At the station, the detectives started summarizing the results of their work. Rudy asked Jim to go first and was given a treatise on something called "intermittent explosive behavior." Rudy groaned, saying, "Jim, I need to get a handle on the possibilities for murderous behavior by a preteen, not a master's degree on the brain and behavior. Get to the point."

Smiling, Jim, in summary, said that callousness, nuanced manipulation, retaliation for any kind of slight, impulsiveness, frustration, hypersensitivity, and abnormal brain MRIs involving the insular cortex and the posterior cingulate are all related to the potential for violence. And the list went on. He further asserted that there were current studies indicating a biological foundation for sociopathy or psychopathy. Many in the field suggested that the two were almost the same. Lack of empathy for another was the big issue for violence. Having no feelings of guilt could camouflage the perpetrator for a long time; the mask would be uncovered eventually. Jim had even explored the possibility that examining twins may have some value. However, from what Jim had heard from the department therapist and what he himself had read, he doubted that the fact that two of the girls were twins was important. He'd learned that identical twins studies showed that twins had the same biological predisposition; one twin hurting the other after either one or both killed six kids seemed to take that right out of the equation.

Jim was most interested in the concepts of nuanced manipulation and retaliation, along with hypersensitivity, which might supply the less understood motives they had been attempting to grasp. As to an adult perpetrator, he thought that Mason's work on alibis may be more important.

Rudy was willing to put the twin theory on the back burner but not willing to eliminate it until a better prospect was found.

Mason took the floor and said that he felt he had maybe a more specific direction for them. In going over all the alibis that had been given, he'd found a few that were supported by family only—the Rozovskys for Mariska, Anya, and the grandmother Albina; the Haygoods for the couple because Jenny's running errands for the time of the assault could not be corroborated; Amy Landers and Suzanna; Mr. and Mrs. Tisdale and Judy; and Mr. and Mrs. Liacos and Evelyn. And that was not including the victims' families, for which he had not had time to check. He said, "I'm assuming that we have one or maybe a second murderer for all the murders. If someone has provable alibis for at least two murders, I'm willing to eliminate the person, but only if those alibis have been supported by disinterested outsiders."

Rudy asked Mason what they had said they were doing or where they all were for each murder and whether, when they vouched for each other, were they all in their homes or elsewhere? Mason said that Amy and Suzanna Landers both seemed to be at home or without a perfect alibi for the murders, and Jenny Haygood was not always with her husband. With the Tisdales, it was difficult to know because Judy sometimes would go home to an empty house; how often, he could not tell from the reports. Her mother would be up to two hours later coming home, and Judy was in the home alone for most of the murders and may have been with her mother for one. Timing for the assault was questionable but probably within a twenty-minute period. "As to the Rozovsky ladies," he concluded, "there was absolute validation for each other, except that we know that they weren't together for the assault on Carol McNamara."

"Petra, Mason, what do we know about all the paths in the woods? How many are there?"

The captain was reminded that there were eight paths starting from the entrance to the park, path number one being the entrance and path number eight ending at the Rozovsky house.

Rudy stated, "Eight paths is a lot. I'd forgotten there were so many."

Petra showed him a map and pointed out that some paths, like paths five and six, went directly from the owner's home to the park, while the others were more diagonal. He could see from the map that there was not a long path parallel to the street, and he could understand now why there may be noise in the woods behind the houses if someone did not stay on a path.

Rudy then asked Petra if she had walked all the paths. She had and had found them lovely, but all were narrow, pined-needled paths that were firmly established, meaning that they were walked on regularly. The paths were all bordered by tall trees and lots of bushes and low-growing ferns and the like. There were several small streams besides the one where Merry was killed. She said that the clearest paths were behind Jenny Haygood's home. It was lovely out there.

Rudy and Jim both questioned her on how difficult it was to walk the paths and whether it took more time to walk than maybe on the sidewalk. She said that it was easy walking, and she'd made good time. She had a sheet with all her times for each numbered path measured as she walked from the houses to the ends of the paths, which all ended in the park. She also showed her time for walking the Sunnyside Street from each house to the park. Then Rudy stopped her in her tracks and looked at Petra with that aha look he was famous for.

"Wait," he said. After a few seconds, he said, "Freida McNamara told me to look for what shouldn't be there, which she thought we would probably already have looked at, and then what was missing that should be there in each scenario. I think we've missed the boat on the second part. Follow me for a minute. Anya and Mariska Rozovsky didn't see each other on the day of the assault until Mariska returned to the house and found Anya at home. Am I right?"

Heads nodded and Rudy in a very slow and controlled voice continued with, "Petra, do we know how Mariska went to the park to get Anya?"

Petra replied with her assumption that Mariska had walked on

Sunnyside to the park. That's why Anya had missed her. Mariska was on Sunnyside while Anya was on that piece of the woods on path two, a diagonal path from the park through the woods out by the Stuart driveway.

Rudy was about to speak when all three of the other detectives shouted, "Nobody saw her on the street."

Heads shook as they saw what they had not seen. After pulling all the reports from the assault scene, they were able to see that many people were on the street near the park, but the only sighting of Mariska was of her returning from the park. She must have gone through the woods to get to the park, but that question was never put to her. If she went through the woods, she still could have missed Anya. Anya could have left the woods before Mariska reached that section. "Could" was a big word! Their analysis of the paths left them to question the ease at which Evelyn, Anya, Judy, and Mariska, who all had imperfect alibis, could have had access to each scene. Mason was busy matching times for Mariska's returning and Anya leaving the park, but there was nothing definitive enough to determine real inconsistencies.

Rudy capped the conversation with a plan to visit the Rozovskys that evening to question the women of the family, and they were to bring a Russian interpreter for Albina. He said that Jim's notes inferred that Albina was shaking her head and insisting she was in her bedroom, therefore implying that she didn't know when Mariska or Anya had returned. His gut announced to him in a growl that there was something wrong with her responses.

It was at that moment that Chief Coyne and the mayor entered the conference room with a frustrated-looking Millie behind them. Rudy welcomed them and told Millie that it was okay, that they were not interrupting.

Mayor Fitshler spoke first. "I'm sorry to be here when I know your team is working diligently, but it is now over seventeen months since the first murder, and the public is not impressed with our progress. Realtors are up in arms. Their worries are not just because of Sunnyside's problems. No, the word on the street is that there may be a continuation of new murders, and maybe it means that the town itself is not safe. That is what's affecting property values for the whole city."

He went on, "I don't think we'll recover from this public relations disaster for years, and it makes your department look ineffective. I know from your faces that you think it's unfair that I say this. I know that we're dealing with a psychotic killer, but people are being hurt. I'm not waiting. I'm pressing the FBI to get in here today. In fact, they're waiting for my call because I've already made an initial call. Now Chief Coyne wants me to wait until Friday. He says there's movement, but I'm telling you you're going to have to convince me that something's brewing, or I'm making that call. I don't want to threaten, but there's a call by some on the council for your heads."

The detectives were crushed at this news, with the exception of Rudy, who with an unexpected quick movement for him, stood up and said, "We have inconsistencies in evidence that lead us to believe we may have a person and maybe several persons of interest. I think that if you give us until tomorrow afternoon or Monday, we'll have some results and maybe an arrest. If so, our making the arrest would be viewed well by the public. Solving the crime locally would be an important indication that this city is well run by its mayor and is safe."

Chief Coyne insisted on details and was told about the focus on details in walk paths, time, absence of perfect alibis, access to murder sites, and the limited group of kids and adults who had access and questionable alibis. During the recitation of details by the detectives, nothing was held back; both the chief and the mayor insisted that they bring the Russian women into the station for questioning and not do the interview in the home.

Rudy expressed concern in a firm voice. "If we bring this family in, it will appear that they're guilty, and we don't know that. I know that we've had persons of interest brought into the station for questioning after the first five murders, but never one of the neighbors. We have some indications that we may be on the right path, but the evidence is not conclusive, not even good enough now for a circumstantial case.

"Further, this family will lawyer up. Mr. Rozovsky has the resources to get good legal help, and we need questions on inconsistencies in their alibis before they stop talking. We were going to go there this evening, but Sergei Rozovsky will be home, and I don't think we will have an effective interview with the ladies with him present. It'd be better if the interview took place tomorrow morning at seven o'clock before Anya leaves for school and after Sergei leaves for work. He leaves every morning, even on Saturdays, at a quarter after six. It will take some time for Sergei to be reached and return home even if he is called. We will use that time to our advantage.

"We'll bring an interpreter for the grandmother. I think from all our interactions with her that she understands everything said in English but pretends otherwise. Also, Mr. Adams, who lives across the street from them, really likes her. I get that feeling because she talks to him, and he sure as hell doesn't speak Russian.

"Meanwhile we can question the other children, Evelyn and Judy, and their parents this evening. We need more detail, and there are some searches to be conducted for tomahawk stones. We will also need the dog again.

"The press will be all over us if we bring someone in; and you know that they interfere with our work. If we're wrong, we will all look like we don't know what we're doing. Two more days, please. We'll make the person of interest decision tomorrow at this same time. If it turns out that we bring someone in from that household, we'll need several uniforms. Sergei could be difficult."

Chief Coyne started to speak when the mayor sharply cut him off and directed his words to them all. "Two more days! This is it! I'll be here Friday at this same time, and I hope there will be an arrest." Speaking to the chief and to Rudy, he said, "Jim, you'd best hang around here to direct, and Rudy, be at that interview tomorrow. Hear me?" With that, he left without the chief.

Chief Coyne's round, healthy face had turned a vivid purple as he turned to the detectives, "I hope, sincerely hope, that you have something. Mayor Fitshler has only a year and a half left before he runs for office again, and he told me there are grumblings out there about his appointment of me. A couple of selectmen are eyeing his office. But believe it or not, Selectman Tisdale is supporting our cause. I never thought of him as anything but a good ole boy, but he's been a stand-up on this issue, and he lives on Sunnyside. He told the mayor that he thought that you guys were the best. I'll be here in my office, but report to me regularly. Don't screw the Rozovsky interview up."

16

Stressed

MILLIE HAD SUPPER SENT in for the detectives from a local pizza parlor before she left the station for home. She was pleased to get out of the station. The stressful environment was killing her, and she responded to it by drinking umpteen cups of coffee. Ordinarily, she truly loved her job. She was the nice lady who smoothed everyone's feathers. She loved the cops and thought their work was truly important work. Further, she was devastated at the public's disdain for the police. Where she came from, cops were part of the community and respected. Of course, nobody in her family ever had problems with the police, other than an occasional parking ticket that was waived away. She thought that she was successful at her work as the administrative assistant to the Major Crimes Unit because it was in her nature to create a positive environment both at home and at work. But now, with murder all around her, her work life brought dreadful nightmares; she wondered how the neighbors on Sunnyside Road could sleep at night. She was fearful, and she didn't understand why. She lived in West Side; but she didn't live anywhere near Sunnyside Road.

As she walked to her car, she mused on all the disruptions in her work and home schedules during the last year and a half. *I sincerely hope that the FBI won't be in again. The last or even the last few times a few agents were at the station, they kind of took over, directing people and bringing in all types of equipment. Behind their pasted, serious faces, they acted like they were doing God's work and like they were the only ones with brains. They're worse than the state cops, who are at least careful about local procedure. At least that's how they make me feel.*

On exiting the station, she saw Mayor Fitshler using his cell phone in his car. His window was opened, and she heard him say, "Look. I've given them two more days. Tomorrow's Thursday. I'll announce in time for the five o'clock news on Saturday that you'll be in on Monday. Don't push me. I don't like that I have to do this."

Millie got in her car. She immediately let Rudy know what she had just heard and left to go home really, really stressed.

Rudy already knew that the mayor and the chief were chomping at the bit to bring in the FBI. He knew that they weren't necessarily being disloyal, but they were mistaken if they thought that they would be off the hook just because the FBI was there in West Side again. Ignoring the pressure, Rudy returned to his duties and directed Petra and Jim to interview Judy Tisdale and Evelyn Liacos and their families again. He reminded them that, before they left, they should review all previous interviews and visual reports by witnesses on all of the murders but particularly on the day of the assault on Carol.

"Noise heard in the park is a subject I'd like to nail down. Also, Petra, talk about that path number two and see how familiar residents are with it. Ask them in a subtle manner if someone could hide in the woods, maybe in the brush along the path; let someone pass by; and then return to the path without being seen. How long is that path, Petra?"

Petra said it was at least four hundred feet. She reported that it wasn't a perfect diagonal but straightened out when it came between the Tisdale and Stuart houses. "Captain, persons walking on that path would not be seen until they hit the front yards of those two houses, unless the Stuarts or the Tisdales were in their backyards or in their garages and looked out the rear garage windows."

The detectives left on their mission and agreed to be at the Rozovsky home at seven in the morning on Thursday. They were not surprised that Rudy said he would meet them there and would bring the interpreter.

———————————

Rudy contacted the community police cruiser patrolling Sunnyside Road and requested the officers call him when Sergei Rozovsky left his home. They confirmed that they saw him every morning like clockwork leaving at a quarter after six and would call him.

Rudy was waiting at the curb for Jim and Petra, who arrived at 6:55 a.m. He allowed them to enter first. Then five minutes later, he entered with Mrs. Moriarty, the Russian interpreter. Born in Moscow, she was in her late sixties. He had chosen her because she had very nice manners; understood the older world culture; had lived in an area close to Buzuluk, Russia; and might appear to Albina as less of a threat than some of the other interpreters he had used in the past.

When Mariska answered the door, she was surprised to see them. Rudy introduced Mrs. Moriarty and was reassured when he saw Mariska greet her warmly. Petra had not started the interview yet but was just getting through the pleasantries and had explained that they were taping these interviews. Anya was eating breakfast while Albina came quickly out to greet Mrs. Moriarty, whom she somehow knew by just looking at her that she was Russian. Every person's action was noticeable at a glance in this large open construction design in rich oiled woods; the whole area encompassed the kitchen, dining room, and family room and was arranged with large windows and bright lighting.

After the detectives explained that they needed additional witness statements from all of them, Anya, with Albina behind her, moved away from the kitchen and questioned why. "We've already told you everything. And why are you taping us this time?" Anya then said that she had to go to school soon because she was having a test.

Petra quickly explained that they were taping all final interviews to use later when they prosecuted the killer. She went on to explain that details were important. She talked at great length, to the point that the other two detectives thought she would never finish and they would fall asleep.

Petra then told Anya that her statement was important and asked if she could just go over again how she had left the park on the day of the assault. The detectives could see that Anya's cell phone was left on the kitchen table, and they wished to direct her thoughts away from it.

Jim stood with his back to the kitchen table while helping Albina find a seat on the couch next to Mrs. Moriarty. Rudy sat in a chair next to Anya, with Petra across from her sitting next to Mariska. Anya appeared to like being involved but still restated her question from before.

Not answering Anya's question, Petra questioned how Mariska had gone to the park that day.

Mariska's face colored a bit and she said that, because she had fallen asleep, she was late and going through the woods was faster than walking on the sidewalk. Petra questioned the difficulty of some of the low brush, reminding Mariska that there wasn't a perfect path all the way down the path.

Mariska answered that she had no difficulty on the path, but when asked how she'd exited the path, she answered, "I just exited at the entrance to the park."

At that moment, Albina started coughing and choking. Anya and Mariska ran to Grandma, but Mrs. Moriarty was already talking to her in Russian, and her eyes waived the family away.

Mrs. Moriarty reassured Anya and Mariska that Albina was fine, but she would take Albina into the kitchen to get some water and relax. She asked Rudy to assist her with Albina. Albina got up slowly and moved to the kitchen counter with Rudy and Mrs. Moriarty.

Since everyone could see each that Albina was being taken care of, Mariska and Anya let the conversation continue. Petra then showed Mariska a map of the eight paths in the woods, and the detectives could see that Mariska realized that if she'd entered directly from any path into the park, then she would have been seen by someone. They could almost see the mechanics of her brain figure it out through her lovely blue eyes. She told them that she had chosen path number three and entered the park that way. She further explained that, when she entered the park, she had seen all the police cars and, frightened, had then run out of the park up Sunnyside, hoping to find Anya. It didn't take long for her to quickly return home, finding Anya with Albina at home.

When asked a second time about her route, she answered, "Yes, I'm sure that I took path number three."

Anya's ears perked up when she heard the question asked twice and said, "Let me see that map." She looked at it and said to her mother, "You're mistaken, Mama. You probably went down path number two. That's how you would have come."

Nervously, Mariska looked at the map again and said, "Maybe she's right. I don't remember for certain." At that point, Mariska appeared to be in distress and in a daze.

Petra questioned Mariska on her normal process of meeting Anya at school every day and her history of making arrangements to have a car sent when she was unable to meet Anya. With what appeared to be uncertainty or anxiety, the detectives could not be sure of which, she said, "Sometimes I fall asleep in the afternoon when I should be meeting Anya. I don't know why. My mother wakes me up. It doesn't happen all the time, but it does happen sometimes. When I wake, I'm foggy for a little time. It never happened before maybe a year ago. I'm not old enough to be sleeping in my chair like the old people. It's confuses me, because I have so much energy normally."

Petra asked if she had seen a doctor for this sleepiness and was told that she had. She'd sought help from Dr. Ornstein, who thought that the sleepiness was related to her feelings of anxiety and worry, which had increased with these murders in her neighborhood.

Mariska was then questioned about any medications she was taking. She said that she kept filling the medication bottles prescribed but never took them because they made her sleepy. She never told Dr. Ornstein that she wasn't taking them.

Petra was actively thinking, *I wonder if she only gets sleepy in the afternoon.*

Mrs. Moriarty, Rudy, and Albina returned to the family room. Albina appeared to be calmer as she inspected the faces of her daughter and granddaughter.

Jim stepped forward and directed some questions to her in a laid-back manner. He generally included conversation about the value of three generations in a family living together and enjoying a happy family life. He went on to ask about Mariska's anxiety and Albina said in Russian, "She is anxious, all the time. She is the best mother and wife and daughter, but she makes herself unhappy with worry. The doctor cannot help her. We don't know how to stop her worry."

While they focused on Albina, Rudy noticed that Anya was moving toward the kitchen counter. He walked over to her and informed her that he really would like them all to come to the station soon to assist in the investigation. He looked at Anya, saying, "Anya, you're a bright girl, so I feel I can talk to you. We think someone was in the woods when both you and your mother might have been on the path. We think that it was someone who always uses the path. We need help with the everyday of who uses the paths, whose use of the paths would not be noticed—you know, that kind of thing. Does your grandmother ever use the paths, other than the path from your house directly to the field?"

Anya's eyes responded in a smile, and she said quickly, "Yes, Babushka uses it to walk to the edge of the field all the way down along the woods because someone planted some wild plants that she knows from Russia. I guess some of the plants are herbs that she then mixes with oils for us. They really work for softening skin, calming bee stings, and for just about everything that could go wrong. She calls one the name in English, which my teacher even knows about, comfrey. She always walks up and down in the woods, but mostly in the early morning before other people are out of bed. In the winter, she's a little later in walking her route."

Again Rudy suggested that it would be helpful for all of them to come to the conference room at the police station soon, saying, "You know, Anya, all our interviewing materials and forensic results are there, not here. Now that I know that your grandmother walks in the area, well, she could be helpful. We do think you all could really assist in the investigation. It may be that you're far away from the murder sites, but everyone in this family walks those paths. It's logical that you may have seen things that you don't know you've seen. I'd like to start interviewing with your mother first and you and your grandmother later. I believe that your mother is a little nervous, but I think that she'd help us first, if you thought it was okay."

Rudy then had further conversation with Mariska as to why her help may be important.

It was then that Rudy explained that the detectives and Mrs. Moriarty needed to return to the station and asked if Mariska could come down the next day to assist. Later, they would invite the rest of the family to assist because tomorrow was a school day for Anya.

Anya, apparently swayed by being included in this detective work, told her mother and grandmother that it was their duty to help solve these awful murders and that she couldn't wait to help them. Mariska and Albina looked at each other, and they seemed to perk up.

Rudy suggested that Mariska, the first in the family to come down to the station to assist tomorrow, would probably be brought back in time for lunch. He also stated, "I'll have Millie authorize Anya's absence from school today. It's taken so long that it's foolish for her to go in so late—unless you want her to attend. In that case, we will take her to school."

Anya excitedly told them to tell the school counselor, Dr. Abbott that she was helping in the investigation, and that's why she would not be in school today.

⟫⟫·◇·⟪⟪

Mason and Chief Coyne had congregated in the conference room, waiting for the detectives' return from the Rozovsky women interview. The chief was holding in his hands a file folder containing search warrants for rocks, twine, pieces of vine, rawhide, sticks, sharpening tools, work gloves, bows, and the like, which one of the officers had had no difficulty in obtaining from a Springfield District Court. The judge who signed them had made himself immediately available. Chief Coyne, who was well liked by just about everyone, had influence, and his detective was given top-shelf and instant service. This was not necessarily a normal process in the slow movements of the court, but just about everyone wanted to assist in solving the infamous child serial murders.

The chief told Rudy he had informed the uniform captain that he should get some uniforms, and he also wanted Mason, to conduct the searches of the Rozovsky, Tisdale, and Liacos homes, garages, and any outer buildings, as well as motor vehicles on each premise. The warrants were specific for what they were looking for but encompassed all areas of the properties.

Petra said, "Chief, when I was walking the eight paths, I looked around the paths in the brush. I saw some things that I don't think the search officers saw or that didn't register to them as important. I remember them listing it as bundles of brush, but they were lean-tos. They were like the type we were taught to build in my Indian forestry experience when I was a kid. These lean-tos are difficult to see unless you're looking for them and were built in the more crowded brush area. I saw two of them—one near path number four and one near path number three. I don't think we need a search warrant for them. But could we have the officers look in there and bag any shaped rocks, tools, personal stuff, and whatever else they find there? I did see a cloth in one. If we're looking at kids as possible perpetrators, then we should think like kids. Also I realize that near some of the murder sites, in fact most of them, the brush is rather dense, as is the brush in about 50 percent of the woods. This brush could help explain how someone could surprise the victim. I don't think that we thought about that before."

The chief nodded, which meant agreement.

Rudy posed the question of whether they needed to search the Liacos and Tisdale homes when they already had the weapons in evidence. They decided they didn't, and he then directed Mason to start the searches as soon as possible, with a group of three officers for the woods and another group to search the Rozovsky area later in the next afternoon after Mariska had been interviewed.

Mason left, and Rudy summarized the conversations from the morning interviews and from interviews conducted the night before. The Liacos and Tisdale families were clearly trying to be helpful but could not support three of the murder alibis with support from outside of the family. Another supported murder alibi was not strong but was based on neighbors thinking they had seen the girls at home at the time. And the assault alibis were left based on the girls leaving the woods and no one seeing them return. Both interviewing detectives believed that the families and their daughters were telling the truth.

The girls also were questioned about making tomahawks and whether they still had the sharpening stone or stones and their extra river stones and wood. Both girls did, and the items were down on their fathers' workbenches. Both fathers had the same inclination as Mr. McNamara that these weapons were not to be left in the girls' hands. They then gave up the stones and wood to Petra and Jim, who bagged them for evidence to be examined. In both cases, the girls had built their tomahawks with twine.

The detectives discussed their morning with the Rozovsky family with the chief. Rudy told the chief that he had requested, before the detectives had left the Rozovsky home, that the women be available to assist again, as some of the other families were assisting. He'd told the women that other families and their kids were willing to come down and look at some of the evidence and help them with their questions.

Jim, in his best psychologist tone, had explained to the Rozovsky women how important it was for the police to listen carefully to all the residents' experiences. He said that evidence could not be removed from the police station, but it would be helpful if neighbors who were out and about more could come to the station tomorrow and assist the police. He had told them, "For instance, we have several weapons. If you see them, perhaps you will remember them. Maybe they were in the woods at some time that you, Mariska, were walking."

Mariska had answered very quickly, "I'm more than willing to assist you, Detective Locke. I want the murders to stop. I want it so badly. I am so afraid for Anya. I'll come down. What time would be convenient for you?"

Jim told the chief that this drama was important—that the family needed to think that they were not different from the other families on the street. He said, "Anya also wanted to come down, but we reminded her she could not miss school on a second day." So it was agreed to have Mariska come down right after she sent Anya off for school the next day on Friday. Jim said he'd ended the conversation with, "Mariska, be sure to inform your husband that you're coming to assist us. I don't want him to get the wrong idea. Have him call me if he has any questions. Mariska, we need you and all the mothers of your daughters' friends' assistance, and I thank the Almighty that you are willing to assist us."

They had been successful and expected Mariska the next morning if her husband did not prevent her, which they all really expected him to do despite their having played their cards perfectly. They hoped to be extremely fortunate. At this time, the detectives did not have a backup plan if Mariska didn't show for the interview.

Rudy had Petra pull up Mariska's previous interviews, and they explained to the chief the problems with her alibi for the assault. Petra immediately said, "Look, on the days of three of these murders, Mariska was late meeting her daughter, if she met her at all. How could we or any of the investigators have missed this? The FBI conducted the interviews as well as us for most of the murders. After the third murder, they at least reviewed all the in-depth interviews on all the neighbors at each murder. Sunnyside Road is very long, with over twenty-five occupied houses on the street at the time of the murders."

Jim said, "The officers just did house-to-house quick interviews and logged the Rozovsky women in as at home together on those days and Sergei still at work. But, you're right, Petra. Other witness reports for at least three of the murders dates have Mariska running late down Sunnyside to meet her daughter. It was right there for us all to see, but we didn't until now. Combine that with Mariska's change in her alibi, which could be a mistake."

But they thought there was something really wrong, and Mariska looked guilty of something.

Rudy said that he would bet that Mariska could not murder anyone but thought that she may have some mental health problems. He suggested that they do a hard interview with Mariska. He had questioned Mrs. Moriarty about the cultural aspects of behavior within the family, and she affirmed that, in her opinion, Mariska and Albina were hiding something and that Anya was the more careful, watchful, and logical of the three despite her youth. Her opinion was that Albina would lie and hide anything to protect her daughter and granddaughter, but she thought that Mariska had difficulty lying.

Chief Coyne had remained quiet throughout the summary and ensuing discussions. His first inclination was to talk again to the psychic and have her take a look at Mariska, but he then caught himself. "Nix that, it's probably not a good idea. I can just see defense counsel making fools of us, saying she solved the case with psychobabble." He reviewed some of the paperwork he'd been handling and finally said, "You have a person of interest. God, no, you have a suspect. Question her alone and not with kid gloves. But get Mariska to release her rights on tape. That is paramount. Don't do it in front of her mother or daughter. The daughter probably watches all those crime shows on television and will get suspicious."

He pushed further with, "You have an opportunity here, when and if she comes in tomorrow morning. There is no motive now. There is a possible means. But can Mariska use these weapons accurately? Can she overpower a strong young boy? Davie was small, but what about Jackson Elsby? How tall is she, Rudy? Is she strong? The file here says she worked in a cleaning service before marriage. That means she's probably pretty physically capable. If she gives you further evidence, then you book her. You have seventy-two hours to hold her.

He added, "So she gets a lawyer! The DA is sending ADA Marion Hetterman over now before you interview her and before you make the arrest. She's a pit bull, and she'll decide whether there's enough to charge her. Shake the bushes. You can hold off questioning the grandmother and daughter until we decide about Mariska, but you have only this weekend.

"Monday, the FBI will be in, and you'll be working the case under them. I think that we must cast suspicion on Anya and Albina to make Mariska confess. She doesn't have to speak to be aware of what we're doing. I'll leave that up to you, Rudy. You'll have about three hours after an arrest before Sergei shows up with a good defense lawyer. Let's hope that Sergei lets her come in. You don't know that yet. We'll talk tomorrow. If we learn something, then delay the arrest if you can. Do you know what time Sergei gets home and whether he's out of town on a job?"

The chief was told what Anya had said when the detectives had been at the Rozovsky house that morning; her father was in Worcester on a big job and would be coming home late for the next two weeks.

The chief suggested that they make the arrest as late as possible on Friday but thought that the grandmother and Anya would be very upset if Mariska wasn't home when Anya came from school.

"We're in luck," Jim replied. "They're having Hoffington School year-end activities at the park until four thirty tomorrow. I think it's called a challenge course—you know, with climbing ropes and everything. We've scheduled a big police presence there to ensure that the kids will be okay. The Hoffington Middle School assistant principal didn't want to call it off. Instead, he demanded cops everywhere and sent a note to parents that it was important for their child's well-being that normalcy in scheduling be carried out—just like school officials. I don't like to be too critical, but what's the matter with administrators when they think murder's not as important as school schedules?"

The chief reiterated that the later in the day the arrest was made, the better, especially on a Friday. He said, "It makes it more difficult for Sergei to hire a lawyer quickly. He's probably smart enough not to get just anyone, and it's not always easy to get a good lawyer quickly. It seems to me that they're always on some exotic vacation for every weekend when they don't have a scheduled trial. This is all iffy stuff because we don't know yet if Mariska will show and, if she does, just what she'll tell us."

Rudy was not convinced that this strategy was best, and he vehemently said so. "Chief, I don't think she did it. My gut tells me she knows more, but I don't think she's capable of killing. The whole neighborhood will be crazed when we arrest her, so we had better be right. If we're wrong, we will have done a lot of damage to her."

The chief said derisively, so much so it really cut Rudy, "No one has greater respect for your gut, Rudy, than I, but the FBI will be here on Monday. And who else do you think did it, Rudy, the kid or the old lady?"

At that moment, Marion Hetterman walked into the conference room with Millie and, without even a hello said, "Give me the basics."

She listened while the detectives laid the case out for her. "Weak," she said, "but possible. Let me see that map. We know she goes down this path easily; she said she has no difficulty walking on it. We know that she doesn't know why she falls asleep, doesn't know why she's groggy when she wakes up, why she's confused about lying to us, is anxious all the time, doesn't listen to her doctor, doesn't take her antianxiety pills, maybe has a really negative background in Russia (we hope), and has no real alibis. We know that she appears to be controlling and insecure, knows everything going on in her daughter's life, and that she lives for her daughter. We know that she lives next door to Henry, the archery boy. We know that she would know all about the girls and Anya making their tomahawks. But motive? Give me a motive. Everyone talks well about her, and she's an immigrant who has become a citizen. She's not ISIS. For God's sakes, she bakes pies for her neighbors. We need history on her. How did she get the ax to murder this kid Jim Derrick? In fact, how did anyone get the ax?

Could anyone else have gotten the ax? Neighbors would have noticed someone walking around with an ax, especially a pretty woman."

Petra said that the problem might be that Mariska was mentally ill. "I think that we need another search warrant for her pills; just what is she supposedly taking and has she, as she has said, not taken them? What condition are they for, anxiety or something else? Can we get a warrant for the pharmacy once we have them? You know the immigrant experience brings all kinds of problems with it. I remember stories about one of my grandfathers, who came from Poland. He would hide in the basement if a police officer in uniform came collecting for the athletic league, which they could do in those days. Motive could be PTSD or hatred of her daughter's friends, competition, or anything. And I do think that we have to have a theory on the ax evidence in the Derrick killing."

ADA Hetterman said that she was frankly just a bit sick of criminal behavior being masked as a poor sick perpetrator suffering from PTSD. She was about to leave when she informed them that she regrettably had to be in Superior Court in Springfield in the morning but would come over after lunch, if she could manage it, to review their success and she said she hoped it was success. "Before I leave, Chief, get a warrant for the pills at the Rozovsky home and check with the pharmacy about how many of that type of pill prescription was ever issued. I hope it's a good and strong antianxiety prescription. I can work with that. The whole country's sick of seeing television programs about these 'unsolved serial killings of kids in rural western Massachusetts in the sleepy town of West Side.' What a joke!" And she left.

Chief Coyne was happy to have the department pull a search warrant, which he planned to have served later for the search at the Rozovsky home on Friday. "By the way," he added, "I've thought about it, and you can give that Marnie a call and ask her if she sees anything in her dreams. The cops in Springfield said that they ignored her dreams, and she didn't push them, but that, in review, after the arrest of the perp, one dream was 'spot on.'"

The chief was reminded that she had already shared her dreams and they would call her after the arrest as he suggested. Meanwhile Jim and Petra went to pick up some sandwiches. They were famished, and it was now past two thirty in the afternoon. They took their lunch and headed over to the woods to join Mason and the uniforms.

17

Search

PETRA LED THE WAY for the uniforms to path number three, pushed the brush around, and discovered the well-camouflaged lean-to. Mason, Jim, and the uniforms had started searching in the main woods first by the Elsby house and then moved to path number two. They were just reaching Petra's area and were surprised to find that Petra had found the treed lean-to so easily; they wondered if maybe they had missed another one in their previous search. She soothed their egos with, "Experience, guys. I built them myself as a kid." Their reaction was to call her "Indian Girl Guide" for the rest of the afternoon.

The lean-to had three sides of branches backed up on an evergreen whose branches had been cut to nubs up to six feet. The nubs were used to hang twine and what looked like Christmas tree ornament hooks, holding scissors, a plastic Target bag, a ball of twine, an oily cloth, hedge shears in a plastic bag, a bunch of small tools in cloth and plastic bags, a switchblade in a plastic case with a tape spelling 43 Sunnyside on it, a bag with a couple of barrettes and ponytail holders, and other debris. The Sunnyside kids' treasures were kept here.

Petra looked on her address list for Sunnyside and saw the number 43 was Sky Erikson's address. She showed it to Jim and Mason. It was a good "maybe we've got something" moment.

Petra took charge, saying, "Bag everything carefully and rope off this area. Also do a search all around in case you see anything. Then continue your search while we head up to path number four, where we know there is another lean-to. We'll see you up there."

Petra and Jim discussed the implications of their find with excitement. Jim said aloud what they were all thinking, "You know what this could mean. The kids kept their treasures here. Jim Derrick was known for stealing and was suspected of breaking into Sky Erikson's garage. Well, we've found what looks to be Erikson's case for his switchblade. If it turns out to be true, then Derrick probably kept a lot of the stuff he stole in there, and maybe he kept an ax in there. Maybe we have a theory on the accessibility of one of the murder weapons. Kids have been here, and maybe one of the adults found it by following their kids. I know Freida McNamara was on a tear about a tree house her husband found the kids building, which was dangerous. Her husband made the kids help him tear it down. Knowing this, the kids would keep this stuff secret. At least, that's what I would have done when I was a kid."

Petra and Mason nodded in agreement.

The detectives were impressed when Petra brought them to a lean-to on the section of path number four, which was behind the Stoteras home. Each one believed that he would never have found it by walking on the path. Petra showed them what Indian trailing was all about and how she had discovered its location. She said that, when she was walking slowly, timing her walks and looking down, she saw the disruptions in the terrain. There was recent pressing down of the trail's pine needles in a kind of messy spot and small broken branches leading off the trail. Those were the signs that made her investigate.

Petra said, "I know that someone was there recently. If there had been no recent visitors, then I could easily have missed it."

This lean-to had the same nubs on the tree as the other one, but had rusty hooks/hangers on each nub with very little stuff hanging on the hangers. There was a collection of river stones and pieces of wood branches, much like what had been used for the tomahawks.

The detectives also found a broken finished piece of a bow, which was about eight inches long. *Could it be part of the first murder weapon? It's too much, too much; we can only hope.*

The three detectives spent the next two hours helping to bag evidence and searching further down path number four near the section by the Haygood home and found no additional structures. They were not surprised, remembering Jenny's account of her tearing down some mess the kids had built. They then hopped over to the other paths but did not find any additional lean-tos.

By this time, it was early evening, and the crew luxuriated in wonderful weather—a respite for all except this hard working group. Jim looked about and, with great earnestness, exclaimed, "I feel the gods have been with us all day. Let's get pizza sent to the station; we'll review the list of evidence tonight and tomorrow maybe get some results from the lab. Rudy will break to have dinner with his family and then return. We'll keep a couple of pizza pieces for him for later. The next few days are all we have. Let's give it our all."

Mason said, "Fine for you. But I'm meeting my sister to pick out a barbeque grill for our mom for Mother's Day. If I don't meet her, I'll never hear the end of it. I'll come back at around eight o'clock and hope by that time I won't be needed. But on the bright side, I'll get all the reports for you early in the morning. I've notified forensics that they need to work all night. They'll do anything to avoid the FBI looking at them like they're Obama's notorious referenced 'JV team.'"

⸺◈⸻

The Red Rose pizza, which one of the uniforms delivered to them, was the best pizza in the area. Red Rose Pizzeria and Restaurant was a city of Springfield landmark, never changing, never needing to change, despite many changes to the city.

One change coming to Springfield was gambling. MGM was the chosen corporation to build a casino in downtown Springfield after receiving authorizing votes from the State Gambling Commission, the state legislature, and the city of Springfield—not necessarily in that order and not without great difficulty. Now the area was faced with a new legalized vice. No one, including the criminal justice system bigwigs, was certain it was the right decision, but all hoped that MGM was creative enough to make it work. MGM's management was not able to convince Red Rose Restaurant, one of the nation's top pizza restaurants, to give up its location and move inside the casino. Everyone cheered the decision the three-generation Italian business owners made. The Red Rose owners knew their own self-worth, and no patron of the restaurant wanted any change in the great pizza offered.

As they buried their noses in paperwork while licking their lips with gusto, Petra counting the offensive calories, the two detectives scribbled notes from the day's work. Jim answered a call on his cell phone from Sergei Rozovsky, who questioned why it was necessary to have his wife come down to the station the next day and whether she needed to be represented by an attorney. Jim asked if Detective Aylewood could join in the call, and Sergei asked if it was necessary. Jim told him it wasn't, but Petra had a good relationship with his wife and could probably better explain why Mrs. Rozovsky would be helpful as a witness. Sergei seemed confused and said that Anya had thought it was the captain's request that Mariska come to the station.

Jim was thoughtful before he answered and said in a deliberate but laid-back voice, "Mr. Rozovsky, Mariska, your wife, is very upset about these murders, perhaps more upset than anyone else in the neighborhood. She knows the neighborhood and is very well thought of by all her neighbors. She is willing to help, and God knows, we need perspectives. Many other mothers and children are coming in tomorrow and next week to assist us with neighborhood information. You know, we can't bring the evidence and files to them to view. Your wife seems to want to help, and we told her to ask you. I hope she will be able to assist."

Sergei's answer was surprising, "Yea, you're right. She's insistent on looking at evidence and a map of the paths. All right, I told her she can go. I'm out of town on a major construction job, or I would come with her. Thank you, Detective Locke. Mariska will be there early tomorrow morning."

Jim's face was beat red and he was sweating when he clicked off his cell phone. He looked over at his partner, whom he now dearly loved and said, "I'm not meant for this, Petra. I'm looking at his wife as a potential murderer, and I'm lying to her husband, who is a good man, about his wife who, if she is the perp, is probably crazy. I'm helping him make a decision that may corral her. No wonder, we're hated."

Looking around her first and seeing no witnesses, Petra touched his face and said, with tears in her eyes, "No, you're not for this part of the job, Jim. You've never had to do something this difficult before, have you? You were truly phenomenal at handling a difficult situation. Granted, the police objective in this instance is not your personal moral objective. If she is guilty, then you have done well. If she's not, then we all have made an error and will do our best to rectify it."

Jim shook his head, and they sat quietly for a moment. He sighed and said, "No, I can't do this again, Petra. I'll have to made changes in my line of work. I love police work but not this part. It won't really be a bad thing if I do make a change. We'd have to make some career choices for one of us anyway if we marry. It seems to me that I've already made that choice. I'll look for a role as a police psychologist. Maybe go back into clinical practice and pick up consulting work for various police departments. I don't know. That decision is, I guess, for another day."

They returned to their paperwork, discussing whether it was strange that the dog had not found the lean-tos. All the while Petra was thinking, *If we marry. If we marry! Love and marriage! God, he's a human love vector. Am I ready, really ready for that?*

Jim called the Weasel and questioned him. He wanted to assure that the dog cop was able to reiterate, in a court acceptable manner, the process used. Weasel recalled that they initially were looking for the blood scent that Carol's blood had left on the river stone, already matched to her clothing and thus using the scent for the hound to find the stick, which the lab results showed positive for Carol's blood. He said that hounds look or smell for the scent it is given—only one scent at a time. Multiple scents confuse the dog. This dog was given only Carol's blood scent, and that's what he found.

"Weasel, when did you find that out?"

Weasel said, "I sent the report three hours after the lab got the sample, which was shortly after it was delivered to the lab. It's on your desk."

Jim scrambled through the papers on his desk and found the report in his in-box, which was flopping over with about nine inches high of paperwork. He thought that there was a serious potential cost to this kind of carelessness. The tomahawk handle with Carol's blood was found by the Stuart house in the bushes, which was right by path number two, the diagonal path from the park used by everyone who lived up Sunnyside on both sides of the street; it was actually used by kids and some parents.

He and Petra looked carefully at the various paths on the map and realized that only paths number one, two, and four went from the field to Sunnyside directly. This was information they already knew but information that now fit their pattern of thought and their current investigative direction. In other words, it was as Rudy had always said: "It's there for us to see. We just don't see it until we're ready to see it."

They noted the lean-to locations on the map and again were surprised at their proximity to all the murders. They now believed that this small area was probably a place of comfort for the killer; truly the killing area was a respite for the killer and a place to maybe hide weapons or maybe something else. What else?

⋙◆⋘

Mariska was anxious as she entered the police station. It didn't help that her mother and Sergei were inundating her with instructions on what not to say and that you could never trust the police. They reminded her that, no matter that these were American police, police were police. They would twist anything you had to say just to help solve their case. Look how foolish they look now. They can't solve these cases. They're now bringing down all the neighbors to the station. Sergei said, "They're just shaking the bushes, hoping a rotten apple will fall."

Anya, on the other hand, had acted like a typical twelve-year-old and was excited. She lectured her mother, as if Mariska were an imbecile, to remember everything, while Mariska instructed Anya not to tell anyone at school. Mariska told her, "Anya, always remember, we keep our personal business to ourselves."

Well she was now here to assist the police, and she was nervous and wondered why they would want her assistance. She wondered, *Do they think I know something? I suppose that if I said I didn't want to help, the police would be at my door every day. Sergei tells me to say no. He wanted to call a lawyer for me and Anya and Babushka.* Mariska remembered telling Sergei, "Call a lawyer, and the neighbors will wonder, and the police will think we're guilty of hiding something. We are all innocent, aren't we? Well, aren't we? No, I don't want a lawyer."

She was greeted by an officer at the desk who requested that she sit while he called for a detective. It took over twenty minutes before Captain Beauregard presented himself to her and directed her to follow him. She did not expect such a hubbub of activity. While she was waiting, she saw a young man, who she knew had been fired by her husband. He was there with his wife and what she guessed was his lawyer. He was not in good shape, and he was arguing. She knew that Sergei had regretfully let him go and told her he had bad habits. Mariska knew that bad habits meant drugs. She thought with frustration, *Why don't they just say that? Why do they call it a bad habit when, in my mind, it is a sickness? It has to be a sickness. You'd have to be sick to ruin your life. Sick people need help, not punishment.*

She was brought into a small room with a big glass-mirrored window. It was labeled Interview Room Number One. The captain asked her if she would like a coffee. He said, "Detective Aylewood brought in some great Italian pastries from Cerrato's today. Would you like one?"

She said yes, even though Sergei had told her not to accept anything from the police. He explained to her that they would use her cup to get her fingerprints. She had reminded him that, when she came to the United States, all immigrants were fingerprinted. The immigration officials had not been able to get her fingerprints. Didn't Sergei remember what a big thing it was for them? They'd thought that she would not be let in. The authority had said she had no fingerprints; they couldn't get any. They had then asked her what kind of work she did. Apparently, heavy chemicals that she cleaned with could help wear off her prints. They thought that she was awfully young for that, but she could not think of any other reason. However, recently she saw on a television program that some people were born without fingerprints. She thought she remembered the show had said it was a slight developmental error in maybe the third or fourth month of development. Maybe that's what had happened to her. The officials put a note on her file and let her in the country. No, Mariska was not worried about fingerprinting.

Detective Aylewood came into the room with coffee and a pastry she called *sfogliatella* or something like that.

The captain then rejoined them with his coffee and a half pastry. He explained that his wife, Mona, would be upset that he was even eating half of one, but they were the best of all Italian pastries—even better than cannoli. And then the captain said, "Mrs. Rozovsky, before I begin questioning you about anything, I have to do what I have done with all your neighbors. I must ask you if you want a lawyer present. If you answer no, and I hope that you will, to avoid all the time and paperwork, then I need you to sign a waiver of your right to a lawyer with the understanding that you may stop all the questioning at any time if you want a lawyer. Is that what you want?"

To his immense relief, Mariska answered, "No. I told Sergei I don't need a lawyer. I'm just answering your questions honestly. I will sign your paper, Captain."

Petra was listening and was thankful that Jim Locke was not in the interview room at that time, although she knew he was listening in. Rudy then told Mariska that the department required taping of all interviews to ensure that the police were doing their job and that, later, the tapes would be used to remind witnesses of their previous testimony, if they were required to be a witness in court. Mariska said that she thought that was a good practice for the police and for the witness.

Captain Beauregard asked Mariska about her life in Russia. He was very interested in the culture in her home city of Buzuluk.

Mariska told the captain, "In many ways, Buzuluk should have been my home for my lifetime. It's near the mountains, located on a tributary of the beautiful and famous River Volga. Even Americans have heard about the Volga River. There were economic changes that occurred at my home before my family left. Pensioners were suffering everywhere, and the government made changes all the time and did not respect workers. The family wanted to leave. It took us over five years and many trips to Moscow for paperwork, but my mother said that I would not have opportunities for a good long-term and secure future in Buzuluk or anywhere in Russia. Our friends who left before us for America returned home and looked prosperous. I don't regret leaving but hope someday to go back for a visit. I have two cousins around my age that I miss."

And she explained that once she'd met Sergei here and they had done well, "Well this is home now."

Petra questioned her about her home on Sunnyside Road, and Mariska talked glowingly about how she and Sergei had purchased the land and built the house and kept adding on. She also said, with an embarrassed smile, "My husband loves the extras—what my friend Amy calls all the Russian glitter. She's right. If it's bigger, Sergei wants it and will work for it, while my mother puts up jams, pickles, and all kinds of vegetables so we won't starve. Detective, I cook American and Russian. In our home, we experience two ways of thinking. It has been good until the murders. Our street now scares me. Life is not so good now for us."

Rudy, wanting to move things along, positioned himself behind her as she was talking. Mariska turned to him, nervously answering his questions about each different victim. It was clear to the detectives in the room that what Mariska knew about some of them was only through gossip and through Anya, Merry, the twins, Judy, and Evelyn's conversations with her. The girls had, in the past, visited fairly often and swam in the pool. Their visits were always short, for an hour or so. There was no sleeping over. Albina didn't approve of girls sleeping over; she thought that privacy for the family was important. Mariska said, "I like all the little girls. I thought Merry was special and a particularly bright little girl. I can't understand why anyone would hurt that child."

Rudy couldn't understand how she could be so convincing in her innocence when he was looking to her as the doer.

When Mariska was questioned about the boys who were victims, she said that she often saw some of them next door when Henry was alive, but she really didn't know them. Jackson Elsby was a guest at Anya's birthday party. She then said that there was an incident with Jackson, but he was just a silly boy who wanted Anya's attention. "It was just a stupid thing, but it ruined the day for Anya. Sergei overreacted. We all felt terrible when we heard of his death. He wasn't bad, just naughty."

Again, Rudy thought that she was just as sweet as rhubarb pie, refreshing like on a hot summer day.

Mariska was then asked about her need to meet Anya after school each day, no matter what else was going on. In other words, was there a reason Anya could never walk home with some of the other girls and did this decision on Mariska's part happen after the first murder?

Mariska reacted. She took a moment before she answered, and her hand shook a little as she brushed her long hair back from her face. This question bothered her, but she answered. "Detectives, I have always walked or driven Anya to and from school, her activities, and appointments—always. I don't think that it is unusual in this day and age. I am able to do it. I am pleased to do it. She is our only child. I don't work. What else would I do? What else is more important to our family than the safety of Anya? And now, with all these murders, well, protecting her when she is alone is just prudent and intelligent."

Petra quickly stated that she had heard that, when Mariska was sick, she hired an Uber driver to pick Anya from school. "Didn't you worry about the driver, who was a stranger?"

Mariska said, "No. You have it all wrong. Sergei's nephew is an Uber driver when he's not at school at Holyoke Community College. I would trust Vladimir with my life and my daughter's life. Vladimir is a good student. He's studying nursing."

Mariska was again calm and controlled, but when Rudy asked her about the days when she would fall asleep and not get Anya on time, her hands started to shake, again. If they were playing cards, it would be called a "tell." He waited for her to respond.

She said, "I get sleepy. I have already told you about that. I just get sleepy, and I don't know why or when it will happen. It only happens occasionally. It seems to happen at the same time when my mother is napping and not long before I am to pick up Anya. Never does it happen at any other time—not ever. It never happens when Sergei is at home. I asked the doctor, and he could not find anything wrong. My psychiatrist said that I'm stressed, and my body is just giving me rest. But why just then, when I have duties, I asked him. But he had no answer. He thought it was the medicine I was taking, but he doesn't know that I don't take it."

Again, Rudy registered the thought, *She's almost glamorous in a nonshowy way. It's surprising given Sergei's obsession with showy stuff. She gives answers very fluidly in a sweet way. Then on some questions, she holds back and is not able to cover up. Mariska is not a good actress.*

Rudy asked, "So on those days that you fall asleep, Anya walks home alone. Why doesn't she wait for an Uber ride or call one herself?"

Mariska was shocked at that thought, telling the detectives, "Anya is only twelve. We would never give her cousin the okay to take her wherever she might decide to go. We make those decisions. I'm surprised you'd think that it would be okay for her to call herself. And you have to understand that I never know when I might fall asleep. So how could I be able to plan a ride for my daughter? It doesn't happen all the time. I feel so guilty that I can't control my own body to do what is my job to do—to take care of my little girl."

Petra wanted to know why she thought that a twelve-year-old girl was unable to walk up a street, dotted with nothing but nice neighboring houses, in midafternoon. Wasn't the age of twelve years old enough for some independence?

With her hand shaking, Mariska whispered, "With all these murders, no! Are you crazy?"

Realizing that she had hit a soft spot, Petra changed tactics, asking Mariska to relate the route she would take if she woke up late for getting Anya from school. Mariska seemed to freeze for a moment. Cautiously gauging Petra's stoic demeanor, Mariska said that sometimes she'd run down Sunnyside Road but that if she were very late she would cut through the paths in the woods. When asked which paths, she would take, Mariska appeared particularly stressed. Petra pointed out that there were multiple paths but not one single path that would easily take her down to the park main entrance, which was where she would look for Anya.

Mariska said it depended on the day; sometimes she'd take one series of paths and sometimes another.

Petra asked about the paths she had taken on the day of Carol's assault, and Mariska raised her voice just a little and said, "I thought I took one path, but Anya says I must have taken another path because nobody saw me in the park. I was only seen walking on the street. I am probably wrong, and Anya is right."

Rudy interrupted with, "Mrs. Rozovsky, Detective Aylewood and I have a meeting with another parent in another interview room. Could you please wait a bit? We won't be long. Also, it is lunchtime, and Millie will bring in a choice of sandwiches for you. I know this is taking longer than we anticipated. But Detective Mason will be ready soon with some weapons for you to view. Everything always takes longer here than expected."

Mariska assured them that they did not have to rush and that she was willing to wait. But she noticed, *They didn't ask me if it is okay; they told me. They're still nice but different. They're probably just busy.*

The detectives dragged the time out for over an hour, during which they and Jim joined Mason, who had pulled together a report on Mariska Rozovsky. It included her immigration records. Unlike all other immigration records they had seen, it did not include fingerprints. Instead, there was a note that immigration could not get her fingerprints due to her history of cleaning with harsh chemicals. Rudy and Mason did know from past history that there was a segment of the population without fingerprints, albeit a small segment. This was the first time that information had impacted one of their investigations.

Still, this fit the scenario of not finding fingerprints on the weapons. Well, they wouldn't have to ask her and raise her awareness that she may be a person of interest.

Mason had already contacted Sky Erikson, who said that the switchblade was not his but the box it was in was his. He identified a couple of other tools as having been stolen from his home. The detectives did wonder if he was being truthful about the switchblade. It was legal to own a big switchblade in Massachusetts, while selling one like this one was not so easy because there were strict limitations on who could sell to whom.

Petra and Rudy returned to the interview room munching on the great sandwiches that Millie had brought. They were using up time, and they didn't want Mariska to think that they would leave her alone, just so they could eat their lunch.

Mariska kidded with them, saying, "The police station is like at school with a lunch hour for teac hers, which is only twenty minutes, forcing them to eat at the interview table too fast. It's not good for the digestion."

Rudy recalled his wife Mona's indictment of the police department.

"Rudy, they plan to hustle you cops into an early grave in order to avoid paying retirement benefits." It was one of the reasons they let police officers retire in their fifties. Between the many adrenal spikes cops experience every day and the atrocious diets they consumed on the run, their mean life after retirement was not long. *Mona may be correct again!*

Mason entered the room with a bunch of plastic-wrapped weapons and other items and placed them on the table. One by one, Rudy questioned Mariska about tomahawks, river stones, grinding tools, the ax, pieces of twine, metal arrows, a piece of a bow, vine, oily cloth, switch blade, shaped sticks, hooks on trees, nubs on trees, barrettes, and ponytail holders. The whole explanation process used by Rudy and Petra took a great deal of time.

The answers were surprising. Mariska replied, "I've never seen tomahawks. Nor have Anya or any of her friends told me about making them. I would not have approved if I knew. I am shocked and disappointed that Anya didn't discuss this camp project; I suppose she thinks we're too strict with her."

Rudy questioned, "How could Anya hide the tomahawk from you the day the kids took them home from camp? It'd be difficult not to notice a tomahawk!"

Mariska defensively said that Anya had a backpack and would never let her open it. She would say, "I have to have some privacy."

Sergei told her that American children had a big thing about their "own stuff." She thought that maybe she didn't understand because, where she came from, children didn't have a lot of stuff. None of the barrettes or ponytail holders they had just showed her belonged to her daughter. Her daughter did not wear anything in her hair, not ever. That was a fetish with her. She said that the stripping of branches to make nubs on trees was something that they did in Russia all the time to use for holding things. She wondered out loud, "Detectives, I don't think we Russians discovered that; maybe that's something people do here too."

Mariska said that the switchblade belonged to Sergei, but she didn't know how it had gotten into the bushes. In fact, she had never seen the lean-tos and she walked in the woods regularly. She said that she would have to ask her mother if she had ever seen them. She denied that Anya walked in the woods regularly. She said that Anya would not dare go in the woods without someone since the murders began. When Mariska was reminded that Anya had come through path number two on the day of the assault, she started to cry and said, "See I have not been able to protect her. She could have been the one assaulted that day instead of Carol."

Petra tried to soothe Mariska while Rudy went for some tea, remembering that she had said that, when she drank tea, she normally liked her tea with sugar. When he offered her the tea, she thanked him and said that she felt so foolish. Both detectives assured her that nobody can be with another person 100 percent of the time.

Rudy pursued questioning concerning Mariska's normal habits. He asked her again if she slept at any other time of the day. Her answer was no. What did she do at that time of day before picking Anya up at school? She said that she would have a cup of coffee to keep her awake, and it did most days. But some days, it seemed to do the reverse. She then said that, once she fell asleep in the afternoon, when she awoke, she would feel groggy.

Petra asked her how she made her coffee. Was it with a Keurig machine?

Mariska answered, "No. We use a regular European coffee press with ground French coffee beans that I keep in a jar for when I have company who want coffee. But that's a lot of work for just one cup of coffee. For myself, and I only drink coffee normally in the afternoon, I use Davidoff Café, a Russian instant coffee. I actually prefer that coffee. I'm the only one in the house who drinks coffee at all. Sergei and my mother both drink mostly Russian tea, while Anya won't drink either tea or coffee."

There was a knock on the interview room door, and both Rudy and Petra excused themselves for a moment.

ADA Hetterman and Chief Coyne were waiting. Rudy said that

the interview so far was not conclusive but was surprised to be immediately contradicted by the other three.

"How can you say that?" said the chief. "We've seen all the video. She had access to the weapons, she's lied about the paths she took on the day of the assault, she has no real alibi for any of the murders, and it's her husband's switchblade found in the lean-to. She says she never saw a lean-to, even though she frequents the woods, and she has no fingerprints. We have no evidence from forensics, whether rubber or fabric, from gloves if they were used. Christ, how many people on the street have no fingerprints? On top of that, she appears to be a nut job to me. Marion agrees with me. Now, stop the sweetness and light and get a confession before her husband finds out she's still here."

Marion agreed with Chief Coyne but said that she thought Jim Locke could bring the ball to home plate, saying, "Jim's a psychologist. He knows where she's vulnerable. It's with Anya. Twist it around so she thinks we have a lock on Anya. She'll confess."

An exasperated Rudy exploded with, "I'm not convinced this lady could kill anyone, but I do think she would confess to anything to protect Anya or her mother or Sergei. This is a mistake. Why does she go to sleep some days and not others? That bothers me. We don't have an answer to that. We have naught in circumstantial evidence directed to her, other than she is mistaken or maybe lied about the paths she took on the day of the assault."

The chief sarcastically said, "Yup, we do. Carbohydrate overload! It makes some people crazy. Happens all the time! She probably eats those Russian tea cookies with her coffee. Rudy, get Jim to do this closing, you hear me?"

Detective Jim Locke did not look happy to take on this job after he was briefed on the interview. He asked everyone if they thought she was really guilty. All but Rudy thought she was guilty.

Hetterman said, "She's too smart to be this stupid, so she's either mentally ill or she's playing us really well with childlike shrewdness. We can find out from Anya whether or not she told her mother about the tomahawk, but we can do that after we arrest Mariska. I'd like to do that house search before Sergei gets home and finds out what maybe going on. The old lady's still there. I think we should get that done after Jim's interview. What do you think, Chief?"

Chief Coyne's only concern was whether there was enough to get a conviction.

Marion said, "Depends on what attorney she gets. But it looks good to me if we find a tomahawk or if we can get her to waiver on her denial of knowledge of Anya's location at the time of the murders or her location or if we get a confession. Go in there, Jim, please."

Upon entering the interview room, Jim remarked that Mariska looked tired and he offered to get her a soda or water.

She ignored that offer. "Where are Detectives Aylewood and Beauregard?"

Jim quietly said that they had a short emergency and that he was taking this opportunity to speak with her seriously about events.

Nervously, Jim thought, Mariska asked if the police somehow thought that she was involved in these murders, and he replied very slowly, "Not you, Mrs. Rozovsky, not now."

Trembling, Mariska said, "What do you mean not me, not now? Who do you suspect? Tell me. How can I help you if you don't tell me?"

Jim, his gut a bit queasy, spoke quietly and with apparent great sincerity. "Think about it. Who else has no alibi for the murders besides you? Your mother and your daughter are the only others on the street with no alibis other than the ones you give each other."

He thought to himself, *Another lie, but it serves our purposes.* He told her, "The police are now checking your personal stories. I don't know what we'll find out about your mother and you. Anya was born here. She is a beautiful young woman with a future, and she's an extraordinary student. However, she is considered cold by some of her friends and there are stories about her anger, which erupts for apparently no reason. Your mother knows the woods well and, in fact, wanders through the woods every day. She is a very direct person and, please pardon me when I say this, appears to have a vindictive aspect to her personality. She could be arrested. Despite what you have said,

Anya has often been seen in the woods. Do you think there's some reason to suspect either one of them? Why do you think we're looking at them?

"You know the truth. It's time that you tell us what you know. I am trying to help you before the captain comes in and grills you or makes the arrest he's thinking about making. I think you're a good person, but this story about sometimes falling asleep after you've had your coffee is a little weak. What do you know that you're holding back? It is far more plausible that Anya is the suspect, rather than your mother. If you've noticed, Anya walks very fast, while your mother walks slowly. Anya is very smart and always has a story line. You know this, don't you? It is that time, Mrs. Rozovsky, to give up; it is that time."

Mariska sobbed and sobbed. Jim did not comfort her, not this time. He held back, and he did not feel good about it. He was sure that she was suffering, and in his heart of hearts, he hoped she would ask for legal counsel. But she didn't!

Mariska whispered, "Get them all in here. I have a confession to make. I don't know why I did it, but I am responsible for killing those children."

ADA Hetterman, Rudy, Petra, and Jim attended the confession. The next hour and a half flew by as Mariska told her story to the detectives after being read her rights and again signing the form. She then signed the written confession. She did not give a motive for the killings but, instead, insisted that she was responsible and that she knew right from wrong and she was wrong. She said, "I will enter hell for what I did and did not do. There is no forgiveness for my actions." She explained in detail everything she did, and the details fit the evidence the police had. She told which paths she walked on for each killing.

Mariska admitted that she had taken the tomahawk that Anya had made in camp and hidden it. She had found the ax used hidden in the lean-to. She had known all about the lean-tos. "We used to build them in the woods in Russia as kids; not so different here after all." She had put Sergei's knife in there just in case. So far, she had not needed to use it. All her statements were made in a voice that exuded nothing but rote and resignation, almost as if she had been rehearsing it.

The problem was that she did not explain why the victims were chosen. She said that she killed some of them because they were really going to grow up to be bad people and have a negative influence on others. But when it came to her reasons for killing Davie, Melvin, and Merry, she did not want to talk about them. She said that killing Merry was a mistake and that killing Davie and Melvin was necessary; but she would not explain.

Petra formally conducted the arrest, and Mariska was taken to a holding cell. Upon leaving the interview room, she looked at the clock in the outside room and saw that it read four fifteen. Almost hysterical, she said to Jim, "Someone must pick up Anya. She cannot be left to walk home alone."

Mariska was assured that the police were searching her home at this very moment and that they would make sure Anya was safe. She then asked if Jim would call Sergei and tell him what had occurred. She said, "I can't tell him. Please call him for me."

In the conference room, there was a great deal of excitement. Chief Coyne had called the mayor earlier when he knew a confession was imminent. The mayor had replied with "The district attorney and I will call a press conference in time for the five o'clock news, and I want all your detectives and Captain Beauregard in attendance. It'll take place outside the station."

The press was already getting ready outside the station.

Rudy was visibly upset. He ranted to his chief and the other detectives, "We're conducting a search of the house right now. The conference could have waited until tomorrow. She doesn't have an attorney yet. And frankly, I don't believe she killed these kids."

Chief Coyne replied, "Rudy, we didn't beat it out of her. She confessed. There's closure. If later you find something to disprove it, then I'll listen. Right now, we're going to a press conference."

Rudy did not embrace being part of this travesty of justice. This was not justice in his mind. He knew that Mariska couldn't kill a fly. He didn't know who was guilty. He knew, however, that Mariska had thought that the police would arrest either her daughter or her mother, and so she had done what her culture trained her to do; she had confessed to protect her family. He thought, *Mariska is an easy target for the police. She's neurotic and compulsive, but she's not a killer. Mariska believes that the police have ruled out everyone who lives on the street other than her family. That's not so, but her family does look better than anyone else for it. Charging Mariska gets the mayor and the chief off the hot seat. This isn't the right way to end this. It's not the truth; of that I am certain.*

At that point, a frazzled Millie called him. "I just got a call from the husband, and he is wild. Will you take the call please, Rudy? I can't get rid of him."

Sergei's response to Rudy's hello was filled with attacks on the police. "You're no better than Russian police. You frame people by questioning them until they will say anything. Mariska would not hurt anyone. You couldn't wait to make charges, could you? Why not wait until I am able to find a good attorney? You should have talked with me, not Mariska. She couldn't hurt anyone. They said on the breaking news that there will be a live press conference at the station at five o'clock. I won't even be there then. What's the rush? It's Friday, and I know they don't hold court on Saturday. Why not wait until Monday for the press conference? You want to hold her until Monday, which is the first day to go to court. I know the system. Mariska can't stay in jail. She's not well. You guys want to be famous on the backs of my family. You're nothing but rotten shits. They said that there's a confession. How could Mariska confess to something she could never do? You tell me! Did you beat it out of her? If there's a mark on her, I will sue your asses—"

Rudy finally cut him off and said, "Mr. Rozovsky, your wife is upset, of course, but she is physically fine. I cannot help you, except to suggest that your wife needs a really good criminal attorney to represent her. Now I must go to the press conference and go now. I am very sorry for you, Mrs. Rozovsky, and your family." And Rudy clicked off.

18

Media Blitz

A PODIUM BORDERED ON either side by metal barriers similar to bicycle racks was set up in front of the station. There were news reporters from every local news outlet and from Boston, Holyoke, Chicopee, Northampton, Worcester, Pittsfield, Hartford, and local television, as well as Fox News, CNN, and so on. There was a crowd; this was important news nationally.

Rudy was not surprised at the crowd. He knew that this murder charge, whether he believed in it or not, would be a catharsis for this community and for the area. But he also knew that this murder charge would hurt this woman, whom he did not believe murdered anyone. It was not the first time he thought the system might not be supporting justice.

The district attorney made the announcement that an arrest for the multiple murders had been made and that there was a confession. He gave credit to all the work done by the state police, the task force, the FBI, and of course the West Side police department. He then said that Mariska Rozovsky had been arrested.

Some in the audience said, "No," loudly enough for others to hear. The district attorney introduced Chief Coyne, who would take questions relative to the arrest. The chief, in a grand gesture, gave much of the credit to his detectives.

Rudy thought, *He did that just in case I'm right, and this arrest proves to be a bad arrest at a later date.* Rudy questioned his own cynicism, which he supposed was not so bad. It wasn't a negative trait for a detective, but it was certainly a no-no for normal life.

The chief answered questions in a most limited fashion, which was what you did before a trial. In substance, he said that Mrs. Rozovsky lived on Sunnyside Road, was an American citizen, and had confessed to all the murders and the assault. He also said that circumstantial evidence supported her confession. When asked why it had taken them so long to find the murderer, he answered in his most political way. "The task force, the FBI, and the state police focused on outsiders and typical serial murderer types, while his department had always thought it was someone who lived in and knew the area. It takes time to properly investigate. We can't make up evidence, and we make mistakes when we are forced to speed up the process."

Rudy thought, *That's why I'm not the chief. I could never say that knowing that we have sped up the process and probably are making a mistake. Chief Coyne will regret this statement if I'm right about Mariska.*

Mayor Fitshler closed the press conference, citing his knowledge that the West Side Police Department was a superior force whose detectives had never lost their focus on solving this case. "I have great conference in their abilities. This is not a day to be proud, but I am able to say the West Side Police Department has conducted this investigation with diligence and endurance."

Rudy, back in his office, met with the uniform captain whose blues had finished the search. There was no evidence of a tomahawk or bow anywhere on the Rozovsky premises. They had searched everywhere for evidence of the murdered kids. The grandmother was vitriolic in her reaction to the search, but she screamed only in Russian, which the cops had little trouble ignoring. Anya, fortunately for them, was not at home when the search was conducted. As they were leaving, Anya came home, and they said that, for a little girl, she had gone ballistic. She had immediately called her father and then screamed at them to get out.

Rudy asked for a count of any prescription medicine by type given to anyone in the family. Mariska was prescribed birth control pills and .5 milligrams of Lorazepam to be taken daily when needed. The pill bottles dated back to November 30, 2015, and were partially empty. He noted that this use of pills was in contradiction to Mariska's story that she'd never taken the pills except that one time.

He thought that it could be that she was ashamed of relying on pills, or maybe she was addicted to them. *Although if she were addicted to them, they'd all be gone!* It was strange that about a third of each bottle was gone. There were five bottles, each with some missing. The average Joe would finish the first bottle and then start the next one; unless the time stamp for usage had run out. Not here, no; so what does that mean if it means anything at all?

He thought, *It seems to me that maybe someone doesn't want Mariska to notice that the pills are gone. Maybe Anya is taking them and doesn't want Mariska to know. This misuse of a parent's prescription drugs is normal for kids today and talked about in all the school and police seminars. Could Anya be under that much pressure that she would steal her mother's antianxiety meds?*

Rudy remembered his meetings with Anya and her control over her family. She didn't look anxious. Mariska and Albina looked anxious, but she did not. He wondered, *Who knows who's anxious? I need to ask Mariska some more questions—questions I should have asked her before.*

He checked the search inventory sheet and found what he was looking for. He then made a call to get fingerprints and chemical analysis. He thought, *It's a long shot, but it's worth fighting over the cost of analysis.*

It was time to go home to Mona and the kids. They would be all excited until they saw his face. They were true detectives when it came to his thoughts, ideas, and moods. But he needed them now because he was certain that justice right now was being subverted and that he had a part in this stage play of subversion. And then, surprisingly, he decided to make a short detour to Holyoke to see Lizette.

He hurried down the concrete walk, not nearly as nice as the ones on Sunnyside but well kept with no debris anywhere near. He saw Lizette peer out between the lace curtains with her black labradoodle, Cheri, barking next to her. Cheri barked at any passerby. Didn't matter if you lived at the pretty little cape-style home, Cheri's job was to let Lizette know that someone was visiting. The door opened. Cheri sniffed his pant legs, while Rudy bent to hug the petite mama Lizette who had saved his life.

Lizette said, "You didn't tell me you were coming. You're just as bad as always. I don't have a big supper for you. Your father has a card game tonight, so we just had those big Italian hero sandwiches he likes. I'll make one for you, Rudy."

Rudy stopped her with his hand up, an old habit he'd used as a kid to stop his mom's chatter. She never took offense. She knew she was given to filling up any vacuum in conversation. "So, what's on your mind, Rudy? Do you have bad news for me? Is Mona okay? Are the kids okay?"

"No, Ma, they're all fine. I'm here because I'm finally ready, like you said, someday I'd be ready. Tell me what you know about my brother and the lady who might be my birth mother. I'm ready to investigate. I'm ready to accept my history."

Lizette wiped a tear as she left the room. He knew she was getting the file—the one she kept in the chifforobe in her bedroom that she'd showed him many times, explaining that it contained unfinished business. She would tell him, "It would be better to explore while I'm alive than after I die, but you must be ready."

Rudy knew lots of adopted kids who knew all about their birth parents, and some of those birth parents were not very nice. Why was his potential truth so frightening to him?

Lizette sat next to him, patted his knee, and opened the file. He looked at the adoption papers. His name was Rudolfo Eaton. He thought, *What kind of name is that? Spanish or Italian for the first name and English for the surname!* The name for the bigger boy was Billy Locario, and he was almost four years older than Rudy.

"Ma, you kept my name. Why? It's not even French. You could have called me Pierre or something."

Lizette responded, "We were very happy with our little Rudy. It was the name you were used to. It's what your brother said your name was. We didn't want a Pierre. We wanted only you. Your brother's name was William, but he insisted to the authorities that he was only to be called Billy because that's what his mother called him, and you were Rudy. They told us that Billy had serious psychological issues. They wouldn't let us see him and said that, at that time, he wasn't adoptable. We tried later, but they said we had no right to further information. It was a different time, Rudy.

"Your mother's name was Mavis Eaton. They never found her. She may have died. Billy was seven, and you were three and a half when the police broke the door and found you. The neighbors said that Mavis came home every morning and that she worked nights. She'd only lived in the small motel apartment for six months. The police said she either ran or was dead. Because both of you children were basically physically healthy, your father and I think that if she was going to leave you, she would have called and reported you to child services. We think she's dead. Rudy, people don't take care of children well enough like that and then risk their lives.

"You were both tied to chairs. The neighbors never saw evidence of addiction; neither did the police. You're an investigator, the best. Investigate, Rudy. I'd like to know before I die that maybe you have someone out there. Go to that ancestry thing advertised on television. Maybe Billy is looking for you. Maybe you can get the police report. It's a long time ago. I don't know if they keep them or not. You're lucky, Rudy. You have Roland, me, Mona, Roland Jr., Jeremiah, and Lucas. Don't be afraid. Get rid of your chains and your nightmares."

Rudy left Lizette's and found that, although his brain was running all over the facts, his heart was light.

Sergei thought long and hard about who he trusted for advice about a lawyer. He knew that he would need a criminal lawyer, but his only experience in choosing a lawyer was with a business attorney for his leases, closings on his properties, and some contracts. First, he contacted his business attorney, but he was on a riverboat cruise in France. He then called his friend Matt, who was not Russian but thought to be "in the know" and asked him for some ideas.

The advice given seemed honest but was disheartening. "Sergei, this is serious, and you can't get just anyone. I'll give you a few good names in Springfield, but maybe they won't take the case because it's too controversial. A Boston attorney would work, but I don't have any names I trust. And you would have to pay all the travel back and forth for the attorney and staff if there's a trial. One of the names I'll give you advertises on billboards and television and everywhere. Look him up. He's supposed to be tenacious, which is what you need—a tenacious attorney. Sometimes a picture will speak to you. At least it sometimes speaks to me.

"You need a seasoned attorney, one who will not be intimidated by all the police who have worked on this case. Find out who's prosecuting, and I'll get you some feedback on the prosecutor. You know I really like Mariska, and I can't believe she could have done these murders.

"Sergei, you are in for an additional nightmare from the press and your neighbors. Remember, do not talk about the case to anyone but the attorney you choose. Don't tell me anything. Don't tell your other friends anything. Anything you say can be used against Mariska. And remember that the attorney will not tell you everything, because the attorney will be Mariska's attorney. Get a price by the hour, for the arraignment, for the trial, and for any appeal. Try to get a fixed price, but they won't go for it because they don't know how much time it will take. Go into this with your eyes open. It's going to cost and maybe a lot, Sergei, and you don't want bargain basement prices."

Sergei said, "What do you mean when you say *if* there's a trial, Matt?"

There was a long pause before he got an answer, which he did not like. "Sergei, if they have a lot of evidence and if Mariska confessed, then one option to consider is a plea bargain. Now I'm not saying that will happen, but going to trial is not always the best thing. Besides, this will be Mariska's decision. So be careful; it's her life."

After his thanks and goodbyes, Sergei cursed to himself and thought, *Why didn't Mariska listen to me last night? I told her not to go. I said that if she went, I'd have an attorney go with her. But no; she wanted to do the right thing.*

Could she really know something? He was very afraid that the big cloud over their heads was about to open up. Mariska knew something. *But why would she confess? Why wouldn't she tell me?*

When Sergei got home, his first chore was to quiet Albina, who was clutching at her heart and hysterically crying. Anya watched, and he saw fear in her eyes.

Anya said that she was watching television and saw that the district attorney said Mama had confessed to killing the kids. "Why, Papa, would she do that? She was with me for practically all of the murders. You must fix this Papa and get her home. She's not right sometimes in the head. She is so anxious. They must have scared her into confessing. We need Mama home now, Papa. I'm afraid for Mama."

Sergei had Albina make some Russian tea and told her that he must get the best attorney for Mariska. He explained that he would be in his study for a couple of hours searching and they were to go about eating dinner and getting ready for bed like usual. He would let them know more in the morning. "Just leave my dinner in the pot. I'll eat when I'm ready." Sergei hugged the two crying women and left the room.

It wasn't more than five minutes later that Anya had the sad Russian song "As I Walk Alone Along the Road" loudly playing. He thought then about the Russian tradition of crying to music when the world is falling apart. Apparently Anya had a little Russian in her after all; she wasn't all American.

Sergei searched the web and read about each attorney whose name Matt had given him. He saw something in the billboard guy's eyes. They looked honest but street smart to him. He thought, *The only drawback is this attorney Norberto Cull looks very American to me. It's not easy for me to entrust my family to a guy who looks like white bread America. But a jury might like him. Maybe I should call one or two of the other names first to see what their reactions are. That's what I would do at work when I need a vendor in a new area. I'd call several vendors to get pricing and a feel for whether the vendor was reliable or not.*

Shopping for professional services probably was not that different. He thought, *I need to be certain that I'm doing the right thing. I'll make some calls and tell each lawyer I call that I'm making a decision about representation. I'll ask whether the lawyer has the time to devote to the case and find out about cost.*

After his first call, Sergei was very concerned. The attorney spent fifteen minutes talking about the seriousness of the case and the fact that his firm would face a public relations nightmare if it took the case. However, he would consider it and asked for a retainer of $50,000; he added that services would be billed against the retainer at $300 an hour for his services and various lesser amounts for that of his assistants and staff. He would only be able to see Mariska early Monday morning before the arraignment because he was in Texas right now. He also said that Boston attorneys' rates were higher and spent a few minutes talking about himself and his record of success.

The second attorney was friendlier but was not able to take the case. He had a conflict and would not say what it was.

Sergei called a third attorney and, after five minutes, realized that he would never be able to work with him.

His fourth call was to an answering service for the firm with the billboard advertisements. The receptionist said that Attorney Cull would get back to him within an hour.

By this time, Sergei was extremely nervous. This was not good. So far, not one of these attorneys had inspired confidence in him for handling this case. He went and ate some dinner left in the oven and checked on Anya. She was in her room reading, and he hugged her and tried to reassure her. He did not bother Albina, who was also in her room, probably praying.

The phone rang, and Attorney Cull's hello was direct and friendly. Sergei then explained that his wife, Mariska, had been arrested for six murders and an assault. It seemed easier to say this time. He talked on and on about themselves as a family and his Mariska and how she could not hurt anyone. He told the attorney that she had gone voluntarily to the station alone that morning, had been kept there all day, and that she had confessed. He wanted to know what Mr. Cull could do.

Attorney Cull said that he would have to see Mariska first; he would need to find out what she had said to the police and why she'd said it. He was willing to talk to her and maybe take the case. But the client, not her husband, would have to want him to represent her. "I am willing to go and speak with her this evening. I will call you after I speak with her and tell you if I will take the case. You know that there is a business side to this, and we can discuss that tomorrow. I need to assess what is going on, but you must understand that your wife will be my client, and I will not be able to share what she tells me with you."

Sergei questioned that with, "I'm her husband, and I can't testify against her without her letting me. I know that. So why can't you tell me everything?"

Attorney Cull patiently said, "I will insist, for many reasons, that she will be the one to tell you what she wants you to know. I take you very seriously, when you say that she is not a woman who could do what she's been charged with doing. If these terms are agreeable with you, then I will get over there immediately. You, as her husband, will only be able to visit at normal visiting hours. She probably has already been moved to the county correctional facility. I will check on that and call you. Mr. Rozovsky, take heart. I will do my best for her. Things are not always the way they seem at first."

Sergei was miserable, as he now finally understood that he had no control. He knew his Mariska. Her decisions were always based on her best moral sense. Something was very wrong here. Why would she do this to herself and him and Anya and Albina? Sergei saw no hope for Mariska and the rest of his family and himself. Maybe he should have stayed in Russia after all.

19

The Neighbors

AMY LANDERS'S PHONE HAD been ringing continually since the press conference had been aired on television. She personally had been devastated when she had seen the news. Of all people the police could find to blame, they'd pick Mariska! This was not good. And why on earth would Mariska confess to something that Amy knew in her heart that she did not do, could not do?

Some of her neighbors were quick to convict her and, shamefully enough, because the Rozovskys were Russian and immigrants. Amy took this opportunity to remind them that the Rozovskys were citizens, that Anya was born here, and that some of them had been the beneficiaries of Mariska's kindness and Sergei's largesse.

Other callers, like her, did not believe it. Mostly all callers felt relief and expressed the sentiment that they could all get on with their lives. She laughed at that thought. Did they think that life would ever be the same for any of them? Her thoughts went very dark, and she realized that she had been fighting those thoughts for two years. Every day she wrestled with dark images of slashing out against the unfair loss of Henry and Henry's painful suffering and the loss of Jeffrey. Where was Suzanna when she needed her?

At that moment, Suzanna entered the door, and she could tell in a heartbeat that she already knew the news. Suzanna was the first to express outrage that anyone could think that Mariska could hurt a fly. She was flamboyant in her language and totally confused as to why Mariska would confess.

Suzie asked, "Do you think they forced her to confess, Mom? There could be no other reason. Remember when I talked with Merry before she was killed. She was convinced it was someone we all knew, and I think she thought she knew who the killer was. But she loved Mariska."

Amy didn't mean to but yelled, "Stop this nonsense, Suzie; they don't have the facts. I'm going to talk with Sergei in the morning and offer assistance with legal counsel. After all, I've become adept with lawyers, after settling your father's complicated estate. She thought, *It's probably too late to call now.* But Suzie begged her to call Sergei now.

Amy said, "I suppose not for a minute do I think that Sergei is sleeping."

Not for the first time since Jeffrey's death, Amy followed Suzie's suggestion. She called Sergei. She quickly realized that this very strong man was completely depleted of his usual "in charge of the world" air. She felt profoundly sorry for him. As she questioned Sergei about an attorney for Mariska, she felt better. Sergei had stumbled onto Norberto Cull. Amy couldn't believe that he could get it right so quickly and told him so.

Sergei said that Attorney Cull had stated that Mariska would have to want to have him as her attorney, and he was worried about whether she would even allow that.

Amy said, "This situation won't be resolved overnight. Be careful with what you say to anyone, even to me. Talk only with the attorney. You don't want anything you say to anyone to come back and haunt you or hurt Mariska's case."

This was not the first time Sergei had been told to keep his thoughts to himself.

The Tisdales were horrified at the news that Mariska was the suspected killer. Mrs. Tisdale was immediately caught up with the implications of Mariska's confession and its probable effect on Anya, with a remark of, "Poor Anya. What will this do to her?"

Her daughter, Judy, was quick to make a snide retort. "Oh, poor Anya, poor Anya, who is the prettiest and smartest girl in class and who only cares about herself. Oh, poor Anya"!

Gerald Tisdale was shocked at Judy. "How can you say those things about your friend? I've never heard you speak out like that, and I can't believe it's my quiet and sweet daughter who is so insensitive."

Judy glared at her parents. They were so clueless sometimes that it made her sick. They were foolish know-it-alls. And without thinking, she spoke her mind for the first time in a long time. "You guys … uh, like you guys think you know it all, but you don't know jack. You—"

"Judy!" her mom said, her voice full of surprise.

Still smarting at their falling for Anya's sweet little girl front, Judy glared at her parents. "What's up? I can't tell you the truth for once? It doesn't fit in your ideas? Got news for you, Mom, you don't know what's up for nothin' about Anya. You're not with her every day. Some days, I just hate her! She's acts so superior and calls me a baby. She's not the only one, just the worst one—other than those boys who were killed. Even Davie and Melvin called me a big baby. And they called her the queen, which made her really fightin' mad. But everyone calls me a big baby, and most kids wouldn't dare call Anya a queen to her face. They're afraid of her; nobody's afraid of me. Daddy, my fearfulness is all yours and Mommy's fault. You think you're protecting me; well, you make me afraid of my own shadow. I'm not afraid anymore. I just act that way because you want me to be a baby; and it's too much trouble to tell you the truth. I don't want to be a baby anymore."

With that she sat and cried as her startled parents held back and did not comfort her for the first time in her life.

Gerald Tisdale, always the politician adapting to new information, said, "Judy, perhaps you've got something there. Maybe it is time that we allow you to grow up and take your place in the world. Your mother and I will do our best to let you bloom. Judy, promise us you'll ask for our shelter when you need shelter."

They both hugged Judy, who looked absolutely in shock that she wasn't being punished.

⟫◆⟪

Nearby, Jenny Haygood was in a battle with her husband, Albert, over her blunt reaction to Mariska's arrest. Albert was wild with anger, spieling sarcasm directly at her. She was fit to be tied thinking of what he'd said—*at me, like always. Everyone outside our world has his respect for his or her higher moral aspirations. Imagine, telling me that Mariska Rozovsky could never commit murder because it was just not in her. But me, apparently I am, as he stated, "viscerally resentful." Of what?! A pretty, oh-too-good Russian immigrant! Did he know that it was an added insult with his inference that I didn't even have the intellect to suffer real resentment? Albert could verbally cut someone's ego like a butcher cuts a side of beef.*

Well, she thought, *they didn't arrest me for those murders. They know that I may not like children very much, but they also know that I live too carefully to ever risk murdering someone even if I wanted to. Right now, I'd like to kill Albert. Look at him pacing the floor with great indignation at the thought of Mariska sitting in the county jail.*

Albert believed that Mariska was an extraordinary and gentle woman who just couldn't deliberately inflict pain; he also was truly conscious that her every word was kind. He couldn't believe that Captain Beauregard was that stupid. He regretted his original assessment of the man. It was one of the few times that he was wrong about character. *Unless maybe,* he thought, *the mayor stepped in for political reasons with a, "Let's push an arrest and see what happens."* That idea was more logical.

Albert remembered explaining to Jenny on Tuesday, "Jenny, the police are looking at someone on the street. The detectives' questions are too focused on what all the neighbors were doing every minute during all the murder times, much more so than in previous questioning. And it makes sense to me. I know that catching this killer will be difficult, even if it is, as they suspect, someone who lives on Sunnyside." Now he thought, *And I know for sure that the killer is not Mariska Rozovsky.*

Albert wondered why he had not stumbled on sociopathy as a field of study when he was young. He remembered a department chairperson at the college who, for several years, had been touted as a boy wonder—until, gradually, his antics had been discovered. No, there were no murders. But boy wonder was known to send letters beautifully worded that, for a while, destroyed competitors' reputations. It took time before the pattern emerged. And that's what had happened here. *The pattern has emerged. But God damn, Mariska is not the one.*

⋙◆⋘

Further down the street, Freida and Frank McNamara were taking a couple of hours of respite from standing watch at the hospital. They were thrilled that Carol would be home on Monday, and there was every reason to believe that she would make a full recovery. The report of the arrest of their nice neighbor truly shocked them, and Freida did not believe Mariska was the guilty one.

She said to her husband, "Frank, you remember Alicia McCarthy who lived near Ashmont Station in Dorchester? She would always offer to visit any sick neighbor while the family was working. The neighbors thought she was an angel. They often would pay her. While she would visit, she would replace the sick person's pills with sleeping or antianxiety pills. The patients got a bit better under her care but a little loopy, requiring the families to continue to have Alicia visit some more. She was careful to just extend their illnesses. And so it took a long time before anyone noticed—until a baby camera monitor in a sick room caught her in action quite by accident."

Frank did remember the event. The woman was never charged

because it would kill her elderly mother with whom she lived, and the neighbors had felt that no real harm was done! She lived a very lonesome life thereafter. She was, in the old way, "shunned" by everyone in her neighborhood and actually died at age sixty.

Neither Freida nor Frank could see any of Alicia's personality in Mariska. Alicia sucked up to people with this phony gushiness. Even before folks knew about her activities, they would talk about her annoying personality. They thought her actions were more like the mothers who had Munchausen syndrome by proxy, which they had seen in that television movie. Those mothers made their children sick in order to bring attention to themselves as doting mothers. Alicia wished to be thought of as a great caretaker, giving her access to everyone's homes and making her life more interesting.

Mariska really didn't need that kind of attention, the adoration of others. She had attention, first, because she was such a lovely individual and, secondly, because she was a calm and reassuring presence when she met anyone. Everyone liked Mariska, except for those few callers this morning looking for gossip and talking about her Russian immigrant status.

Frank had set one of them straight with, "Mariska is an American citizen, as is her daughter," as he clicked off his cell phone.

Freida felt deeply for the family and worried about Anya. She did not think that Anya would be able to steer through this mess. As an only child, she was perfect in every way and really had never faced much difficulty before. Probably first or second in her classes all through school, a good athlete when she wanted to be, and certainly pretty almost beautiful, Anya had no problems that Freida could see. For any child, the arrest of a mother would be horrible. But Freida thought, in this case, it may be a catastrophic. She thought, *I will have to tell Carol about the arrest if she has not already heard; if she had, she'd most likely already have called home.*

Claire did not know what to think, and she and her siblings all remarked that Mariska was never anything but kind to them. They were confused.

Claire was thinking, *What if I'm wrong about Anya's mother? What if she did this to my sister? Well, I can't think about that today. I'm like Scarlett O'Hara, like my mother's always comparing me to. I'll worry about it tomorrow.*

⋙◆⋘

Ricky Bowes was crying, and his mom and dad and Maynard were having difficulty soothing him. He kept repeating, "She was always nice to us. Why did she pick Merry and Carol to hurt? I don't understand it, Mom. I really liked her, and she's a killer of little kids."

Maynard, the mature brother although the younger brother, who also watched more television than Ricky, tried to explain, "She probably didn't do it. The cops get it wrong all the time, and then the suspect sues the police and gets a lot of money."

Looking at the boys, Mr. and Mrs. Bowes envisioned a long afternoon before them. They later discussed the possibility of culture and whether there were things they didn't understand about Mariska. They would leave it to the courts to sort it out because, as Mr. Bowes recalled from an old radio show called *The Shadow*, which his father would quote, "Who knows what evil lurks in the hearts of men."

⋙◆⋘

Barnett and Neil had spent the morning explaining to Jonah about the formidable unfairness of life and what can happen to us all. Jonah, in their eyes, was an old soul and seemed to accept the unacceptable with grace and little drama.

Barnett, who tended to embellish and not reduce drama, was always impressed with Jonah. However, in this case, both men were having difficulty accepting the validity of this arrest of Mariska Rozovsky.

Barnett said, "Neil, you know that I'm quite a good judge of character, but maybe not after all."

Neil pooh-poohed him and tried to think of Mariska in the act of each murder. No matter how he tried, he could not even envision any possibility of her guilt. Neil was all logic, and when the news said that Mariska had confessed with detail, well that was problematic. Confession meant something, he explained to Barnett. But what did it mean here?

He and Barnett knew a lot about subversive behavior, based on their upbringings and their not-so-comfortable fits within their individual families. Much of that discomfort was removed now, but he remembered all the pushes and pulls of parental disappointment and how angry it used to make him feel. He wanted to be considered normal, not different. But he now understood. He was part of a new normal, not part of the old normal.

How would the rest of the Rozovsky family cope? That was the question now. The two fathers had reassured Jonah that, as far as they were concerned, it was important not to make Anya feel bad when they saw her in school and to stop anyone from bullying her. They explained to Jonah that this was the time to talk to school authorities if Anya was being victimized, not a time to resolve things himself.

Barnett reminded Neil about how their views on life had changed since the murders and now, even more so, since the announcement of the arrest. "Remember, Neil, when we thought this place, Sunnyside Road, was Nirvana, a paradise for us? We thought then that the three of us would live here and have a wonderful life, expecting we'd make lots of memories. We would be without the horrible city gang problems, and our neighbors seemed so civilized. Our family would offer Jonah a calm upbringing, not the stress we faced. It's all gone wrong, and we couldn't have planned for any of it. Not only are we faced with what we don't want, but I, for one, have now lost any trust in planning for the future. This whole experience has been devastating, and it reminds me to respect my father more. He always thought that life bites us all in the ass in the end. I thought he was just an old man spouting off."

Upon hearing the news, a disturbed Jeb Stuart thought that his newfound equilibrium was in jeopardy. How could a mother, a nice ordinary woman, kill his kid? Camille had spent the morning with him trying to reassure him that this chaos had now probably ended, and they could continue with their normal living.

He laughed at her. "Camille, how can I look at any of my neighbors without thinking, who's the next sociopath? Did you ever think that Mrs. Rozovsky would kill our kid? What the hell motive could she have? You tell me. Maybe I'm not seeing straight, but why kill Jared?"

They sat in silence, and then they both cried.

Camille now believed, *There will never be an end to this. There will be the trial, and they will drag Jared's reputation through the mud again. They won't understand the whole little boy that he was and the changes he had made.*

Could she and Jeb also make dramatic changes like the ones Jared made before he died? She just hoped that her son's spirit for change and life was in them too. But she wondered!

The Wafters family was at home. Zachary had called from college when he had gotten the news. They were bereft again, the scabs newly opened on their recently scarred over hearts. Cliff and Lorraine hugged each other, and they cried. They discussed this arrest and if this arrest was a good arrest. How and why could their neighbor have done these murders? And why Merry?

The truth was Merry had really liked Mrs. Rozovsky and had felt that the liking was returned in kind. Merry, the smart and savvy twelve-year-old who loved Mrs. Rozovsky more than any of her other friends' mothers, was the victim of this same woman. How could that be? This couldn't be true.

Vivian Stoteras stopped her husband's rants about the arrest within a very short time, thinking *How easy it is to stop him in his tracks.* The resulting aftermath on Chris's behavior after Melvin's death was shocking. *I now know that I have been as much at fault in our problems as Chris has been.* She realized. *I never stood up to Chris before. If I had, then Davie would have been able to also. The girls don't have that problem with their dad because he expects nothing of them except that they be pretty—just as he previously expected of me.*

Viv now realized that the weight of responsibility of the family on Chris was too much. He had previously not understood the concept of her sharing his responsibility as part of their marriage. Melvin had probably saved their marriage. She wondered, *How can I be so forgiving of Chris's previous behavior toward Melvin, who was just a little boy? I've always loved Chris and understood that the pushy front was a disguise for his insecurities. Now I wonder if I can ever forgive Mariska. I don't know how to forgive her, but I know revenge is not an answer. This beautiful home on this beautiful street and my beautiful daughters and my now compliant husband are what I have. Will they be enough to mitigate my loss or erase my anger?*

⪼◆⪻

Meanwhile, there were protesters at the police station with a variety of signs. There were a few crazies, some Sunnyside Road residents, and a bunch of outsiders holding signs that said things like: "What took you so long?" "Don't bother with a trial!" "Investigate all immigrants!" "We'll never be safe!" "Psychotic child killer!"

The cops standing outside the station thought various versions of, *Just another day in the criminal justice system!*

20

Cull

NORBIE CULL CONSIDERED THE volcano of his conflicting thoughts as he walked out on the bluestone patio. He was thinking, *The weather is mild. The stars are out. And yet, on this beautiful spring night, I get this kind of shitty case. If she's innocent, that's one thing, but ...*

He went and sat by his pool and admired a border of shrubs hiding the fenced-in pool, thinking, *They did better surviving this winter than last year. Won't have to replace any of them!*

Cull sighed, took a long swallow of his vodka martini, and lit a cigar. The rich tobacco smoke filled the air around him in a cloud. Restless, he walked to the edge of the pool and said softly to himself, "Is this Rozovsky lady crazy? Must be. And do I want to represent another crazy? The husband described her as an innocent angel. He's been married for quite a while; maybe he's right. Sergei talked with balance; he sounded normal under the circumstances. I do this every day—talk to people. Maybe she is innocent; maybe it's worth a shot."

His conversation with Sergei had not prepared him for his interview with Mariska. Norberto thought, *Sergei is a rational and hard-nosed businessman.* He had hoped that Mariska would have some of that in her. Instead, he found a frightened woman, resolved to her situation as she saw it. *How could she be so accepting of a potential life sentence? Her looks are of an upper-class soccer mom. Something's very wrong with this picture!*

Defending murderers was not new to Cull. What was new was a client who insisted she was a multiple murderer and couldn't convince him that she was. He remembered asking Mariska how she had committed the murders and why she would murder her daughter's friends.

"Mr. Cull, that's nothing I want to discuss. I did the murders, and I'm sorry. Why do I need you anyway? I confessed. Why can't the judge put me in jail and be done with it?"

Most of the time it was the other way; the client insisted he or she was innocent when Norbie believed his client had great culpability. Among his disturbing memories of his interview with Mariska was her continual insistence, "I told you I don't need a lawyer because I'm guilty. Why should Sergei spend the money on me when I'm guilty? A trial will just make the situation worse; it will prolong my punishment, which I gladly accept."

To make matters worse, he got a call from Carlo, a legal colleague and a resident of Sunnyside Road, who fueled the truth of his instincts and insisted that Mariska was not a murderer. Carlo gave him an assessment of her character that supported his own belief in her innocence. Could she commit six murders? He thought, no, a resounding no. He was sophisticated enough to believe that, in the right circumstances, anyone could be caught in a moment of extreme passion, where violence was a potential possibility. But he believed most of those times were rare or involved impairment or mental illness.

He thought, *Lots of work before me in defending Mariska. I want to defend her if I can work my way around her stubbornness and ignorance about the system.*

His interview with Mariska was odd. It had taken him fifteen minutes of careful discussion before she would even consider that she might need a lawyer. In fact, what had truly convinced her was when she'd heard that the court would give her an attorney, who may want publicity and thus create more of a public relations storm for her family to face, if she didn't accept counsel now. Cull explained the process of a plea agreement. "In order to plead guilty, Mariska, you must give the facts. If the judge does not find what you say persuasive, then the judge could still insist upon a trial."

She cried, saying, "That's stupid. I confessed. I had not considered this."

That thought stimulated Mariska's asking many questions about the process. One question that stood out was, "Attorney Cull, can you find out everything the police know about each of the murders, especially about the first two murders?"

He asked her why that was important, and she was vague, expressing that her "sometime" headaches blurred her memory. "Attorney Cull, I want the plea deal I'll make to stand."

Much of his interview was getting to know her, her view on her family, her history in Russia, her neighborhood, her health history, and the substance of her interview with the police.

Mariska was forthright about most areas discussed, with the exception of her final police interview. She was all over the place. He had reviewed all the press records on the case before he had seen her last evening and had a feel for what the police had as evidence. They had very little circumstantial evidence before the last assault. He guessed that they were honing in on the neighborhood before the last assault. He personally had thought earlier that the murderer was a local who knew a lot about the neighborhood. The killing area on one street told him a great deal about the murderer. He guessed that the killer, although bright enough to leave little evidence, was stupid to confine the killings to kids who lived on one street. Therefore, the killer had an important reason to kill these kids, and it was personal.

Now could Mariska be that killer? No, he didn't think so, which made him uptight. Defending a killer who, under the law, had the right to an attorney was a lot different than defending an innocent, albeit maybe a crazy innocent. He knew that the pressure was now on him.

Additionally, his view of Mariska was supported by his conversation with Carlo, whom he thought was a shrewd assessor of the accused. Carlo, who lived on Sunnyside, was a truly cynical man, especially since his wife's death. Carlo said that the killer could not be Mariska. But if it were Mariska, then she was crazy—maybe multiple personalities. The only Mariska he'd ever seen was a good neighbor, kind and giving but never overstaying her welcome. The family was a good family. Carlo then told him everything that he had told Jim Locke about his thoughts.

A call from Sergei interrupted his thoughts. Sergei said that he had been able to see Mariska. He said, "And I told her to only talk to you, not to anyone else about the case, not even me. She nodded her understanding and said that you had already told her that."

Norbie asked that Sergei not talk on the phone and agreed to meet him at his office in a half hour.

At Norbie's office, Sergei spent the first forty minutes ranting to Norbie about the police. When he quieted down, Norbie questioned him about Mariska's mental health with a soft statement that was, he hoped, persuasive. "Mariska is a very sensitive woman, Sergei, and I wondered if she has found living in the United States difficult. Does she have any anxiety or depression emanating from her adjustment to this country?"

Sergei took not a second to tell Norbie that Mariska was more American than the neighbors on the street. She was the force behind their becoming citizens so early. She studied with him, and her English was better than his. "And I'm in business."

Norbie had noticed that both the Rozovskys' English was quite good. In fact, Mariska's was probably too good to be American born; it was a bit more formal and used fewer contractions than Americans typically did.

Norbie then asked Sergei why the police would have taken all of Mariska's medicines and the coffee and container from their kitchen in their search.

Sergei thought it was probably for fingerprints, as Mariska was the only one in the house who drank coffee. "She only drinks coffee in the afternoon. I don't know why they would take her medicines. What kind of medicines did they take?"

When Sergei was told that the police found multiple bottles of Ativan, he seemed confused. "Why would the police take them when they are completely filled? Mariska never took those pills. It always annoys me. Dr. Ornstein gives her prescriptions, and she likes Dr. Ornstein but won't take the pills he gives her. What good is going to a doctor and not doing what he says? He's the specialist. And it won't do the police any good to take them if they're looking for fingerprints. Mariska doesn't have fingerprints. It caused some problems when we first came here because immigration couldn't get her prints. Mr. Cull, there's a note in her file. Immigration didn't know if she never had fingerprints because some people don't or if her cleaning materials wore them off. They said that she was awfully young to have them worn off."

Norbie pushed him on the Ativan, asking him if he knew what kind of a doctor Dr. Ornstein was and what Ativan was supposed to do for her. Sergei understood very well that Ativan was given to treat Mariska's great anxiety, which the doctor felt stemmed from her previous life. Sergei assured Norbie that he and Mariska both felt that her previous life, although not perfect, was good. He said that Mariska's paternal grandmother was an evil woman, but Mariska was protected from her influence.

Norbie continued to ask questions about the family but was assured that her childhood was wholesome. He questioned a family unit of three generations, including Mariska, Sergei, Anya, and Albina living together, but Sergei's answers left him thinking it was as good a three-generation family living together in harmony that he had ever witnessed, outside of Mariska's anxiety.

They then discussed the legal representation agreement that Mariska had signed, with a separate financial agreement section for legal services for Mariska, which Sergei was to sign as guarantor. Sergei had no problems signing the financial contract but questioned why he was not a party to the representation agreement, but only a guarantor. The explanation finally brought to Sergei complete understanding that Mariska would make all decisions for her defense, and his only role was as a possibly influencing friend.

This was not satisfactory, and he complained vigorously. It took Norbie twenty minutes to convince Sergei why he could not be a party to the contract. This was a criminal case, and Mariska needed every protection the law allowed. Only she could determine what actions to take; it was her life that was at risk, not Sergei's life.

To this, Sergei replied, "No it is also my life and my family's life at risk now."

Sergei finally left with instructions not to discuss the case with anyone, including Mariska. Norbie told Sergei, "If you have a problem, talk to me. You don't want to give Mariska advice that would put her at legal risk more than she already is. I'll discuss your concerns with you, okay?"

Norbie did not feel certain that Sergei would completely conform to this requirement.

Norbie considered the information he had to date. Instinctively he knew that he had to get Mariska out of jail. And he hoped that, at her arraignment on Monday, she would be released on bail, albeit a high bail. Normally he would not worry about the case until Monday, but there was a problem here. He believed that Mariska had not done it. Therefore, if he were right, the neighborhood was still at risk. He needed some more information.

Mariska had told him a great deal about the neighborhood and the layout of the murder scenes, but her descriptions were just kind of a crying documentary, not a description of how she had done it, except in the most general manner. At any other time, the police would not have accepted this confession, and he was surprised that Captain Beauregard would fall for this.

Norbie had some ideas about an alternate theory and thought, *The sooner I pursue it, the better it will be for Mariska. I don't want any more information from her. If what I fear is true, I may be walking an ethical tightrope. Maybe I can get some feedback from the police without waiting for formal depositions and requests for evidence.*

Well, he'd start with the Springfield Police and see what they heard through the grapevine, thinking, *They're a talkative bunch. Perhaps they can be useful. Then I'll try to see Rudy Beauregard. I guess the search for the pill bottles was important to them.*

Cull recalled that Mariska had said, "I never took any of the pills; except for one or two."

What if some were gone? He couldn't wait to find this out. It wasn't the first time he had gone fishing. His last resort would be the district attorney, but he may have to call on him. Meanwhile, he would research legal ethics. He knew that he was on a legal hot seat now, thinking, *I'm pretty certain I know why Mariska is lying. If I act counter to my client's wishes, I have a problem; and I am going to do that!* The additional thought that he would have to also rely on others to do the right thing made his stomach a bit queasy.

Rudy got a call at home on Saturday night from Mark Spaulder, a Springfield police detective. His opening was, "What the hell is going on there, Rudy? You've arrested a Russian woman, supposedly a really nice lady, for serial murders. Norbie's representing her. You know, Rudy, Norbie's no walk in the park. He told me that this Rozovsky, or whatever her name is, is 'an innocent.' Norbie said, 'She's innocent, or I've lost my criminal radar.' You know he ain't naive, and his radar is the best in the business, maybe better than most cops."

Well, Rudy thought, *neither am I naive.* Rudy could see Mark trying to corral him into giving information he had no business asking about. Then again, he thought, maybe Spaulder could serve a good purpose for once in his life.

Rudy started questioning Mark, hoping to find out what he thought he knew from Norbie. He was not surprised that Norbie insisted that the case had some serious problems, because Norbie was a good defense attorney and his MO always included the phrase, "Your case against my client is rife with problems."

Mark reported that Norbie had said that, in the search of the

Rozovsky house, the police had picked up pill bottles of Ativan that weren't completely unused, and that alone has given rise to Norbie developing an alternate theory of the crime.

Rudy was immediately riled thinking that maybe someone in the lab or his department was talking out of turn or that Norbie was looking for an answer by fishing. No one else knew that the pill bottles were not completely filled.

Rudy decided to play the game and said, "You mean that she was under the weather when she murdered six kids and assaulted a seventh?"

Mark said, "Nah, Rudy. That would be a normal possibility for an alternate theory. I think he was redirecting the case, but he was vague about what direction he was going in. What was pretty clear is that he thought you were the person he wanted me to tell. You know I served with Jim Locke in Iraq, but he pushed me toward you. What do you think? Norbie doesn't make up stuff, and he was, you know, wired the way Norbie is when he thinks he's onto something. What could he possibly know? The lady confessed to it all. Are there problems with the confession?"

Rudy, thinking that Norbie was as shrewd a defense lawyer as they came, concluded that he'd guessed without too much information that Mariska could never murder anyone. What else could he have learned that would support his reaching out to him? What would have him take this risk? His client had confessed.

He must know somehow that I have my doubts. He knows about the pills. How the hell does he know that, unless Mariska told him she took the pills? More troubling for Rudy was the possibility that someone at the station or lab had told him. *Christ, I hope Jim didn't say anything. I know he's not completely convinced Mariska murdered anyone, even though he actually was the interrogator who obtained the confession.*

Rudy thought that Norbie probably needed some corroborating evidence. He needed to think more carefully before he moved forward, but first he had to get Spaulder off the phone. This took a couple of minutes of explanation that dinner was ready for him and the kids, and Mona would kill him if he didn't come to the table when the food was hot. Actually, it was a lie, because Mona was out serving at some scholarship supper, one of the many events she worked at to assist in the goals of whichever organization needed help. He was free to think about what info Norbie was looking for.

What did he have that Norbie couldn't wait to get? After all, Norbie would get everything in the end. He'd already know most of the stuff from the newspapers. His knowledge of the last assault and the search warrants results would be unknown, and Mariska couldn't help him with the search warrants because she wasn't there. Sergei would not have known about what had been taken because he was not there. Only Anya and Albina would have known that the pills were taken, but would they have known that the bottles were not full? The officer in charge of the search warrant had seven days before he was required to return it to the court with a completed inventory of what was seized.

No, Norbie had inside information, or he'd made a good guess. If he'd made a good guess then his alternate theory would maybe coincide with Rudy's theory. Rudy thought, *Chalk one up for the defense and thank God.* Mariska would also have told Norbie that at first she'd lied about knowledge of the tomahawk and then corrected herself. Well, maybe he could help Norbie along. He laughed. *What a nightmare when a cop helps out the defense.*

Rudy picked up the phone and called Sergei's cell phone. Sergei was not friendly and said he didn't want to talk to him, but Rudy pushed on saying, "Mr. Rozovsky, I'm looking for the missing Ativan pills. All the bottles weren't full."

Sergei immediately accused him of lying. He was vehement when he said Mariska had never taken but one pill and none after that. Rudy, in a serious but deliberately cynical voice, said, "Come on, Sergei. There were at least one-third of the pills missing from each bottle? And what about the coffee?"

Sergei stopped the call, but Rudy knew that Sergei's next call would be to Norbie. He hoped this would help the defense attorney. After all, the policeman's lot was to support the pursuit of justice. He knew that he had stepped out beyond his police parameters and would not have done this if the attorney on the other side were a bigmouthed idiot.

◆

Norbie got the call from Sergei in the middle of his dinner at the Springfield Country Club. He was sensitive about taking the call because Sheri, his wife, did not like him taking calls when they were out with friends for dinner. He thought, *But she knows that this murder requires all my attention; after all she's got years with me. I know Sheri resents my taking this case after she told me that it's the one case she didn't want me to take; but she knows I have to do what I need to.*

Norbie remembered her remarks, "Oh, no, Norbie, you do what Norbie wants to do. You don't worry what our friends say about you defending a murderer of kids—no, not my Norbie. And now you insist that you believe this monster may be innocent. Hell, you never believe anyone, but you believe a woman accused of killing six kids. I think you're the naive one in this marriage."

Norbie's mother-in-law was not impressed that Norbie represented murderers but was impressed that Norbie had bought her a new condo after his father-in-law had died.

Sheri knew that Norbie was a complicated man. She also knew that she would never find a more interesting man, although he confused her. She thought, *I trust him because my history with him has taught me he is worthy of that trust. But his work doesn't allow him to take me into his confidence; and if I'm honest, I deeply resent it.*

Sheri once asked Norbie if he didn't trust her. His answer had been firm and final. "One slip, Sheri, just one slip, and you could place a client in jeopardy. This way only I can do that. Do you want that responsibility?" No. She knew she didn't. Why, oh, why hadn't she married a doctor or a businessman? This was the question she often asked herself.

Norbie left the dining room and scowled as Sergei repeated his conversation with Rudy. It didn't take a brain surgeon to see through the obfuscation. Sergei and Mariska both didn't know about the pills being taken by the police and that some pills were missing. It was time to make a visit to the district attorney and not ADA Hetterman. He made the call and was pleasantly surprised that the DA agreed to see him at his office at ten o'clock on Sunday morning after the nine o'clock Sunday Mass at Sacred Heart. Norbie smiled, thinking, *It's always good to have a DA who knows when something's happening without having to spell it out.*

They met the next morning, and Norbie was as forthcoming as he could be without disclosing privileged information. He pointed out that there may be a conflict between his duty as an officer of the court and his duty in the defense of his client. He thought that his role as a defense attorney on this case may be much shorter than he and his client had ever planned.

He even suggested that Captain Rudy Beauregard could bring about supporting his alternate theory with very little effort. He explained that he could not really be a part of the investigation. As he forwarded the details of his theory, he pointed out that if it were true, it would not be a panacea for anyone—the family, the neighbors, the district attorney, or himself. But it would prevent an additional injustice.

When Sergei clicked off from his conversation with Norbie, he realized that both Albina and Anya were listening, and they both looked terrified. They had been difficult to deal with all day, before he'd left for his visit to Mariska; but their anger had increased after he returned home. He had insisted that they not go with him to visit her. In retaliation, they were waiting to inflict punishment on him when he returned. The women accused him of being a "Russian man," both of them saying the same thing, one in Russian and one in English. "This is America, and we are equal to you. We should have been able to decide if we could go."

He was furious, thinking that this was typical American botched thinking. They were just like the crazy university kids on television with their "isms"—communism, racism, sexism, ageism, and on and on. He told Anya that if she paid attention to all the crime shows on TV she would know that Mama couldn't talk to them about anything related to her case and that Mama would not want them to see her in jail.

Albina was the first to give a little and cried. She told him that he must protect Mariska and them. She said that she could not keep up the house like Mariska, for which Anya piped in that they needed a cleaning lady.

Albina said in Russian, "Sergei, I don't know where Mariska keeps all the numbers for the pool man, the lawn man, the cleaners who picked up laundry, and all the other people needed to maintain the house. Anya has to go to school. She can't make calls. They won't understand my English."

Anya complained vociferously, "I'm eating Russian food all the time. It gets boring, and Babushka doesn't cook hamburgers well at all. Who's taking me to school? I need to be safe. And the murderer has not been caught yet. We know that Mama didn't commit those murders."

Sergei's world was coming apart, and Anya's question about who would take her to school every day occupied his thoughts. It was one of the first questions Mariska had asked him. Albina was not a great driver and had little geographical knowledge of the area outside of the mall on Riverside and Anya's school. He left for work early each morning and couldn't take her to school on a regular basis.

Sergei called his cousin and made arrangements thinking, *Thank God for family.* His cousin said he could do it every day but Wednesdays. Sergei then reached out to Amy Landers, who was happy to help. She also offered him the name of an older Latino woman who cleaned houses and who could be trusted not to gossip. Sergei poured vodka on ice, sat in his enormous skin-covered den chair, and sank into the aftermath of too much energy spent.

Rudy got a call on Sunday afternoon from the district attorney, bypassing the chief and the mayor. He was relieved by this expression of discretion. He thought, *Finally, maybe we'll be able to do the right thing.* The challenge was how to get out from under the effects of Mariska's confession.

He thought about his kids who were always texting, chatting, or tweeting, which he called "buzzing" like bees. Well the "buzzing" was now from him, Norbie, the DA, and the lot of them. He didn't think that Mariska could help or would help, even though he was convinced that she knew the murderer. But Mariska's vision about duty was distorted with what he suspected was guilt, and perhaps a misguided sense that she could protect someone. Sergei wants to help. He would do just about anything to help Mariska. But Sergei was not the avenue Rudy was going to use. No, he was going to visit the Landers family with Jim and Petra. They were sitting on some truths; that he knew.

Amy and Suzanna were having afternoon coffee and cake and were surprised at the arrival of the police. Amy let them, the captain, and Detectives Aylewood and Locke, into the entry. She tried to act hospitably but could not hide her distress over Mariska's arrest. They all settled into the living room, not the kitchen, which was the usual hosting norm in Amy's house. The living room was for hosting guests, not necessarily friends, by which she was telling them that this was formal, not friendly, in the subtlest way she knew.

The, at first, stilted conversation focused on the Rozovsky family, and Amy limited her comments, while Suzanna, perhaps because of her youth, had something to say in answer to all of the detectives' questions. Rudy heard nothing new until Jim honed in on Anya's brilliance, looks, and personality.

Suzanna's initial answer was not unkind but unexpected. "Anya is certainly beautiful and very smart, but nobody thinks she's charming. In fact, like any only child, she has to have things her way. Her mother has real personality. And, believe it or not, Sergei is fun to be around. Even Albina is funny. Anya, she is not funny, except when she's competing with someone who is entertaining the kids. Then she is a planned funny—you know like a comedian's script, not like naturally funny people. My mother calls people who are truly funny engaging. Anya is not engaging. In fact, she's annoying. You feel like you're on eggshells when you're with her. Only Merry was not intimidated by her."

Jim said some inane thing about differences in kids, and Suzanna told him that he was misunderstanding her. "Detective Locke, Anya is very different and, in many ways, not a kid at all."

Petra, perhaps to keep some emotional lightness in the room, asked them both if they could remember their locations specifically on each of the days that the murders occurred. Amy spoke up and questioned why, now, did they want this information and whether they were examining their alibis.

Petra explained that she really wanted help with Mariska's presence on all those dates. If, for instance, either one of them saw her at a particular place and time for any one of the murders, then maybe that fact could remove her from suspicion; maybe it could be helpful to Mariska.

Bingo, Jim thought, *Petra is on to something.* He saw it on the women's faces. *They want to help Mariska.*

Suzanna said, "I keep a diary, and sometimes it's really in depth by the hour. I'll get it. Mom, you used to keep receipts for two years to mark off anything on your grocery list that you can use for Dad's office expenses. Do you still do it? Maybe it will give you some dates and times that correlate. Also look at your checkbook on vendors for the house that you pay. You normally cut a check right after the service; you never wait for billing, even with Russ Landscaping Service. Those dates are firm and could help trigger memory. You know their normal times for being here. Detectives, if we have it, you will have it. But you're going to have to give times of the murders for us to match. Can you give them? Or are you not allowed to give us that kind of information? Give us a little time to get this stuff, while you have more coffee."

Rudy wondered, *Who is the adult here? Who is the detective? Suzanna has a future in detective or audit work. I can't believe she's just a teenager.*

It took nearly half an hour before the women returned, and Suzanna had a complete history of four of the murders. They started the matching process. On the Saturday murder, Suzanna had seen Anya come up the back way in the woods within fifteen minutes of the murder. On two of the murders, she had seen Mariska running down Sunnyside within five minutes after the murders. She was so excited and said, "How could Mariska have murdered those kids? It takes longer than five minutes to get to the park."

Petra pointed out that, although this was helpful, murder times were estimated and not exact. Amy found one piece of perfect information in her diary—a note that Mariska agreed to donate to the food pantry. On the day that Merry was murdered, Amy had encountered Mariska walking or, rather, staggering down the street to pick up Anya. Amy had stopped her to ask for a donation for the food pantry. Mariska was having trouble focusing and asked Amy to put in fifty dollars for her and she would repay her. Mariska said that she couldn't stop, because she had fallen asleep again, and when she had woken up, she'd had trouble walking.

Suzanna was excited and said, "Doesn't this mean that Mariska doesn't know what she's doing, like in the case that Springfield lawyer handled talked about in the news as the 'Sleepwalking case'?"

Rudy asked if they had ever seen Mariska like that before. Amy said she had on one other occasion, but she couldn't remember the date. He then asked if they had ever had coffee at the Rozovsky home.

The answer from Amy was, "No, Russians drink tea. And it's really good but strong tea, Detectives."

Jim changed the subject to bows and arrows and questioned whether Mariska had ever joined classes with Henry at their home. Both ladies said that Mariska did not like weapons at all and made Sergei hide all his rifles in a locked case.

Mariska had been upset when Suzanna had told her that Anya was pretty good at archery. But Anya had just explained that her mother was overly protective. Naturally, she wouldn't like Anya taking archery lessons, much less finding out that she was good at archery.

Petra stated that it would have driven her crazy if her mother was with her all the time when she was twelve years old and wondered if Anya rebelled at all.

Suzanna said, "I don't think that Anya would ever openly rebel because her father and grandmother are pretty tough about rules. But if Anya saw an opening, well, she was pretty good at taking advantage."

Rudy asked what Suzanna was doing the day she had seen Anya in the woods on the day of the murder. Was she also in the woods or was she in her yard? Suzanna quickly said that she had cut into the woods directly from the field and had just reached her backyard when she saw that Anya was behind her.

Rudy questioned what she was doing at the field and was told that she was meeting a friend.

Amy frowned and said, "I know just who that was, and I'm certainly happy that you don't see him anymore."

"Mom, he is, or shall I say was, a good guy; it's all over between us—mostly because he's like all the guys; they won't come near

Sunnyside now because they're afraid they'll be stopped by the cops. He's had a difficult life, but he's not all bad. You should trust me."

A touchy subject between mother and daughter, but the detectives could see that Suzanna wanted to please her mother and did not pursue the conversation further.

Jim asked Suzanna why Anya was in the woods alone that day when her mother claims that Anya is always with her or a group of friends.

Suzanna, with great glee, told the detective, "Just like my mother didn't know I was meeting someone she didn't approve of, so sometimes Anya got away from her mother. Somehow, she'd know when her mother would fall asleep. I'm not sure how she escaped her grandma, who has eyes in the back of her head. But she found ways. Mr. Rozovsky always works at least half a day on Saturdays, so Anya just has to find a way around the other two. They are really good to Anya, but I would hate to have to report everything I did to my parents. For Anya, I think it's just another challenge that she beats."

Rudy questioned Suzanna and Amy about the grandmother and whether or not Albina was honest. He was told that she kept family business to herself, but in every other way, she was a really nice person. She was always making homemade remedies and sharing them with them. One remedy worked particularly well according to Suzanna. "When I had a bout with acne when I was fourteen, Albina gave me some drink for the acne. It worked better than the pills I got from the skin doctor."

Rudy looked out the window and saw Sergei alone in his car. He mused that Sergei was probably going to the county jail to visit Mariska, but he did not have the two women with him. He excused himself and made a call to Mrs. Moriarty, after which the detectives left the Landers home.

21

Truth

RUDY; MRS. MORIARTY, THE interpreter; Jim; and Petra entered the Rozovsky home at Albina's invitation about forty-five minutes after Sergei had left to see Mariska. Rudy had planned the time frame, knowing that cell phones could not be used when Sergei was visiting but could be used in the waiting room. He'd given Sergei enough time to drive to the facility and to wait until he could visit, which, on a Sunday, might take a while. Albina was now alone with Anya; and that bothered Rudy, as well as Petra and Jim.

Petra asked where Anya was and was told that she must be in her room because all that teenage American music was being played. Albina was annoyed that Anya hadn't answered the doorbell. Petra offered to go get her and bring her out to the main room and, without waiting for an okay, and with Albina following her, went to the source of the music. She knocked, got no answer, and entered the room.

Anya was not there. Petra wondered aloud about her whereabouts and could see that Albina was upset, although she only said that she must be in the yard or meeting her girlfriends. Albina was shaking a little bit, and Mrs. Moriarty started talking her down while Petra, on her own, went outside.

The detectives could not help but remember what Suzanna had said, "If as we believe Mariska didn't do it, then the kids on Sunnyside are not yet safe. Have the police stopped watching the street, because I don't think that they should stop?"

Rudy assured Albina that Petra was going after Anya to keep her safe, and Albina was not to worry about her.

Petra, familiar with the trails and knowing that Anya would not want anyone to know except her friends that she had escaped the vigilance of her family, ran through the trails following parallel to the houses from one trail to another. She had not taken the direct route to the park but the multiple routes that would bring her near the park entrance, which she thought would be the meeting place for kids.

Petra pushed herself hard. She ran down the path leading to the park entrance. The spring air was slightly humid. Sweat trickled down her back. She felt her muscles strain, and it felt oddly good—like she was alive! Then she slowed down and stopped. She cocked her head at the sound of footsteps in front of her near a dense stand of underbrush. "Anya?" she yelled. "Stop! Police!"

Petra caught up with a very angry Anya. So angry was Anya that she actually shouted at the detective, "Are you now my mother following me everywhere? I don't have to stop for the police. I don't have to talk with you. Go away."

Instead of reacting, Petra just said that she was looking for evidence to help prove that Mariska couldn't have murdered the children. Anya stopped walking and seemed to take this information in, stating something to the effect that it certainly took the police a long time to figure things out.

She then directed a question to Petra, "If Mama didn't do it, do you know who did? I mean you must know by now who did it, or you wouldn't be looking for stuff to clear Mama."

Petra realized that his kid was more analytical than the average twelve-year-old and not too emotional.

Meanwhile, at the house, Rudy, through Mrs. Moriarty, was attempting to educate Albina about the United States federal and Massachusetts state criminal justice systems. He talked about first-degree and second-degree murder charges and the possible resulting punishments for those charges and for manslaughter. He also explained problems with an insanity defense. Her astuteness was quickly evident from her questions. She asked about the insanity defense, and she didn't like his answers.

Rudy took this opportunity to push her on Mariska's confession, asking her why Mariska would confess to something she didn't do. He asked Albina about Mariska's sense of obligation to others. Would she confess to protect someone whom she thought had suffered too much already? Albina said that Mariska would.

Albina then asked him what jail was like in America. She said, as translated, that her own mother-in-law had deliberately trumped up charges on her own daughter, Albina's sister-in-law, and caused her to be sent to jail because she was a serious delinquent. The mother-in-law, when later confronted, explained her actions, stating that the daughter was an embarrassment to the family and would learn the hard way. That daughter died in jail. Her mother-in-law never felt any guilt about it. She personally thought that her mother-in-law really didn't love anyone but herself.

Albina said that Mariska was petrified of that grandmother and would hide when she came around. She wondered if Mariska had heard the story about the girl's death from a cousin; she herself had never told Mariska the story. But she remarked how stories, however suppressed, always get known. Truth be told, the girl who died in jail was really an evil one, as was her mother.

Rudy asked how old the girl was and was told she was fourteen years old when she was incarcerated. He asked what her prison sentence was and for what crime.

Albina said that the mother planted drugs on the girl when she went to hang out with her friends. Her sentence was fifteen years because the police also found some stolen goods in the house where she was found. They had all gone to jail.

Rudy took the opportunity to tell Albina about Massachusetts law and that a child can be tried as an adult at age fourteen years. But prior to that, a child would be considered a youthful offender, and the most that would happen is the child would be sent to a youthful detention center until age twenty-one. Then the child would be free.

Albina was suddenly very interested and said, "You mean that a child under fourteen years of age could commit serious crimes and only go to a youth house until reaching twenty-one years, while an adult could be electrocuted or get a life sentence for the same crime? This is because the child doesn't know any better, right? Do you believe that, Detective? Do you believe that children who murder don't know any better?"

Instead of answering her, Rudy told her a story about Brian, the little boy he had seen on his trip to L.L.Bean in Maine with his wife, Mona. He described the boy's actions and the mother's awareness of her child's problems. He also described how only the mother understood that the child had serious tendencies, which may not easily go away in the future.

Albina stoically said, "The mother always knows. The mother always knows."

Jim quietly said, "Albina, you know, don't you? You know that Mariska is covering for someone? Is it Anya? She doesn't have an alibi, and she also does not seem to have feelings about the loss of her friends, does she?"

Albina cried and, in a volume of Russian, told Mrs. Moriarty that she did not want to be impolite, but family business is family business.

Jim pushed ahead. "From this day forward, you will be responsible for any child killed, and you know that Anya has escaped for the day; she's under great pressure with her mother gone. Think about it, Albina. The kids will ignore her in school because her mother is deemed a murderer. Think what that will do to her. She will be punished and her mother too. That is not fair. Anya is a child who needs professional help—help that her family cannot give her. She will not go to jail. She will not die in jail. And other children will live. What do you know, Albina, that can help us? It's your duty. Just direct us and nobody will know."

Albina cried and wailed and, in the end, told them to go to the edge of the woods by the park behind the large strip of meadow near the bottom of the street. There they would find stuff. That was all she could say—all she would say.

It was at that moment that Anya and Petra walked in.

"Babushka, what have you been telling the detectives?" she said in Russian.

The captain told her that Albina just said that they were discussing what Mariska was facing—a life sentence in jail.

Anya then said, "It will never happen. She is going to win the case because she doesn't know the facts, because she never killed anyone. Her lawyer, Mr. Cull, well, Papa says he's really smart and will get her off." Anya seemed quite happy with that statement and looked at the detectives and Mrs. Moriarty and asked if they wanted coffee.

Rudy said yes, which surprised Jim because Rudy really tended to watch his caffeine lately.

Anya said that she would make it and then realized that there was not coffee in the house because the police had taken the coffee, along with some sugar and cream when they searched. She made them tea with honey. Rudy asked if she had a paper cup because he would take it with him. It was too hot to drink now. The other detectives and Mrs. Moriarty had no problem drinking the hot tea.

As the police were leaving the house, Rudy said to Anya, "Things are closing in on the guilty one. I want to assure you that the killer, whoever he is, should rethink any stories he told so far. We have found some serious discrepancies in several stories and alibis. Don't you worry, Anya. We are closing in. The killer should have a better story." As he was leaving, he thought that it was important to keep her thinking and away from the park.

On leaving and outside the house, Rudy sent Petra and Jim to find out what was in the strip of meadow before Anya thought about it. He also ensured that uniforms would be present immediately in the woods to prevent Anya from acting out. Rudy said what they were all thinking, "She's a cold one. She would never need a motive to kill, just like we thought about before—an instant desire unmet. Maybe murder calms her down from the frustration of her unmet perceived needs. I've had the inklings of distrust about Anya for a long time and suppressed them. Now I know her, but I don't really want to know that about a kid."

⬅◆➡

Anya, and they were all certain it was Anya, had left trophies of her victims. The trophies were such that the families had never realized the items were missing. The items had been touched and had fingerprints. The detectives were able to guess which item belonged to each victim, and they quickly matched the prints on four items to the prints from four victims' bodies.

There was other evidence, for example Suzanna having identified Anya as coming through the woods a short time after Merry's murder—near the murder. The timing was telling for both of them. Fortunately, Suzanna's diary putting her in other people's company ruled Suzanna out on two murders. Rudy had his paper cup with Anya's prints. It would allow them to match prints he expected to be Anya's on some of the things recovered from the search.

Added to that evidence, the lab in Springfield called about the chemical analysis. The instant coffee that some Russians use and was used by Mariska was laced with Ativan. Rudy was told that if you had a cup, it was a wonder you weren't dopey for a few hours. Anya had not only acted to murder her classmates and probably doped her mother but had kept trophies as well. Rudy hadn't expected that.

All four detectives were in the station's conference room on Sunday night working on a plan to close these cases before the next day. The chief was coming in shortly. Rudy had informed him about the new evidence and the new suspect. And his response was, "Figure it out before I get there. Figure out, Rudy, how you're going to close this case."

All the detectives were agreed that there still was not enough evidence to close the case now. They believed that Mariska would insist she had committed the murders. Anya would deny it. Albina would say nothing more.

Rudy said, "We'll never be able to get anything out of Anya now because Sergei will lawyer her up. But what about Sergei? He has no idea that Anya could do any of this. To him, Anya's his perfect little girl. Albina knows that Anya is a problem, but she is afraid to talk to us. She's afraid to cross family lines and be ostracized. After all, Albina has no means of support, and her bank account balance is limited. Sergei is the only one who we can approach. She's going out to kill again, don't you agree, Petra?" Rudy asked.

Before she could answer, he reminded her that very soon after Sergei had left the house, Anya had gone out into the woods. Rudy thought that she was stressed and was either going to see her trophies or was going to pick someone to murder to get her mother freed. "This has to stop. We have nothing to lose and everything to gain by talking to Sergei. I don't want to muddy the waters by bringing Norbie into this. I think that Jim and I should go and see Sergei. Call patrol over there. We need to know when he comes home from seeing Mariska."

Petra told Rudy that, although she agreed with him and had thought, earlier in the day when she'd caught up with Anya, that Anya was on a mission, she also thought that Sergei may not say a word to them. "Captain, his attorney would have told him not to talk to us, and maybe he won't even let us in the house."

The visit to the Rozovsky home was dramatic. Albina opened the door and was startled to see them again. She yelled to Sergei, and both Sergei and Anya entered the room. Rudy asked if they could speak to him alone, and Anya reacted.

She said to her father, "They were just here today. What do you have to do, Daddy, with these murders? You have perfect alibis. They're just trying to get you involved. Don't trust them, Daddy. We need you at home. You have to work to take care of us."

Sergei, in a soft, strong voice, told both Albina and Anya to go to their rooms. They could hear Anya slam the bedroom door.

Rudy started the conversation. "Sergei, I'm going to talk in hypotheticals. Do you know what I mean by hypotheticals?"

Sergei asked if he meant the *if* this happens, then *that* will happen, like in Excel "if statements." Rudy knew nothing about if statements in Excel, even though he used the program, but thought that Sergei knew what he meant.

Rudy then, with Jim's assistance, told Sergei a story about a child who murders and whose mother confesses to save the child.

Sergei yelled, "No. What are you saying? Not Anya! Are you nuts? She's wonderful, perfect, always has been the perfect child. I'm not listening to this shit. Get out now." Although he was yelling and visibly disturbed, he did not push them out of the house.

Rudy told him to just listen to what they had to say. The child, he said, was the serial murderer. They could prove it. It would go to trial, but it would be very difficult on the family if that were to happen because the world and the prosecutor would tend to think that mother and daughter were in it together or, at the very least, that the mother knew what was going on.

Jim then said, "Detective Aylewood found Anya in the woods today, and we fear for her motives, to either visit her trophies for comfort—and she had trophies—or to commit another murder."

Sergei got up from his chair and started pacing the floor, almost shouting, "You have to be wrong." He fought back tears.

Jim, in a soft voice, summarized what he thought was best for the family. "Sergei, Mariska is innocent of these murders, and Anya is guilty. Anya is only twelve years old and is, therefore, a juvenile defendant. They won't even put her name in the paper. Mariska is facing a life sentence for something she didn't do. Anya would get the help she needs. She would get the help you can't give her. She is a very sick little girl—a sickness that no one in this family and no one in her school ever picked up on. She will continue to murder if left uncharged, and I don't think you can live with that. Your wife would not have confessed to something she didn't do, except to save her child. She cannot save her child. You know I'm telling the truth."

"Sergei, you also can't live with your wife, Mariska, taking the fall for Anya, which she has proven she's willing to do. I'm banking on you doing the moral thing here and, at the same time, actually doing what is best for your family. Mariska doesn't know what we know. I can't tell you everything, but you must talk to your wife and Attorney Cull before tomorrow morning. The district attorney and we will be there at the court, and the police will be at this house. It would be best for you to bring Anya in with you. But if you don't, she will be arrested here. We have an arrest warrant."

At that moment, Anya walked into the living room. They wondered from her belligerent stance if she had heard the discussion. She looked at her father, and something passed between them—something that was almost telepathic—because she then turned to Rudy and screamed, "You don't know anything. And whatever you told my father is a big fat lie. I can tell by looking at him that you're trying to blame me. I was with my mother. You can't convict her, and you can't convict me, because I was always with her. We were always together."

Albina, hearing the shouting, walked in the room. She told Anya to stop yelling and to go in her room. Anya shouted at her grandmother, telling her to say that they were all together all the time.

Sergei did what Rudy imagined was an almost impossible task for a loving father. He said, "Anya, sit down." She did not and he continued talking, "The detectives have come here to arrest you for these murders. I won't ask you about them. That will be your lawyer's job. They believe that you are very sick and under a lot of stress. I am going to get a very good lawyer for you, but you will be taken to a juvenile facility tonight. Your mother and I and Babushka will never abandon you. But you need help that we can't give you. I am sorry, but you can't stay here any longer."

Petra felt suddenly cold deep into her core. The little girl looked almost demonic. She literally changed physically from a pretty little thing to something evil. "You should die!" she screamed, advancing slowly toward her father. "You should die! Die! Die! Just like the others!"

"No, Anya," Sergei said, moving toward her.

"Stop!" Petra yelled as Anya using what appeared to be no effort at all grabbed a heavy vase from the sideboard and rushed in so swiftly Petra barely had time to act.

Anya swung the vase at her father's head. Petra blocked the blow, catching Anya's right arm with a blow from her left. The vase flew through the air and crashed against the wall.

"Die! You will all die! All of you!" Anya screamed.

Petra managed to block Anya's punches. Jim rushed up behind the girl. In seconds, he had her by both wrists.

Anya cried, "Mama will never let this happen. Mama will hate you and Babushka for the rest of your lives. You believe the police and not me. You think I could do those murders; you think that I could do them—all by myself? You're fools to believe that. You're not taking care of me. I won't forget that."

Rudy's antennae went up. He did not like what he heard. *What does she mean?* He thought, *What does she mean "all by myself"?*

<hr />

The Monday-morning arraignment for Mariska did not go as the press had planned. While they were busy trying to figure out why Mariska was not being arraigned, Anya was brought to juvenile court. It took only a few minutes before the press moved over from one courthouse to the next courthouse building where the juvenile court shared real estate with the housing court. The press had been well informed by those special personnel in all courts who trade information for a little glamour as an inside source, resulting in a call made from one public employee snitch to another.

Word on these kinds of matters gets out quickly—and, in this case, very quickly. Sunnyside Road neighbors were again shaken. How could that pretty little girl commit six murders?

<hr />

There was, however, one young girl who understood not only that Anya could commit these murders but also why Anya had assaulted her. Carol McNamara had partially recovered her memory and recalled that Anya had a brilliant blue print jacket that she sometimes wore—a jacket color that was to be remembered. And she remembered a hint of that color, that exact color, when she was hit with the hatchet. She also recalled how angry Anya was when she'd told Anya that her brother Nick would never look at her, even when they got older, because her brother liked blondes. Carol knew that it didn't take much to set Anya off. She had seen her reactions several times when someone would get in Anya's way. She thought, *I should have known it was Anya all along who murdered our friends. But really, even if I had opened my eyes sooner, who would have believed me—about beautiful, perfect Anya?*

———⟫◆⟪———

Freida McNamara, the mother of eight, was sad, angry, and, rare in her experience, bitter. She said to herself, "All I've heard on the news lately is that young people today feel entitled, but entitled to murder? How Frank and I worried about living in a tough neighborhood! How we scrimped and sacrificed to live on Sunnyside Road. But living here is no guarantee for the perfect life. There is just no assurance ever that we will be able to protect our loved ones, our children. Can I ever be certain that my judgment about people, even little kids, is insightful or even halfway right? No! What is left for any of us after living through this nightmare? Just live and continue to live and maybe trust again—someday—maybe?"

Acknowledgments

Family: To Joe, my husband, for his unquestionable loyalty, kindness, and love. To my children—Kerstin, Joseph, Raipher, and Julian—the lights of my life. To my grandchildren—Dream, Persevere, and Prevail!

I am grateful for all *technical assistance* I received from my good friends. On *police matters*, thank you to Retired Springfield Massachusetts Chief of Police Paula Meara. Thank you to *attorneys* Charles E. Dolan, Joseph A. Pellegrino, Sr. (ret. Justice, Mass. Trial Courts), and Raipher D. Pellegrino. For *all things Russian*, thank you to Vitaliy Yanyuk.

And to my *editors*, I thank you for your support and counsel. To all of you, all errors on implementation are mine, solely mine.

Care to Review My Book? (or "Honest Reviews Don't Kill")

Now that you've read the story to the end, I'd love to know what you think of it – and read your honest review about the book on Amazon, Goodreads or another major online book site where it is featured.

Thank you for your interest in my books!

Kathleen

More Books by K. B. Pellegrino

Kathleen B. Pellegrino – Author & Storyteller
EVIL EXISTS IN WEST SIDE TRILOGY :
Sunnyside Road – Paradise Dissembling (Liferich Publishing)
Mary Lou – Oh What Did She Do? To be published Fall 2018
(Liferich Publishing)
Brothers of Another Mother – All for one -- Always? Expected to
be published 2019

You can find K.B. Pellegrino's books on all major online Book Stores,
such as Amazon, Barnes & Noble, kobo, I Books Store, SCRIBD, as
well as on her website at:

KBPellegrino.com/books

Preview: "Mary Lou — Oh What Did You Do?"

If you want to get a taste for Kathleen's upcoming book, **download a free Chapter** of the Trilogy's book #2 "Mary Lou — Oh What Did You Do?" at <u>KBPellegrino.com/mary-lou-free</u>

BONUS

"I am grateful for every reader who picks up my books to read them. I'd like to give something back that you might find interesting."
Kathleen

To access **freebies** like book Giveaways, Free Books or Free Chapters of published and upcoming books, and more, visit:

kbpellegrino.com/bonus